ME AGAIN

ME AGAIN

UNCOLLECTED WRITINGS OF

STEVIE SMITH

ILLUSTRATED BY HERSELF

EDITED BY
JACK BARBERA & WILLIAM McBRIEN

WITH A PREFACE BY
JAMES MacGIBBON

VINTAGE BOOKS

A DIVISION OF RANDOM HOUSE · NEW YORK

First Vintage Books Edition, May 1983
This arrangement, introduction and commentary
© Jack Barbera and William McBrien 1981
Preface and Endnotes to Letters ©James MacGibbon 1981
All Stevie Smith writings and drawings © James MacGibbon
1937, 1938, 1942, 1950, 1957, 1962, 1966, 1971, 1972, 1981
Sylvia Plath letter © Ted Hughes 1981

Library of Congress Cataloging in Publication Data
Smith, Stevie, 1902–1971.
Me again.
Includes index.
I. Barbera, Jack.
II. McBrien, William.
III. Title.
PR6037.M43A6 1983   828'.91209   82-40430
ISBN 0-394-71362-1

Manufactured in the United States of America

CONTENTS

POEMS

PREFACE

Ever since Stevie Smith died in 1971 the question of her biography has cropped up from time to time. One of her closest friends undertook to write it but gave up: another wanted to take it on but had to abandon it. There was an impediment: what was there to record that had not already been expressed in her writings?

She was always reticent about her private life; I myself took the view that the essence of it is in her novels and poetry and that, her work apart, anything like an official biography would have to depend too much on surmise and speculation, be it on her personal relationships or professional life. One good friend of hers, for example, assured me that she had had an affair with George Orwell, but I agree with Professor Bernard Crick (*George Orwell: A Life*) that they were just 'chums' when they saw something of each other at the BBC during World War II. Stevie had a great talent for this kind of friendship, affectionate, even intimate for a time but not lastingly deep, and I was one of the many who benefited from it. After all, does it *really* matter whom she loved? Her poetry and novels make clear enough that she knew all about the joys and agonies of being in love. Her beliefs, experiences and relationships are described in almost everything she wrote.

Something, though, had to be done, for world-wide interest in her work has aroused curiosity in her as a person. The rise in her popularity over the past decade has been wellnigh phenomenal: four impressions of the posthumously published *Collected Poems*, new editions of her three novels and increasingly frequent use of her poetry in anthologies in Scandinavia in the north, Germany and Italy to Japan in the east and of course the United States in the west. As her executor, I was therefore glad to respond to the approach made by William McBrien and Jack Barbera for permission to compile this volume. Stevie kept few records and the task was formidable.

What they have chosen for *Me Again* is tantamount to an autobiographical profile. Some of the letters and reviews, for example, reveal her attitudes to religion and politics with an authenticity that no biographer could have achieved.

Much as I admire the editors' assiduous research, I do not always agree with their conclusions in the introduction. They never met Stevie and have had to depend on her writings and on conversations with friends. The letters inevitably express moods of the moment. Her interest in death, for instance, was metaphysical and practical, not an ever-present pre-occupation as might be inferred from her poetry. Close friends of Stevie knew that she could overcome her depressions and that she had a bubbling zest for life, and its comedy in particular. She was marvellous company with a highly-developed appreciation of the ridiculous.

Also, although like many writers she had her troubles with libel, she was not worried about it incessantly as might be inferred from some of the letters and 'The Story of a Story'. It was again a concern of the moment, she was not persecuted by the dangers; she had, after all, a cavalier side to her character—in writing as well as in her relationships.

For me an extra pleasant factor in the publication of this book is that during her lifetime Stevie made very little impression in the United States, and so she would have been gratified that two American scholars have now taken the initiative. She would have been surprised and amused, throwing back her head, laughing with pleasure that the 'little nugget of genius' recognised early on by the critic, Sir Desmond MacCarthy, had been spotted by *American* editors.

I am grateful to them both, I must add, for tracking down the poems in that section of the book. None of them has been published in book form. When Stevie put together two collected volumes, *Selected Poems* and *The Frog Prince*, she omitted some of the poems that had been published in the previous small collections. Just before her death, however, she sent her publishers the last small volume, *Scorpion*, and it was of course included in *The Collected Poems* together with what had been left out of *Selected Poems* and *The Frog Prince*. I considered book publication to be the criterion in deciding what, in the final judgment, she would have wanted to be preserved. However, ten years later it seems appropriate to have anything worthy of hers in *Me Again* and I was happy to allow the editors to include these virtually unknown poems. The poems quoted in other sections of the book have been very slightly edited to conform with Stevie's definitive versions in *The Collected Poems*.

Lastly, I must record that the much wider recognition that Stevie

Smith's writings have enjoyed since her death is in no small part due to the enthusiasm of Allen Lane and Penguin Books who have published her poetry and the equally enthusiastic vigour of Virago Press whose new editions of her three novels have had a success never attained in her lifetime.

James MacGibbon, Devon 1981

ACKNOWLEDGEMENTS & BIBLIOGRAPHICAL NOTE

Janet Watts allowed us to see Stevie's typescript of *The Holiday* from which we learned 'In the Beginning of the War' was originally a part of that novel. Judith Hemming showed us Margery Hemming's copy of *The New Savoy* (eds. Mara Meulen and Francis Wyndham) in which Margery Hemming wrote a key to the identity of the characters in 'The Story of a Story'. The story was reprinted in Peter and Wendy Owen's *Springtime Two: An Anthology of Current Trends in Literature*, Peter Owen Ltd., 1958, and we have incorporated some minor changes Stevie made for the reprinting. Except where noted, all publishers and publications mentioned in our Contents and this Note are London based.

'Getting Rid of Sadie' was reprinted in *Did It Happen?*, Old-bourne Press, 1956. 'Sunday at Home' is preserved on microfilm at the BBC Written Archives, Caversham Park, Reading. 'Syler's Green: a return journey' was published in *From the Third Programme: A Ten-Years Anthology*, ed. John Morris, Nonesuch Press, 1956. We have incorporated a few minor changes Stevie made in her copy of the text. 'Private Views' was reprinted in *Turnstile One: A Literary Miscellany From the New Statesman and Nation*, ed. V.S. Pritchett, Turnstile Press, 1948. When 'Surrounded By Children' was published in the *New Statesman and Nation* it was listed as a prose-poem.

Eve's Journal was published by Newnes, Pearson (Stevie's employers) from 1937 to 1939. All copies in the British Library were destroyed in the bombing. Four copies are preserved as part of the Stevie Smith Collection of the Brynmor Jones Library, the University of Hull. It is from this collection that we obtained the 'Mosaic' article. *Cats in Colour* was published by B.T. Batsford, Ltd, and in the U.S.A. by Viking Press. Other books listed in our Contents are: *Allsorts 2*, ed. Ann Thwaite, Macmillan, 1969; *The Windmill*, No. 2, eds. Edward Lane [Kay Dick] and Reginald Moore, William Heinemann, Ltd, 1945; *T.S. Eliot: A Symposium for his Seventieth Birthday*, ed. Neville Braybrooke, Rupert Hart-Davis, 1958; *Holidays and Happy Days*, ed. Oswell Blakeston, Phoenix House, 1949; *At*

Close of Eve: An Anthology of New Curious Stories, ed. Jeremy Scott [Kay Dick], Jarrolds, 1947; *Presenting Poetry: A Handbook for English Teachers*, ed. Thomas Blackburn, Methuen & Co., Ltd, 1966; *Flower of Cities: A Book of London: Studies and Sketches By Twenty-Two Authors*, 1949, Max Parrish, Max Parrish & Co., Ltd; *The Holiday Book*, ed. John Singer, Glasgow: William Maclellan, 1946. Although Stevie's poem, 'Pretty Baby', was published in her volume, *The Best Beast* (New York: Knopf, 1969), it was inadvertently omitted from *The Collected Poems*, and so it has been included in *Me Again*.

As far as we know, the poems by Stevie which are not attributed on our Contents pages have not been published. All such poems, and the poem 'Why d'You Believe?' which is mentioned in our Introduction, are in undated typescript or holograph form in the McFarlin Library, The University of Tulsa, Tulsa, Oklahoma, U.S.A., except for the following: 'Mother Love' is a typescript in the possession of Terence Kilmartin; 'The Old Poet' is a typescript in the files of P.E.N., London; 'They Killed' is a typescript in the McFarlin Library, but our date comes from Kathleen Farrell's holograph, now in the possession of Jack Barbera; 'My Earliest Love' is a rejected proof sheet in the possession of Rupert Hart-Davis; 'The Ballet of the Twelve Dancing Princesses' is a typescript, dated June 1939, in the possession of Kitty Hermges. Stevie sent typescript copies of 'Goodnight' to Rupert Hart-Davis and Naomi Mitchison. Rupert Hart-Davis retains his copy and Naomi Mitchison has put hers on deposit in the Department of Manuscripts of the National Library of Scotland: it has been published in her book, *You May Well Ask: A Memoir, 1920–1940* (Victor Gollancz Ltd., 1979). The last stanza of 'When One' appears in *The Collected Poems* as 'Why do I'. The *Scotsman*, which printed 'Sapphic', is published in Edinburgh.

Stevie's copy of the Autumn 1966 *Agenda*, mentioned in our Introduction, is in the McFarlin Library. Sylvia Plath's letter to Stevie, printed in our Introduction, is in the possession of James MacGibbon. It is copyright Ted Hughes, 1981, and is reproduced by permission of Olwyn Hughes, to whom all enquiries should be directed.

Me Again contains *all* of the stories written by Stevie which we know to exist. It also contains *most* of her essays and uncollected poems. We have omitted some uncollected poems and some essays because they do not seem to be worth publishing in *Me Again*. This is also true of many of Stevie's book reviews, although some very interesting reviews have been sacrificed because of limitations of space. A more extensive account of Stevie's writings will appear upon publication of our Stevie Smith bibliography, in progress.

Our selection of Stevie's letters is comprised of the most interesting and well written of those we were able to locate before *Me Again* went to press. Stevie's letters to the following people are in their possession: Patricia Beer; Anna Browne; Robert Buhler (published in his essay, 'Heads—I Lose!', *Chelsea Arts Club Yearbook 1979*); Dr James Curley; Doreen Diamant; Helen Fowler; John Guest; Rupert Hart-Davis; Ladislav Horvat; Denis Johnston; Elisabeth Lutyens (published in her autobiography, *A Goldfish Bowl*, Cassell & Company, Ltd, 1972); Jonathan Mayne; Naomi Replansky; Anthony Thwaite; David Wright. The letters to Ian Angus and John Gabriel are in the George Orwell Archive, University College, London (the letter to Mr Angus is in the administrative papers of the Archive). Stevie's letters to Diana Athill and Vanessa Jebb are in the files of the publisher, André Deutsch; her letters to Sally Chilver are in the Manuscripts Division of the British Library; and her letters to Richard Church and R.A. Scott-James are in the Humanities Research Center, The University of Texas at Austin, U.S.A. All of Stevie's letters to Kay Dick are in the Manuscripts Division of the Washington University Libraries, St Louis, Missouri, U.S.A.; and her letter to Kathleen Farrell is owned by the London booksellers, Bertram Rota. The letter to L.P. Hartley is in the Manuscripts Collection of the John Rylands University Library, Manchester; and letters to John Hayward and Rosamond Lehmann are in King's College Library, Cambridge. The BBC Written Archives has Stevie's letters to Anna Kallin and George Orwell: the letter to Orwell has been published in Bernard Crick's *George Orwell: A Life* (Secker & Warburg, 1980). Stevie's letter to Terence Kilmartin is in the files of the *Observer*; and her letters to Rachel Marshall are in the possession of Geoffrey and Kitty Hermges (née Marshall). We have printed the letter to Jack McDougall from Stevie's carbon copy, now in the possession of James MacGibbon. Letters to Naomi Mitchison have been published in her memoir, *You May Well Ask*, but for *Me Again* we have consulted the originals on deposit in the Department of Manuscripts of the National Library of Scotland. Stevie's letter to Hermon Ould is in the files of P.E.N., London; and her letter to

Osbert Sitwell is in the Boston University Library, Boston, Massachusetts, U.S.A.

All drawings in this book are by Stevie Smith, and we believe none of them, except those on pp. i and 104, has been published before. The two exceptions, we discovered after the book went to press, appeared in Stevie's sketchbook, *Some Are More Human Than Others*, Gaberbocchus, 1958. The drawings on pp. iii, viii, 79, 170, 185, 198, 206, 221, 230, 248, 326, 327 are in the possession of James MacGibbons; those on pp. 39, 44, 50, 147, 158, 183, 201, 225, 250, 251, 279 are in the possession of Rupert Hart-Davis; and those on pp. i, 11, 27, 81, 104, 111, 125, 134, 137, 171, 181, 192, 211, 213, 216, 218, 223, 228, 236, 241, 243, 333 are part of the Stevie Smith papers owned by the McFarlin Library. The photo at the front of *Me Again* is by Howard and Joan Coster, *c.* 1937, and the photo at the back is by Jane Bown, *c.* 1969.

We thank all of the individuals and institutions mentioned in this Note who have provided material and information for *Me Again*. The research necessary to assemble, edit and introduce the book was supported by grants from The American Council of Learned Societies, Hofstra University, The National Endowment for the Humanities, and The University of Mississippi (all U.S.A.).

INTRODUCTION

You have weaned me too soon, you must nurse me again.

So says the ghost in Stevie Smith's poem 'The Wanderer', as she taps on the windows of the living. But the poet rhetorically asks if the ghost *would* be happier within, for Stevie delighted in death as an 'end and remedy'. She did respect, however, the kind of afterlife writers achieve when others continue to read their work. Ten years after Stevie Smith's death we have what was never available in her lifetime: her *Collected Poems* and all three of her novels in print at the same time. Now, here she is again, in hitherto uncollected writings —some of them never before published. They reflect the wide variety of her talent as well as the volume of her writings.

For most of her life, in her own neighbourhood, Stevie was not celebrated: 'Very few in this suburb know me as Stevie Smith, & I should like it to stay that way', she wrote in 1956. The neighbourhood was Palmers Green, a setting in Stevie's third novel, *The Holiday*, and the focus of her essay, 'A London Suburb'. She called it 'Bottle Green' in her first two novels, in the short story, 'The Herriots', and in a series of special articles entitled 'Mosaic' which she wrote for *Eve's Journal* in the late 1930s. Palmers Green is also the 'Syler's Green' of an essay read on the BBC Third Programme by the actress Dame Flora Robson, who had been in Stevie's class at the Palmers Green High School. (Stevie later went to the North London Collegiate School for Girls). These disguises worked, but in 1969, when Stevie again celebrated her suburb in an essay called 'The Same Place' (written for *Allsorts 2* and not included here), the secret was out; so she called it by its real name.

Palmers Green is a 'high-lying outer northern suburb' of London, where 'the wind blows fresh and keen'. Stevie thought it 'beautiful kindly bustling', and for most of her life she lived there with 'Aunt', 'the Lion of Hull'. In Aunt's Yorkshire accent Stevie was 'Paggy', for she was christened 'Florence Margaret' and acquired the nickname 'Stevie' only when, at the age of nineteen or twenty, she was riding with a friend and some boys shouted 'Come on Steve!' (after the great jockey, Steve Donoghue). The name stuck. Her mother died when Stevie was sixteen, and her father went to sea shortly after her birth and saw very little of his family thereafter. But sturdy Aunt was always there. Stevie never married, and it was her Aunt who provided her with freedom from domestic responsibilities, and an emotional security, to which many of her friends attribute something childlike in her manner and vision. Others are acerbic: Stevie had a 'quite deliberate "child*ish*" manner', wrote the composer Elisabeth Lutyens in her autobiography, adding, with spirit, 'who in hells wants "innocence" from an adult—or a child?'

There was no innocence about Stevie nor did she believe that children were innocent—the underlying point, for instance, of her story, 'Getting Rid of Sadie'. 'Sadie' and 'To School in Germany' were written for a series published in the *Evening Standard* under the title 'Did It Happen?' The requirement of this series was that its stories could have happened to their authors. The next day's *Standard* would tell readers if the stories were fact or fiction, and, in the case of Stevie's stories, did tell them that the stories were fiction. If the fictional 'Getting Rid of Sadie' is knowing about the hearts of children—that they are not so different from adult hearts—still, Stevie had an affection for childhood. It is her metaphor for human passion in the poem 'At School', as she says in her essay of the same name, and it is contrasted with growing up—her metaphor for something mysterious and cold. In 'Syler's Green' she evokes her own childhood as a 'golden age', and in the story of 'The Herriots' she seems to be imagining the sorrow she might have encountered had she left the security of life with her aunt for the demands of marriage. An old woman in that story is associated with the eventual happiness of 'Peg'. The old woman loves to sit in a cemetery, and she counsels Peg to be reconciled to her lot, telling her that 'in the lofty and ethereal conception of the aristocrat' the only escape is death. She is like Seneca, who said to the unhappy slave, 'Dost thou see the precipice?'—meaning, as Stevie loved to explain (and does explain in her essay, 'What Poems Are Made Of'), 'he could always go and jump off it'.

For Stevie, Death was a friend and she used to say that the notion of Death coming when called cheered her up so much she was able to face life. This idea is not far from the theme of childhood, for entombment and womb return are two sides of the same fantasy. It was not just Eve Stevie was thinking of when she wrote in a review titled 'A Life of Christ': 'some people do not want eternal life; they

would rather, if possible, "storm back through the gates of birth." '
Although she did not say so in the review, the quotation is from her
poem, 'A Dream of Comparison' (included here in the essay 'Too
Tired For Words'). Stevie imagines, in a similar vein, a return to the
pram in her fascinating prose-poem, 'Surrounded by Children'; and
there are other examples of this yearning, in her poem 'Childhood
and Interruption' and in 'To Carry the Child' (*The Collected Poems*),
in which she says that 'To carry the child into adult life/Is to be
handicapped':

> But oh the poor child, the poor child, what can he do,
> Trapped in a grown-up carapace,
> But peer outside of his prison room
> With the eye of an anarchist?

In her anarchic attempt to climb into the perambulator, the sad
beldame of 'Surrounded by Children' sees the real children closing
in, staring and laughing.

It is true that Stevie sometimes saw children as rivals. She spent a
beach holiday in 1961 with a family of her acquaintance. The young
son was home from school, and his parents told Stevie she should
know, if she joined them, their time would be devoted to the boy and
his wishes. She joined them, became annoyed when their attention
centred on the boy, and wrote her poem, 'The holiday' (with its line
about the peace she 'did not know') which appeared in the *Observer*
several weeks later. The story 'Beside the Seaside', written in 1948,
grew out of a beach holiday Stevie spent with a different family. It is
perhaps Stevie's best story, and was praised for its charm in a note to
Stevie by the mother of that family. But the mother did not like the
way Stevie had written about her son—called 'Hughie' in the story.
Indeed, in its lyrical nostalgic ending is the characteristically Stevie
pinch: 'Oh, what a pleasant holiday this was, how much she had
enjoyed today for instance; hitting Hughie had also been quite
agreeable.' In her letter about not wanting to be known in Palmers
Green, Stevie expressed her wish that the neighbourhood would not
be '*stirred up in any way*', because many of the residents were 'in the
novels & poems'. But the families of the seaside holidays were not
from Palmers Green, and they did know Stevie as a writer, and they
were 'stirred up'. In fact, the family in 'Beside the Seaside' broke

3

with Stevie, and never again saw her socially.

Stevie's use of real people and events in her writing not only resulted in broken friendships, there was the threat of libel too. 'One has to be careful with these transcripts from life', Stevie wrote to the discerning critic and bibliophile, John Hayward, about her 'concentrated and strrong' poem, 'Goodnight'. In her powerful essay, 'My Muse', she wrote that poetry 'makes a strong communication', it 'never has any kindness at all.' Among other things, fears about libel probably entered her mind when she noted: 'It is not poetry but the poet who has a feminine ending, not the Muse who is weak, but the poet.' The whole of 'The Story of a Story' is concerned with the strains to which a writer can be subjected by anxious friends who find themselves turned into subject matter. Is the writer's obligation to the Muse, or to the sensitivities of others? In 'The Story of a Story' Helen is accused by Roland in a dream: 'You go into houses under cover of friendship and steal away the words that are spoken.' We must admit that here Stevie is giving the other side its due. Her own feelings are expressed by Helen who says the law of libel 'is everything that there is of tyranny and prevention'. Margery Hemming, in her copy of 'The Story of a Story', wrote a key to the identity of its characters: Stevie, of course, is the writer Helen; Margery Hemming and her husband Francis (eminent civil servant and lepidopterist) are the couple, Roland and Bella; Ba is the art historian, Phoebe Pool; and Lopez is the writer, Inez Holden. The story Stevie was writing about in 'The Story of a Story' is 'Sunday at Home'. One clue is the references to goldfish that appear in both.

'Sunday at Home' was originally titled 'Enemy Action'—a witty reference to the marital discord of its characters Ivor and Glory, and its macrocosmic parallel in the fall of doodle bombs. It was accepted in early 1946 by the editor of an anthology called *The Holiday Book*. A month later he returned it, after hearing from Stevie that the story was based on real people. She kept trying to place it until December 1948, when it was accepted for consideration in a Short Story Contest run by the BBC Third Programme. Stevie's work had already been broadcast on BBC Radio—a script on Thomas Hood for the Eastern Service, and 'Syler's Green' for the Third Programme—but she would have liked to read it herself. Her desire to have this opportunity is seen in the vehemence of a letter she wrote to George Orwell (then working for the BBC) in 1942, accusing him of cheating her of a chance to read her poetry on the air. It was typical of her profes-

4

sionalism that Stevie did not attend her father's funeral in February 1949, because she was occupied with auditions and rehearsals for her first broadcast. She requested the title 'Enemy Action' be changed, perhaps thinking a less pointed title would reduce the chance of stirring up trouble. 'Sunday at Home' was accepted as a runner-up, and Stevie's voice went out on the air in April 1949. Thereafter she often broadcast book reviews, interviews, and poetry readings.

Stevie wrote to Kay Dick in February 1946, describing the changes she had made in 'Sunday at Home' so that Ivor and Glory could not be equated with the Hemmings. She changed her own name to 'Greta', but Greta's conversation will be familiar to readers of such poems as 'At School' and 'From the Coptic'. The central detail of Ivor sitting in a cupboard while the doodle bombs fall, talking to his wife through the door, she would not change. 'I do not think this can be laboured into an imputation of cowardice,' Stevie wrote to Kay Dick, 'because . . . the doodles reminded him of the "experiment" in which he had been wounded.' Francis Hemming was not involved in bomb experiments, but he was wounded in France during the first World War, and he did repair to cupboards when the bombs fell (a sensible act, by the way) during the second World War. To Margery Hemming Stevie became 'a plain simple symbol of betrayal and treachery', as Stevie put it in a letter. Another door was shut tight against her.

'The almost absolute dearth of companionship in Palmers Green does drive one into writing', Stevie wrote to a friend in 1964, and some twenty years earlier, discussing her motivation for writing in a letter to John Hayward, she told him: 'it's not the fame, dear, it's the company'. Ironically, as we have seen, the writing sometimes estranged her from the company, and this was no less true of her book reviews than it was of her fiction and poetry. But this is one-sided. There were also in Stevie's life the families she cherished, families who loved and cosseted her, families who became her families and to whom she wrote many of the letters in *Me Again*–the Marshalls, the Brownes, the Fowlers. As she became famous there were the country houses to which she had entry: Biddesden House in Hampshire, for example, the home of Lord Moyne (the writer Bryan Guiness) and his wife; and Chastleton House in Oxfordshire, home of the Clutton-Brocks. She enjoyed leading the conversation on such visits just as she appreciated the outlets for poetry readings and recording studios that were now available to her.

It had all begun when her first book, *Novel on Yellow Paper*, was published in 1936. But who was this Stevie Smith? Virginia Woolf has recorded in her letters that Robert Nichols, the poet, wrote her a six-page letter telling her that, without doubt, *she* was Stevie Smith and this novel was her best by far. When he learned the truth he wrote Stevie a fan letter, and so did Clive Bell. Her reputation had been established and this led to the publication of her poems and to reviewing. Although her career started and ended with *éclat*, her commercial success did not match her literary renown.

Since first publication, though, she had always a select band of admirers ranging from Noël Coward to the author and monk Thomas Merton, and including the critic Desmond MacCarthy and Robert Lowell. Sylvia Plath discovered her relatively late:

Monday: November 19 [1962]

Dear Stevie Smith,
  I have been having a lovely time this week listening to some recordings of you reading your poems for the British Council, and Peter Orr has been kind enough to give me your address. I better say straight out that I am an addict of your poetry, a desperate Smith-addict. I have wanted for ages to get hold of 'A Novel on Yellow Paper' (I am jealous of that title, it is beautiful, I've just finished my first, on pink, but that's no help to the title I fear) and rooted as I have been in Devon for the last year bee-keeping and apple growing I never see a book or bookseller. Could you tell me where I could write to get a copy?
  Also, I am hoping, by a work of magic, to get myself and the babies to a flat in London by the New Year and would be very grateful in advance to hear if you might be able to come to tea or coffee when I manage my move—to cheer me on a bit. I've wanted to meet you for a long time.
  Sincerely,
  Sylvia Plath

They never met, for Sylvia Plath died less than three months after writing this letter.

It is tempting to surmise that the undated holograph of Stevie's poem 'Mabel', which is the only copy we know to exist, was written after Stevie heard of Sylvia Plath's death. Of course it might have been her own fantasy: a list of poetic self portraits Stevie sent in a letter to Kay Dick concluded with the phrase, 'and all the others that are about being dead or dotty'. On the list is the poem 'Croft' ('He is soft'), which somewhat explains the drawing of a *woman* Stevie chose to illustrate it. Some of the poems in *Me Again* which were not discovered in time to be included in *The Collected Poems* may surprise readers familiar with her work. Certainly 'Goodnight' and 'On the Dressing gown lent me by my Hostess the Brazilian Consul in Milan, 1958' are atypical. So is Stevie's imitation of Milton. Although 'Satan Speaks' was published in 1945, Stevie's note on a typescript of the poem indicates it was 'written about 1925'—so it was an early and accomplished exercise. 'Sapphic', Stevie's lovely poem in 'mixed speech', is also atypical. A signed version of it is written in her copy of *Agenda* (Autumn 1966), on the same page as Peter Whigham's translation of Sappho's 'Loneliness'. Tom Scott's Lallans poems on subsequent pages of *Agenda*, especially 'The Annunciation' which Stevie notes on the cover of her copy, probably gave her the idea to put 'Loneliness' into 'mixed speech'.

Loneliness as a theme is common in Stevie's poetry, and the previously uncollected poems are no exception, especially the touching 'None of the other birds' and the amusing 'Telly-me-Do'. Also common in Stevie's work and represented in *Me Again* are poems on death and on poetry. The first group of character sketches, from 'A Portrait' to 'He preferred . . .', evokes another of her themes—that one must have the courage to try. Often in poetry readings she would contrast the brave Harold of 'Harold's Leap' with the cowardly monk of 'The Weak Monk'. 'Pretty Baby' is a good example of Stevie's 'religious' poetry: the child in the poem, who looks 'imperially', is reminiscent of the child who is described as 'Noble and not Mild' in Stevie's poem 'Christmas'. 'Pretty Baby' ends sweetly, with mention of angelic song, and the observation that 'we will try to sing songs too'. But it raises one of those conundrums Stevie was always finding in Christian dogma—freedom from sin seen as a limitation on Deity. The same thought arises in her poem, 'Was He Married?', which Stevie included in her essay, 'Some Impediments to Christian Commitment': 'All human beings should have a medal, / A god cannot carry it, he is not able.'

'Some Impediments to Christian Commitment' has not been published previously. It is the talk given by Stevie, a little more than two years before her death, to parishioners of St Cuthbert's, Philbeach Gardens in London. She included in the talk several of her poems which question Christian dogma in a teasing way—one of them, 'Thoughts about the Christian Doctrine of Eternal Hell', being considerably longer than the familiar version first (?) published in *The Listener*, 9 July 1959. However, in *Me Again* this poem and all other poems in Stevie's essays and in the radio play have, at the request of her executor, been made to conform to the definitive versions printed in *The Collected Poems*. Stevie also included in her talk a stanza from a poem which exists in typescript under the title, 'Why d'You Believe?'. (The stanza begins, 'Oh Church of Christ, oh bride of mien ferocious': although 'Why d'You Believe?' is not in *The Collected Poems*, we have elected to omit it from *Me Again*. It is not a good poem.) She said of 'Why d'You Believe?' that it is 'rather intolerant perhaps, but . . . not tinged with uncertainty, as later sometimes I again came to be, and my poems too'.

Although there is a ring of conviction in her poems that challenge Christianity, Stevie had another mood: one of her favourite quotations, cited as such in *Novel on Yellow Paper* and in one of the reviews in *Me Again*, was, '*les natures profondement bonnes sont toujours indécises*'. And towards the end of another review she writes: 'who is upside down—Fr D'Arcy [a Jesuit priest at Farm Street Church, London, much consulted by the intelligentsia with Roman Catholic leanings] or the unbelievers—we cannot know'. And there is the splendid definition she gave of herself in an interview: 'I'm a back-slider as a non-believer.' Her hesitations extended to other areas: 'I wish there was some litmus paper test you could have for your poems, blue for bad and pink for good', she wrote in a letter to Rosamond Lehmann. 'Can I leave it to you?' she asks the poet and editor David Wright, referring to her indecision about whether to use the adjective 'warm' or 'cold' in a poem. And to Rachel Marshall she wrote, 'I am not sure that I don't sometimes get the wrong poems into print.' Another kind of hesitation, which will give heart to some, comes up at the end of her review, 'A Private Life':

> Read the stories and poems the sinners write, but leave their private lives (as we should like our own sinning lives to be left—remembering that equation which cannot truly be cast by any human being) to heaven. So one feels. One may be wrong.

Biographies often came her way for review, and despite the sentiment which concludes 'A Private Life', she seems to have enjoyed them. Other books she wrote about with relish were those on religious topics. Only rarely did Stevie review poetry. As she reviewed books for three decades, what we have included here is of course only a tiny percentage of the whole; and we have not given examples from all the newspapers and journals to which she contributed: none, for example, from *Modern Woman*, *World Review*, *Tribune*, and *The Daily Telegraph* for which she often wrote. Surprisingly, one of the journals to publish her reviews (and, once, her poems) was *Aeronautics*, in which they were not signed, but initialled. A letter included in *Me Again* confirms that the *Aeronautics* reviews initialled 's.s.' *were* hers. Our selection of reviews for this book has been guided by Stevie's description of the critic's virtues in *P.E.N. News*, which is why the section begins with that statement.

In the reviews, essays, poems, stories, letters, and radio play, one hears the same Stevie—her rhythms, her wit, her obsessions. Her presence in the various forms of writing contained in *Me Again* rides above the book's diversities, and often calls them into question. She herself continually plays with these diversities. About the distinction between argument and poetry she says in her talk, 'Some Impediments to Christian Commitment': 'You may find it curious to write poems so much on argumentative subjects—but so did the Arians, you know, when they rushed about Alexandria, singing their popular song: "There was a time when the Son was not"—what was this but a poem?' The dividing line between story and poetry is another distinction (a modern one) challenged in her work. Her story 'Over-Dew', for example, which she slipped into *The Holiday*, reappeared years later as a poem, 'The House of Over-Dew'. She challenges our very conception of poetry in a poem such as 'Torquemada': 'Uncle Torquemada, / does Beppo know about Jesus?' The drawing which accompanies these lines—of the famous inquisitor (or prelate named after him) thrown a bit off balance by the child's question concerning her dog—is part of, and essential to, the poem. We might call it an especially powerful cartoon, or we might echo Stevie: 'what is this but a poem?' Note the Interlocutor's question, in Stevie's radio play, and her reply:

INTERLOCUTOR: . . . Those prose passages you said, about where you had seen me, with the hour-glass on the moire ribbon and in the sunshine of Homer, these are also poems, are they not? Just as much as the girl in the dark wood was a poem?
s.s.: There is no very strong division between what is poetry and what is prose.

The passage about seeing a man with an hour-glass and moire ribbon, and a later passage—which begins, 'There is a little laughter where you are going and no warmth'—are both taken from Stevie's novel, *The Holiday* (as is the passage about a cat on a raft in her Introduction to *Cats in Colour*). The radio play is itself an excellent example of how she blurred distinctions between one form of writing and another, for it is in fact a poetry reading, like so many others she gave, with a final twist when the Interlocutor is revealed as Death. The convention of Death as a man who takes Stevie away is the same one employed so successfully several years after her death, by Hugh Whitemore, in his stage play, 'Stevie'. Literary boundaries are crossed again—those between life and art—when Stevie cites the words of a neighbour (in her essay, 'A London Suburb') as an 'unconscious poem that happens sometimes when people are talking':

> Seven years old 'e is.
> Ever so sweet 'e is.
> Ever such a neat coat 'e's got.
> Ever so fond of kiddies.
> But a dog likes to know oo's going to 'it 'im and oo isn't.

'Poetry does not like to be up to date, she refuses to be neat'—Stevie writes in an essay. Her own oddities of manner may keep some from her work, but there seems to be a growing number of readers who appreciate what she is doing. To them she is like the actress mentioned in the essay 'Too Tired for Words': however odd her exterior she has 'a poet's mind' and what goes on inside her is 'superior'. For such readers *Me Again* is published.

Jack Barbera, William McBrien, London 1981

STORIES

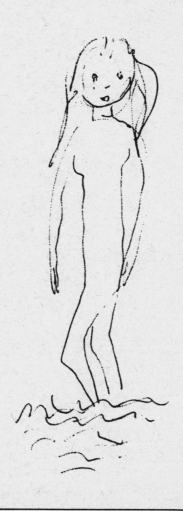

BESIDE THE SEASIDE
A Holiday with Children

It was a particularly fine day. The calm blue sea at unusually high flood washed the highest ridge of the fine shingle beach. It was a particular moment of high summer.

'In England,' said Helen, 'the hot August day is sufficiently remarkable to make an occasion.'

'One could roll off into it,' said Margaret dreamily, looking at the bulging sea.

The beach shelved steeply and the deep water lay in to shore; the water was also clear, you could see the toes of the paddlers, perched like fishing birds upon the upper shingle, knee-deep in the sea.

The two girls were in bathing dress, but Margaret's husband Henry sat in his sports shirt and flannel trousers in a deck-chair with his hat on.

'Yes, one could,' said Helen, 'but you won't, Margaret, you know you always stand up and take fifteen minutes to get right in.'

Helen now turned over and lay flat on her back looking from under her hands at the seaside people at their seaside pleasures.

'It is rather like the moral poem I wrote,' she said. 'Do you mind if I say it to you?' She looked anxiously at Henry.

'Not at all,' said Margaret.

'Oh well . . .' Henry sighed.

'Children . . .' said Helen firmly . . .

> *Children who paddle where the ocean bed shelves steeply*
> *Must take great care they do not,*
> *Paddle too deeply.*

Margaret, who was happy, took the poem with a smile, but Henry, who was never really happy, began to speak about the political situation.

'It is certain that the Russians have the atom bomb,' he said, 'otherwise they would not be pushing us so far over the Berlin business. Professor D.,' he went on (naming a once well-known Russian scientist), 'used to work with us at the Cavendish Laboratory in Rutherford's day, he went back to Russia several times, and then one day he went and did not come back. He was a most able man, no doubt he is still working, they say nothing about him. . . . '

'Oh, please drop it,' said Helen; but she was not speaking to Henry, she was speaking to Hughie. Henry and Margaret Levison had two children: Hughie who was ten and Anna who was eight. Hughie was now coming along the beach from the next breakwater with a large shrimping net in his hands, and in the shrimping net was a jelly fish so large that it brimmed over the net, and all its strings hung down through the holes of the net and waved about as Hughie ran.

'Oh do drop it, Hughie,' said Helen again, 'or better still put it up at the top of the beach under the sea-wall in the full sun, where it may fry to death and quite burn out. Oh what a wicked face it has.'

'I think it looks rather beautiful,' said the gentle girl Margaret.

Well, perhaps it did, after all, look rather beautiful. It looks like a fried egg, thought Helen. The frills waved prettily around a large yellow centre, this was the yoke of the egg; it was the underneath side that seemed to have a face. Hughie had disobediently turned it upside down out of the net just beside his father's deck-chair, so now the wicked face was hidden.

'They reproduce themselves by sexual congress,' said Henry grudgingly.

Margaret and Helen lay baking in the sun, laughing silently to themselves. Henry was so brilliantly irascible and gloomy, truly he was a care-ridden person, but so simple and open, and of such a violent honesty and of such a violent love of what was beautiful and truthful, one could not help but love him.

Helen began to whisper in Margaret's ear (the two friends were both writers and had a great appreciation for each other's writing, which was quite different): 'That poem I showed you the other day, with the drawing of the man riding the old tired horse, and the old woman close behind him, is rather like Henry.'

'What poem was that?' said kind Margaret, who knew how Helen liked to say her poems aloud.

> *Behind the Knight sits hooded Care,*
> *And as he rides she speaks him fair,*
> *She lays her hand in his sable muff,*
> *Ride he never so fast he'll not cast her off.*

Margaret sighed, and turned her head away from Helen. 'That poem has rather a gothic feeling,' she said; 'it is sad too.'

At this moment Major Pole-Curtis came galloping by with his little boy David.

'Hallo, hallo, hallo,' he cried in his deep musical voice, 'not been in yet, and a lovely day like this? Slackers,' he said, 'the water is quite warm, isn't it, David?'

'So long all,' said David, who looked rather blue. 'Helen,' he cried, as his father tore off with him, 'H-e-l-e-n!'

The baby-wail of 'Helen' came back to them on the wind of their flight, and Hughie, who was squatting rather restlessly beside his mother, began to jeer.

'Helen!' he mimicked. He got up and began to prance round Helen, shouting in his shrill penetrating voice, 'David loves Helen, David loves Helen'.

The major and his family were at the same hotel as Helen and her friends, and had the next table to theirs in the dining-room. David told everybody in the hotel that he was going to marry Helen.

'Will you be quiet, Hughie,' said Henry. 'Ah, the Major,' he said, as if he had just woken up to the fact that they had been running past. There they were, now in the distance, still running.

'He was awfully cross because David and Colin were late for lunch yesterday,' said Hughie. 'Do you know he gave Colin a terrific thrashing.'

'What!' said simple Henry, as impressed and horrified as his son had meant him to be. He turned to his wife, 'I suppose that is the correct way to bring children up; you and I, Margaret, are of course quite wrong. I expect he is unfaithful to her frequently, and then he comes home and confesses "all" and says, "Muriel" (or whatever her name is), "Muriel, I have behaved like a cad." '

Henry looked pleased with himself for this flight of fancy, and especially pleased because it was so well received by the girls, with such a lot of laughter.

'I think I shall bathe now,' said Margaret.

She stepped into the sea and stood with the sea washing gently round her knees looking out to the horizon of the sea where the heat mists played tricks with the passing ships. The great liner that was passing down channel from Tilbury seemed to be swimming in the high air, because the dark band of mist that hung below her made a false sea-border.

Margaret always took a long time to get into the water, when she was at last right in she would begin to swim strongly up and down parallel with the beach in a leisurely way that was full of pleasure.

'Oh,' she said, 'I wish there was no such thing as politics and problems, how wicked people are, how beyond hope unhappy, man is the most wretched of all the animals.'

'I do not think so,' said Helen, who had rushed quickly into the water and was now swimming alongside her friend, 'I think men are splendid hopeful creatures, but they have not come very far yet.'

How beautiful the water was, warm and milky; the sun burning through the water struck hot upon their shoulders washed by the sea. Helen turned on her back to rise and fall with the swelling sea (there was quite a swell on in spite of the calmness).

'It does not look as if they would come much further,' said Margaret.

'Because of the atom bomb, you mean?'

'And a good riddance to them.'

'*Them?*' said Helen. '. . . we are also the children of our times and must live and die with them. But oh what nonsense. Have you not, Margaret, seen babies trying to destroy themselves, they feel that they will burst for all that is in them: men and women are like that.'

'And perhaps they will burst,' said Margaret.

'If they do,' said Helen, 'they will still have been the high summit of creation, both great and vile beyond dreams.'

'Well, I don't think so,' said Margaret.

'Well, I do.'

'We have been having a rather deep philosophical argument,' said Margaret, as the two wet girls flopped down beside Henry, who never bathed.

'I think I shall take my shirt off for a few minutes,' said Henry.

He peeled it off over his head and replaced his large straw hat. 'How you girls can stand so much hot sun, I do not know,' he said. 'And now look at Margaret putting all that cream on her face.' Henry sighed. 'It is no good nowadays, there used to be a natural vegetable oil in the face creams, but now what is it? nothing but petroleum oil, no good at all, in fact, harmful.'

Helen, who was slopping about in the water again at Henry's feet, her elbows on the shingle ridge to keep her steady and her body afloat in the deep water where the shingle dipped, looked up into Henry's anxious face. In his intelligence, she thought, is all his care.

The child Hughie who had run off, now came back, pushing his sister Anna in front of him. 'I think Anna has poliomylitis,' he said.

16

'She has a stiff neck.' (Hughie was going to be a doctor when he grew up.)

'I think my breasts are beginning to grow,' said Anna.

'Breasts,' jeered Hughie, 'at eight years old, breasts, ha ha ha!'

He turned to Henry. 'Daddy, can I have sixpence, please, for another boat ride?'

'Nothing but boat rides, ice creams, pony rides. Well,' said Henry, giving him sixpence, 'I suppose that is what you think I am here for.'

'I'll come with you,' said Helen, 'so will Anna.'

They all ran off to the *Lady Grace* which, with Mr Crask in charge, was just about to start on a trip.

'Off with you,' cried Mr Crask, chivvying the children away from the stern seat where he kept his motor. He tapped them in a friendly way upon the behind. 'Oh, beg pardon,' he said, when he had tapped Anna, 'it's a lady.'

Anna went and sat beside her brother. She was a happy, silent child, easily silenced by her clever brother, a fair, silent child, a clever child, far cleverer than Hughie, but she was his loving slave. She had a strong neat comfortable body and wore only a pair of pants. Helen loved Anna; she thought she was like a seal.

Just as they were starting off, Major Pole-Curtis came running up. 'Just in time,' he said, and popped David on board. 'Good-bye, children,' he roared as the boat shot off, 'don't be late for lunch.'

Hughie began to entertain Mr Crask with his famous imitation of a train coming into King's Cross main-line station. His bright red hair flamed in the sunshine, his thin straight body moved delicately with the movement of the boat. He stood upright on the seat and let out a wild whistle.

'What's that, Mr Crask?'

'I dunno, me boy, a whistle, eh?'

'It's a goods train going into a tunnel on an incline,' said Hughie. He gave three short barks and a groan. 'That's the trucks closing up as the engine slows down. Chug, chug, chug, it's all right now, they're gathering speed again and coming on to the flat.'

Helen smiled at Hughie and then sighed. Hughie made himself rather unpopular sometimes, he was devoured by restless energy, he must do his train noises (or whatever it was), and he must have an audience.

'That Levison boy . . .' the Major had said one day with quite a critical eye . . . he had stopped talking when Helen had come up, but

17

there was no doubt he would like to have smacked Hughie. *Levison*, oh of course, Helen sighed again, of course the Major would feel like that . . . he had just come back from Palestine.

She looked down at the Major's little boy David who was lying alongside with a devoted air. David had pale yellow hair and great charm; he was five years old. Helen stroked his hair and, slipping her hand under his chin, turned his face up to hers. The sun-speckled face, she thought, the smiling eyes, the assured and certain eyes, the easy authority of certain charm, there is the quality of sunlight about you, of ancient sunlight in privileged circumstances.

'Daddy is going to take us to church tomorrow,' said David. 'You come too, Helen. Helen, do!'

Hughie paused in his train noises and glanced furiously across at them. What a nuisance David was, couldn't Helen *see?*

'We are going to that old church at Lymne,' went on David in a confiding tone. 'Oh, Helen, do come, do . . . *where that nice vicar is.*'

'Oh, I don't know, I don't know,' she said, stroking again the daffodil hair, 'I don't know, David . . .'

David moved closer. 'Come on, Helen, come on, do . . . *it's the best glass in the south of England.*'

Helen laughed, she knew there would be no room for her in the major's car, with mamma who liked vicars, and papa who liked church glass . . . 'I haven't got a hat.'

'Never mind,' said David, 'I never wear mine in church.'

In the evening the hotel children, marshalled by Hughie, played cricket in the field at the back of the hotel. This was a fine wide closely-mown piece of grass stretching for a distance under the hills where the old town stood. There was also the military canal and the beautiful gardens before you came to the main road. It was now seven o'clock and the sun dropping to the soft hills threw a golden light upon the cricket field and long shadows.

The grown-ups sat on the pavilion steps and watched the game. Anna, who only played with boys, was batting; she made thirteen runs.

There were a lot of other people in the field, doing different things. An old mild person stood himself in front of the children's wicket with his back turned to them; he was watching the tennis players on the other side of the wire netting.

'Would you mind moving, please,' said David firmly; he was wicket-keeper.

Some runners came charging by. Never mind, they were soon gone.

Suddenly Henry said that he would play too.

'Oh yes,' said Margaret, 'do play, Henry.'

Helen squeezed her friend's arm affectionately as Henry took his place. 'How happy you look,' she said and began to laugh softly. What an irritating girl.

'Oh, why is it,' said poor Margaret, 'why is it that there is something so sad and tense about fathers when they play with their children; it really tears at one when they take part in the sports. Why is it?'

'Yes,' said Helen, 'it is never very touching when the mothers run in the three-legged race at schools; no, it is different.'

She squeezed Margaret's arm again, 'It will be all right, you'll see.'

Margaret said, 'Henry is more locked up in being a Jew than it seems possible.'

Oh dear, thought Helen. 'Well,' she said, 'you are Jewish too, aren't you, and you do not feel locked up in it.'

'No,' said Margaret. 'But, Helen, you cannot know quite what it is like; it is a feeling of profound uncertainty, especially if you have children. There is a strong growing anti-Jewish feeling in England, and when they get a little older, will they also be in a concentration camp here in England?'

'One sometimes thinks that is what they want,' said Helen flippantly, getting rather cross, 'they behave so extremely. Well, that is rather an extreme remark of yours, is it not, about the concentration camps, eh, *here*? If there is an anti-Jewish feeling in England at the moment it is because of Palestine.' Helen paused and went on again more seriously, 'I do not hold with the theory that the Jewish people is an appeasing, accommodating people, knowing, as some say, on which side their bread is buttered, and prepared to make accommodations with conscience for their own advantage. No, I think that they are an obstinate and unreasonable people, short-sighted about their true interests, fanatical. They have not the virtues of a slave, you see, but also they have not the virtues of a wise person.'

'Do not speak like this to Henry, please, Helen,' said Margaret. 'Oh, please, do not.'

'Of course I will not,' said Helen, and was about to pursue the subject when a closer glance at Margaret's gentle face showed that to do so would be untimely and indeed fruitless.

Darling Margaret, she thought with a pang, darling darling Margaret.

Margaret liked to live in a vegetable reverie; in this world of her vegetable reverie the delicate life of the plants, and the stones, too, for that matter, and the great trees and the blades of sharp grass and the leaves that were white when they turned upon the breeze, had a delicate obstinate life of their own. Margaret thought that people were the devils of creation. She thought that they were for ever at war for ever trying to oppress the delicate life of the plants and to destroy them; but this of course fortunately they could not do.

After the cricket match Henry went back to town, travelling late by moonlight in the car of a friend. He had to attend a conference early the next day. Margaret and the children and her friend Helen were now alone.

They spent the long days bathing and sunning themselves, and in the evenings they left the children and climbed to the downs at the back of the town and lay to watch the moon come up far out to sea; the turf was soft and the nights were warm.

Helen's old school-friend Phoebe lived in the little seaside town, and now that they were alone Phoebe often came to visit them, bringing her car.

Phoebe was a quiet girl, enjoying a private income and no cares.

They took the children for a picnic on the banks of the military canal far into the country where it turned inland from the coast three miles over the flats. From the banks of the canal that were covered with long grass and shaded by trees that were planted at the time the canal was built to keep Napoleon out, you could see the Martello towers that marked the line of the coast, and in the distance the pale sea that was as pale as the sky, baked clean of colour.

Helen wandered off on her own and explored the marshes which, cut by little sluggish streams, lay over towards the sea. The little quiet streams were like dykes, the water did not seem to move in them, the tall reeds stood up and every now and then a cow, mistaking the reedy margin for firm land, floundered in the soft mud. Swishing her tail the cow stood puzzled; the flies made a black patch over one eye which gave her a dissipated look.

Helen took off her shoes and walked barefoot over the soft marsh grass, and barefoot over the bare patches where the mud lay caked in squares. She sat down on the bank of the stream and looked up from below at the tall reeds and the thick bushes on the river-side. The cowparsley towered above her head as she sat close down by the water's edge. How hot and solitary it was here on the marsh by the river, and what a hot muddy watery cowparsley smell it had.

Helen fell into her favourite Brobdingnagian dream . . . if she were so high (say three inches) and the rest of the world unchanged, how very exciting and daring would be this afternoon excursion; each puddle a solitary lake, each tussock a grass mountain, the cowparsley mighty jungle trees, the grass, where it rose high by the river, to be cut through with a sharp knife for a pathway. Helen's enjoyment of scenery was as great as her friend Margaret's, but very different. She was rather childish about it and liked to imagine herself on some bold quest, travelling, with gun and compass and perhaps a fishing rod, exploring, enduring—for some reason, of course. But what reason? Ah, that she had never been able to determine. Never mind, it was the movement, and the sun and the grass and the lakes and the forests that made it exciting, and so agreeable. Sometimes there would come the steep face of a great inland cliff, and up the baked surface of its caked mud slopes the intrepid adventurer would slowly climb, hand over hand, step by step, half crawling, half climbing, the sun hot on her back. Until at last, and only just in time (for really it was hard work), she would come to the top and, pulling herself over by a fistful of tough grass most happily to hand, fling herself down on the grassy plateau, saying, 'Well, that's over, and not bad, if I may say so.'

Full of these agreeable fancies, soaked in sunshine and spattered with smelly mud, Helen now made her way back to where her friends were setting the tea-things on the river bank.

Hughie was grumbling and tossing. 'I hate this place,' he said, as Helen came up to them. 'I wish I was in London again; I would rather be in the Edgware Road. Do you hear, mother?—the Edgware Road.'

Helen sighed. She thought there must be something in Margaret's gentleness that drove her son mad. Hughie must wish to see her round on him, to make her angry, to make her cry?

'Do we have to have Hughie with us?' she said coldly.

One day Phoebe came again to fetch them in her car.

'Would you like to come to Dungeness?' she said. She wanted to go

21

there herself, it would make a nice afternoon trip, and they could get some tea at the Ship Inn on the way.

'Would you like to come, Hughie?' she said.

'Yes,' said Hughie. 'No, I don't know. If it is fine I should like to bathe again.'

He ran off to spend some time jumping from the high stone wall on to the beach.

Anna lay in the shade of her mother's deck chair.

'My little seal,' said Helen, holding the painting water for her so that she could colour her drawings. She had a temperature and could not bathe or walk or ride.

'Shall we go to Dungeness?' said Phoebe lazily.

'I don't know. Shall we, yes, let's go quickly to Dungeness, now,' said Helen, jumping up. 'Let's take Anna because she can't ride or swim. Let's go quickly before anyone notices.' (She meant Hughie.)

Helen and Phoebe gave Margaret no time to think about it; the three girls and the child Anna ran laughing through the hotel and climbed into Phoebe's car—there was an exciting air of conspiracy.

'To Dungeness, to Dungeness,' sang Anna as the car leaped along.

There will be hell to pay, thought Helen glancing quickly at Margaret and away again.

'It is an escape,' she said, 'an escape from the men.' (From Hughie, she thought, from the restless son, the troubled father.) 'Hurrah. A car full of women is always an escaping party,' she said. The women laugh, their cheeks flush with excitement. They are off again, laughing they say, as they say of giggling schoolgirls, 'They're off again, that's set them off!' The boiled mutton is forgotten, the care of the children, the breadwinner's behest, the thought for others; it is an escape.

Phoebe drove with enthusiasm, well and quickly. Now the long line of bungalows gave way to black buildings of military significance, and now on their left, half out of the sea, stood up the great black wheel that had carried Pluto's cables, they were coming now to the home of Pluto and to the great lighthouse of Dungeness. Black barbed-wire curled over the landscape and ramshackle fishing huts straggled to the water's edge, with sparse dry grass growing up from the shingle gardens. The lighthouse establishments and the lighthouse itself were prinked and spry, untouched by the litter of war, bearing their neat fresh colours in stripes of grey, black, ochre and white.

They parked the car and made off through the barbed-wire entanglements to the brink of the sea at the very point of the land where it dropped to fathoms deep so that great ships drew safely close. They sat with their feet dipping in the sea, watching the porpoises at play and the seagulls dipping for fish. Where the North Sea met the Atlantic the waves drove up against each other, but in the lee of the land a great calm left the surface smooth to the winds' track.

Margaret began to be unhappy. She felt that she had been persuaded—over-persuaded—by these bold friends. Already the temperament of Hughie that was the temperament of his father Henry, stretched an accusing finger. They would certainly be late for dinner.

How beautiful the air was, how hot and singing and full of salt and dry. The sea was quite navy blue where the two seas met; out to sea lay a band of white mist: it was a heat haze. 'All through the war,' the lighthouse man had said, 'the lighthouse kept its light burning. Yes, they tried to bomb us once or twice, but then they gave it up, we were too useful to them, too.'

Yes, it was Pluto they were after, though they didn't know what it was, but just to be on the safe side; they'd hear rumours—oh no, they'd never got anything, except them bungalows.

'Margaret, dear,' said Helen, 'do cheer up. It won't do Hughie any harm; in fact, it will do him good.'

(Oh no, they did not understand.)

'The wife is the keeper of the peace,' laughed Helen, 'but take a long view, Margaret, the long peace is not always the peace of the moment. Hughie must learn.'

They were fifteen minutes late. Hughie met them with a speechless fury.

'I will explain, darling,' said Margaret. Hughie, who was quite pale with passion, would not speak to them, but began an affected conversation with the major's eldest child at the next table. ('Hallo, Helen,' said David the lover, 'hallo.')

Margaret and the two children slept in one room. After dinner Helen went up with them, and now Hughie began to speak.

'You are low, disgusting women,' he said in a low, fast voice getting louder. 'You are liars. I curse the day I was born.'

Hughie was beginning to enjoy himself now, he was beating himself into a great passion and Margaret was getting frightened. He went on in a mad voice: 'It is always Anna who must come first,' he said, 'always Anna, naturally Anna. Mother,' he shrieked, 'you have deliberately humiliated me to give me an inferiority complex to cripple me in my whole life; later I shall go mad, I feel that I am going mad now, and how will you like that, mother? The people will point to you in the street and they will say, "There is the woman who drove her son mad." ' He began to scream, 'Mad, mad, mad! When I am in an asylum you will be sorry.'

Helen picked up a rolled bundle of *Life* that had come from America. 'Shut up,' she said, and hit him sharply across the shin with the rolled magazine, 'shut up, you fool; whose car was it, anyway?'

'Anna is the second-born,' went on Hughie, 'she has displaced me in my mother's affection, as soon as she was born this is what she did.'

'You are practically word-perfect,' said Helen, with a fearful sneering expression. She hit him again. 'Stop putting on an act, shut up.'

At this moment the door opened and in walked Henry with his suitcase in his hand.

'Babies,' he said, 'babies, what hope have they? They are wheeled in prams along the sea-front like lords; often there is a coloured canopy between them and the sun. You can see them from the window, look.' He crossed the room and stepped out on to the balcony looking down at the sea walk. 'Look, it might be Lord Curzon. No wonder they are megalomaniacs. I've had a most difficult day,' he said, 'the people at the Clinic, really, it hardly seems worth while going on, really no idea . . . hum, hum, hum . . . ' (He began to sing under his breath.)

Suddenly everybody was talking at once.

Daddy, Hughie, Helen, Children, Mother, Anna . . . .

The words tumbled out all together at the same moment. Henry, washing his hands at the washbasin, did not seem to notice, he was still lost in thought for the babies he had seen in their prams along the promenade on his way from the station. 'Megalomaniacs,' he muttered.

'Well, good-bye,' said Helen, choking back the laughter that was now rising in hysterical gusts. 'I am staying the night with Phoebe you know. I'll see you all at breakfast. I'll be back for breakfast.'

She ran along the beach picking up some mussels as she ran. The moon was coming up in the twilight sky over to the horizon; but on the west there were long red and pink and green streaks where the sun had just settled below the hills: these were a dark soft olive green. She and Phoebe, Helen thought, could cook those mussels and have them for a late supper. One could always eat two suppers these lovely hungry seaside days. Oh, what a pleasant holiday this was, how much she had enjoyed today for instance; hitting Hughie had also been quite agreeable. How much she enjoyed the company, the conversation, her darling friend Margaret, the stormy Hughie, the sleek child Anna, and that excursion to Dungeness, and now dear Henry's unexpected return.

She sat down for a few minutes before turning inland across the fields to Phoebe's house. She sat on the beach by the tall posts of the breakwater where the sea was lapping up quickly to high tide again. The shingle was still warm on the surface with the day's sunshine, but underneath as she dug her fingers deeper it was cold and wet. She leant her head back against the post and closed her eyes and took a deep sniff of the sea-weedy salt smell, that had also some tar in it. Presently there would be the mussels for an extra supper with dear Phoebe, but not just yet, just for a time she could stay here. Helen shifted a bit from the post and lay flat back upon the beach, looking up at the sky. There was the sun and the moon (well, almost the sun) and the stars and the grey sky growing darker, and there was this fascinating smell, and on the other side of the breakwater the sea was already getting deep. If only the beach were really as empty as the moon, and she could stay here and lie out all night, and nobody pass by and no person pass again ever. But that no doubt was what it would be like when one was dead (this was always what Helen thought death was like), and then of course the poor soul would weep for its loneliness and try to comfort itself with the memory of past company. Was not that what Hadrian had been thinking so cold and solitary of the sheeted dead—*quœ nunc abibis in loca?* Best, then, to make best use of the company that was now at hand. Helen got up and walked slowly up the beach and across the fields towards Phoebe's house, pausing only for quite a short time to lean over the bridge that crossed the dark river, and only then because there was a fish swimming that came suddenly into the track of the moonlight, rising to snap at a mosquito that lay out late on the water.   *1949*

25

SURROUNDED BY
CHILDREN

Under the shadow of the trees in Hyde Park the mothers are nursing the babies, and in the long grass of Kensington Gardens and on the banks of the Serpentine the sisters are caring for the brothers, under the trees the aunt walks. What is the aunt doing, under the trees walking? She is thinking of the young man who has the ice-cream vendor's cart; the cart of the ice-cream vendor is upon the road, he is peddling briskly away from the walking aunt.

The brothers of the sisters and the babies of the mothers have no care at all; theirs is a careless fate, to be pampered and cared for, no matter if there is no money the brothers will have the sisters to jump around after them, the babies will have the mothers to nurse them, the aunt will have the pleasure of sweet dreams under the tree and the ice-cream vendor will have his escape upon the saddle of his bicycle cart.

It is a pleasant English summer's day in the Gardens and in the Park. The brother of the sister has an ice-cream which he is eating, it is plastered upon his mouth, it is all over his whole face; he relishes the ice-cream. The sister anxiously combs back from her brow with long soiled finger the lank lock; she is worried to keep at the same time an eye upon the eater of the ice-cream and upon the younger brother who will paddle in the Serpentine, nobody shall say him no.

The little brothers and sisters who are the children of rich parents play also in the Park, but their play is watched by ferocious nannas. The children are fat and pink-cheeked but listless rather at their pleasures; their voices are the high-class English voices, the baby accents of the ruling classes, the clichés too, already they are there, a little affected is it not? and sad, too, that already the children are so self-aware almost already at a caricature of themselves—'we are having fun.' 'Did you enjoy your walk in the Park?' says Mama upon the child's return. 'Why, yes, it was fun you know, just rather fun. Did we enjoy the walk Priscilla?' Priscilla sneers with tight lips above baby teeth. 'Why yes, I suppose so, it was fun, rather fun.'

Towards both these groups of children is now coming a famously ugly old girl, she has wisps of grey hair carelessly dyed that is rioting out from under her queer hat, as she walks she mutters to herself. Very different is the walking dream of the old girl from the walking dream of the love of the ice-cream vendor. Ah, upon the old girl is no eligible imagination for the nurture of a love-life of entertainment value. As she walks she talks, and also her hands that are delicate and long, like delicate long birds' claws, clasp the air about her. She fetches up to a standstill beneath the rich chestnut tree; in the shadow of the tree is reposed a grand pram for a rich child. The pram is empty but the covers are turned back. How invitingly securely rich is the interior of this equipage that is for a grand infant of immensely rich parentage, how inviting indeed the interior where the covers lie backwards upon the pram beneath the green tree!

The famously ugly old girl is transfixed by this seducing vision of an open and deserted perambulator, she will get into it, come what may that is what she will do, that is her thought. Her hands now stretch upward to remove the queer hat to fling it down upon the grass, the toque lies at her feet. Tearing apart the lapels of her tightly buttoned coat she will not wait, the flimsy bombazine tears, the coat is off; with one hand she props herself against the dear perambulator, kicks shoe from shoe, stands stockingfoot.

But now the children gather round, close in upon her fast, for what is going on here? The children of the rich parents and the children of the poor parents are now united in a childish laughter, the sisters of the brothers have forgotten their care, the nephews and nieces of the aunt are here, the rich children have escaped their nannas, laughing and staring they close in upon the poor old girl, they join hands and laugh.

'Ah,' cries the sad beldame, transfixed in grotesque crucifixion upon the perambulator, stabbing at herself with a hatpin of the old fashion so that a little antique blood may fall upon the frilly pillow of the immaculate vehicle, 'what fate is this, what nightmare more *agaçant* so to lie and so to die, in great pain, surrounded by children.'

1939

IN THE BEGINNING
OF THE WAR

The British Nation is biological, said the refugee professor to the girl, who was attending some political parties. This party was left-wing political-literary.

There was a young refugee doctor of science who had been speaking about underground movements in Germany before the war, messages handed round on cigarette wrappings, it was very exciting, like *I was a Spy*, it had all that appeal.

She spoke to the young doctor afterwards and said he must not think this party was representative of England, the people at this party, she said, were vociferous but had little influence. A shrewd expression came over the doctor's face as she said this and he glanced apprehensively around. I have often wondered, he said, where are the right wing intellectual persons? Place hunting, said the girl, they are in office perhaps or hope to be. These people . . .? They are writers to-night, their emotions are conditioned by christian ideas, although they would not admit it, a lot of the younger ones are against Christianity they say, but for all that their thoughts have a christian impetus, politically they are immature and vanity is evident in their speeches. (She had been saying this to the professor when he, wishing to dispel her depression, said the British nation was biological.) The girl sighed. I suppose, she said, the groups and societies that these people form have a high nuisance value, but now that the war has started it is I think only a matter of time before Government takes steps against them. That the Government has not already done so, said the Professor, is I suppose a measure of the Government's contempt for them. Yes, sighed the girl, these people are good but they are not wise.

The next day she and the doctor and the professor went to a meeting in a committee room at the House of Commons. It was held by the Inter-University Peace Aims Group. On the platform sat brilliant Sir Sefton Choate, MP for North Devon, flanked by three undergraduates on either side, looking pretty serious. Sir Sefton spoke in detail about a book he had written. The girl had read his book and was interested in his ideas, but, she thought, to put them into action would necessitate a complete upheaval, both social and political, was war the time? She became sunk in gloom and the professor and the doctor too looked grey with sadness. They had so recently come from Halle an der Sale and Vienna. They knew how strong Germany was in the strength of a lie, and how a lie is strong because it can be so much simpler than the truth. Truth, thought the girl, is so many-sided, how long indeed it may take for truth to prevail.

The meeting was now open to discussion. Many people who had been holding their breath for this moment sprang to their feet, but the Chairman decided who was the first. This one was a clergyman and after coughing a little he said he noticed with something akin he might almost say to consternation that he alone of his cloth had seen fit to come forward in public witness to the ideals for which we were, were we not, fighting, fighting, he would add, a battle not on the Flanders fields but in the hearts of our own people, there must be there, he said, a rebirth, a resurrection, a regeneration . . . he felt . . . After five minutes he sat down although there was a three-minute limit. Three members of the CP then rose simultaneously but after talking it over one stayed standing. He spoke about the unrighteousness of war, the bogey of nazi-ism, the bogey of atrocity stories, the bogey of war sacrifices. Almost before he had finished the Peace Union person was on his feet. All right, the Chairman let him stand. It was much the same. The girl and the professor and the doctor came out during this speech and went to a coffee bar just along the passage. The girl was sorry for the doctor he was so sad. Never mind, said the girl, they have little influence. The bogey of nazi-ism, screamed the doctor. Never mind, said the girl again, for them you must know there is only one bogey, Chamberlain. They also have no experience of war, they will forgive the Germans for the pain they have given to other people. It is not so good to be stoical about other people's sufferings. The Germans have inflicted little pain on England because England is so strong. The conversation went on over the terrible coffee and the sandwiches. In the street, said the girl, the common people are saying: The Germans are asking for it, now they will get it. That is a greater truth than they realize. But perhaps they do realize it. After coming from the committee room I feel humble about the common people because the others are such fools. The girl thought she would write a jingo poem about it, 'For every blow they inflict on Jewry, And other victims of their fury, They ask for death on bended knee, And we will give them death and we, Will give them death to three times three.'

From the cosy House of Commons they looked out on to the bleak plains of war. It will take England a long time to warm up, said the girl, feeling more wretched and like Sam Hoare than ever. Oh, said the professor, certainly England is biological but oh if she would only come to it more quickly and in the end I would say, though it may sound not right with less cumulative strength, there will be very little left when she has finished. They are asking for death, kept on the girl, Freud said the German race had a stronger death wish than any other people. They ask for death, only on death can a new Europe be built. They hold out their hands and ask for death, when we do not give it to them they behave more and more extremely, they cry at last 'Have we not yet earned death?' It is not suffering they ask or I would give, it is death; their peace is the peace of the grave.

After the professor had left them the girl hooked her arm affectionately into the doctor's. As a matter of fact, she said, I feel even more grey with sadness than he. My thoughts go in a dance round my head but the music is sad. They walked in silence by the river. Then she said: I remember before the war none was more fertile and emphatic in atrocity stories than the political person with left wing inclinations. Then there was indeed revelations. But now because Government sings the sad song at once it becomes for them not true. For they no more than Government care for absolute truth but only for party expediency. The atrocity stories are always true, there is nothing that has been written that has not been done over again many times. The Government book about the atrocities is keyed down, it is not half the truth; the scatological and sexual nature of nazi cruelty Government will not present to the British people because of the law about obscene publication and because of la pudeur anglaise that is so famous.

The doctor now began to weep and silently the tears fell down, he did not sob. He was thinking of the cruelties and that the times was set to death. There is a time in history when death is petitioned, no one shall say the people nay, death they will have. 'From the manure of our corruption . . .' cried the doctor. Yes, said the girl, interrupting, that is the food of our vanity, an age flatters itself on its evil and in a bath of abasement looks to the future for a grand and different birth, we are impatient and death is the scope of our immediacy, pat-come upon command.

1942

A VERY
PLEASANT EVENING

Helen darling I am so glad to see you, Lisa ran up the steps and kissed Helen, it was so long since she had seen her the last time in Cambridge at the Newnham Senior Student's Party, or was it at Professor Lichtenstein's at Oxford, that time Rudi upset the custard? Dear Helen, never would Lisa forget her dear friend. And now here was Helen in London suddenly, staying with the Hicksons in Moon Street, W.

Behind Helen in the wide Regency doorway stood a man. This must be Mr Hickson, but no of course he was dead. Helen introduced Mr Rambeloid. Oh yes of course, Anita Hickson had married again. How do you do, How do you do. Roland Rambeloid took them into the sitting room of the old grand but rather empty house. We are hardly settled in yet, he said, We have as you see very little furniture, we expect to get the rest out soon, but I expect it will be rather smashed up. Oh dear, the bomb, yes. But, said Lisa, you will be able to get an emergency supply with special permits. Oh yes, said Helen, but it all takes so long. I am so glad you escaped with your life, said Lisa. Roland Rambeloid looked rather startled, Oh thank you, thank you, yes, my wife and I as a matter of fact were at the play when it happened, it was Richard the Third.

They were now sitting drinking some pre-war sherry and some Irish whisky. How did you manage to save the sherry and the whisky? asked Lisa. Oh well, as a matter of fact we only borrowed this house from a friend. Oh yes, thank you, I will have some more whisky. How jolly good of your friends it was. Would you like to come down and see the cellar? asked Roland Rambeloid. You two run along, said Helen, I'll stay here, I have some buttons to sew on. She took some piles of mending and some reels of thread from under the cushion on the couch and a needle from the ashtray, and sat down again to sew.

You see, said Roland, prancing down the basement steps, this is such a fine old house, such wide shallow steps, on the main staircase I mean of course, steady now, mind this corner, there's a step out here and the light is off. Down they went. In the basement was a wide cool old kitchen where Anita Rambeloid, formerly Hickson, *née* exactly what Lisa forgot though she had been at college with her, was cooking the dinner. How nice it smells, said Lisa, slipping a tomato into her pocket and advancing to the stove where Anita was boiling a stew. Run along, said Anita laughing, show her the cellar and the coal house Roland, off with you. What a happy house it was. Won't you have a tomato Lisa, said Roland, I may call you Lisa, mayn't I?

For dinner they had potato soup, Irish stew, a chocolate pudding with some frozen milk from the frig, some sardines on toast and black coffee laced strongly with the Irish whisky. There was also some Stilton cheese. We found this in the cellar, said Roland, pour some whisky into it, Lisa. The talk now turned to dialectical materialism. After the war, said Roland, England will be of no importance whatever, there will be only America and Russia, but we shall have our famous character of course, he went on hurriedly, seeing that his wife who was very pro-English was about to speak, And so we shall always suppose we amount to something, so everybody will be pleased.

Helen threw a Berkleyan remark into the conversation, fearing that it might lose its Cambridge flavour and become vulgar. Nonsense nonsense, said Roland, just words, baby-talk. If a man falls off a cliff in the dark because he cannot see it that is a proof that the world exists apart from the mind's thought of it, said Lisa. They had some more whisky. Well, Lisa went on, he does not know the cliff is there and yet it is there with a vengeance, it is the death of him. Helen's husband who had done little up to the moment except sniff took up the conversation, but it was now time to turn on the radio and listen to the budget speech. Practically everything they had eaten and drunk was to be taxed double, Roland looked hungrily at the Stilton. It is better to parcel it out slowly I think really, said Lisa, it would only make you sick, and with care it will last a very long time. Jolly nice of our friends, said Roland absentmindedly.

Lisa had some more whisky and went and sat by Helen and took her hand and asked, How are the children, how is Caroline, and how is Clorinda and how is Sarah? The children all had these smart Cambridge names, everybody of that age in Cambridge had these names. Nothing common like Doris, said Lisa. The sea mouse, said Helen's husband, and began to talk about the kangaroo and the young kangaroo that is, he said, born a worm. How can that be, said Lisa, a worm. No the kangaroo, it is like this, he is born with his claws and his fur on, but he is not quite finished off yet for all that, so the mother puts the child kangaroo into her pouch . . . or poosh, said

Roland rather irritatingly. Well, she puts the child into her pouch then the child kangaroo keeps warm and grows finished; it is attached to the mother kangaroo by some attachment of a sort, so that she can run and jump and leap without a fear that her child will fall out. Nonsense, said Helen's husband, it is a worm and from the worm it grows to the young kangaroo. Helen said hurriedly that no doubt the term worm was used in the widest sense. Oh I see, said Lisa, the worm, the way the mediaeval people used the word, it might be the dragon that Guy of Warwick hunted. Or the worm of the bible that dieth not, said Roland, or the worm of Milton that tempted the fairest of her daughters Eve. The mediaeval people were very imaginative, said Helen's husband, with a precise child's imagination, very visual. 'Spiritual ambition and imaginative loves,' said Lisa pat, for she felt there was about to be a quotation game and she would get in early. Helen's husband sniffed loudly, but Roland was pleased, he liked to talk about poetry in this easy gamey way. He said that he allowed himself to doubt whether any writer writing poetry to-day would so many centuries from now as we are from Milton be quoted easy by easy reading people apart from the research hounds.

Anita got up to go and fetch some more coffee. When she got to the glass door leading through into the garden and through again to the backstairs there was a bright red flash in the sky over the wrecked low rubble of Heartbright Street. Roland, she cried out, that must be a doodle. Roland looked at his stop watch and counted out the seconds, nobody spoke. He had got up to forty-five before the crash came. The house shook and the glasshouse windows fell out with a crack. Oh dear, said Anita, that happened only last month, we had them put back but we shall never get them done again, old Bonesey slipped them in for us on the quiet because Roland helped his son to get into the Blue Coat School, she sighed. She said that old Bonesey had now had a bomb on his house and had gone to live with his brother-in-law at Peckham.

Roland looked at the red skyline and said that it was awfully like the skyline in the last war with the red light now fading dark over Heartbright Street. He was restless to get back to his poetry. In the last war, he said, I used to sit in my dugout and read Childe Roland to the Dark Tower Came, nobody reads Browning nowadays, he looked in a challenging way at Lisa but went on quickly, Childe Roland is such an exact spiritual description of the detail of the

Flanders battlefield, he sighed, the bits of broken machinery, and the mud and the dampness and the greyness and the longness and the horse. He fell into a muse. Lisa took Helen's hand and said: One stiff grey horse his every bone astare, stood stupified however he came there, thrust out past service from the devil's stud, With that red gaunt and collopped neck astrain and shut eyes underneath a rusty main, seldom went such grotesqueness with such woe, I never saw a beast I hated so, He must be wicked to deserve such pain. Helen thought Lisa was getting rather drunk, What is that? she said. Lisa looked at Roland, It is Childe Roland, she said. The Victorian age, she said, for Roland was looking at her rather closely, Was a great age, a very great age, she laughed thinking that this was what old fashioned people said when old fashioned people died, A very great age. It would be surprising, she said if we should be so great as that. Well, said Roland grudgingly, that is rather like Childe Roland, but it is not quite right of course. No, said Lisa, the lines do not seem to have come right, they are not quite in the right order perhaps. I have my school Browning at home. She remembered the book quite well, it was congealed ox-blood red with gold embossing and on the fly leaf was written 'With love from Daddy.' Inside there was a bookmark with the word 'No' embroidered at the top and then an embroidered cross, and then the word 'No' again and underneath an embroidered crown.

Now, she said, I must go home. Roland said he would fetch her to the tube station. Good-bye Anita, good-bye Helen. Roland led off by a short cut through the back streets to the tube station. You are not cold, Lisa? No, no, not at all thank you. In the dark patch outside the lighted tube station Roland fell suddenly upon Lisa and began to kiss her. Oh Roland, how furious you are, sighed Lisa, as he gasped and panted. His right arm went round to the back of her shoulder, he caught hold of her hair and took a pull at it, forcing her head back, it was a furious adroit grip. Lisa began to laugh, Oh Roland, she said, and put her arms round him and kissed him, Now I must go. Lisa fell away from him and walked into the bright light of the station, but Roland came after her and took her in his arms and began to kiss her again under the bright lights and the approving eyes of the friendly porters. Good-bye Roland dear, Lisa drew apart and shook him politely by the hand, Thank you for a very pleasant evening.

1946

TO SCHOOL IN GERMANY

How much harm may one do at 16–being egotistical, argumentative, infantine of heart being then, absolutely, 'oneself at 16'? This begins as a comic story, a summer anecdote of not much account. How far it thrust into the future casting shadows I do not even know; perhaps I am flattering my 16-year-old self thinking she thrust into the future at all.

At 16 I was at school in Potsdam. Infantine of heart I may have been, even for a schoolgirl, but I was beginning to have a faint inkling of how extremely inconsistent one can be and how little difference it makes to one's comfort, opinions and behaviour having this brought home. As it was, almost daily.

For we were an international lot at Fraulein Plotzler's academy and opinions ran strong. There was, for instance, my friend Steppy. Steppy was an American of Polish ancestry. The cause which had our public voice–hers and mine–was a lofty internationalism, but this did not prevent fights between us at a lower level.

'We beat you British.' 'You were in Poland at that time grinding the faces of the poor.' 'America beat Britain.' '. . . or slinking in the Ghetto. They were British on both sides, bar the Hessians on ours.'

'Slinking in the Ghetto?' 'Ha, ha, how can you pretend to be liberal when you won't even speak to Flossie Silbermann?' 'She is a Jewess.' And so on.

Yes, at sixteen I was disputatious rather than sentimental and it was in nothing at all of a sentimental mood that I went to spend the holidays, as often I did, with some friends of my mother, the von Rs.

This 'R.' name has since become rather notorious, so let the initial stand. Herr von R. was 'a nice old thing' (forty-five I dare say), of a humour more Berlinish than East Prussian. His wife was asthmatic, but self-effacing, there was a daughter, Bella, and there was Maxi. That summer was wonderfully hot and long. Maxi, Bella and I used to go riding and bathing in the shallow Baltic that I liked so much, and sailing too.

Maxi was in his first year in the university and liked holding forth. He was dreadfully taken up with those historico-hysterical pseudo philosophical ideas one used to laugh at then, not guessing what was coming up out of them, or wanting to guess.

At mealtimes he did not say much, because German sons, even

student sons, did not talk when their fathers were there. But on the rides and bathes Maxi would grow very extreme indeed about the Jews and about how cynical, corrupt, of poor moral fibre and generally disgusting the English were.

Bella took no part in these arguments; she was a calm girl and thought only of catching shrimps and pounding them into a paste which she wolfed down on slabs of cold toast.

'She has no mind,' Maxi used to say, 'but she is very pretty.' There was a great deal of tension between Maxi and me. But it was not on my side—or at all, I thought—a sentimental tension of the sort that so comically drives engaged couples to dispute with violence some trivial question, say of party politics.

It was all the same unnerving; 'worse than Steppy' I used to think, quite often ferocious. And as the names Maxi cast at me of persons the English were supposed to have mistreated or bamboozled meant little to me or positively nothing, I spent much time in Herr von R's library looking up an answer for him. But by then, of course, he had gone on to something else.

Maxi was a handsome-looking boy, I could see that, but my mind was on other things. So one day when he suggested we should go off together and leave Bella in the kitchen with her shrimps, I sighed a little, thinking of the arguments to come up, but said yes.

You know those inland seas that lie behind the strips of coast up by Pillau getting on for Koenigsberg? The von Rs' land lay there, the great flat fields running by the lakesides down to the sand dunes and the sea.

At once Maxi began to speak of the Jews again. 'Oh, heavens, Maxi, not again.' And I said there were moments when one liked to be quiet and think. And that this was such a beautiful day, so hot and still, we should do better to enjoy it in silence, and swim silently, rather than for ever to rattle round those hackneyed exascerbating and wicked sentiments vis-à-vis the Jews, the English or any other persons, institutions or opinions.

And as we strolled together through the pinewoods towards the sea shore I began to have some curious thoughts—as for instance that a fine sunny day can make one feel more separate than ever, especially if one's companion is in a frame of mind noticeably different from one's own, for there the creature is in the physical lump, the disturbed playmate, and how on earth can one wrap oneself from him?

36

'I am trying not to be aggressive,' I said, 'I am really very fond of you, Maxi; I don't want to be cross because it is such a hot day and just the day for a swim and soon I shall be going back to England, so do not be so beastly cross.'

And to cheer him up I began to read out aloud from a letter I had had from my sister Elizabeth who was still at school in England.

I sighed as I read. I had been in Germany for more than a year now and would be glad to go home. 'Isn't it marvellous,' Elizabeth wrote, 'Ocean Swell and Ephesus beating Teheran? I'm simply thrilled. And I'm terribly pleased about Dicky Boy, he's a very nice-tempered horse and of a queer spotty colour. I'm simply dumbfounded, Ian has got engaged to Caroline, much to Nat's disgust. I can't get over it. Must dry up now, tons of love though.'

I looked up. Maxi was looking quite extraordinary, his eyes very odd, boiled slightly and bursting and his face of a most peculiar shade of dark red. 'I don't believe you've heard a word I've been reading.' I was going to walk off aloofly and get the picnic things out when Maxi leapt at me. 'Don't you know I love you?'

'No I don't,' I said. 'Heavens, you must be stark staring mad. I mean I didn't. I think it's soppy all that, all right for Caroline I dare say. What on earth's the matter?'

'Don't you love me at all?' 'Well, Well, I never thought about it. (Oh do shut up.) I'm very fond of you. I'm fond of Bella too and I think your father is heaven and . . .'

But I stopped because of the way Maxi was looking. 'I say, you aren't serious, I suppose? I say, look out, you'll break my arm.'

He got a grip on my plaits and pulled my head back. 'I say, look out, you're pulling my hair. Maxi, do shut up!'

He began to shout that he loved me, that he was serious and wanted to marry me. 'But we can't' I said, 'we're not old enough.' 'We could be engaged.' 'I know I'm not in love with you, Maxi (oh, do shut up!) and I couldn't marry you, anyway. I've nothing against it in principle but it wouldn't work.'

'Why not?' So out it came with nothing much more behind it than crossness for a spoiled day you might say and yet—was it not for me at that moment a sort of truthfulness, the summing up of a situation? 'Why not?' 'Because you're German.'

I wish I might say I never saw Maxi again and so leave it as a summer anecdote. But I did see him again, many years later and in dreadful circumstances. It was after the war in a restaurant in the British Zone not far from Berlin. I was with my cousin Eustace, who was in the Army. We went into this restaurant and it was very crowded. We sat down at a table in the corner. There was one other person there, a thin, twisted-looking oldish man.

Only when he looked up with those blue eyes of old did I recognise this person for Maxi.

'Good heavens, Maxi!' I cried and turned to Eustace.

'This is Maxi von R. you know, I stayed with them ages ago; in another world.'

My cousin stiffened up at the name von R.

'I could make a bolt for it, I suppose,' said Maxi with a quite ghastly smile. 'I don't think I should,' said Eustace. Maxi turned to me.

'He's not got it quite right, has he?' and then in an echo that fell from a long way off, in a thin mincing false voice that came as my own voice from a long ago afternoon in East Prussia he said: 'I've nothing against it in principle but it wouldn't work.' My cousin took him off then. Maxi was a war criminal on the run. I had guessed that, of course. Later, Eustace told me his record. It was vile beyond words.

'Don't worry,' he said when I told him the summer story, 'if it hadn't been that it would have been something else.' I stared at the coffee in the bottom of my grubby cup. 'How beastly and bitter it all is: I hate this "holier than thou" situation we are all in now.' 'We ARE holier than him,' said my cousin.

Maxi got 15 years.

1955

GETTING RID OF SADIE

'Crumbs,' said my brother, 'if this isn't old Sadie. No, seriously, old girl, just look here. Well, isn't it?' He threw the paper across to me.

We were sitting—it is some time ago now—in the old playroom at Staithe overlooking the bay—and a good deal nearer to it since the last winter's landslide. You could have tossed the ash-tray spit into Skeddles Wash.

'What?' I said, 'where?' Edward came across and jabbed a finger. 'There.' It was a short paragraph and said that Miss Elizabeth Findlater, aged fifty, had been convicted 'of attempting to extort money by menaces.'

'It was a day like this, too,' I said, when we could speak for gaping, 'the day of our famous dress rehearsal, our *plot* . . . sunny, with the wind blowing hard off the sea . . .'

Did we remember?—did we not. We were about ten and fourteen at the time, Eddy rather grown-up and sick to have to spend eight weeks' holiday in Aunt Slippy's house (as it was then) with only two beastly girls, myself and cousin Beth, for company.

Oh, and the governess, Miss Elizabeth Findlater.

'She's a sadist,' Eddy said to me on our second day there, 'you wouldn't know what that means but it's being cruel and liking it.'

And he began to thump and sing, 'Sadist-Sadie, You are a shady lady . . . ha, ha, ha.'

'Look out, you fathead, she'll hear you.'

'Not a chance, anyway she likes us.'

39

As a matter of fact, she did, perhaps because we weren't frightened of her. Like poor Beth. Perhaps again, and the glum thought dogs us still, because she thought we were more 'her sort'.

'She *beats* her,' I said. 'Fancy being beaten by a governess.'

'And she isn't a lady anyway, she's just a common old bag.'

'She's a bag, she's a hag. All the same, we can't have a relation of ours being banged about by a bag of a hag who isn't a lady.'

We turned solemn then thinking of poor Beth.

'It's awful in every way,' I said, 'because, well, it isn't only beating, though that's simply awful . . . .'

Eddy struck in. 'Girls aren't beaten, they're not, it's just not civilized.'

'Oh shut up. Well,' I went on, 'that couldn't be worse, but also you know she's got Beth absolutely dumb with fright, oh it's sickening. Old Sadie just plays cat and mouse with her.'

'It's the power complex,' said Eddy.

'Do you know the other day,' I said, 'I found Beth crying in the corner by the banisters and do you know what it was? Sadie had sent her to fetch her spectacles from her bedroom and Beth couldn't find them. And all the time they were in Sadie's ghastly reticule thing.

'I'd seen them as I ran past to go upstairs, the reticule hung open on Sadie's lap. She must have *known*. And when I got upstairs there was Beth crying and shivering, it was awful, like poor old Prince when he's going to be sick.'

(Prince was the dog, a heavenly old Labrador we all adored.)

Well, that settled it. Sadie had got to be got rid of.

Of course, you might have thought Beth could have told her mother, our Aunt Slippy—that is if you hadn't known Aunt Slippy.

She was one of those females who care for nothing but horses, never spoke to Beth and paid the governess to keep her out of the way. Also she was hardly ever there.

We supposed she was out with the horses (wrongly, as it turned out, but that comes later). Anyway Beth's case, poor, tormented, sweet Beth's horrible case, obviously lay in our hands. What could we do?

We had endless confabulations, Eddy and I, and meanwhile time was running short.

'Sadie likes us,' I remember saying, 'she does like us, Eddy, so we'd better work on that.'

Well, we did. We played up to Sadie, we flattered her, we told her she was 'different', 'such a brick' you know, 'a sport', etcetera.

The old thing (she was quite forty, I suppose) really came on wonderfully. Oh, she liked it, lapped it up and asked for more.

It was finding the passbook that finally hatched out our plot.

'I say, look here, Eddy,' I said, 'old Sadie's got £700 on current account.'

It may seem odd that an infant of ten should know about passbooks and current accounts, but our dear father had ideas about education and especially about giving a practical turn to arithmetic lessons by linking them up with cheque books and company promotion and so on, and not a bad idea either.

'Crumbs,' said Eddy (as he still does), 'that's a lot for a governess —and on current account.'

The plan we finally decided on was really rather clever. I still think it was, though Eddy says it was too complicated and couldn't have worked out.

We were going to persuade old Sadie to accompany us on a picnic to Skeddles Wash some afternoon—that is almost any afternoon— when poor Beth was being 'kept in' doing long division sums for a punishment (she never mastered the Italian method though heaven knows we toiled to teach her).

The cliffs at Skeddles Wash run up sheer in a sharp-angled cleft with a cave at the end and another on top of it at the back and a fairly sticky climb up to it, which would flatter Sadie's vanity—'So different' you see, 'such a sport' (well, she was pretty agile for her age)— and an even stickier climb out to the cliff which only I could do because it got so narrow.

At high tide the lower cave would be ten feet deep in water.

Well, the plan was for Eddy to tie Sadie's wrists as he was helping her up (he was huge even at fourteen, and she was barely five feet and skinny), then we'd tie her feet, too, and keep her there till the tide ran high.

Well, after that it really wouldn't have been difficult. We'd stick her up for £400. If she jibbed at writing the cheque (we'd have pinched the cheque-book from her bag, she always carried it around with her)—cash, of course, and a covering note to the bank requesting payment in one pound notes—we'd simply threaten to untie her and push her into the cave, we knew she couldn't swim—and that would be that.

Oh, she'd write the cheque, we were sure of that, and I'd hare off with it up the cliff, get Beth to take it to the bank, as she was always being made to do these dog errands and they knew her there, then I'd post the money in an old chocolate box or something to our London house addressed to myself 'To Await Arrival'.

(Daddy was most punctilious about our letters and there was only about a week to go by now.)

Oh, we'd thought of everything—even to getting the bank's receipt signed by Sadie, though we guessed some more of the water threat would be necessary here. Our point was this—Sadie would get the £400 back when she'd got herself another job.

(We put that in because we didn't want her getting the money and turning up again.)

Well, as I say, that was the plan. It was a bright, sunny day with a strong north-easter blowing when we staged our dress rehearsal. Eddy insisted on a dress rehearsal, with careful timing for the high tide, and dear old Prince, the Labrador, who weighed about a ton, was to 'stand in' for Sadie.

Dear old dog, it was Prince who sent things wrong. We were hauling him into the upper cave, with a handkerchief tied round his front paws, when the poor old boy began to make the most extraordinary noises.

We let him down again, and Eddy jumped down, too, and then poor Prince was most terribly sick—he was always being sick but this was different, somehow, it was absolutely frightful, we thought he was going to die.

Eddy went deathly white and I was crying.

We carried the old man home and got the vet and as a matter of fact he was his own sloppy, sweet self in a day or two and nothing to show for it.

But that was the end of the great plot to get rid of Sadie. Because —and this is where Aunt Slippy comes in again. Apparently she *had* been thinking of something besides horses, she'd been thinking of a chap called Captain Harry Satterthwaite.

Well, the upshot was that Daddy bought the house and Aunt Slippy went off with this Satterthwaite person to somewhere in America where he had a ranch (he'd been staying with nearby friends of Aunt Slippy's on a stock-buying visit).

So Beth went to boarding-school and spent her holidays with us, and Sadie, our Sadie, 'Miss Elizabeth Findlater,' off she went too and not a squeak was heard of her till this cutting turned up, to bring

42

it all back again, our plot, our bloodthirsty, perfectly criminal plot.

Sitting now, ten years after, in the old playroom, I said to Eddy, 'You know even if it didn't come off, we meant it to, we would have enjoyed threatening her.'

I turned to the cutting again. '. . . extorting money by menaces.'

'Perhaps we were rather alike, us and her.'

'I've often thought that,' said Eddy. 'It's the thing that's kept me straight.'

So we couldn't help laughing then, yes, in a way it finished in laughter. But not for Sadie, no, not for Sadie.

'Well,' I went on, answering this thought that must have been in both our minds, 'she was a cruel beast, wasn't she? It would just have been a case of one cruel beast meeting two cruel beasts, too bad. And I don't think we would really have pushed her in.'

'I wouldn't count on it,' said Edward glumly.

'Well, I don't suppose it would have been *necessary*.'

My brother squinted slightly, pushed to the point.

'I wouldn't count on that, either,' he said.

1955

SUNDAY AT HOME

Ivor was a gigantic man; forty, yellow-haired, gray of face. He had been wounded in a bomb experiment, he was a brilliant scientist.

Often he felt himself to be a lost man. Fishing the home water with his favourite fly Coronal, he would say to himself, 'I am a lost man.'

But he had an excellent sardonic wit, and in company knew very well how to present himself as a man perfectly at home in the world.

He was spending this Sunday morning sitting in his bedroom reading Colonel Wanlip's 'Can Fish Think?' letter in ANGLING. '. . . the fallacious theory known as Behaviourism.'

As the doodle bomb came sailing overhead, he stepped into the airing cupboard and sighed heavily. He could hear his wife's voice from the sitting room, a childish, unhappy voice, strained (as usual) to the point of tears.

'All I ask' sang out Ivor 'is a little peace and quiet; an agreeable wife, a wife who is pleasant to my friends; one who occasionally has the room swept, the breakfast prepared, and the expensive bric-a-brac of our cultivated landlord—*dusted*. I am after all a fairly easy fellow.'

'I can't go on' roared Glory. She waved her arms in the air and paced the sitting room table round and round.

Crump, crump, went the doodle bomb, getting nearer.

'Then why,' inquired Ivor from the cupboard (where he sat because the doodle bombs reminded him of the experiment) 'did you come back to me?'

Glory's arms at shoulder height dropped to her side. There was in this hopeless and graceful gesture something of the classic Helen, pacing the walls of Troy, high above the frozen blood and stench of Scamander Plain. Ten years of futile war. Heavens, how much longer.

She ran to the cupboard and beat with her fists upon the door. 'You ask that, you . . . you . . . you . . . '

'Why yes, dear girl, I do. Indeed I do ask just that. Why did you come back to me?'

'Yesterday in the fish queue . . . ' began Glory. But it was no use. No use to tell Ivor what Friedl had said to her in the fish queue . . . before all those people . . . the harsh, cruel words. No, it was no use.

The doodle bomb now cut out. Glory burst into tears and finished lamely, 'I never thought it was going to be like this.'

Crash. Now it was down. Three streets away perhaps. There was a clatter of glass as the gold-fish bowl fell off the mantlepiece. Weeping bitterly Glory knelt to scoop the fish into a half-full saucepan of water that was standing in the fender.

'They are freshwater fish' said Ivor, stepping from the cupboard.

Glory went into the kitchen and sat down in front of the cooking stove. How terrible it all was. Her fine brown hair fell over her eyes and sadly the tears fell down.

She picked up the french beans and began to slice them. Now it would have to be lunch very soon. And then some more washing up. And Mrs Dip never turned up on Friday. And the stove was covered with grease.

From the sitting room came the sound of the typewriter. 'Oh God' cried Glory, and buried her head in her arms, 'Oh God.'

Humming a little tune to himself, Ivor worked quickly upon a theme he was finishing. 'Soh, me, doh, soh, me. How happy, how happy to be wrapped in science from the worst that fate and females could do.'

'If only I had science to wrap myself up in' said poor Glory, and fell to thinking what she would wish, if she could wish one thing to have it granted. 'I should wish' she said, 'that I had science to wrap myself up in. But I have nothing. I love Ivor, I never see him, never have him, never talk to him, but that the science is wrapping him round. And the educated conversation of the clever girls. Oh God.'

Glory was not an educated girl, in the way that the Research Persons Baba and Friedl, were educated girls. They could talk in the informed light manner that Ivor loved (in spite of Friedl's awful accent.) But she could not. Her feelings were too much for her; indeed too much.

'I do not believe in your specialist new world, where everybody is so intelligent and everybody is so equal and everybody works and the progress goes on getting more and more progressive,' said Glory crossly to Friedl one day. She shook her head and added darkly, 'There must be sin and suffering, you'll see.'

'Good God, Glory,' said Ivor, 'you sound like the Pythoness. Sin and suffering, ottotottoi; the old bundle at the cross roads. Dreams, dreams. And now I suppose we shall have the waterworks again.'

'Too true,' said Friedl, as again Glory fled weeping.

'Sin and suffering,' she cried now to herself, counting the grease drips down the white front of the stove. 'Sin, pain, death, hell; despair and die. The brassy new world, the brassy hard-voiced young women. And underneath, the cold cold stone.'

Why only the other day, coming from her Aunt's at Tetbury, there in the carriage was a group of superior schoolgirls all of the age of about sixteen. But what sixteen-year-olds, God, what terrible children. They were talking about their exams. 'Oh, Delia darling, it was brilliant of you to think of that. Wasn't it brilliant of Delia, Lois? But then I always say Delia is the seventeenth century, if-you-see-what-I-mean. And what fun for dear old Bolt that you actually remembered to quote her own foul poem on Strafford. No, not boring a bit, darling, but sweet and clever of you—especially sweet.'

At the memory of this atrocious conversation between the false and terrible children, Glory's sobs rose to a roar, so that Ivor, at pause in his theme, heard her and came storming into the kitchen.

'You are a lazy, slovenly, uncontrolled female,' he said, 'You are a barbarian. I am going out.'

'Round to Friedl's, round to Friedl's, round to Friedl's,' sang out Glory.

'Friedl is a civilised woman. I appreciate civilised conversation.' Ivor stood over Glory and laughed. 'I shall be out to lunch.'

He took his hat and went out.

'The beans,' yelled Glory, 'all those french beans.' But it was no good, he was gone.

Glory went to the telephone and rang up Greta.

Greta was lying in bed and thinking about hell and crying and thinking that hell is the continuation of policy. She thought about the times and the wars and the 'scientific use of force' that was the enemy's practique. She thought that evil was indivisible and growing fast. She thought that every trifling evil thing she did was but another drop of sustenance for the evil to lap up and grow fat on. Oh, how fat it was growing.

'Zing,' went the telephone, and downstairs padded Greta, mopping at her nose with a chiffon scarf which by a fortunate chance was in the pocket of her dressing gown. The thought of the evil was upon her, and the thought that death itself is no escape from it.

'Oh yes, Glory, oh yes.' (She would go to lunch with Glory.)

The meat was overcooked and the beans were undercooked. The two friends brought their plates of food into the sitting room and turned the gas fire up. Two of the asbestos props were broken, the room felt cold and damp.

'It is cold,' said Greta. 'Glory,' she said, 'I like your dressing gown with the burn down the front and the grease spots, somehow that is right, and the beastly dark room is right, and the dust upon the antique rare ornaments; the dust, and the saucepan with the goldfish in it, and the overcooked meat and the undercooked beans, it is right; it is an abandonment. It is what the world deserves.'

'Let us have some cocoa afterwards,' said Glory.

'Yes, cocoa, that is right too.'

They began to laugh. Cocoa *was* the thing.

'When you rang up,' said Greta, 'I was thinking, I said, Hell is the continuation of policy. And I was thinking that even death is not the end of it. You know, Glory, there is something frightening about the Christian idea, sometimes it is frightening.' She combed her hair through her fingers.

'I don't know,' said Glory, 'I never think about it.'

'The plodding on and on,' went on Greta, 'the de-moting and the up-grading; the marks and the punishments and the smugness.'

'Like school?' said Glory, waking up a bit to the idea.

'Yes, like school. And no freedom so that a person might stretch himself out. Never, never, never; not even in death; oh most of all not then.'

'I believe in mortality,' said Glory flippantly, 'I shall have on my tombstone, "In the confident hope of Mortality". If death is not the end,' she said, an uneasy note in her voice, 'then indeed there is nowhere to look.'

'When I was studying the Coptics,' said Greta, 'do you know what I found?'

'No, Greta, what was that?'

'It was the Angels and the Red Clay. The angels came one by one to the Red Clay and coaxed it saying that it should stand up and be Man, and that if the Red Clay would do this it should have the ups and downs, and the good fortune and the bad fortune, and all falling haphazard, so that no one might say when it should be this and when that, but no matter, for this the Red Clay should stand up at once and be Man. But, No, said the Red Clay, No, it was not good enough.'

Glory's attention moved off from the Coptics and fastened again upon the problem of Ivor and herself. Oh dear, oh dear. And sadly the tears fell down.

Greta glanced at her severely. 'You should divorce Ivor,' she said.

'I've no grounds,' wailed Glory, 'not since I came back to him.'

'Then you should provoke him to strangle you,' said Greta, who wished to get on with her story. 'That should not be difficult,' she said, 'And then you can divorce him for cruelty.'

'But I love Ivor,' said Glory, 'I don't want to divorce him.'

'Well, make up your mind. As I was saying,' said Greta, '. . . . . so then came the Third Angel. "And what have you got to say for yourself?" said the Red Clay, "What have you to promise me?" "I am Death," said the Angel, "and death is the end." So at this up and jumps the Red Clay at once and becomes Man.'

'Oh Glory,' said Greta, when she had finished this recital, and paused a moment while the long tide of evil swept in again upon her, 'Oh Glory, I cannot bear the evil, and the cruelty, and the scientific use of force, and the evil.' She screwed her napkin into a twist, and wrung the hem of it, that was already torn, quite off. 'I do not feel that I can go on.'

At these grand familiar words Glory began to cry afresh, and Greta was crying too. For there lay the slop on the carpet where the gold-fish had been, and there stood the saucepan with the fish resting languid upon the bottom, and there too was the dust and the dirt, and now the plates also, with the congealed mutton fat close upon them.

'Oh do put some more water in the fish pan,' sobbed Greta.

Glory picked up the pan and ran across the room with it to take it to the kitchen tap. But now the front door, that was apt to jam, opened with a burst, and Ivor fell into the room.

48

'They were both out,' he said. 'I suppose you have eaten all the lunch? Oh, hello Greta.'

'Listen,' said Glory, 'there's another bomb coming.'

Ivor went into the cupboard.

'Do you know Ivor,' screamed Greta through the closed door, 'I had a dream and when I woke up I was saying, "Hell is the continuation of policy".'

'You girls fill your heads with a lot of bosh.'

Glory said, 'There's some bread and cheese in the kitchen, we are keeping the cocoa hot. Greta' she said, 'was telling me about the Coptics.'

'Eh?' said Ivor.

'Oh do take those fish out and give them some more water,' said Greta.

'The story about the Angels and the Red Clay.'

'Spurious,' yelled Ivor, 'all bosh. But how on earth did you get hold of the manuscript, Greta, it's very rare.'

'I don't think there's much in it,' said Glory, 'nothing to make you cry. Come, cheer up Greta. I say Ivor, the doodle has gone off towards the town, you can come out now.'

Ivor came out looking very cheerful. 'I tell you what, Greta,' he said, 'I'll show you my new plastic bait.' He took the brightly coloured monsters out of their tin and brought them to her on a plate. 'I use these for pike,' he said.

There was now in the room a feeling of loving kindness and peace. Greta fetched the cheese and bread from the kitchen and Glory poured the hot cocoa. 'There is nothing like industry, control, affection and discipline,' said Greta.

The sun came round to the french windows and struck through the glass pane at the straw stuffing that was hanging down from the belly of the sofa.

'Oh, look,' said Glory, pointing to the patch of sunlight underneath, 'there is the button you lost.'

Silence fell upon them in the sun-spiked room. Silently, happily, they went on with their lunch. The only sound now in the room was the faint sizzle of the cocoa against the side of the jug (that was set too close to the fire and soon must crack) and the far off bark of the dog Sultan, happy with his rats.

1949

THE STORY OF A STORY

'I am so awfully stuck,' sighed Helen. 'You see it is a monologue, it is Bella's monologue, it is saying all the time how much she is thinking about Roland all the time, and thinking back, and remembering, and so on. It is like a squirrel in a cage, it goes round and round. And now I am stuck. Tell me, Ba, how can I come out of it to make a proper ending,—ah, that is difficult.'

The two girls were having lunch together in the Winter-garden, the potted palms were languid, but underneath the palms stood out like tropic flowers the keen dark faces of the yellow-skinned business men. Everybody was drinking strong bitter coffee that was served rather cold and soon became quite cold. The yellow of the skins and the yellow of the whites of the eyes of the business men spoke of too many of these cups of coffee drunk too often.

'You do not mean to say,' said Barbara, 'that you are writing a story about Roland and Bella?'

'Well, I am trying to,' said Helen, 'but it is very difficult, but I am doing my very best.' She sighed again. Oh, how difficult it was.

'But,' said Ba, 'you know that Roland will not like that.'

'Pooh, nonsense,' said Helen, 'he told me that he would not mind.

But it is so difficult, but difficult, always so difficult to write.' Helen sounded rather desperate. 'It must be right,' she said, 'quite right.'

'But Roland,' said Ba again.

Helen began to look rather dreamy. 'Human beings are very difficult,' she said. 'You know, it is like the lady in Maurice Baring, she was one of these foreign countesses he has, and she was sitting at dinner next to an English writer. "And vat is it you write about, Mr So-and-So?" she said. "Oh, people," he said, "people." "Ah, people," said the countess, "they are very difficult." '

'But Roland . . .' went on Ba.

'I do wish you would stop saying "But Roland," ' said Helen. 'I tell you Roland said to me, "Helen, I suppose you will write a story about us." And I said, "Well, perhaps I shall, but it is very difficult." "Well, do," said Roland. "write whatever you like Helen, I shan't mind." '

'Ah,' said Ba, 'he only said that to trap you.'

'No, no,' said Helen, 'he could not be so base.'

That evening Ba tidied herself and went round to see Roland and Bella. Bella was not very pleased to see her. Bella was a warm-hearted person, but this girl was rather tiresome, she was *devoted* to Roland.

'I think I ought to tell you,' said Ba, 'that Helen is writing a story about you.'

This is how the war broke out, the war that was to carry so much away with it, the personal war, the war that is so trivial and so deadly.

Bella loved Helen.

'Oh, Helen, how could you do such a thing?'

'What thing is that, Bella?'

'Why, to write a story about Roland and me.'

'Oh, that,' said Helen, 'why that is very difficult. I am so terribly stuck, you know. It is difficult.'

'But Roland . . .' said Bella.

'How is Roland?' said Helen. Helen admired Roland very much for his fine intelligence, and because this fine intelligence was of the legalistic variety, very different from Helen's.

'Roland is furious,' said Bella, 'simply furious.'

'It is so frightfully difficult,' said Helen, 'to get it exactly right.'

'He says that if you do not give him your word that you will not publish the story he will not see you again.' Bella was now in tears, she loved Helen and she loved Roland. 'It is all so difficult,' she said, 'and Ba with her student-girl devotion does not help, and this story makes it all so difficult.'

'Yes, yes,' said Helen, 'it is difficult. I am most frightfully stuck.'

'You mean you are going on,' wept Bella. 'Oh Helen, how can you?'

'Well, that is just it, I do not know that I can. But,' said Helen, 'I shall try.'

'But Roland says . . . '

'Pooh, *that*. He cannot be so stupid.'

The two friends walked together across Hyde Park to Hyde Park Corner. Coming down the long grass path between the trees towards the statue of the great Achilles, Helen saw a horse drawing a cart full of leaves and bushes. 'Oh look, Bella, look,' she said. The horse had broken into a gallop, he drew the cart swiftly after him. He was a tall heavy animal, dappled grey and white, his long flaxen hair flew in the wind behind him, the long pale hair streamed on the gale that was blowing up between the April trees.

'What is it,' said Bella, who was in the middle of saying something about Roland. 'Well, what is it?'

'That horse,' said Helen.

'How can you look at a horse at such a moment? You want it both ways,' said Bella.

Helen looked at Bella and laughed. 'It is the moment to look at a horse.'

She went home and went on with the story. It was building up slowly, it was not so bad now, it was coming right.

When she had finished it she took it round to Lopez, who was also a writer. Lopez was a very clever quick girl, she had a brilliant quick eye for people, conversations, and situations. She read the story right through without stopping. 'It is very good, Helen,' she said, and then she began to laugh.

When Helen had gone Lopez rang up all the friends, and the friends of the friends, the people who knew Lopez and who knew Helen, and who knew Bella and Roland, and even those who knew the devoted girl Ba.

'Look,' said Lopez, 'Helen has written a most amusing story about Roland and Bella. It is very amusing, exactly right, you know.'

Everybody was very pleased, and the soft laughter ran along

the ground like fire.

Cold and ferocious, Roland heard about it, coldly ferociously he sent messages to Helen. Bella came running, bringing the ferocious messages. 'Pentheus, ruler of this Theban land, I come from Kithairon where never melts the larding snow . . . ' Yes, it was like the Greek messengers who have the story in their mouths to tell it all. 'Where never melts the larding snow,' that was surely the cold Roland, so ferocious now and cold.

'He says,' cried Bella, 'that he will never see you again if you do not give him your word that never shall the story be published.'

'Pooh,' said Helen, 'we have heard about that. Very well then, I shall never see Roland again.' But she, too, began to cry. 'It is so easy,' she said, 'to close a door.'

'But he says,' went on Bella, 'that he will have his solicitor write to you, that he will have his secretary ring you up, that if the story is published he will at once bring a libel action against you.'

'It is so difficult to get these stories right,' said Helen, her thoughts moving off from Roland to the dear story that was now at last so right, so truly beautiful.

Bella shook her ferociously. 'Listen, Helen, he will bring a legal action.'

Helen began to cry more desperately and to wring her hands. 'He cannot be so base, indeed it is not possible, he cannot.' But now through the thoughts of the beautiful story, so right, so beautiful, broke the knowledge of the cold and ferocious Roland, that was now standing with a drawn sword.

'Ah, ah, ah,' sobbed Helen.

Bella put her arms round her. 'It is no good,' she said, 'no one and nobody has ever got the better of Roland.'

'But I love Roland,' said Helen, 'and I love you, and I even love the student girl Ba, and I love my story.'

'You want it both ways,' said Bella.

'There is no harm in this story,' wept Helen, 'and he is condemning it unseen. He has not seen it, it is soft and beautiful, not malicious, there is no harm in it and he is destroying it.'

'Roland,' said Bella, 'is a very subtle person, he is this important and subtle character.'

'For all that,' said Helen, 'he does not understand, he does not understand one thing, or know one thing to know it properly. He is this legalistic person.'

'He is the finest QC of them all,' said Bella.

'He knows nothing,' said Helen, and at once her thoughts passed from the benign and the happy, to the furtive, the careful, the purposeful and the defensive.

'You are childish about this story,' said Bella.

'You shall see that I am not.'

'What are you thinking of now?' said Bella, watching Helen and watching the ferocious intent expression on her face.

'I am thinking of Baron Friedrich von Hügel,' said Helen.

'Eh, who might he be, and what are you thinking about him?'

'I am thinking of what he said.'

'And what did he say?'

Helen screwed up her face and spat out the words, the terrible judging words. 'He said, "Nothing can be more certain than that great mental powers can be accompanied by emptiness or depravity of heart." He was thinking of Roland, be sure of it.'

Helen went home and knelt down and prayed, 'Oh, God,' et cetera. She was a Christian of the neo-Platonic school. She prayed that she might do the right thing about the story. This matter that had been so trivial was now running deep, deep and devilish swift. It was time to pray. She prayed that all might come right between herself and Roland and her dear friend, Bella. She knelt for a long time thinking, but it did not seem the right thing to do to suppress the story because of the threat of legal action and for the fear of it. But she knew that Roland could have no idea of this, he could have no idea of Helen but the idea that she was a friend of Bella's, a rattle, a literary girl, a desperate character, a person of no right sense or decency. 'But I will go on with it,' said Helen, and she began to cry again, and said, 'It will be the death of me.' For now the human feelings were running very swiftly indeed, and on the black surface of the hurrying water was the foam fleck of hatred and contempt.

She did not see Roland because she would not give him her word. Driven by Bella, whose one thought was that the story should not be published, because of the trouble that would follow, Helen cried, 'I will give my word in contempt, using his own weapon, for my word shall mean as much as his word meant when he said, "Write about us, write what you like, I shall not mind." '

Bella felt that her heart would break, the violence and the obstinancy of Roland and Helen would break it quite in two.

'He denies that he ever said such a thing.'

'But Bella, you heard him. You were coming out of the bathroom carrying the goldfish. You heard him, you told me that you heard him.'

'I heard him say, "Go ahead, write what you like," but it was a threat.'

Helen began to choke. 'It was no threat, he spoke most friendly, very open he was, he was treating me as a friend, he was anxious that it should be right.' She sighed and smiled and gave Bella a hug. 'It was difficult, but now it is right.'

She did not see Roland, but still she saw her dear friend, Bella. But always Bella was telling her of the affair, *Roland versus Helen,* and how the situation lay, and what Roland had said only yesterday, and what the part was that the girl Ba was playing.

The weeks went by, the story was now accepted and to be published. Nobody had seen the story as it now was, worked upon and altered with cunning and furtiveness and care and ferocity, it was now a different story, hedged and pared from legal action, but as good as it had ever been, good, shining bright, true, beautiful, but pared from legal action.

Helen prayed that the story might come safely through. The friends said that Roland would not bring an action, that he would not do it, that he was playing a game of bluff to frighten Helen, to make her withdraw the story.

But now Helen had the thought that she was dealing with a maniac, *a person who would go to all lengths.*

The danger of the situation and the care for it made her grow thin, and every time that she saw Bella the harsh cruel words of Roland were repeated, and what Ba had said was repeated, and all of it again, and again; and then again.

'Ba says that it is a good thing that she has done informing against you,' said Bella, 'for in this way the story will not be published, and everybody's feelings will be spared.'

'But the feelings and truth of the story will not be spared,' said Helen, and a bitter look came across her face. 'That does not matter I suppose?'

Bella tore on, 'Roland was saying only yesterday, "Helen will have to write a story to say how the story was not published," and he laughed then and said, "Helen must be taught a lesson," and he said, "Now that she has learnt her lesson I am willing to see her again." '

Helen put her head on the tablecloth of the restaurant where they were having lunch and wept, and she said: 'I wish Roland was dead.'

It was now Good Friday. Restlessly, sadly, Helen moved about the wide empty garden. The sun shone down through the fine ash trees and the lawn was bright green after the heavy rain. What a terrible day Good Friday is as the hour of twelve o'clock draws near. Her Aunt was at ante-communion, her sister at the mass of the pre-sanctified, but Helen would not go to church because she had said, 'I wish he was dead.' She went into the garden to fetch the book that she liked to read on Good Fridays and read:

> The third hour's deafened with the cry
> Of crucify Him, crucify.
> So goes the vote, nor ask them why,
> Live Barabbas and let God die.
> But there is wit in wrath and they will try
> A Hail more cruel than their crucify.
> For while in sport he wears a spiteful crown,
> The serious showers along his decent face run slowly down.

She thought of the crucifixion that was now at twelve o'clock taking place, and she thought that she, in her hatred of Roland and her contempt for him (because of the violence of the law that he threatened to use) had a part among the crucifiers, and she wept and hid her face, kneeling against the cold bark of the fine ash tree. 'The cruelties of past centuries are in our bones,' she cried, 'and we wish to ignore the sufferings of Christ, for we have too much of a hand in them. Oh I do not wish Roland dead, but what is the use to love him and to love my dear Bella? They will not receive it and the door is now closed. But even now,' she said, 'if I withdraw the story, and give my word that neither here nor in America—(for it was not only British Rights that Roland was asking her to give up)—shall the story be published, nor after his death, will that door be opened again and shall I be received? Oh, no, no'—Helen screamed and twisted and beat her head against the cold ash tree bark—'I cannot do this, and if I did never could it be the same between us, for it would be the act of a slave person, and no good thing.' And she knelt at the foot of the fine ash tree and prayed, 'Come, peace of God,' et cetera.

She went into the house and fetched out her writing pad and wrote to Bella: 'Dearest Bella, I think we had better not see each other for a bit. I like to think agreeably of you and Roland and even Ba, but I cannot do this now while I am seeing you, so we had better not see each other.' She paused and then went on, 'We can think of each other in the past as if we were dead.' Helen's face brightened at this idea, 'Yes, as if we were dead. So with love to you and Roland and Ba.'

When she had written her letter she thought, 'One must pay out everything, but it is not happy.' She thought of Bella's beautiful house and the beautiful pictures that Roland had collected, especially there was such a beautiful picture in the hall, the Elsheimer, ah, that was it, *it was the gem of his collection*. Helen wept to think that never again would she see her dear friends, Roland and Bella, in love and friendship, and never again would she see the beautiful house, the Elsheimer, the trees in the shady garden or the goldfish swimming in their square glass tank. She thought that she must pay out everything and she supposed that the Grünewald prints that Roland had lent her must now also be given back.

She fell asleep in the garden and dreamt that she was standing up in court accused of treachery, blasphemy, theft and conduct prejudicial to discipline. Roland was cross-examining her:

'Do you think it is immoral to write about people?'

'No no, it is very difficult.' She held out her hands to Bella and Roland, but they turned from her.

'You go into houses under cover of friendship and steal away the words that are spoken.'

'Oh, it is difficult, so difficult, one cannot remember them, the words run away; when most one wants the word, it is gone.'

'You do not think it is immoral to write about people?'

'It is a spiritual truth, it is that.'

The dream-girl breaks down under cross-examination by the cold and ferocious Roland. She is cross, lost and indistinct.

'The story is beautiful and truthful,' she cries. 'It is a spiritual truth.'

The girl cries and stammers and reads from a book that she draws from her pocket, 'Spiritual things are spiritually discerned, the carnal mind cannot know the things of the spirit.' She weeps and stammers, 'Of the Idea of the Good there is nothing that can be spoken directly.'

The dream-girl glances furiously upon the Judge, the Counsels for Defence and Prosecution, upon the tightly packed friends, who have come to see what is going on. She reads again. 'Let those be silent about the beauty of noble conduct who have never cared for such things, nor let those speak of the splendour of virtue who have never known the face of justice or temperance.'

There was now a mighty uproar in the court, but the dream-girl cries out high above the clamour, stuttering and stammering and weeping bitterly, and still reading from her book, 'Such things may be known by those who have eyes to see, the rest it would fill with contempt in a manner by no means pleasing, or with a lofty and vain presumption, as though they had learnt something grand.'

'He that hath yores to yore,' said the Judge, 'let him yore.' And he pronounced the sentence, 'You are to be taken to the place from whence you came . . .' The police constable and the wardress in the dock beside her took hold of her.

On the Tuesday after Easter there was a letter from Bella. 'How could you lump me with Ba?' she wrote.

Helen sat in her office, here were the proofs of the story come by post for correction. How fresh and remote it read, *there was no harm in it*.

Her employer, who was a publisher, came into the room where she was sitting. 'What's the matter, Helen?' he said, seeing the tears running down her cheeks.

She told him the story of the story.

'Look here, Helen,' said the employer, 'just you cut them right out, publish the story, tell him to go to hell.' Then he said, 'I am afraid the editor will have to be told.'

The moment, which had been so smiling when the employer first spoke, now showed its teeth. 'Of course, I don't expect he'll mind,' he said. But mind he would, thought Helen.

She took the bath towel from the drawer in her desk and held it in front of her face. 'The law of libel,' she said in a low faint voice, 'is something that one does not care to think about.' She pressed the towel against her face. 'It is everything that there is of tyranny and prevention.'

'Yes, yes,' said the employer, and walking over to the mantelpiece he pinched the dead lilac flowers that were hanging down from the jam jar, 'Yes.'

Helen wrote to the editor to tell him. He regretted that in the circumstances he could not publish the story.

When Helen got the editor's letter she wrapped the raincoat that Bella had given her tightly about her and walked along the rain swept avenue that led to the park. She sat by the bright pink peony flowers and she thought that her thoughts were murderous, for the combination of anger and impotence is murderous, and this time it was no longer Good Friday and the soft feeling of repentance and sorrow did not come to drive out the hatred. The rain fell like spears upon the dark green leaves of the peony plants and the lake water at a distance lay open to their thrust. It was not enough to know that the door against Roland and Bella was now locked tight, she must forget that there had ever been such people, or a door that was open to be shut. But how long would it take to forget, ah, how long, ah, that would be a long time.

1946

IS THERE A LIFE
BEYOND THE GRAVY?

It was a wonderfully sunny day; the willowherb waved in the ruins and the white fluff fell like snow. But alas—Celia glanced at the blue-faced clock in the Ministry tower—it was eleven o'clock.

She shook herself free of the rubble and stood up. The white earth fell from her hair and clothes.

'Are you all right?' said her cousin Casivalaunus, who was standing looking at her.

'Oh yes, thank you so much. Oh, hallo, Cas.'

'Hallo, Celia. Well, I'll be off. See you at Uncle Heber's.'

Celia took hold of her cousin's arm and hung on like grim death.

'You're sure you're all right?' said Cas, flicking at the white fluff with his service gloves. 'I say, would you mind letting go of my arm?'

'So long, Cas.'

'So long, Celia. You'll soon get accustomed to it.'

He saluted, and walking quickly with elegant long strides made off down an avenue lined with broken pillars.

Celia leaped over the waterpipes that lay in the gutter and tore across the garden in the middle of the square. This was a short cut to the Ministry. She was already an hour late, but she thought it was a good thing to take the short cut, and very important to run.

'How do you do, Browser?' she called out, as she ran past the porter and up the stairs.

'Same as usual, miss,' said the porter with a wink.

Well, it *was* much the same really; for one thing Celia had never in her life been early.

'You've never in your lifetime been early.' Browser's parting shot (what a very carrying voice he had to be sure) followed her up the stairs and across the threshold of her room.

Tiny was standing over by the window squashing flies on the curtain.

'Hallo, Tiny.'

'Hallo, Celia.'

Celia flung her gloves into the wastepaper basket and put her hat on the statue of the Young Octavius. What a really fine room it was, she thought, so high and square, with such a beautiful moulded ceiling. But rather untidy. Celia sighed. She began to count up the number of things that would have to be put away one day, but not just now. Perhaps Tiny would put them away.

There was a leather revolver holster on the radiator, a set of tennis-balls on the table by the window, a tin, marked Harrogate Toffee, with some cartridges in it, a large feather duster and a jigsaw puzzle. On the floor lay a copy of Sir Sefton Choate's monograph *Across the Sinai Desert with the Children of Israel*, and sticking out of the tall bronze urn by the fireplace were a large landing-net and a couple of golf-clubs with broken sticks. A long thin climbing plant had managed to take root in the filing tray and was already half way up the wall.

Celia sighed again and closed her eyes. 'Anything in today, Tiny, darling?'

'Just a telegram,' said Tiny, and read it out:

'To Criticisms Mainly Emanating Examerica He Anxiousest More Responsible Ministers Be Associated Cumhim But Sharpliest Protested Antisuggestion Camille Chautemps'—wang wang, Tiny struck a note and intoned the rest of it—*'Quote Eye Appreciate Joke Buttwas He Who Signed Capitulation Abandoned Allies Sentenced Leaders Deathwards Unquote General DeGaulle Postremarking He Unthought Hed See Andre Maurois Again.'*

'It is from our cousin,' said Tiny. ' "Eye appreciate joke", I do not. Look,' he pointed to the signature, *Casivalaunus.*

Tiny and Celia began to laugh their aggravating high-pitched laugh. This noise was very aggravating for Lord Loop—Augustus Loop—Tiny's brother, who occupied the adjoining room. He began to pound on the wall. Tiny turned quite pale. 'Oh, lord, there goes Augustus,' he said. He flicked at the papers on his desk and put a busy expression on his face.

'This cablegram,' he said, 'is dated 1942.'

'I tell you what,' said Celia, 'I'll do the washing-up.'

Celia had a large red Bristol glass tumbler, out of which she drank her morning milk. She was delighted with the appearance of this tumbler in the wash-basin and swam it round for some time, admiring the reflection. 'But of course,' she said, for she had acquired the habit of talking to herself, 'it is to be seen at its best only with the white milk in it.' There was also Tiny's old Spode cup and saucer to be washed—he had pinched this from Augustus—and a rather humdrum yellow jug that belonged to Sir Sefton. Celia suddenly remembered Sir Sefton and wondered if he was in yet. She was Sir Sefton's Personal Assistant. How grand that sounded! Personal Assistant to Sir Sefton Choate, Bt, MP, MIME—yes, he was a famous mining engineer, or had been, before 'like the rest of us' he had been caught by the Ministry. Had he not written in his famous monograph on the Children of Israel, 'It is probable, in this rich oil-bearing district, that Lot's wife was turned into a pillar of asphalt, not salt'?

From somewhere in the distance came the sound of a harp—the thin beautiful sound. That must be Jacky Sparrow in Publications. He was a graceful harpist. Celia remembered that she was lunching with Jacky today. She must hurry up and get on with the morning. The morning was like a beautiful coloured ball to be bounced and played with till the next thing came along to be done, and that was lunch-time.

Tiny came and banged on the door. 'Hurry up, Celia! Crumbs, what ages you take. Sefton wants you.'

' 'Morning, Miss Phoze.'

' 'Morning, Sir Sefton.'

'I had a rotten night last night,' said the baronet. 'I don't know. This way and that. Couldn't get a wink. Then I got up and sat on the side of the bath with my feet in hot water. No good. So I took a tablet. Thought it was Slumber-o, but must have got the wrong bottle. Turned it up next morning. D'you know what it was? Camomile. I was up all night.'

Sir Sefton was sitting at his desk doing the *Morning Post* crossword puzzle.

'What's a difficult poem by Browning?'

'Paracelsus,' said Celia, who was trying to write an article for the *Tribune*—where was that envelope with the figures on it? Was it two-thirds or two-fifths?

'*Eight* letters,' said the baronet.

'Sordello.'

'Hrrump, hrrump! Yes, that's it. Thank you very much, Miss Phoze . . . I don't think there's anything very much here.' He began to rummage under his blotter, holding it up with one hand and paddling underneath with the other. 'Oh, here's a note from the LCC.

Let's see, March 1942? Well, it's answered itself by now.' He went back to his puzzle.

'Where did the Kings of Israel reign?'

'Jerusalem,' said Celia.

'Now now, it's not as easy as that.'

'The Kings of Israel,' said Celia, and began to stare round the room rather desperately. 'I say, the charlady has left a packet of sandwiches in the curtain loop.'

'Good heavens!' said Sir Sefton absentmindedly. 'The Kings of Israel, the Kings of Israel?'

'Stead,' said Sir Sefton. 'I asked Jacky Sparrow about it, as a matter of fact; he's a dab at these things.' He grinned delightedly. ' "And Jeroboam reigned in his stead." Smart, isn't it?' he said. 'Well, well, Miss Phoze, I think I'll buz off now. I'm going to this lecture on Oil Surrogates at the Institute. Thought I'd take Bozey with me—cheer him up you know—he's never been the same since his wife died. I said to him: "Bozey, your good lady's gone, hasn't she? Very well, then, she's gone. No good moping, is there, we all have to go some time." '

'Don't forget the hare,' said Celia, as Sefton padded towards the door.

This was a large, dead animal, half wrapped in brown paper, that lay across the floor. Augustus had brought it up for Sefton from his farm (the beastly Augustus, thought Celia, for neither she nor Tiny could stand him). All the same, it was a fine animal, the hare, and stretched right across the room.

Sefton picked it up and went out rather burdened, with the creature trailing over one arm, and his umbrella on the other.

'God bless you,' he said, with a happy smile. 'God bless us all and the Pope of Rome.'

There was a message from Jacky Sparrow on Celia's desk, to say that he would not be able to lunch as he had to rush off to the dentist's.

Celia and Tiny decided to have lunch in their room, and Celia went to get it from the canteen, because Mrs Bones always gave her more ice-cream than Tiny. Halfway through their picnic lunch, Augustus came into the room with a made-up boisterous expression on his face.

'Hallo, you two, pack up there; we're off to the countryside for an excursion.'

Hand in hand Tiny and Celia went and stood in the garden of the square while Augustus went to get the car out. The garden now stretched for miles and was more full of flowers than it had been in the morning; indeed there was a rather alarming air of quickly growing vegetation.

'Perhaps we had better make a move,' said Celia.

They walked together down a narrow pathway, between the giant blue flowers which grew and flowered high above their heads. Suddenly, coming round a hairy oriental poppy plant, they ran full tilt into Sir Sefton.

'Good heavens,' he said, 'I must hurry, or I shall be late for the meeting. I shall see you next week at the Ministry, Miss Phoze? Ah, howdedo, Loop? So long, all.'

He went off in a fuss in the opposite direction.

'Next week?' said Tiny. 'What can he be thinking of?—the poor old gentleman.'

'Why, *this* week is the holidays, of course,' said Celia. 'We are going to stay with Uncle Heber.'

'Oh yes,' said Tiny, 'I'd forgotten. How quickly the time comes round.'

'Well, we'd better be getting on,' said Celia, disengaging her foot from a young oak tree that was shooting up from a split acorn.

'But Augustus told us to wait for him.'

'I don't care about Augustus,' said Celia recklessly, and tossed back her fine dark hair. 'After all, he can soon catch us up in his motor-car.'

'Perhaps we had better keep to the pathway,' said Tiny slyly.

The pretty grey grass was soft under their feet, but there was hardly room for the two of them to walk abreast.

'Yes, perhaps we had,' said Celia, laughing. 'It will save a lot of bother.'

'Why, look,' said Tiny, 'here comes Jacky Sparrow.'

Jacky came running along the narrow path towards them, jumping gracefully over the young shoots as he ran. He was carrying his harp in his outstretched arms.

'Hallo, hallo, hallo,' he said, 'can't stop, can't stop, can't stop. Sorry about the lunch, Celia; got to get me harp-string mended, got to catch the old chap before he lies down for the afternoon.'

'Phew!' said Tiny, as Jacky disappeared from sight. 'Everybody seems to be going in the opposite direction.'

The vista now opened before them upon a slight decline. There was a fine white marble viaduct down below them to the right, and upon the viaduct was an old-fashioned train, with steam coming out of the coal-black engine and the fire stoked to flame upon the fender.

'Hurry, hurry, hurry,' cried Tiny, catching Celia by the hand. 'We have just time to take the train!'

The train was beginning to move as they tore up the steps and into the last carriage.

'Jolly good show,' said Tiny; and then he said, 'I hope Uncle Heber will be pleased to see us.'

They both lay down on the carriage seat, and ate the sandwiches which Celia had brought with her from Sir Sefton's room.

The train was now running between high embankments. On the top of the embankment and down the side was the soft grass waving like beautiful hair; also on the top, against a Cambridge-blue sky, there were some poppies.

'Beautiful,' said Tiny; 'might be Norfolk.'

'One always comes back to the British School,' said Celia dreamily.

'What a dreamy girl you are,' said Tiny.

The train, gathering speed at the bend, shot through an old-fashioned station. There were rounded Victorian window-panes in the waiting-room and a general air of coal, sea, soot and steamer oil.

'What station was that?' asked Celia.

'Looked like Dover,' said Tiny.

'Can't be Dover,' said Celia. 'Dover isn't on the way to Uncle Heber's.'

After another mile or so the train pulled up with a jerk and they sat up quickly to look out of the window. It was an enormous, long, busy station. People were hurrying down the platform towards the refreshment-room; soldiers, sailors and airmen stood about in groups drinking cups of tea from the trolleys.

'Just time to get dinner if you hurry,' sang out a familiar voice, and there was Sir Sefton carrying a couple of bottles of hair-oil as well as the hare and the umbrella. 'So long,' he said, raising his hat to Celia and dropping one of the bottles, which smashed against the platform and released a beautiful odour. 'So long, all, see you later.'

'Must be Perth,' said Tiny. He pulled the blind down with a snap, and pushed Celia on to the bunk.

Celia looked round the carriage, at the wash-basin, the lights just

65

where you wanted them, the luggage-table, the many different sorts of racks, the air-conditioning control, the neat fawn blankets and clean pillow-cases.

'What a good thing we managed to get a sleeper,' she said.

'I fancy we have to thank Sir Sefton for that.'

'I think Sefton is simply ripping,' said Celia.

'One of the best; jolly good show, sir,' said Tiny.

'Can't be Perth,' said Celia. 'Perth isn't on the way to Uncle Heber's.'

'We shall be in the mountains soon,' said Tiny; 'the mountain air is always so delicious. I trust that we shall catch a great many trout. It is a pity that we left the landing-net at home.'

'Uncle Heber's country,' said Celia, 'is as flat as a pancake.'

Tiny said, 'We must continue steadfastly to look on the bright side of things,' and promptly fell asleep.

There now came a great pounding at the door. It was Jacky Sparrow with his harp in his hand, and an inspector's cap on his head.

'All change, all change, all change,' he cried out. Then he said, 'So long, I simply must fly.'

Celia and Tiny got the suitcases shut at last and tumbled out on to a grass-grown platform. There were a couple of donkeys grazing on the siding, but no people at all. The train gave a shiver and a backward slide, then it pulled itself together and rushed off, leaving a patch of black smoke hanging in mid-air. The smoke bellied out and hung, first black, then grey, then white, against a pale-blue sky.

'Thornton-le-Soke,' read out Tiny from the station nameplate.

'You see,' said Celia, 'no mountains at all.'

The station was set in a beautiful sunbaked plain under a wide skyline. The sea could be seen in the far distance, and a soft fresh wind blew inland over the samphire beds.

Tiny looked very happy. 'We have arrived,' he said. 'It is curious, do you know I have not thought of Augustus for several moments?'

'I fancy,' said Celia, 'that Augustus has taken the wrong turning.'

'Indeed?' said Tiny.

'Augustus was looking rather weird,' said Celia in her dreamy way. 'There he was, sitting high above the road in his old-fashioned motor-car, with his dust coat and his goggles, and the dust flying up behind the car and the chickens running away in front of it.'

'Oh, did you see him?'

'Did *you*?'

'Yes, as a matter of fact I did see Augustus in his motor-car. I said nothing about it,' said Tiny kindly, 'because I did not wish to disturb you.'

'Oh, not at all,' said Celia; 'thanks awfully all the same.'

They now sat down on their suitcases like a couple of schoolchildren waiting to be fetched.

'Do you know who will fetch us, I think?' said Celia.

'It will be Uncle Heber for one.'

'Uncle is an old and established person, he may not come, but if he comes there will also be another one, and that other one will be our cousin, Casivalaunus.'

'Good heavens!' said Tiny. 'He was seconded to Intelligence, was he not? I fancied he was in the mountains.'

'You seem to have got the mountains on the brain.'

Celia began to count the wooden palings opposite, counting aloud in German, *'Ein, zwei, drei, vier, fünf.'*

'Mark my words,' said Tiny, 'that car of Augustus's will *konk out* on the hills.' He coughed. 'If you will excuse the expression.'

At this moment a long, thin person came in an elegant stroll along the platform towards them; he was wearing the uniform of a high-ranking British officer.

'There you are. What did I tell you?' said Celia. 'It is Cas.'

'I can't stand these clothes,' said Cas. 'You'll have to wait a minute while I change. Uncle's down below in the pony-trap. We drove it under the bridge, as Polly likes the shade. I'll just pop into the waiting-room, I won't be a tick.'

'I do think our cousin has a vulgar parlance,' said Tiny.

Celia tore down the station steps and climbed into the pony-trap beside Uncle Heber, and put her arms round him. Heber was wearing his shabby old clergyman's clothes, a clerical grey ankle-length mackintosh and a shovel hat. He was crying quietly.

'We must get home quickly,' he said. 'I have set the supper table because it is Tuffie's night out, but there is much to do; we must hurry.'

He pulled gently on the reins and Polly moved off at an amble, with the grass still sticking out of her mouth. Cas, in a light-green ski-jacket and flannel trousers, came running with Tiny. They caught hold of the trap and jumped in.

'All aboard,' said Heber in a hollow voice.

As they drove the quiet country miles to the rectory, Celia began to sing, 'Softly, softly, softly, softly, The white snow fell.'

'Now, Celia,' said Cas, 'we can do without that.'

They were bowling along the sands by this time, bowling along the white sea sand down below the high-tide level where the sands were damp and firm. The sea crept out to the far horizon, where some dirty weather was blowing up; one could see the line of stormy white waves beyond the seawhorl worms, and the white bones and white seashells that lay in the hollow.

'There's some dirty weather coming,' said Tiny.

'True, Tiny, true,' said Cas.

'I hope we shan't be *kept in*,' said Celia.

'I am sure we shall be able to *get out of the wind under the break-water*, and that we shall be able to go for a *stretch*, a *blow*, a *turn*, a *tramp* and a *breather*,' said Cas, giving Tiny a sly pinch.

When they got to the rectory they had some sardines, some cheese, some bread, some margarine and some cocoa.

'There are some spring onions in the sideboard cupboard, if any person cares for such things,' said Heber.

The dark fell suddenly upon them as they sat at supper, and the rainstorm slashed across the window-pane.

'Off to bed with you all,' said Heber. 'There are your candles, take them with you. You are sleeping in the three rooms on the first floor at the back of the house overlooking the beechwoods. The rooms are called Minnie, Yarrow and Florence. You, Celia, are in Minnie. The boys can take their choice.'

'Oh, thank you sir, thank you so much,' said the boys.

'I must buzz off now,' said Heber, 'I have some business to attend to.'

He took his white muffler from the chest in the hall where the surplices were kept and a horn lantern from the porch. 'So long, all,' he said.

Tiny looked rather frightened.

'He is certainly going to the church,' said Celia.

They spoke in whispers together, and together went up the shallow treads of the staircase to bed.

Tiny pushed past Cas and went into the Florence room.

'Just what one might expect,' muttered Cas furiously. 'You know perfectly well, Tiny,' he called through the door, 'that I detest Yarrow.' He turned to Celia. 'I shall not be able to sleep a wink.'

Tiny sat on the window-seat crying. He leant far out into the night and his tears fell with a splash into the water-butt that was under the Florence window.

Then he got up and went into Celia's room. 'I keep thinking of Augustus,' he sobbed.

'Now, Tiny, now, Tiny,' said Celia, 'why do you do such a foolish thing?' But she was crying too.

'Then why are you crying, Celia?'

'Since I thought of Uncle going alone to the old, dark, cold church,' said Celia, 'I have had a feeling of disturbance.'

'One must continue to look on the bright side of things,' said Tiny.

As he spoke they heard the church bell tolling.

'It is tolling for the dead,' said Celia.

She went and stood in the middle of the room with her fingers in her ears. Her white cotton nightdress flapped round her legs in the wind that blew in from the open window.

'Be sure Augustus will not come,' she said. She stood quite still in a dull and violent stare. 'Do you not remember,' she said, 'what Augustus did to Brendan Harper the poet?'

'No,' said Tiny, cheering up a bit. 'What was that?'

'If you do not remember, then I shall not tell you. All *that*,' said Celia, 'belongs to the dead past.'

'To the *living* past,' said Tiny, rather to himself.

'Augustus is an abject character,' cried Celia, her voice rising to a high-pitched scream that quite drowned the wireless coming from Yarrow, where Cas sat sulking. 'Do you suppose for a moment that our uncle would have such a person to darken the threshold?'

'Well, it is already rather dark,' said Tiny. 'I say, Cas has got the radio on, I do think he's the limit.'

He began to pound on the wall.

'Starp that pounding!' yelled Cas.

'How vulgar he is,' Tiny sniffed in a superior manner. 'Well, so long, Celia, I'll be off.'

The next morning, after a broken night, they assembled early for breakfast. Tuffie, who had spent her evening at the pictures, brought in a large jorum of porridge and set it in front of Heber, who was looking rather severe in a shiny black suit and a pair of black wool mittens. The three visitors lolled in their chairs waiting for the porridge to be served.

Heber looked severely at Celia. 'Instead of lolling forever with your cousins in a negative mood, you should strive to improve. Do you all want to be sent back to school?' he inquired.

'Oh no, Uncle—oh no; oh, *rather* not!'

'Oh, Uncle,' said Celia, 'I will *try*.'

Heber gave them an equivocal look and rapped the table with a small silver crucifix. 'You will please stand,' he said. And then he said, 'For what we are about to receive.'

Cas intoned 'Et cetera' on a bell-like note, and they all sat down.

'What did you see last night, Tuffie?' inquired Celia politely.

'It was a lovely piece, duck,' said Tuffie; 'it was called Kingdom Kong.'

'Thy kingdom kong,' said Tiny with a giggle.

Cas kicked him under the table and turned to Heber.

'Who was it that arrived so late last night, sir, and was bedded down not without disturbance?'

Heber, who at Tiny's words had turned quite pale, spoke in a reed-like whisper.

'Sir Sefton Choate,' he said, 'has honoured us by an unexpected visit.'

'My word!' said Tiny. 'Not old Sefton? Well, I never!'

'Shut *up*, Tiny!' said Cas.

'You are so frivolous, Tiny,' Celia sighed. 'It is something one does not care to think about.'

'Will he be making a long stay, sir, and where have you put him?'

'To the first part of the question, I do not know,' said Heber in his ghostly voice. 'To the second part, in Doom.'

'Good heavens!' said Tiny, his mouth full of porridge. 'Not in Doom?'

'And why not in Doom, pray?' said Heber. 'Is not Doom our best bedroom, and does it not look out upon the cemetery?'

'It may be the best bedroom,' said Tiny, with a wink at Celia, 'and it may look out upon the cemetery, but the bed is pretty well untakable, sir, since Celia broke the springs last hols.'

'Shut up, Tiny!' said Cas, but they all began to giggle furiously, stuffing their handkerchiefs into their mouths.

'Poor old chap,' said Tiny, who was purple in the face by this time. 'He won't get a wink.'

'Not a wink, not a wink, not a tiddly-widdly wink,' sang Celia, beating time with her porridge spoon.

They all joined in.

Celia said, 'Mark my words, *he'll be up all night.*'

Heber rose to his feet like a lion in anger.

'It is Sunday today,' he said, 'you must all go to church.'

'I make it Thursday,' said Tiny. 'What do you make it, Celia?'

Celia answered in German, with a strong North German accent, finishing up with her aggravating laugh: '*Bei mir ist's Montag um halb sechs.*'

'No, no,' said Tiny, 'it is Thursday.' He smiled in an infatuated manner upon Celia and pointed to the lake that could just be seen from the kitchen window where they had set the table, '*C'est le lac de jeudi*,' he said, 'for, you see, it is Thursday today.'

Cas, who was getting rather restless, said, 'Heads Sunday, tails Thursday.' The coin came down heads.

'So long, Uncle,' they said.

When they got to the church the service was already over, so they turned back along the grass path bordered with poplar trees. The weather had cleared again and it was hot and fine.

'I am afraid we shall not be able to get our church stamps for attendance,' said Celia.

'I'm sorry about that,' said Tiny.

'I thought our uncle's sermon was extremely to the point,' said Cas.

'Quite affecting,' said Celia.

'I always think that is one of his best sermons,' said Tiny with a generous smile.

'I enjoyed the hymns so much,' said Celia.

'I thought Mr Sparrow's voluntary on the harp was in excellent taste,' said Cas. 'Was I right in detecting a slight flaw in one of the strings?'

The white butterflies flew round their heads in the hot sunshine and the tall flowers, red, white and blue, waved against their shoulders as they walked along.

'Marguerites, cornflowers, poppies,' drawled Celia, pressing the stalks in her hands.

'Don't pick the flowers, Celia,' said Cas. 'Do you wish to raise the devil?'

'How tall they grow,' said Celia.

'Very fine,' said Cas, with his eye still upon her.

'They would make a nice bouquet for the lunch-table,' said Celia.

'Don't pick the flowers,' said Cas and Tiny together, edging nearer to their cousin.

Celia now looked down at her clothes and found that she was dressed in a pink-and-white-striped sailor suit, white socks and black strapped pumps. She took off her hat to look at it and to ease the discomfort where the elastic was biting into her chin. It was a large floppy leghorn hat trimmed with cornflowers and daisies and a white satin bow.

'Do you realize, boys, that you are both wearing Eton suits?' she said, and took them by the hand.

'Why, look,' said Tiny, as they came up the drive to the rectory, 'there is old Sir Sefton standing in the doorway with our uncle.'

'Howdedo, little girl?' said Sefton, pressing a bar of Fry's chocolate cream into Celia's hand. 'We've put the hare in the fridg,' he added in a confidential aside.

Celia shook hands with Sir Sefton, and gave a little nick of a curtsy.

'Celia has recently returned from her school in Potsdam,' explained Cas, who was rather embarrassed by the curtsy.

'She had become quite Prussian,' said Tiny.

Cas trod on his toe. 'Shut up, Tiny,' he said.

'Well, well, well, very nice, I'm sure,' said Sir Sefton, who had not quite taken it in. He gave a large coloured ball to Tiny.

'I bought a model motor-car for you, my lad,' he said, turning to Cas, 'but it has not come yet.'

'Oh, hurrah,' said Cas. 'Oh, thank you so much, sir.'

'Are they going back to school after the holidays?' Sir Sefton inquired of Heber.

'Well,' said Heber, '*that depends.*'

Cas and Tiny and Celia sat in the long, cool nursery.

'That depends . . .' said Tiny, with a rather fearful look at Celia. 'Oh, Celia, I do hope we do not have to go back to school.'

'Not likely,' said Cas; 'nothing more to learn.'

'Cas is awfully smug,' said Celia, putting her arms round Tiny, who was beginning to cry. 'Cheer up, Tiny, you won't have Augustus, anyway.'

'I was flogged twice through Homer at Eton,' said Cas, with an ineffable smug smile.

Celia began to print a sentence in coloured chalks in her copybook, there was a different chalk for each letter. Cas looked over her shoulder and read out what she had written: 'Is there a life beyond the gravy?'

'It's an "e",' he said, 'not a "y".'

At this moment there was a black shadow across the open window and a large, dark, fat boy fell into the room. He picked himself up and swaggered over to where Tiny was crouching beside Celia.

'I couldn't make anyone hear,' he said.

Then he looked round the room with a sneering expression. 'Crumbs,' he said, 'what a place, and what smudgy beasts you look! Why, Celia, the ink is all over your dress. There's no life here,' he said; 'you people simply don't know you're alive.'

It was Augustus.

Cas came over to him and stood threatening him with the heavy ruler he had snatched from Celia's desk.

'*You* don't know you're dead,' he said.

'It's better to know you're dead,' said Tiny.

'Oh, much better,' said Cas.

'There's no room here for anyone who doesn't know he's dead,' said Celia.

They took hands and closed round Augustus, driving him back towards the window. He climbed on to the window-sill.

'We're all dead,' cried the three children in a loud, shrill chorus that rose like the wail of a siren. 'We're all dead, we've been dead *for ages.*'

Tiny rushed forward, breaking hands with the others, and gave Augustus a great shove that sent him backwards out of the dark shadowed window.

'We rather like it,' he said, as Augustus disappeared from view.

1947

THE HERRIOTS

When the Herriots first went to Bottle Green to live it was in the wicked old spacious days of King Edward. Dr Climax went his rounds in a carriage and pair; he wore a silk top hat and had a manner that was agreeable and distinct. Everybody in Bottle Green hired a maidservant, and the better families had two and called them by their surnames.

It is now after the war. At number 54 Colefax Gardens there lives this family of Herriots. They are well connected 'you know' on their father's side, coming down from Sir Edward Coke the Great Chief Justice. The eldest son is called Coke, he pronounces it 'coak'—Coke Herriot.

Bottle Green is now a very large suburb. The Greek bankers have sold their landed estates to speculative builders who have made a good thing out of it. They have built rows of small houses. The sons and fathers of the families who live in these new small houses are no longer lawyers and stockbrokers, they are clerks and commercial travellers.

But in an old tall house at number 13 The Pound (this is where the old cattle pound still stands) lives Peg Lawless and her aged great-aunt, Mrs Boyle. There is another aunt also living there, a Miss Cator, Peg's mama's sister. The parents of this child are both dead. She has been brought up in a way that does not appeal to some people in the suburb.

Old Mrs Boyle felt every now and then that Peg should be taught how to keep house, but Miss Cator, who was affectionate and impatient, preferred to do it herself, and about this there was always disagreement between the two ladies.

When Peg was a child she used to play with the Herriot children. One day she was coming home from school when a schoolboy pulled her hair. Coke Herriot was coming along behind, Peg ran back and said: 'Please fight that boy, Coke.' Coke punched the boy's nose and it began to bleed.

Coke was seven years older than Peg and passed straight from the VI form into the Army. One day when Peg was twelve Coke came round in his officer's uniform. Peg was in trouble at home with Mrs Boyle. Mrs Boyle had won a battle against Miss Cator and Peg had been sent out to buy three bloaters. She was an absent-minded child and brought home in the shopping basket three lobsters instead of three bloaters. Peg had a sort of absent-mindedness that worked in a queer way. Always between lobster and bloater there was this indecision. She said lobster and saw bloater. Her great aunt was exasperated, although in a way it was a support for her argument that Peg should have more housekeeping practice. She was a splendid rigid old lady with old fashioned ideas about discipline. She was talking in the sitting room with Coke when Peg came in. 'You deserve a good whipping,' she said. Peg was putting a log of wood on the fire and Coke wanted to help her but as he touched her arm she stumbled, dropped the log and would have fallen, but Coke caught her and she fell on to his knees. He put his arm round her and laughed: 'Shall *I* whip you?' he said.

When Peg was eighteen she married Coke. He had given up his commission (he could not live on the pay) and taken a job in the City; it was the most foolish thing he could have done, the office work irked him and the orders fell off. No good, he gave it up and became a salesman in cars for a time. He had an adventurous streak in him and would have made a career in the army—if there had been a war. He lost his salesman's job and went back to the City. He hated the work but could do nothing else. He was not clever; he was warm-hearted and affectionate and quick-tempered.

Peg and he had so little money that when the first baby was coming they had to give up their flat and go and live with Mrs Herriot. (Old Mrs Boyle was dead and Miss Cator had gone to keep house for a married brother with an invalid wife.) They had a room on the ground floor, a bedroom at the top of the house and of course the 'use' of the bathroom and kitchen. Peg fretted at first, they could do nothing with the house, it was awful. Instead of their beautiful fresh seersucker curtains they had the old people's Nottingham lace curtains looped back with olive green silk sashes.

Peg was absent-minded and not good with money and now she felt that the happy feminine-independent days of her childhood were over indeed. Mrs Herriot unquestioningly put the wishes of the men first. Peg had been brought up to think that men were to fetch and to carry. She felt that she had married into an Indian or Turkish family. But she loved Coke and Coke loved her. As the baby got nearer Peg began to have nightmares about the Indian-Turkish idea and the curtains.

When the baby was born it was a lovely boy with bright blue eyes like Coke's. They adored the baby and used to play with him up in the bedroom on the ugly old-fashioned bed.

Mrs Herriot had not the buoyant temperament of Mrs Boyle and Miss Cator, she was depressed and she had the idea that Coke's shiftlessness was Peg's fault. When the baby was teething it used to cry a great deal. Mrs Herriot would come upstairs and open the door and sigh and go out again. Peg was very anxious and overwrought. One day she was rather rude to Mrs Herriot. 'Do not come in here,' she said. 'Please go away.' When Coke came home Mrs Herriot complained to him. Coke was very tired and dispirited after a long day at the 'terrible' office and he was cross with Peg. She would not say anything, she looked desperate. It drove him mad. He struck her.

Peg had nowhere to go to get away from them. She wandered round the house distraught. She looked into the sitting room, old Mr Herriot was reading his paper. Mrs Herriot was in their room, looking for something. Peg went into the scullery (they had no maid now) and began to do the vegetables for dinner. She began to cry; now that she was alone she could think again. She thought that Coke had struck her but that if they could go away it would be all right.

Coke and Peg went to church on Sunday to take the baby to be christened. He was called James after his uncle—James Coke Herriot. The vicar was a practical kind wise man, very much one with his parishioners. The church had always been the centre of the life of Bottle Green, but until a few years ago they had had a scholarly eccentric vicar called Mr d'Aurevilly Cole. He was not married and became so eccentric that he had to retire. When he retired he married the organist; the ladies of the parish had always thought he would marry her. The London papers had a paragraph about it—'Vicar marries organist after twenty years'.

The present vicar was not so much a 'recluse' (they said) as Mr Cole, but he was splendid with the people, hard-working and sensible. Everybody helped everybody. At the church it was a very happy community.

But when the people came home so many of them were like old Mr and Mrs Herriot and Peg and Coke. The big houses of the pre-War period were let out in flats, nobody could get away from anybody, there were always nerve storms and people crying themselves to sleep, but also laughing when there was some money and the little cars could go along.

After the christening people made a good appearance, and the vicar came back to the Herriots to tea. Everybody's secret—it was no secret in the family that Peg and Coke had quarrels and that Coke had struck her—was put away; Mrs Herriot had excellent hostess manners, the tea came in on a trolley. They were so poor by now that the family had margarine, but butter was given to the vicar and the friends.

Peg and Coke had a sleepless night after the christening. The baby cried and cried. Peg nursed the baby and tried to quieten him. Coke called to her. She put the baby down and got into bed. She put her arms round Coke and pressed her hands over his ears so that he might not hear the baby. He began to cry, too, his head against Peg's shoulder.

One day Coke came home very cock-a-hoop. He had met an old friend who was running a flash amusement park in the poorer part of Bottle Green. 'I'm giving up my job at the office, Peg,' said Coke, 'I told old Snooks exactly what I thought of him. You ought to have seen his face.' 'Oh, Coke, what are we going to do now?' 'Trust me, dear old girl, Tommy is a good chap, and he knows what's what. I'm going into the fun fair business with him.'

To begin with there was a lot more money. Peg went out and about with Coke and Tommy. Tommy was a dashing sort and used to come to the house and flirt with Mrs Herriot. He had vulgar hearty manners and Mrs Herriot would never have had him in the house if she had not thought it might help Coke. One day Tommy came round and found Peg alone. 'Peg,' he said, 'I'm hard up, I must have £20, it's a dead cert. I can pay it back next Friday, but if I don't get it now it's all up with the business.' Peg gave him £20 out of the tin box where Mr Herriot kept his papers.

There was no more news of Tommy and the men came round and shut up the fun fair, and came round to the Herriots to see Coke. Peg was in disgrace. They were so poor now with Coke out of a job that there was very little food in the house and they could not afford a fire.

On Sunday morning very early Peg went to church. She prayed that she might find some work to do to help Coke. She cooked the Sunday dinner. It was eaten in silence, there was a little soup and some cheese and bread, afterwards she made some tea. They sat in the sitting-room for a time behind the lace curtains, and then Peg and Coke went upstairs. It was very cold in the bedroom, the baby was quiet now, sleeping in his cot. Coke sat in the armchair with Peg in his arms. She fell asleep with her head on his shoulder. She dreamed about Bottle Green. She was walking along and round. She knocked at all the doors down a long street, at each door there was a woman who answered the bell. There was no conversation between them, only gestures. A refusal, and the door was closed. Inside each house there were little rooms. The rooms were the homes of the people. There were old ladies and gentlemen, nodding on separate chairs; there were young married couples with babies, the babies were crying, the women were laughing sometimes and talking with their husbands; sometimes they were silent and angry.

At the end of the street there was a tall house with a flight of steps leading to the front door. In her dream Peg knocked and knocked. There was no answer. It was number 101.

When Peg woke up she kissed Coke and put on her hat and coat. 'Where are you going, Peg?' 'Just out for a few moments, darling Coke, I won't be long.'

She went to the house at number 101. It was kept by an old lady who was very eccentric; she gave Peg a job as companion at £1 a week.

Coke was left at home all day; he went off sometimes in the morning early, he walked round and round the streets looking for work. Mr and Mrs Herriot were very quiet now; there was no conversation.

The old lady at number 101 began to be in love with Peg. Every day she made her take her to the cemetery. There they sat; the old lady, Mrs Barlow, talked to Peg, holding her hand: 'When I am dead I shall be laid out in a beautiful white dress, the candles will burn round my head, you will kneel there at the foot of my couch. I shall be laid on a beautiful couch. You will pull down the blinds and kneel there by the light of the candles. That will be for me the greatest moment. And you will be with me.'

'I must go home now, Mrs Barlow, my baby must be fed, I have my baby to see to. Will you let me go now?'

'Not yet, wait a little while, it is only dusk, wait till the light fails.' Then she said: 'You must bring the baby to see me. We shall get on well, the little rogue, next time you come you must bring him.'

When Peg got home that night Coke said: 'Peg I am a poor sort of failure, how can you love me, I am no good to you at all, I might as well be dead.'

'If only we could get away,' said Peg, 'life would be so different. But I love Bottle Green so much, too; sometimes I think I could *not* go away, but always I say this: If we could get away. It is the sort of thing one says, nothing really.'

'I don't wish to go away either,' said Coke.

The next day Mrs Barlow said to Peg: 'Your husband has not found work yet?' 'No, but he is happier now and quieter in his mind. I think his father will find some sort of work for him where he is. He is an old man now and must retire soon. Perhaps Coke could have his place.' 'You are happy here with me?' 'Yes, very happy.' 'You, too, feel easier in your mind since you have been with me?' 'Yes, I feel so quiet too, and happy. I used to feel if I could get away from Bottle Green I should then be happy. But now I do not wish to go away.' 'Coke will have his job, you will see. And now we must go, we shall be late for the cemetery.'

They went up to the cemetery and sat on a seat beneath the yew tree. Mrs Barlow said: 'It is very vulgar to think in the absurd terms "you can get away". There is only one way in which you can get away, in the lofty and ethereal conception of the aristocrat, and that is to die and be buried.'

At this moment Coke came through the cemetery gates. His face was lit up like a flame. He came straight towards them and pulled Peg to her feet. 'How do you do, Mrs Barlow?' he said. 'Darling Peg, it is all right, I have got the job of travelling plumber, father is going to retire at the end of the month.' Mrs Barlow began to cry, 'I am so happy,' she said. Peg and Coke sat down on each side of her, and Coke gave her some chocolate he had bought for the baby.

1939

ESSAYS

SYLER'S GREEN:
a return journey

Syler's Green, Syler's Green, dear suburb of my infancy. How well I remember the first time I ever saw Syler's Green. It was on a September afternoon, many many years ago. I was four years old. My mother and my Aunt, my sister and myself, had just arrived from Hull, in Yorkshire. My Aunt, who had gone on ahead, had taken this house in Syler's Green as a short resting place until we could find something that suited us better. My sister aged six and myself thought at once it was a very beautiful house and a beautiful garden.

We went round the corner to our Landlord's shop—he was a plumber—to make some arrangements and to get me weighed. I was always being weighed for some reason or another. He had some enormous weighing machines, the sort they use for luggage.

'You are a fine package,' said Mr Blom our landlord.

'Ah came on a train and then on a tram,' I said with a fine strong Yorkshire accent.

'Why you're a furriner,' said Mr Blom, 'you're a foreign package, yes you are.' And he lifted me down from the scales.

That is my first memory of Syler's Green. Needless to say we children were right about the house. Although our cautious elders would at first only sign a lease for six months, we stayed in that house for a great many years, and in the end we bought it from Mr Blom.

The next thing I remember is the woods. Syler's Green in those days was more of a country place than a suburb. And just behind our house, on the other side of the railway cutting, were these vast mysterious dark and wonderful woods. They were privately owned and trespassers were forbidden. This of course made it all the more exciting.

You are never to cross the railway line, children, now Pearl (this to my sister) you are to see that Patsy (that was me) never crosses the railway line.

We promised that we would never do such a thing. But we found a large pipe that ran under the railway line, and we used to crawl through that and run up the high grass slopes of the cutting. At the top was the beginning of the wood, and this part of the woods we used to call Paradise.

Now the whole of Syler's Green when we first went there was a very beautiful place to live in, especially for young children. There were fields to play in and shady country lanes, and farmhouses with their cows and the pigs and there was a toll gate, with its barred gate a-swing and a little house at the side of it for the toll-keeper. It was a long time ago you know, and a ripe September time with the autumn sunshine in the air and the rich smell of acorns and damp mould and the michaelmas daisies, especially there was the smell of the large rich michaelmas daisies that grew in the churchyard. Of course it wasn't always September or always sunny but that is how one is apt to remember past times, it is always a sunny day. This sunny time of a happy childhood seems like a golden age, a time untouched by war, a dream of innocent quiet happenings, a dream in which people go quietly about their blameless business, bringing their garden marrows to the Harvest Festival, believing in God, believing in peace, believing in Progress (which of course is always progress in the right direction), believing in the catechism and even believing in that item of the catechism which is so frequently mis-quoted by the careless and indignant . . . 'to do my duty in that state of life to which it shall please God to call me' (and not 'to which it has pleased God to call me'); believing also that the horrible things of life always happen abroad or to the undeserving poor and that no good comes from brooding upon them—indeed it is not wholesome to do so—although an interest in one's neighbours' affairs is only natural. And indeed how can society be wholesome if everything is not above board?—believing in fact a great deal of nonsense along with the sense.

And much we children cared about all this, indeed we never gave it a thought. We were far too busy with our wonderful deep exciting devilish woods, for devilish they seemed as we came into them from the bright sunshine and dived into their dark shadows, devilish and devilishly exciting. Paradise as I have explained was that part of the wood which lay just behind the railway cutting, an open pleasant place it was with a little stream, all open and sunny as the day itself. But behind that again lay the dark wood, with the trees growing close together, the dark holly trees, the tall beeches and the mighty oak trees. And there too was the Keeper's cottage, and it was the Keeper's business to keep us out. This Keeper was our ogre, our dragon and our enemy. We devoted a great deal of our time to out-witting the creature. He would walk silently with a woodman's-red-

Indian's silence upon the twigs through the undergrowth, and he was always accompanied by a large black curly-coated retriever dog, who answered to the name of Caesar.

The grandest of all the paths in this wood, Longmans path, was a really beautiful path—but dangerous, for it led straight to the Keeper's cottage. It had almost everything that a path through a wood should have, it went up and down, it ran through bracken, it was crossed by a stream that was wide enough to make a running jump necessary—and even then one might if one's legs were short and one's take-off careless, land in the shallow water and go well up to the knees in black loamish mud. It also had a witches' pool, about halfway down the path and still just far enough from the Cottage to make a picnic safe, well fairly safe. Our witches' pool was a pool of water fed by a spring, it had a beach of fine white sand and it was overhung by a very old and knobbly oak tree, whose roots, half exposed, struck down into the water. The sandy banks harboured hosts of rabbits and their holes made a handy cache for our various treasure. I remember I once left a copy of my Aunt's favourite book —Francis Younghusband's *The Relief of Chitral*—in one of these holes, and never recovered it. Perhaps the rabbits devoured it with as much enjoyment as my Aunt.

Yes, in those early days Syler's Green was more of a country place than a suburb, but already the fields were beginning to be broken up and the woods parcelled out and the trees marked for cutting down.

The railway station at Syler's Green bears the date of the Franco-Prussian war—1870, and has the endearing style of its period, the wood-lace frill to the canopy over the platform, the Swiss Chalet appearance of the very sooty-brick station, and the black brick walls thrusting back against the grass banks and made bright by the coloured advertisements pasted on them. I remember these advertisements too.

'The Pickwick, the Owl and the Waverley pen, they came as a boon and a blessing to men,' and that early Jeyes Fluid advertisement. There is the nurse, there is something one feels of Lady Macbeth in her character, she is slowly washing her hands. Her eyes are staring straight ahead. She knows that Jeyes Fluid will not wash out that stain, but it will perhaps disinfect it a little. There was also a very handsome soldier, or so I thought him—but a little caddish perhaps, a thought too well appointed?—who with his tight laced body, his devilish cap and his black swirling moustache, advertised

Dandy Fifth tobacco. But these advertisements, with the date on the station bridge, were anachronisms and had really no business in the Syler's Green of my childhood, that was already thrusting ahead and bustling along to the first World War.

There were two or three large estates in Syler's Green which after a while were sold. One of them is especially vivid in my memory. This estate belonged to a Greek banking family. The Greek family had children of our age, and every year in the summer they used to give an enormous hay party. I remember wearing a stiffly starched white sailor suit and going to this party with my sister and the little boy from next door, who was, we thought, rather a muff. Alan did not live next door, he only stayed there sometimes with his aunts. These two ladies, and their companion lady, were neighbours of ours all through my childhood. The two property-owning ladies were called Jessie and Emmeline, and their companion was always called 'Miss Baby'. They had a stone statue of a Roman boy in their garden, they also had a fat white fox terrier dog called Beano. Miss Baby used to do a lot of work for Foreign Missions. She asked us once if we would let her have any old gym stockings that we did not want. 'What do you want them for?' I asked her. 'For the 'eathen,' she said. She used to cut them down and make them into jersey suits.

Miss Baby was a cheerful happy person in spite of 'the 'eathen' and the fact that she had once been to a bonesetter who had so mishandled her poor frame that she could now walk only with the aid of the furniture, from piece to piece of which she would fling herself in search of Miss Jessie's spectacles or a cup of morning milk for the employers, but Miss Emmeline was full of doom. It was from Miss Emmeline that we first learnt about the White Slave Traffic. Our mother was rather annoyed when we asked her about this—though Miss Emmeline like a true prophetess of gloom had been far from explicit. 'I have told you, Patsy,' said Mama, 'that you are never to speak to strangers in the street or to accept sweets from them, so run along and do as I tell you and don't bother your head about the White Slave Traffic.' But Miss Emmeline had fired our imaginations.

'If a lady comes up to you in a closed cab and leans out of the window and asks you to get in, don't you have anything to do with her,' said Miss Emmeline. And then she seized my hand and pulled me close up to her (I can smell her old-lady smell now, the lavender and mothball, the dusty velvet ribbon, the menthol lozenges she used to suck and sometimes the faint smell of the old dog Beano clinging about her skirts). 'It is the White Slave Traffic,' she said. And one day she said again, 'If a lady comes up to you and tells you that your dear mama is lying in a faint on the pavement round the corner, don't you believe her, don't have anything to do with her, do not go with her into the cab. It is the White Slave Traffic.'

It seemed that if you yielded to the blandishments of this lady in a cab you would become a White Slave. And what would happen to you then? Ah, that we did not know.

Now of course children always play what they hear. And just as, during the recent war, you might see the children at their war-games (for instance the little boy who lived opposite us used to scoot round on his scooter-cycle crying out, 'Coming in to attack, Coming in to attack') so we, in those far off days of our childhood, used to play this game of the White Slave Traffic that was so very much a game of *that* period, for all the apparently sunny innocent and pastoral nature of our suburb. For might not the Lady of the Cab come bowling along those country lanes at any sunny moment, herself more fearful grisly and truly sinister by reason of the sunshine that shone on the black boxlike vehicle in which she travelled and the black satin and jet in which she would no doubt be clad, and the befeathered black hat and veil which would conceal her pale and wicked face? Our imaginations in fact, fired by Miss Emmeline's stories, were very far from boggling at such a proposition, and we used to play the game with great gusto, trundling our dolls downstairs on teatrays—they were the white slaves—and bundling them off in the dolls' pram—the 'cab' of course—to some rather shadowy destination. I remember for a long time I used to think that the waxwork child-models displaying clothes in the drapers' shop windows were really the white slave children who had been changed into statues, and that here indeed might truly be discerned—The Sinister Hand of the White Slavers.

As a matter of fact I was rather fond of Miss Emmeline and I think she was rather fond of me because she often used to take me up to the cemetery for an afternoon's walk. The memory of these graveyard excursions fired me later on to write a very solemn poem indeed, which, for a reason I do not remember, I called 'Breughel'.

The ages blaspheme
The people are weak
As in a dream
They evilly speak.

Their words in a clatter
Of meaningless sound
Without form or matter
Echo around.

The people oh Lord
Are sinful and sad
Prenatally biassed
Grow worser born bad

They sicken oh Lord
They have no strength in them
Oh rouse up my God
And against their will win them.

Must thy lambs to the slaughter
Delivered be
With each son and daughter
Irrevocably?

From tower and steeple
Ring out funeral bells
Oh Lord save thy people
They have no help else.

At the age of five one must of course go to school. And now, if you will please picture my schooldays against a background of new houses sprouting up, of muddy roads, with the drain pipes being laid, of tall brick stacks and curb-stones at crazy angles at the road-sides, I will tell you about the early suburban schooldays. Our schooldays were directed by a most unusual woman. She was a Quaker lady and had a real devotion to teaching. She had gathered several of her relations around her and they had pooled their money and set up this school. She was a very staunch lady and believed in herself and her gifts. She was a very outspoken woman too and at the beginning of the first World War made herself quite unpopular because she thought that a certain poem that was in favour at that time was nonsense. Do you remember that poem I wonder? 'You have boasted the day, You have toasted the day, and now the day has come.' It was called 'The Day' and was aimed at the Kaiser. It was written by a railway porter.

But in the Kindergarten all was dash and gaiety, we had no time for the Kaiser. We were hearing about the Transvaal and the covered wagons and moreover we were making the covered wagons out of matchboxes, with linen buttons for wheels, and cartridge paper, cut to size, for the canopy.

When I was promoted to the Transition Class, life seemed even more wonderful. We were told the story of Beowulf and how he tore off Grendel's arm in the depths of the lake (and this tale we used of course to play later in the woods and by the great lake in Scapelands Park); and above all we were learning in our geography lessons about the tropics. Oh those tropics, how much I loved them (although I had and still have a horror of snakes). But our form-mistress who combined geography with painting—and subsequently left us for ever to study Egyptology under Flinders Petrie and go out digging with him to Egypt—had a real gift for bringing the jungle home to a young child of tender years.

'Now children,' she would say, 'have you got any large hat boxes or dress boxes at home?'

Yes, yes, our mamas had plenty of such boxes.

'Then bring them along with you tomorrow, and bring some moss to lay flat in the bottom of the box and then we can begin with our jungle scene.'

The next day we would set to work in earnest. With rich indigoes and blues and ochres and greens we would slosh the inside of the box lid until it looked, to our inspired imagination (inspired by our mistress's description), exactly like the jungle and the tropical forest scene. And in this jungle would crawl and fly and climb and jabber and whine and shriek all the animals, birds and reptiles we had heard about, and seen in visits to the zoo, and seen in the bright pictures our mistress used to hand round.

This school was extremely strong in history, literature and geography but I fear it was an unorthodox education and today would be frowned upon. Indeed today such a school could not exist. For the headmistress and her assistants were none of them qualified in the academic sense to teach anything. But we learned a lot from them for all that.

We also had a very good selection of poems to read from in our literature lessons. I do not know who made this anthology but it had a great many poems in it that we liked to recite. There was

'The Pibroch of Doneil Dhu'.

> *Pibroch of Doneil Dhu*
> *Pibroch of Doneil*
> *Wake thy wild voice anew*
> *Summon Clan Conneil*
> *Come as the winds come when forests are rended*
> *Come as the waves come when navies are stranded*
> *Faster come faster come, faster and faster,*
> *Chief, vassal, page and groom, tenant and master.*

Needless to say we learnt the whole of 'Horatius' by heart and took great pleasure in those lolloping lines.

> *But nearer fast and nearer*
> *Doth the red whirlwind come*
> *And louder still and still more loud*
> *From underneath the rolling cloud*
> *Is heard the trumpet's war note proud,*
> *The trampling and the hum*
> *And plainly and more plainly*
> *Now through the gloom appears*
> *Far to the left and far to the right*
> *In broken gleams of dark blue light*
> *The long array of helmets bright*
> *The long array of spears.*

I am quoting without the book as I remember it, so it may be wrong. We also liked

> *North looked the Dictator north looked he long and hard*
> *Then spoke to Caius Cossus the captain of the guard*
> *Caius of all the Romans thou hast the keenest sight*
> *Say what from yonder cloud of dust*
> *Comes from the Latian right?*

Then Caius says those wonderful lines ending up with:

> *I see the dark blue charger and far before the best*
> *I see the dark blue charger I see the purple vest*

> *I see the something something that shines far off like flame*
> *Thus over rides Mamilius Prince of the Latian name.*

How grand it sounded, 'Prince of the Latian name.'
    But our headmistress was rather against war and used to try and interest us in anti-war poems like Longfellow's poem.

> *This is the arsenal from floor to ceiling*
> *Like a huge organ rise the burnished arms*
> *But from their silent pipes no anthem stealing*
> *Wakens the village with strange alarms*
> *Oh what a sound shall rise how dim and dreary*
> *When the Death Angel touches those swift keys*
> *What loud lament and dismal miserere*
> *Will mingle with their awful symphonies.*

But this one was pretty war-like too, we thought, although it was saying how awful it all was, so we liked this poem and we liked the lines that come later on.

> *And Aztec priests upon their Teocallis*
> *Beat the wild wardrums made of serpents' skins.*

And how we liked that other poem of Macaulay's, at least how I liked it, but if I have no right to say what the other children liked, at least I can say that we all seemed to enjoy saying this poem out loud:

> *The still glassy lake that sleeps*
> *Beneath Aricia's trees*
> *Those trees in whose dim shadow*
> *The ghastly priest doth reign*

and then the final appalling lines, heavy and haunting with their secret meaning:

> *The priest who slew the slayer,*
> *And shall himself be slain.*

Our headmistress believed in discipline and she had a high—some people might think a rather simple—moral code. But there was a fine touch of melodrama about one of our headmistress's favourite poems which went something like this:

> *Tomorrow she told her conscience*
> *Tomorrow I mean to be good*
> *Tomorrow I'll do as I ought*
> *Tomorrow I'll think as I should*
> *Tomorrow I'll conquer the passions*
> *That keep me from heaven away*
> *But ever her conscience whispered*
> *One word and one only, Today.*
> *Tomorrow tomorrow tomorrow*
> *And thus through the years it went on*
> *Tomorrow tomorrow tomorrow*
> *Till youth like a shadow was gone*
> *Till age and her passions had written*
> *The message of fate on her brow*
> *And forth from the shadows came Death*
> *With the terrible syllable, Now.*

Yes, we liked that one, and our headmistress, like other more professional readers of verse, did not pull her punches when it was a matter of 'expression', that 'Now' fairly shot us away.

We were supposed to be ladylike at our high school. Our headmistress used to talk about 'my girls', especially when 'my girls' had been guilty of some misdemeanour, this, we were told, was not like 'my girls'. We were in fact to hold ourselves distinct from the less fortunate infants who attended the County School, or those even more benighted who picked up their three R's at the Board School. As a part of this separateness, we never wore common gym tunics, no we wore neat navy blue dresses with green buttons and belts and white collars, and for drill we wore navy blue kilts and jerseys with pale Cambridge blue collars and sashes. At drill one of our favourite exercises was the rowing boat exercise. We used to sit on the brightly polished floor and row ourselves backwards and forwards, and all the time we were singing our beautiful rowing song:

> *Here we float*
> *In our golden boat*
> *Far away far away*

Here we float in our golden boat
Far away
See how we splash
And water dash
While in the air
The sun shines fair
Singing of birds
And lowing herds
Far away.

More serious but equally popular were the hymns we sang at morning prayers. These we were allowed to choose for ourselves. I remember my first kindergarten hymn, the first I ever remember singing, I remember it word for word, and I remember the tune, though I cannot have been more than five when we sang it:

Great big wonderful beautiful world
With the wonderful waters around you curled
And the wonderful grass upon your breast
World you are wonderfully beautifully dressed.

But with added years our sense of responsibility grew. A not unfavourite hymn contained some serious matter, although the tune was as gay as a jig:

Opportunities of little passed unheeded by-y-y
Make one sad gigantic failure for Eternity

Phew, that was no laughing matter.

As you see, in those early days at Syler's Green, we were a small community with common interests, and a little harmless snobbery to give zest to life.

I think it was a fairly harmless snobbery, for my family as a matter of fact was always hard up and we lived in a small house and never had a maid, but it never seemed to make any difference, although I suppose it would be better for the drama of the thing, if I could tell you how persecuted I was and how my schoolmates held off from me for that reason, but this was not the case.

I had one particular crony, a half-French child of my own age, who was then about ten. She was called Nica. I am afraid Nica and I did not always behave like our headmistress's 'girls' for our chief delight was to climb a wall and crawl along the top of it past other people's gardens right down the whole length of the road. In this way we had a wonderful view of a variety of gardens and we had also the difficulty of dodging under the overhanging trees and shrubs, and of course of 'not being seen'. To screw up our courage against the hazards of this journey, we used to sing under our breath a song that was a particular favourite of Nica and myself, and I may say with this song we used to drive our parents pretty mad; it went like this:

> Flee-va-la flee-va-la flee-va-la flee
> The animals went in two by two
> Flee-va-la compagnie
> Flee-va-la flee-va-la flee-va-la flee
> The elephant and the kangaroo
> Flee-va-la compagnie

And so on.

And it was about this time I think that I wrote my first poem about which I had a very high opinion. This opinion was not shared by my aunt who I am afraid, along with certain other of my activities, thought it 'unnecessary'. My poem went like this:

> Spanky Wanky had a sister
> He said, I'm sure a black man kissed her
> For she's got a spot just here
> Twas a beauty spot my dear
> And it looks most awfully quaint
> Like a blob of jet black paint
> But when he told his sister that
> She threw at him her gorgeous hat
> And with airs that made her swanky
> Said, I hate you Spanky Wanky

The civic and cultural sense of our suburb developed early. As quite a young child I was taken to the Literary Society's lectures and lantern shows. I remember one fascinating lecture on the Moon; it was given by an old clergyman called Dr Iremonger. He had a slight impediment in his speech, but such was his enthusiasm for the moon and so remarkable were his illustrating slides, that he was one of the Society's most popular figures and was often required to repeat his lecture.

We also had a great many dramatic societies, and of course tennis clubs, croquet clubs, Shakespeare Societies, swimming clubs, rambling clubs; politics also were not forgotten, we had the Labour Party, the Liberal Party, the Primrose League and later the Communist Party.

But there is no doubt about it, our early life in Syler's Green centred naturally enough in the church and the school. Church was exciting, there always seemed to be something going on. The Reverend D'Aurevilly Cole was a scholarly rather eccentric but very loving person. But I believe he was something of a trial to the church council because he was so very absentminded. I remember my aunt coming home one day in quite a furious mood. 'He really is a trying individual,' she said, 'he is really very trying. All the time Mr Harbottle was giving the estimate for the new cassocks and for the heating plant that is to be installed in the new hall he was laughing quietly to himself. The doctor,' she said, 'who was sitting beside him on the platform, kept nudging him to stop laughing, and the vicar said, "What's the matter Blane, why do you keep nudging me?" Everybody could hear what was going on, it was most unfortunate. So then the doctor explained that Mr Harbottle was rather hurt that the vicar was laughing, and the vicar said "Oh I wasn't laughing at you, Harbottle, it was just something that I was thinking about, just something that was passing through my mind." '

But he was a very kind man and sent an invalid girl who used to go to church to Italy for a holiday with her brother, and as they had hardly a penny to bless themselves with, he paid for the whole holiday himself.

We used to be taken to church in the morning to attend Matins, and I always used to decide before we went to church which hymn I was going to sing. This was generally 'Once in Royal David's City', and I sang it, and it did not matter at all that everybody else was singing something different.

My sister and I used specially to enjoy the festivals when the great banners were carried round the church. There was one that had been given to the Scouts' Company by the wife of the old Scoutmaster who had died. He was called Edwin Alton Crumbles, and his name was printed in full on the back of the banner and when it went round and back again to the altar my sister and I used to chant, under our breath I hope, 'Edwin Alton amen, Pray for me and all men.' In the afternoon we used to go to Sunday School, and here we sat in small classes in the church hall, and I can still smell the smell of the scrubbed flooring and the rather dusty smell of the hassocks and the great red velvet curtains, that hung down upon the raised stage at the end of the hall. Just as I can still smell the quite different pine wood, leather and brick smell of the church itself. I was once given a copy of *King Solomon's Mines* as a prize but rather also I think, since it was given to me in class by Miss Frond our Sunday School mistress, to keep me quiet. I remember that I borrowed her fountain pen and wrote on the paper cover at the back of the book my name and address: 'Syler's Green, North London, England, North West Europe, The World.' I then sat down on the book and blotted the ink address on my white muslin dress. But that address is rather true in a way, for I do not think you can know anything very much about the world unless you are fortunate enough to know something about that address as you read it backwards.

It is very fortunate to grow up as we grew up, in a quiet place that has the appearance of going on being the same really for ever, instead of growing up to wander homeless, to be driven homeless from place to place, and to know hunger and to know what it is to have no home and no parents, but to take as matters of course that ruins are your home and that persons unrelated to you, remote if friendly, and in uniform, are to direct your lives; as now is the commonplace of Europe.

Our suburb nowadays is very large and very bustling, but the bones of the older situation are still there. I suppose in the social sense it has 'gone down'. It was once a place for bankers, stock-brokers, doctors and naval officers; but now the larger houses are let off in flats, sometimes they are just as they were but several families live in the houses; now there are no such things as lantern slides, there are two large cinemas instead, and there are dancing halls and I believe, yes it is true, there is even a fried fish shop. But the people are bustling and happy as ever, and one thing they seem to me to have in quite extraordinary abundance, and that is babies. The busy shopping streets are crowded with prams and of course dogs. Oh those dogs, it is about the dogs of Syler's Green that I wrote my poem called the Dogs of England.

> O happy dogs of England
> Bark well as bark you may

If you lived anywhere else
You would not be so gay.

O happy dogs of England
Bark well at errand boys
If you lived anywhere else
You would not be allowed to make such an infernal noise.

But no doubt the dogs of Syler's Green are excited by the fine air of these parts, for ours is a very high-lying healthy suburb and at the top of our hill they say with pride that we are the highest spot between where we are and the Ural Mountains. Of course if you happened to look west instead of east it would be a different story because of the Welsh Mountains.

And now can you guess which suburb it is? Well, I dare say you can. And for my part when I climb that hill again I shall look firmly towards the east and I shall think about being the highest spot between where I am and the Ural Mountains, and I shall say that we are not only this healthy suburb where babies may flourish but we are also to be *envied* and *congratulated* because we have our rich community life and are not existing in a bored box-like existence that is what people think of suburb life, and that all this is due to the fact that by the mercy of heaven we are not one of those new suburbs but have our roots in the old country place that was there before the houses grew up, and that because we have been kind to the country and have kept the beautiful oak trees and the wide estates in which they grow, that we have kept them for wide spacious parks, so because we have done this the country has also been kind to us. For we might have sold them to make more money and cut down the century old fine trees and filled in the vast deep lake that is in Scapeland's park and on which when the frost is hard we wheel out the babies and skate and slide, we might have done away with all this and built more roads and more houses. And this we did not do.

But do you know sometimes in a black-dog moment I wish that the great trees that I remember in my childhood and the even greater trees and the dense forests that were in these parts long long before I was born, would come again, thrusting up their great bodies and throwing up the paving stones, the tarmac roads and the neat rows of pleasant houses, and that once again it could be all forest land and dangerous thickets where only the wolves and the wild boars had their homes. And there in the green depths of Scapelands Lake lay

97

the body of Grendel with her arm torn off. She is mourning her son, the Monster, slain by Beowulf.

Those gentle woods of my remembered childhood have had a serious effect upon me, make no doubt about it. Half wishing for them half fearing them, it is like the poem I wrote about them:

> The wood was rather old and dark
> The witch was very ugly
> And if it hadn't been for father
> Walking there so smugly
> I never should have followed
> The beckoning of her finger.
> Ah me how long ago it was
> And still I linger
> Under the ever-interlacing beeches
> Over a carpet of moss
> I lift my hand but it never reaches
> To where the breezes toss
> The sun-kissed leaves above.
> The sun?
> Beware.
> The sun never comes here.
> Round about and round I go
> Up and down and to and fro
> The woodlouse hops upon the tree
> Or should do but I really cannot see.
> Happy fellow. Why can't I be
> Happy as he?
> The wood grows darker every day
> It's not a bad place in a way
> But I lost the way
> Last Tuesday
> Did I love father, mother, home?
> Not very much; but now they're gone
> I think of them with kindly toleration
> Bred inevitably of separation.
> Really if I could find some food
> I should be happy enough in this wood
> But darker days and hungrier I must spend
> Till hunger and darkness make an end.

Only those who have the luxury of a beautiful kindly bustling suburb that is theirs for the taking and of that 'customary domestic kindness' that De Quincey speaks of, can indulge themselves in these antagonistic forest-thoughts. And of course we may observe that only these ever do. And was there ever such a suburb as Syler's Green for the promotion of briskness, shrewdness, neighbourliness, the civic sense and *No Nonsense?* There was not. And so with this sniff of regional pride and smug self-righteousness I will say goodbye to the happy place of my childhood. And where is it, where is it?

Syler's Green,
Syler's Green,
Listener, have you ever seen
Syler's Green?

1947

A LONDON SUBURB

I like old suburbs that have grown from country places. They stand ten miles from London and ten miles from a countryside that is still unspoilt because the train service is so bad. The railway station is of the Swiss chalet pattern and has a wooden lace canopy over the platforms. It once took a prize for the beauty of its flower beds.

The shops in the High Street of the suburb are rather ugly. There are a great many shoe shops and sweet shops and hair-dressers' shops and drapers. There is an undertaker's shop with a china angel standing on a mauve table cloth. In the office of this shop the undertaker has a blotting pad of mauve blotting paper mounted on a piece of artificial green turf. The pub in the High Street has Georgian bay windows and a Tudor doorway; the turrets on the little tower are from chateau-panto-land; the flagpost mounts a golden fox. There is a Ritz Café where the ladies of the suburb gather for morning coffee and there are two cinemas, the Palmadium and the Green Hall.

Round the corner from the High Street are the old houses and the village pound and the old pubs and the old church. The old houses have names like Hope House and The Wilderness. They are not very convenient to live in and are frequently let as offices, or they may be museums holding pictures, records and the bones of old animals who roamed in past days.

In the straight streets planted with trees and fringed with grass plots stand the modern houses where the families live. These houses have quite different sorts of names from the old houses. The modern names are written on the garden gates or slung in fretwork over the porch. The Cedars, Cumfy, Dunromin, the more original Dunsekin, Trottalong. There is the house that is called Home Rails (a happy investment, fortune-founding?). There is Deo Data for the learned, Villa Roma for the travelled, Portarlington Lodge for the socially ambitious. Ella, Basil and Ronald live at Elbasron. There is also Elasrofton which is 'not for sale' written backwards.

The place names on the way to the city where the fathers go daily to earn their living are countrified—the mysterious Cockfosters, Green Lanes, Wood Green, Turnpike Lane. Coming nearer to the city there is Manor Park. And what is that curious building, an exact copy of Stirling Castle, that stands to the left of the bus route? It is the Waterworks.

In the high-lying outer northern suburb the wind blows fresh and keen, the clouds drive swiftly before it, the pink almond blossom blows away. When the sun is going down in stormy red clouds the whole suburb is pink, the light is a pink light; the high brick walls that are still left standing where once the old estates were hold the pink light and throw it back. The laburnum flowers on the pavement trees are yellow, so there is this pink and yellow colour, and the blue-grey of the roadway, that are special to this suburb. The slim stems of the garden trees make a dark line against the delicate colours. There is also the mauve and white lilac.

Many years ago the suburb was a great woodland country-side, it was a forest preserve and across its wooded acres tore the wild boar and the red deer, and after them came the mounted nobility who made sure by the ferocity of the game laws that none but they should hunt.

In Scapelands Hall at the beginning of the century (that is now Scapelands Park and a fine public place) lived the great Lord Catter-mole, and he rode with his little son and put his horse Midas at the moat that lies round the Vanbrugh House that is now a Hospital of Recovery: he cleared the moat, but his son did not; the son fell with his head against the brick moat and ever afterwards he was weak in his head. They moved away before the wars came.

Behind the thick laurel bushes which border the drive that leads to Hope House there lay one day the body of Thessapopoulos Thereidi the international financier, the great Greek banker. The hand of the assassin had struck him down as he came one night late from his carriage. The body lay three days before it was found by his cook-housekeeper. Hope House is now the Offices of the Metropolitan Water Board, and the coach house that adjoins the main building is in the hands of the agent for the Recovery of Income Tax.

Suburban fast life centres in the club-houses above the shops and cinemas, and in the funfairs at the London side of the suburb which are thought to be rather 'common'. These funfairs, they say, 'let the suburb down'. The fast ladies wear plaid slacks and have long yellow-dyed hair and the cigarette is firmly stuck to the lower lip as they trundle out the babies and the beer bottles. The pubs where these ladies are also to be found have names that are older than the suburb—The Fox, The Dog and Duck, The Woodman, The Pike, The Cattermole Arms, The Cock, The Serpent of Hadley, The World's End.

There is much going on in the suburb for those who seek company. There is the Shakespeare Reading Society, the Allotment Growers' Club; there is a Players' Society in connection with the local theatre; there are the amateur dramatic societies (that are such a delicious hotbed of the emotions—chagrin, display, the managerial mind; pleasure in becoming for one evening a spiv or a lord; ingenuity, competition, meeting young men). There are also the games clubs and the political clubs—tennis, golf, cycling; conservative, labour, communist. There is skating on the indoor rinks, and when the frost is hard, skating too on the great lake in Scapelands Park. There is also riding on the spavined hack or, for those who like danger, on the 'chaser whose temper is as vile as his price was low. The anglers who fish the inshore waters of Scapelands Lake have also their club, but theirs is a silent fellowship. Even the young boys fish silently, but sometimes a bite will stir them to words—'Hang on, man'.

The most beautiful place in the suburb is Scapelands Park, especially when the weather is wild and there is nobody about except the anglers. When the wind blows east and ruffles the water of the lake, driving the rain before it, the Egyptian geese rise with a squawk, and the rhododendron trees, shaken by the gusts, drip the raindrops from the blades of their green-black leaves. The empty park, in the winter rain, has a staunch and inviolate melancholy that is refreshing. For are not sometimes the brightness and busyness of suburbs, the common life and the chatter, the kiddy-cars on the pavements and the dogs, intolerable?

Christianity in the suburb is cheerful. The church is a centre of social activity and those who go to church need never be lonely. The stained glass windows in the church, which are of the Burne-Jones school and not very good, have been subscribed for by loving relations to commemorate the friends of the church and the young men killed in the wars. There is cheerfulness and courage in the church community, and modesty in doing good.

Now turn for a moment to the inner suburbs of London, those places of gloom and fancy. The names of these suburbs, although at first sight they seem pretty enough, have dank undertones—Mildmay Park, Noel Park, Northumberland Park. They suggest November fog and sooty chimneys and visions of decay. Behind heavy rep curtains, and an inner curtain of yellowing net, a parrot swings in his cage. At the corner of the street is a tin chapel with a crimson roof.

The advertisements at the tobacconist's are enamelled in royal blue and yellow on iron sheets. A canal moves sluggishly between mildewed stone bannisters. There is always a fog in the cemetery. London has captured these places, and the cheerfulness of their pubs and music-halls is a London cheerfulness; they must not be counted as suburbs.

The true suburb is the outer suburb and it is of the outer suburb that I am writing.

In Scapelands Park of a fine Sunday afternoon you may snuff the quick-witted high-lying life of a true suburban community. Here the young girls swing arm in arm round the path that borders the still lake-water. As they swing past the boys who are coming to meet them, the girls cry out, to the boys, 'Okey-doke, phone me'. In the deck chair beside the pavilion the old gentleman is talking to his friend, 'It is my birthday today and my wife would have me adorned. She put this suit on me' (he points to the flower in his buttonhole) 'and sent to have me adorned.' By the cage of budgerigars sits the ageing Miss Cattermole, who is rather mad. She wears a pink scarf 'to keep the evil spirits away'. She says the vicar is plotting to kill her.

If you sit by the brink of the lake you may catch the flash of a large fish as he passes at depth; or you may lie on your back and look up at the summer leaves of the tall poplar tree that are always moving. They are like fish-scales of pale green. They make a clattering sound as they turn on the wind. The bad-tempered swan hisses at the barking dog, the swan's neck is caked with mud and has a lump on it. At the corner by the woods the water of the lake is very dark, it is forty feet deep, and speaks again of the past, for here it was that the old Lady Cattermole drowned herself.

'Mother,' says the child, 'is that a dog of good family?' She is pointing to a puppy bull-dog of seven weeks old; his face is softly wrinkled. His tight velvet skin has already the delicate markings of the fullgrown brindle dog. His stomach is fat as the new-born.

Dogs in suburbs are very popular and are not trained at all not to bark. 'Why should my dog not bark if he wants to?' is rather the idea. It is a free country, they also say. But not apparently so free that you do not have to listen to the dogs barking.

Once, waking early, I heard the dog-loving woman from the next house but one talking to her friend in the street below my window. This is what she was saying:

'Seven years old 'e is.
Ever so sweet 'e is.
Ever such a neat coat 'e's got.
Ever so fond of kiddies.
But a dog likes to know oo's going to 'it 'im
     and oo isn't.'

This is the unconscious poem that happens sometimes when people are talking.

It would be wrong to suppose that everything always goes well in the suburbs. At Number 71, the wife does not speak to her husband, he is a gentle creature, retired now for many years from the Merchant Navy. He paces the upstairs rooms. His wife sits downstairs; she is a vegetarian and believes in earth currents; she keeps a middle-aged daughter in subjection. At Number 5, the children were taught to steal the milk from the doorsteps. They were clever at this, the hungry dirty children. Their father was a mild man, but the mother loved the violent lodger. When they were sent to prison for neglecting the children, the lodger bailed the mother out but let the father lie.

Life in the suburb is richer at the lower levels. At these levels the people are not selfconscious at all, they are at liberty to be as eccentric as they please, they do not know that they are eccentric. At the more expensive levels the people have bridge parties and say of their neighbours, 'They are rather suburban'.

The virtue of the suburb lies in this: it is wide open to the sky, it is linked to the city, it is linked to the country, the air blows fresh, it is a cheap place for families to live in and have children and gardens: it smells of lime trees, tar, cut grass, roses, it has clear colours that are not smudged by London soot, as are the heath at Hampstead and the graceful slopes of Primrose Hill. In the streets and gardens are the pretty trees—laburnum, monkey puzzle, mountain ash, the rose, the rhododendron, the lilac. And behind the fishnet curtains in the windows of the houses is the family life—father's chair, uproar, dogs, babies and radio.

1949

MOSAIC

Friendship and the revolt from friendship is the stuff of life. I am so grateful to my darling friends, to all my darling friends, but for the moment adieu. When I get home my noble aunt is reading the papers. At the time I was writing this the number of people reading the papers was more than usual. To keep out or not to keep out of war, that was at that time the question. Now, perhaps we are already again at war, perhaps not. My aunt is a staunch Tory, and equally staunchly she is regarding Germany as the ultimate enemy. Unlike many of the people who live in my own high-class suburb, she is well read in the political game. To-night is the night of the announcement of the flight of the Premier. Flight into darkness, say some, echoing the beautiful title Schnitzler chose for his suicide novel. I am listening at the house of a friend, an old mamma, she is really the church friend of my aunt, or the church sweet enemy, since my aunt carries on her church work in a fury of disagreement with the other ladies. Mrs A., we will call her, has a radio, which my aunt and I have not. My aunt does not like 'the noise.' Mrs A.'s radio announces the flight. On this great day of stress Mrs A. has not seen a paper. She has been too busy. So I say: 'The news looks serious. Japan is coming in with Germany. That will be not so hot for Australia.'

Mrs A. pants rather; she is making a wool rug and the colours must be matched nicely. She pants: 'Oh, yes, Australia! Mr A. has bought a new car.' So now the great news comes through that the Premier is flying to Berchtesgaden. 'So that is the best news I have heard today.' 'What is?' says Mrs A. 'That the Premier is flying to Berchtesgaden.' 'Oh,' Mrs A. says. 'Oh.' Then she says: 'Mr Parker was just in. He said: "Why are we interfering in Czecho-Slovakia?" ' I am rather intrigued by this piece. Bottle Green, I guess, is calling all suburbs. Now, I hurry to say to you that I am not high hatting the suburbs; suburbs are very O.K. in many ways. I use the term spiritually, not geographically. I am thinking of the people who say: 'Where the hell is Czecho-Slovakia?' These people often don't live in suburbs at all; suburbs (it is unfortunate for suburbs) is a term of abuse, and these people earn abuse. Their forefathers, I guess they said: 'Where the hell is Waterloo?' 'Where the hell is Trafalgar?' But they would have known what the hell all right if Napoleon had invaded England. So they will know what the hell all right if Germany goes on her *Drang nach Kolonien*, like hell they will, like hell. So Mrs A. has two sons just down from Oxford, just the right age. I said, *just the right age*. So Mrs A. says now something so sad to make the angels weep, and so ridiculous. Alas, that human beings have the special privilege to be so often at the same time ridiculous and sad. So what does Mrs A. say? 'Whatever happens my boys will not be involved—because we have all signed the Peace Pledge.' Oh, sad echoing of fiendish laughter! Oh, the hollow laughter that goes echoing round the halls of hell upon these words. 'We have signed the Peace Pledge.' And already upon my eyes there is darkness and a great wind blowing over dead battlefields, and the stench of death without honour, and the ridiculous sad cry: We never knew. 'Oh, now I must go!' I say. 'Yes, you have heard the news,' says Mrs A. with a meaning note. Oh, yes, I suppose I am very rude, to hear the news and go.

I think of the old man flying to Berchtesgaden with his umbrella, this famous son of a famous Joe. Later the American papers said: *The mountain has gone to Mahommet.* They said: *An incomparably dramatic moment.* They begin later to hint that one can pay too high a price for an insecure peace. America? Their own cruel Civil War was fought on this issue only. To deny to the Confederate Government the right to secede. America is a signatory of the Versailles Treaty. Will she with men and money defend the Czechs against partition, against Germany, against Hungary? Where does America stand? And England? Is it not better that three-and-a-half million German-Czechs should secede than that Europe and the world should be at war? Is it not expedient that one country die? One country? How many others? Where will it end? The Germans are very good road builders. When I was in Germany we did eighty miles per hour upon those magnificent surfaces . . . After all, what is Czecho-Slovakia? The frivolous, pompous questions and answers, the irrelevant comments fly backwards and forwards; they are like dead leaves before a wind that is blowing up storm-strong. This is a record of dead leaves. A friend of mine says: 'I know of two Austrian Nazis who helped their Jewish friend to escape. Yes, he was forced to scrub the pavements of Vienna, but he laughed while he did it; he took it in the right spirit. Some old Jews begged not to be made to do it; they were forced to. They did not laugh; you see they did not take it in the right spirit.' I think, and think. My friend says: 'You see I do not see people as nations; I see them as men and women.' Ah, the honey-sweet falseness of that vision. Men are good and evil, and women, too; some must die. They are not good and evil in essence, but in the sum of their actions they are good and evil, and on that plane only to be judged, to live or die. This is the scope of human judgment, and human judgment within this scope must upon occasion act. And so with nations. If there is no possibility of two opposed ideologies existing side by side, then the choice must be made, even the choice of war. And 'my boys' who will not be involved because 'we have signed the Peace Pledge'? Ah, bitterest choice of all! For when war has broken out there is no existence of a private peace; you fight for your country or, refusing to fight, you yet fight, and directly for the enemy. That is perhaps the ultimate most horrible demand of war; the State must have your conscience. War does not initiate a moratorium upon the Sermon on the Mount. The thoughts and actions, the jealousy and greed that led to war, our own most favourite imperfections, so long ago began it first. The phrase itself, attractively coined by Lord B—in the course of the last upheaval, upon scrutiny, is empty of sense. 'Stuff and nonsense,' says my aunt. Stuff and nonsense is a song of high explosives. How many wars has she seen, this dear aunt? The Franco-Prussian—well, almost—(no, the lady is not so old), the Boer War, Egyptian, Burmese, African and Chinese affrays and annexations. For a peace-loving people we are somewhat frustrated in our affections. So you won't fight? 'Czecho-Slovakia,' says Germany, this anchronistic sad monster, begotten by falsehood upon weakness, this savage mystic, this unutterable bore, Germany. Already in the lazy English people there is a feeling of exasperation running so easily to hatred. Germany might be a menace and we should not care (where *is* Czecho-Slovakia?)—but a bore, ah, that is something.

1939

SIMPLY LIVING

You must have some money if you are going to live simply. It need not be much, but you must have some. Because living simply means saying No to a great many things. How can you say No to travelling up and down to work and being competitive if you do not have money? If you have a little money and are a poet, there is no greater pleasure than living simply. It is also grand. In my present circumstances I am grand. I can say No when I want to and Yes when I want to. It is important to say Yes sometimes or you will turn into an Oblomov. He stayed in bed all day and was robbed by his servants. There was little enjoyment there.

Le Plaisir aristocratique de déplaire also lies open to those who live simply. But again you must be careful, or you will cut your nose off to spite your face, and so defeat the purpose of simplicity, which is enjoyment.

> *My heart was full of softening showers,*
> *I used to swing like this for hours,*
> *I did not care for war or death,*
> *I was glad to draw my breath.*

I wrote this poem, accompanied by a drawing of a little creature swinging on his stomach on a swing, to show the enjoyment that lurks in simplicity. 'Lurks' is the word, I think. You do not seek enjoyment, it swims up to you. The writer John Cowper Powys, in his sneering, fleering humility, and from the depths of that sardonic laughter which echoes through his books and takes in the whole universe of rocks, pools, animals and human beings, knew all there is to know about the pleasures of simplicity. And its grandeurs too. For as I have hinted, there is a great lordliness in simplicity, very aggravating to bustlers, whether they bustle by choice or necessity. However, they will probably write off the simple ones, as they wrote off poor Croft:

> *Aloft,*
> *In the loft,*
> *Sits Croft;*
> *He is soft.*

I enjoy myself now living simply. I look after somebody who used to look after me. I like this. I find it more enjoyable than being looked after. And simpler. I used to have very complicated feelings about not being able to cook, supposing I ever had to, and not being able to keep house, and wondering if it might not be better being dead than not being capable. Now I cook and do not worry. I like food, I like stripping vegetables of their skins, I like to have a slim young parsnip under my knife. I like to spend a lot of time in the kitchen. Looking out into the garden where the rat has his home, and the giant hemlock is now ten feet high. (I sat next to a man at dinner the other day who during the war specialised in slow-working poisons for use by the resistance movements. He said: You want to distil the roots.) Looking at the date—1887—on my mincing machine . . . at the name 'The White Rose' on my rusty iron stove. We should thank our lucky stars for these masters of incongruity who give names . . . A Dutch blue decorated lavatory pan in a friend's house called 'The Shark'. A cruiser called Harebell. A cat, mother of 200 kittens, called 'Girlie'.

But—*Looking*. That is the major part of the simple life. Yesterday the cupboard door in my Aunt's bedroom stuck. When I wrenched it open, her father's sword fell on my head. I peeled off the perishing black American cloth it was wrapped in and looked at the beautiful sword. Its hilt was dressed in pale blue, white and gold. I looked at the blade with its beautiful chasings. *Looking at colours*. The roof-colours opposite are like the North Sea, in rain they are sapphire.

Looking at animals. The aged dog from the Dog and Duck, wobbling in fat, takes itself for walks. I met it once a mile away from home. When it crosses the road, it looks right and left like a Christian. The man in the round house collects front doors. They stand in his front garden—pink, blue, green. There is a ginger cat near us, born blind. This cat walks like an emperor, head in the air. But he is wild and if touched will fly for your throat.

Regular habits sweeten simplicity. In the middle of every morning I leave the kitchen and have a glass of sherry with Aunt. I can only say that *this is glorious*. There is a great deal of gloriousness in simplicity. There is, for instance, the gloriousness of things you only do seldom. We have not got television. But once, on a friend's set I saw 'The Trojan Women'. What laughter and argument came to me from the strong impact of this rare treat. Why make Helen out a baggage? She was royal, half-divine, and under the compulsion of a goddess. Why present the play as an argument against war, yet leave in Euripides's ironic line (which he puts in the mouth of his captive women, princesses and slaves, being led into captivity), the line: 'If we had not suffered these things we should not be remembered'. What an earth-shaking joke this is. Yet, if my life was not simple, if I looked at television all the time, I might have missed it. There are moments of despair that come sometimes, when night sets in and a white fog presses against the windows. Then our house changes its shape, rears up and becomes a place of despair. Then fear and rage run simply—and the thought of Death as a friend. This is the simplest of all thoughts, that Death must come when we call, although he is a god. It is a good thing at these moments to have a ninety-two-year-old creature sitting upstairs in her dignity and lofty intelligence, to be needed and know that she is needed. I do not think happiness in simplicity can be found in solitude, though many must seek it there, because they have no other choice . . . like this poor man I wrote a poem about and will end with:

> Rise from your bed of languor
> Rise from your bed of dismay
> Your friends will not come tomorrow
> As they did not come today
>
> You must rely on yourself, they said,
> You must rely on yourself,
> Oh but I find this pill so bitter said the poor man
> As he took it from the shelf
>
> Crying, O sweet Death come to me
> Come to me for company,
> Sweet Death it is only you I can
> Constrain for company.

Is it to avoid this *final* simplicity, that people run about so much?

1964

TOO TIRED FOR WORDS

Being everlastingly 'too tired for words' might seem a serious handi-
cap to a writer. I cannot complain myself that it has turned out quite
like that, though of course the Muse complains endlessly; (or, feeling
guilty, one complains on her behalf:

> *My Muse sits forlorn*
> *She wishes she had not been born*
> *She sits in the cold*
> *No word she says is ever told.*

The fact is one works one's fingers to the bone for the peevish beast).
Well, one is tired and the devil take it. One forces oneself, one gets a
bit feverish (and much more tired) and eventually, out of the strain
and exasperation, the words come headlong. A bit oddly too sometimes. Why, the scene shifts wonderfully in the light of the words
that are, by reason of the tiredness, just a bit off-beam. So I have
written 'affable circumstances' for affluent circumstances, and
'nagative' for negative, and are not these richer thoughts? And
yesterday, writing about the great Freud, instead of Austrian Jew
which I meant, I wrote 'Autumn Jew'. And that too is an eerie shift.
One may get a poem out of these shifts. Like this one, with its tired
reading of Lobster for Lodestar.

111

'DUTY WAS HIS LODESTAR'
A song.

Duty was my Lobster, my Lobster was she,
And when I walked with my Lobster
I was happy.
But one day my Lobster and I fell out,
And we did nothing but
Rave and shout.

Rejoice, rejoice, Hallelujah, drink the flowing champagne,
For my darling Lobster and I
Are friends again.

Rejoice, rejoice, drink the flowing champagne-cup,
My Lobster and I have made it up.

But sometimes the shifts of tiredness are too eerie by half. Riding home one night on a late bus, I saw the reflected world in the dark windows of the top deck and thought I was lost for ever in the swirling streets of that reflected world, with its panic corners and the distances that end too soon; lost and never to come home again.

One gets strained, feels guilty, sad, and bad. And so falls into despair. It is then that the great thought of Death comes to puff one up for comfort. For however feeble one may seem, however much 'of poor tone' as they say at school, and negligible, Death lies at one's command, and this is a very invigorating thought and a very proud thought too. I remember once when I was feeling too tired to write an original poem I fell to translating Dido's Farewell to Aeneas, putting something into the last two lines that is not quite in Virgil, to express this proud thought of commanding the great god Thanatos (you remember she is stabbing herself). So the lines go like this:

'Come Death, you know you must come when you're called
Although you're a god. And this way, and this way, I call you.'

Yes, that thought of Death at command is a great relief to the tired. Indeed, if one is tired all the time I do not see how one can accept the Christian religion that is so exhausting and neat, and tied up neatly for all eternity with rewards and punishment and plodding on (that

112

too much bears the mark of our humanity with its intolerable urge to boss, confine and intimidate.) And no, it will not, Christianity absolutely will not allow us this delicious idea of command over Death, preferring to team up on this point with Old Mother Nature, that bloody-minded Stakhanovite with her brassy slogan 'Production at all costs'. But one wants that idea of Death, you know, as something large and unknowable, something that allows a person to stretch himself out. Especially one wants it if one is tired. Or perhaps what one wants is simply a release from sensation, from all consciousness for ever (the Catullus idea of *nox est perpetua una dormienda*.)

I often try to pull myself together, having been well brought up in the stiff-upper-lip school of thought and not knowing either whether other people find Death as merry as I do. But it's a tightrope business, this pulling oneself together, and can give rise to misunderstandings which may prove fatal, as in this poem I wrote about a poor fellow who got drowned. His friends thought he was waving to them but really he was asking for help.

NOT WAVING BUT DROWNING

Nobody heard him, the dead man,
But still he lay moaning:
I was much further out than you thought
And not waving but drowning.

Poor chap, he always loved larking
And now he's dead
It must have been too cold for him his heart gave way,
They said.

Oh, no no no, it was too cold always
(Still the dead one lay moaning)
I was much too far out all my life
And not waving but drowning.

Of course there's another thing tiredness can do, (and this is always so welcome)—it can provide an excuse for not writing at all. One hugs one's disabilities, one cultivates them, one becomes—like the wretch I have put in the next poem—a deserter to ill health. (The wretch was

113

a writer but now he lies in his hospital bed—and let the Muse go hang).

THE DESERTER

The world is come upon me, I used to keep it a long way off,
But now I have been run over and I am in the hands of the hospital staff.
They say as a matter of fact I have not been run over it's imagination,
But they all admit I shall be kept in bed under observation.
I must say it's very comfortable here, nursie has such nice hands,
And every morning the doctor comes and lances my tuberculous glands.
He says he does nothing of the sort, but I have my own feelings about that,
And what they are if you don't mind I shall keep under my hat.
My friend, if you call it a friend, has left me; he says I am a deserter to ill health,
And that the things I should think about have made off for ever, and so has my wealth.
Portentous ass, what to do about him's no strain
I shall quite simply never speak to the fellow again.

Perhaps it is better to keep striving though tearful, even if it means staying one's hopes on some future existence where one may (or may not) find oneself with a little more energy. As here:

LONGING FOR DEATH BECAUSE OF FEEBLENESS

Oh would that I were a reliable spirit careering around
Congenially employed and no longer by feebleness *bound*
Oh who would not leave the flesh to become a reliable spirit
Possibly travelling far and acquiring merit.

A poem like that cheers one up.

The pleasures of tiredness are as exquisite as the pains. Take loneliness for instance, that runs with tiredness. How rich for poets is this sad emotion.

114

LOVE ME!

Love me, Love me, I cried to the rocks and the trees,
And Love me, they cried again, but it was only to tease.
Once I cried Love me to the people, but they fled like a dream,
And when I cried Love me to my friend, she began to scream.
Oh why do they leave me, the beautiful people, and only the rocks
    remain,
To cry Love me, as I cry Love me, and Love me again.

On the rock a baked sea-serpent lies,
And his eyelids close tightly over his violent eyes,
And I fear that his eyes will open and confound me with a mirthless
    word,
That the rocks will harp on for ever, and my Love me never be
    heard.

And then, of course, if one's lonely, one often feels rather superior
too. One *is* different from other people, is one not? . . . (Aloft/In the
loft/Sits Croft/He is soft . . . may be *their* point of view about it, but it
is not ours.) Well, here is an actress, a middle-aged actress. Look at
her! She is walking a tightrope, tears roll down her cheeks, she
carries a spangled wand and wears a crown. She is quite sure she is
superior and wishes other people could see it, but my word, she looks
pretty awful.

THE ACTRESS

I can't say I enjoyed it, but the pay was good.
Oh how I weep and toil in this world of wood!
Longing in the city for the pursuit of beautiful scenery,
I earn my bread upon the Stage amid painted greenery.
I have a poet's mind, but a poor exterior,
What goes on inside me is superior.

But this feeling of superiority is a thin cloak. It drops, and one sees
loneliness as something to be despised and condemned. In the war I
thought lonely people became happier, but in myself I condemned
it:

THE FAILED SPIRIT

To those who are isolate
War comes, promising respite,
Making what seems to be up to the moment the most
    successful endeavour
Against the fort of the failed spirit that is alone for ever.
Spurious failed spirit, adamantine wasture,
Crop, spirit, crop thy stony pasture!

But seriously, you know—and this was meant to be a serious composition, a *cri de coeur* from the doctor's waiting room—this tiredness, propping itself upon the thought of Death at Command, is dangerous. It brings to the stricken writer dead moments of absolute insufficiency, when no thought can be thought and no word found, and these moments, of which the French poet wrote '*et dans ces mornes séjours les jamais sont les toujours*' are dangerous. Especially as the years draw on they are dangerous. To live all one's life with no great feeling for life, though one's appreciation of natural beauty and the beauty of animals may be as sharp as knives—as deadly too, as one feels so separated from them—invites life's revenge . . . 'You won't play? All right then, you shan't.' All the writer can do then is to offer his life, which seems to him so shadowy and inconsiderable, to some god or other for him to chew upon and make the best of.

GOD THE EATER

There is a god in whom I do not believe
Yet to this god my love stretches,
This god whom I do not believe in is
My whole life, my life and I am his.

Everything that I have of pleasure and pain
(Of pain, of bitter pain and men's contempt)
I give this god for him to feed upon
As he is my whole life and I am his.

When I am dead I hope that he will eat
Everything I have been and have not been
And crunch and feed upon it and grow fat
Eating my life all up as it is his.

I remember reading Book Ten of *Paradise Lost* one day. Milton puts a very curious anti-life argument into Eve's mouth. Eve says in effect (they have just been expelled from the Garden of Eden) 'If all our children are to be condemned to discomfort in this life and the probability of eternal torment in the life to come, would it not be better not to have any children?' It is interesting to compare Eve's attitude (or Milton's rather, but of course he quickly pulled himself together, drawing back the delicate toe from the swamp of heresy) with the brave '*fiat mihi*' of the Virgin Mary, the fiery authoress of the Magnificat. About this I wrote a poem:

A DREAM OF COMPARISON
After reading Book Ten of 'Paradise Lost'.

Two ladies walked on the soft green grass
On the bank of a river by the sea
And one was Mary and the other Eve
And they talked philosophically.

'Oh to be Nothing' said Eve, 'oh for a
Cessation of consciousness
With no more impressions beating in
Of various experiences.'

'How can Something envisage Nothing?' said Mary,
'Where's your philosophy gone?'
'Storm back through the gates of Birth,' cried Eve.
'Where were you before you were born?'

Mary laughed: 'I love Life,
I would fight to the death for it,
That's a feeling you say? I will find
A reason for it.'

They walked by the estuary,
Eve and the Virgin Mary,
And they talked until nightfall,
But the difference between them was radical.

Well, there it is. The difference between the person who is everlastingly too tired for words and the person who is not is radical. And there does not seem to be anything that anybody can do about it. I would say just this to the medical profession. Treat your tired patients gently, and do not scold them, for guilt runs with tiredness and a sort of farewell mood too, a desire to go, at all costs to go. So that quite easily, if you make your tired patient feel that he is a criminal (or a failure—a doctor said to me once, 'Your whole life is a failure') he will begin to think the dangerous thoughts of a little child I wrote about. This child stands in his flannel sleeping suit beside his bed and he is saying to himself these two lines:

> *If I lie down upon my bed I must be here,*
> *But if I lie down in my grave I may be elsewhere.*

1956

AT SCHOOL

I have never taught children anything and so can only speak from my own memories of being a schoolgirl, and always with the greatest sympathy for teachers, especially teachers of English Literature. I suppose where so much has been worked over, one may well want something new, but Something New as an Aim can be rather dangerous I think for young children learning to judge. For I take it that to judge well is one of the purposes of education, and how can you judge well if you are not grounded in the classics? Well—that is how they thought at my school. There we studied only the classics of our language, the good poems and the bad-good poems, alike honoured by Time. As our English mistress read the poems aloud to us, a line would strike across to me, a story grip, a picture take colour. I liked grand words and story poems. I liked 'Arethusa arose from her couch of snows, in the Acroceraunian mountains' (the first poem I learnt by heart) for its grand words. And—of course—best of all the story-picture poems I liked 'The Ancient Mariner' . . . tasting the salt on my blackened lips . . . panting for rain . . . seeing for ever and ever the sea creatures twining for their pleasure. It was their inhumanity I loved. Away from school we had our nursery rhymes, and—in the *Playbox Annual* I remember—a rhymed alphabet very dear to me, 'Admiral A., Blithe and gay, In a paper boat, He sailed away.' We learnt a lot by heart at my school, for homework, and also as a penalty if we broke rules. This, far from putting one off, put one on (at least so I found) and as sometimes, when we got older, it had to be Latin, I acquired a good deal of Catullus—'*Paeninsularum Sirmio insularumque*'—along with Tennyson's 'Ulysses', some Milton ('Me worse than wet thou findst not' seemed to me awfully funny. Well, I think it is) and Browning's 'Childe Roland to the Dark Tower Came'. How that repulsive horse . . . 'thrust out past service from the devil's stud' does stick in the mind, the whole poem was for me a landscape of Passchendaele. I also liked and liked to declaim 'The Solitude of Alexander Selkirk' . . . 'I am lord of the fowl and the brute' and certain picked lines with malice intent: 'In pride of power and beauty's bloom, Had wept o'er Monmouth's bloody tomb' ('Please, Miss Donovan'—our English mistress—'what was he doing so far north, did she mean Montrose?') And Dryden's ever-useful: 'When parents their commands unjustly lay, Children are privileged to

119

disobey.' I think it is a good thing for children to be made to learn by heart, most of them do it pretty easily anyway, then later, thinking about the poems and saying them over, one finds they stretch out and take fresh meanings—not always, I dare say, what the poets intended. The Hamlet speech I had to learn by heart, for instance—'Oh that this too too solid flesh would melt'—seemed at first to have only its surface connotation of someone turning away from life. But then I began to wonder if Hamlet was not rather 'working it up' because of those dutiful feelings towards his father, and that the dutiful feelings too were worked up, and that perhaps he had not really liked his father very much. Then it seemed to me that in that bloodstained play, Gertrude and Claudius were the only true lovers, middle-aged people of our own day almost, liking as well as loving each other, caught up in a Dark Ages trap, yet easy in their ugly skins. Ah yes, my dear Hamlet, I thought, it is that easiness you envy, though you think it is also rather banausic of them. ('Banausic' was a word I fished out for myself—and adored!). You never know what a poem may mean to a child. Why should I so much like the lines 'Drop, drop, slow tears, and bathe those beauteous feet, That brought from Heaven the news and Prince of peace' yet find 'See where Christ's blood streams in the firmament' (and so much of Marlowe) pash-stuff for schoolgirls? I am grateful to my schooldays for the poems I got by heart and the books I studied, and the books and poems my studies set me on to reading long after I left school. You may think it is not a good thing to have such a hotch-potch of the good and not-so-good running together in my mind, but there is so much pleasure in it; a child should lay this pleasure up for himself. Such pickings as these, for instance—picking as they come: 'The trees beneath whose shadow, The ghastly priest doth reign, The priest who slew the slayer, And shall himself be slain' . . . 'My father, Time, is weak and grey, With waiting for a better day' . . . 'The judge of Torments and the King of sighs, He fills a burnished throne of quenchless fire' . . . 'thou bringest back to sunny light . . . the blessed household coun-tenances, cleansed from the dishonours of the grave' . . . 'Lo, we adore Thee, Dread Lamb and fall, Thus low before Thee.' 'Cause by the covenant of Thy cross, Thou hast saved at once the whole World's loss' . . . 'Look behind, look behind, there's blood upon the shoe, The shoe's too small, the one behind, is not the bride for you'. Yes, of course, the fairy-story lines. If the children are studying German, what could be better than '*Wer auf mir trinkt wird ein*

Tiger'? But at least with these pieces, Time has done some sorting out. It must be difficult to cut swathes through the jungle-grass of modern poetry. Nothing is decided. Nobody knows. How pick? Anthologies help. (Are there any as good for children as *Come Hither*?) I believe one idea of studying modern poetry is to encourage children to try their hand. I can think of no better way of killing true talent. Of course, if the children have not got it in them to grow later into true poets, no harm is done and some pleasure given. But true poets when young tend to be derivative and they can best—and only safely, I think—derive from the classics. A pseudo-Wordsworth, for instance, will easily find himself out. A pseudo-Modern-Whoever-it-is might easily not. Here is one of mine I have been asked to choose, and to give the thoughts that lay behind it when I wrote it—a poet's meaning I suppose, though not the last word, being still worth something. (Another favourite of mine, by the way, left out from above: 'Vex not thou the poet's mind, For thou canst not fathom it'.) But before I start on this, let me say that my schooldays, though not rich, were privileged, because in those days classes were small (never more than twelve to a division) and our homes were 'booky'. There was nothing but books in those days for our entertainment, we did not go much to the cinema—country walks, books, an occasional grand trip to a London theatre . . . (I remember once being taken to the wrong theatre by our French mistress and so seeing—accompanied by much tut-tutting from Mademoiselle—*La Chocolatière* instead of Molière) nothing much else. Here then is the one of mine I have picked. It is a story-poem, a ghost-story poem, of two children who loved each other and are now at school. Yes, but they are not quite children and it is not quite school they are at. (The sub-title tells you that at once.) It is the girl who does most of the talking, she is absolutely idiotic.

AT SCHOOL
A Paolo and Francesca situation
but more hopeful, say in Purgatory.

At school I always walk with Elwyn
Walk with Elwyn all the day
Oh my darling darling Elwyn
We shall never go away.

121

This school is a most curious place
Everything happens faintly
And the other boys and girls who are here
We cannot see distinctly.

All the day I walk with Elwyn
And sometimes we also ride
Both of us would really always
Rather be outside.

Most I like to ride with Elwyn
In the early morning sky
Under the solitary mosses
That hang from the trees awry.

The wind blows cold then
And the wind comes to the dawn
And we ride silently
And kiss as we ride down.

Oh my darling darling Elwyn
Oh what a sloppy love is ours
Oh how this sloppy love sustains us
When we come back to the school bars.

There are bars round this school
And inside the lights are always burning bright
And yet there are shadows
That belong rather to the night than to the light.

Oh my darling darling Elwyn
Why is there this dusty heat in this closed school?
All the radiators must be turned full on
Surely that is against the rules?

Hold my hand as we run down the long corridors
Arched over with tombs
We are underground now a long way
Look out, we are getting close to the boiler room.

We are not driven harshly to the lessons you know
That go on under the electric lights
That go on persistently, patiently you might say,
They do not mind if we are not very bright.

Oh why do we cry so much
Why do we not go to some place that is nice?
Why do we only stand close
And lick the tears from each other's eyes?

Open this door quick, Elwyn, it is break-time
And if we ride quickly we can come to the sea-pool
And swim; will not that be a nice thing to do?
Oh my darling do not look so sorrowful.

Darling, my darling
You are with me in the school and in the dead trees' glade
If you were not with me
I should be afraid.

Fear not the ragged dawn skies
Fear not the heat of the boiler room
Fear not the sky where it flies
The jagged clouds in their rusty colour

Do not tell me not to cry my love
The tears run down your face too
There is still half an hour left
Can we not think of something to do?

There goes the beastly bell
Tolling us to lessons
If I do not like this place much
That bell is the chief reason.

Oh darling Elwyn love
Our tears fall down together
It is because of the place we're in
And because of the weather.

Now if I had to 'present' this poem to children in class—but of course as its author I should have an obvious advantage—I think I should ask the children to read the poem overnight for homework and put down what they thought about it. Then I should start off in class by saying what *I* thought about it. This: that the children in the poem are young, loving and sad. That they do not understand yet about the school they are at. It is a sort of Purgatory, a school where they have to learn to be better and wiser and 'older'. Already, though they do not know it, they are making progress, because even the little goose of a girl can say 'They do not mind if we are not very bright'. But this school is a bit of a forcing ground too, with the harsh lights, and the radiators turned full on. And the shadows are not friendly. And when they ride out together, it is a melancholy landscape, and where they think they would like to go . . . the 'sea-pool' . . . is never quite near enough for the time they have. It is an ominous place, running up close to panic. But learn they must. And the skies above them are ominous, with a hint of barbed bayonets, grown rusty ('The jagged clouds in their rusty colours'). Those who teach them are 'patient'. And one knows it will take a long time. The idea is also this: that human affections and passions, likes and dislikes, are 'young' (hence the children-idea) . . . and that all this must be burnt away, taught and learnt away, before the children can 'grow up'. But what are they supposed to grow up into? Ah, that is a mystery—something that seems cold to us, cold with more than the touch of death. And the written comments of my imaginary 'class'—the 'homework'? Well, I would read them some time—chiefly to see if these ideas of mine had come through to any of the children, and then, and only of very secondary interest I fear, to see what ideas, if any, the little beasts might have of their own.

1966

MY MUSE

My Muse is like the painting of the Court Poet and His Muse in the National Gallery; she is always howling into an indifferent ear.

It is not indifference but fear. It is the fear of a man who has a nagging wife.

It is like a coarse-grained country squire who has a fanciful wife. It is like an uneasily hearty fellow who denies his phantom. These notions of the Muse are as false as the false-hearty fellow who bites his nails because of the false picture he is making. (If he were really hearty he would not know there was anybody to listen to.)

Why does my Muse only speak when she is unhappy?
She does not, I only listen when I am unhappy
When I am happy I live and despise writing
For my Muse this cannot but be dispiriting.

This comes nearer to the truth. Here are some of the truths about poetry. She is an Angel, very strong. It is not poetry but the poet who has a feminine ending, not the Muse who is weak, but the poet. She makes a strong communication. Poetry is like a strong explosion in the sky. She makes a mushroom shape of terror and drops to the ground with a strong infection. Also she is a strong way out. The human creature is alone in his carapace. Poetry is a strong way out. The passage out that she blasts is often in splinters, covered with blood; but she can come out softly. Poetry is very light-fingered, she is like the god Hermes in my poem 'The Ambassador' (she is very light-fingered). Also she is like the horse Hermes is riding, this animal is dangerous.

> Underneath the broad hat is the face of the Ambassador
> He rides on a white horse through hell looking two ways.
> Doors open before him and shut when he has passed.
> He is master of the mysteries and in the market place
> He is known. He stole the trident, the girdle,
> The sword, the sceptre and many mechanical instruments.
> Thieves honour him. In the underworld he rides carelessly.
> Sometimes he rises into the air and flies silently.

Poetry does not like to be up to date, she refuses to be neat. ('Anglo-Saxon', wrote Gavin Bone, 'is a good language to write poetry in because it is impossible to be neat.') All the poems Poetry writes may be called, 'Heaven, a Detail', or 'Hell, a Detail'. (She only writes about heaven and hell.) Poetry is like the goddess Thetis who turned herself into a crab with silver feet, that Peleus sought for and held. Then in his hands she became first a fire, then a serpent, then a suffocating stench. But Peleus put sand on his hands and wrapped his body in sodden sacking and so held her through all her changes, till she became Thetis again, and so he married her, and an unhappy marriage it was. Poetry is very strong and never has any kindness at all. She is Thetis and Hermes, the Angel, the white horse and the landscape. All Poetry has to do is to make a strong communication. All the poet has to do is to listen. The poet is not an important fellow. There will always be another poet.

1960

WHAT POEMS ARE MADE OF

Colours are what drive me most strongly, colours in painted pictures,
but, most strongly of all, colours out of doors in the fresh cool air, the
colours I see when I am walking in London streets, in the country or
by the sea. In this northern suburb where I have lived all my life, the
colours are exquisite. The streets with their bordering trees hump
over red brick bridges and curve into the blue-green and white pavement perspectives where once the country lanes ran. The railway
station has beige wooden canopies, lacy-edged; the advertisements
are navy blue enamel with yellow lettering, the grass banks are full of
flowers. When we first came here it was a country place and we still
have the great parks that were once private estates, with their great
oak trees and grasslands. There is also a great deep lake which in
hard winters is frozen so that you can walk on it.

> *Underneath the frozen water*
> *Steps the Lord of Ullan's daughter*
> *She is a witch of endless might*
> *And treads the borders of the night.*

I like to walk across Hyde Park where the loving couples lie:

> *I fear the ladies and gentlemen under the trees,*
> *Could any of them make an affectionate partner and not*
>   *tease?—*
> *Oh, the affectionate sensitive mind is not easy to please.*

And then cross into Wilton Place and see the pale grey Italianate
houses that stand so delicate in their crescent curve they seem, like St
David's Cathedral in Pembrokeshire, to be made of Indian paper.
There is much to be seen in city streets that stirs the heart:

> *Sisley*
> *Walked so nicely*
> *With footsteps so discreet*
> *To see her pass*
> *You'd never guess*
> *She walked upon the street.*

Down where the Liffey waters' turgid flood
Churns up to greet the ocean-driven mud,
A bruiser in a fix
Murdered her for 6/6.

But I like sea and country best—and the parks. I like to watch people in our park. What are they talking about? Perhaps this:

He told his life story to Mrs Courtly
Who was a widow. 'Let us get married shortly',
He said. 'I am no longer passionate,
But we can have some conversation before it is too late.'

Our park is a happy place even when it is raining.

I also like to watch the birds, animals and children, and to think how fortunate I am they are not mine. I do not know how people can manage to have animals, wives and children and also write. Of course isolation can be very painful. Many of my poems are about the pains of isolation, but once the poem is written, the happiness of being alone comes flooding back. In this next poem the lonely person was so foolish as not to recognise his nature and its solace. He should have remembered the schoolroom tag: *Fata nolentuem trahunt, volentem ducunt* (the fates drag the unwilling, the willing they lead). Instead he tried to do some war work:

To those who are isolate
War comes, promising respite,
Making what seems to be up to the moment
   the most successful endeavour
Against the fort of the failed spirit
   that is alone for ever.
Spurious failed spirit, adamantine wasture,
Crop, spirit, crop thy stony pasture!

It is not a stony pasture.

Why are so many of my poems about death, if I am having such an enjoyable time all the time? Partly because I am haunted by the fear of what might have happened if I had not been able to draw back in time from the husband-wives-children and pet animals situation in which I surely should have failed.

I admire very much the people who make a success of this difficult situation, that can be also so rich and splendid, for love and comfort. I see a mother and her child, standing by a greengrocer's stall; they are poor people, poorly clad:

> *Mother, I love you so.*
> *Said the child, I love you more than I know.*
> *She laid her head on her mother's arm,*
> *And the love between them kept them warm.*

But sometimes love is demanded. That does not go so well. I imagine this: that a little child has been turned to stone in his mother's lap. She clutches him and cries:

> *I'll have your heart, if not by gift my knife*
> *Shall carve it out. I'll have your heart, your life.*

Not all my poems come to me from what I watch and see and from the colours I love. Many come from books I read (I almost never read poetry), especially from the books I am sent for reviewing, which are often books on controversial subjects, such as history and theology. From the printed page, a counter-argument will strike up in my mind. From this poems often come. There is pleasure in this, but pain, too, because of the pressure on the nerves; for all human beings it is like this. I love Death because he breaks the human pattern and frees us from pleasures too prolonged as well as from the pains of this world. It is pleasant, too, to remember that Death lies in our hands; he must come if we call him. 'Dost thou see the precipice?' Seneca said to the poor oppressed slave (meaning he could always go and jump off it). I think if there were no death, life would be more than flesh and blood could bear:

> *My heart goes out to my Creator in love*
> *Who gave me Death, as end and remedy.*
> *All living creatures come to quiet Death*
> *For him to eat up their activity*
> *And give them nothing, which is what they want although*
> *When they are living they do not think so.*

1969

129

PRIVATE VIEWS

The summer show of the Royal Academy is a beautiful national institution, very tough and bouncing, weird you know, too, in a way, and sad with the perfume of lavender water and the lighter toilet scents, fleeting, wistful, nostalgic and robust. It is a flower that bloomed to perfection in the Edwardian era, but that is a little remote now, and ever since then it has been dying off, and the fact that it is not even yet quite dead, goes to show you how robust it is. All the people have their friends from the country to come along with them, and the whole opening vista of any private view day from 1906 to 1938 is very full indeed of this light, warm current of friendship between the friends and the friends of the friends, for they are all there, and there is this very strong feeling, too, in the part of the room where I now am, that the friends from the country are outnumbering their hosts and hostesses who, maybe, have a town address. That is perhaps why there is this wistful and robust feeling, for nothing is more wistful than the scent of lilac, nor more robust than its woody stalk, for we must remember that it is a tree as well as a flower, we must try not to forget this, and there is, of course, about these friends this suspicion of a lilac *motiv* for memory and kindest messages.

So that, sitting on this elegantly buttoned leather sofa in Room III, we know again the soft moment of excitement when the rather queer dress was taken from the wardrobe, and the queer hat was placed at an incorrect angle to the face, that is for to-day slightly made-up (this is delicious, this quite wrong, distressing, funny maquillage that makes the women look a little too bold for their candid eyes). There is one lady who has a white lace arrangement that cascades from the crown of her hat across and beyond the wide brim, falling in a soft movement of a very good lace over her left eye, so that the remaining one eye, forced into contrasting prominence to do the work for two, holds and repels enquiry from anxious friends.

The men are very staunch and loyal to their ladies at any time during the period under retrospect, they have been brought here a little perhaps noli-voli, but they are splendid, such sports, really you know it is ripping of them to be so kind and docile, not to fall over the trains that some of the ladies wear, and even every now and then to make the right remark, to glance here and there, observe and comment; for they, too, have their part in the merry game of chat and smile, and well they bear it. The fashionable town patrons of our academy artists are without the bouquet of their country cousins, ordinary enough in every way, they are ordinarily fashionable, hardened and regimented in their emotional arteries; but these country others, they are quite extraordinary, and never anywhere else at all ever except at Burlington House on private view day might you see them all together, excited a little, happy and unique. 'Tom is back,' the merry news bell-tones a country voice. 'Did you know? Nell gave a party for him. Tom's back. Harry came. Bob's through and Mary's coming.' The country narrative runs on and eddies round. 'Can't hear a word,' cries Lady Nod, who will not let us forget that this remark, current on every public occasion for many years past, has won her a reputation for wit; clever Lady Nod. The queer white faces of the country cousins, far too whitely powdered, smile and beck. 'I come,' they say, and the words of this poet are most appropriate to the moment, 'I come from haunts of coot and hern, I make a sudden sally . . .' So they do, but Lady Nod got in first, it is a pity. Over there, in the populous far corner, is another of this poet's fancies, a town friend, I am sure. 'The slight Sir Robert with a watery smile, and educated whisker.' Perhaps we might write 'whisper' for 'whisker' in deference to the calendar, and indeed there is nothing so educated as some of the whispers on private view day.

In physique the people who throng the galleries are all rather tall, except for some of the ladies who are rather thin, but still tall, so that for all this it is a little difficult to come near to the pictures on the wall. But these people are happy, oh happy band, how happy they all are, and the pictures, for one must come to the pictures, they are so happy, too, smug in a mediocrity that is sometimes quite excruciating, entirely so pleased with themselves, and happy on this day to receive their dear friends the spectators. 'Our Academy', 'Our dear pictures', like children the spectators have this possessive feeling; they are very worked up, too, you know, very apt to be provoked; but always, of course, a dignified control operates, loosed only for a toss of the incorrectly poised hat brim, or a muffled howl within a masculine throat.

The portraits of these happy people, for they are hung in oils upon the walls as well as pressed in flesh upon each other, have nothing of their delicate peculiar spirit, are nothing but bright masks, coloured competently to last a year or two, cheer none, appal but artists, woo oblivion. When these people have so much in their faces that one may look upon them for a long time and then not reach the end of it, be held and fascinated in conjecture and pursuit, why is it that the painter, catching nothing of it, must be so tired, abandoned to disinterest before the first sitting is at end? It is certainly the painter's fault, and not the fault of the enthralling ladies and gentlemen who sit for him; the soldier, the public house keeper, the simpering débutante, her older sister, the alderman, the admiral and all the people of the cherry stones. If Goya could paint his revealing Isabella and not have the canvas torn by outraged lady so for all posterity betrayed, might not our artists venture something in pursuit of revelation; no human being is so empty of all virtue and all vice as these poor dummies; so it must be that the artist cannot, and not dare not. Not cowardice but lack of skill restrains, and he, in colouring so often excellent, technique so facile, only dummy-paints; ah, so to paint so well, and yet paint nothing; this is where the sadness lies, too deep to run beneath Edwardian fancies. How deeply sad, with only slight exception, the show of all these pictures is; so many miles of competently covered canvases, and hardly ever at all anything to excuse the paint, the canvas and time spent.

The landscapes in the Academy are mostly representational; one thinks not: 'This is a lovely painting,' but: 'This must be a lovely field, a hedge, a roadway; why, it is for a memory of a dear countryside, this happy England.' There is a picture of sea breaking upon a Cornish coast—'Ah, that is the sea.' But with a great sea painter, one thinks at once: 'That sea is special to him,' to the artist, it may be Van de Velde. And later, if you are on the seashore and the lighting of the seascape is in such a manner, you think: 'the sea is Van de Velde'. This ruthlessness of a great artist who takes what he did not make and makes of it something that only he can make, is absent from many of our academy canvases.

Of the conversation pieces, Mr Robey might say that he was not able to follow the conversation. The nudes are very lean and hungry looking; haughty, refined, they are the sum of their separate parts and without sensuality. They sometimes have a highly polished shrimp surface. There is a young girl who has this idiosyncrasy, she is resting upon a small bath towel upon a green bank, she looks rather absurd, you know. Some of the nudes, even the quite young ones, have an odd look about the eyes, haughty and vulgar. 'You need not think that because I took my clothes off I am not as good as you.'

There is this undertoning the slant of their eyes. It is depressing, and when the body itself is so sentimentalized as to be not sensual at all (these unfleshed ladies especially of the symbolic pieces) it becomes quite horrible.

In the Academy, this pretended home of traditional painting, our comparisons may be traditional, we have no special quarrel that Matisse, Picasso, Dali, are not here; but how disappointed we may feel that among the fine soldiers on the wall there is no hint of Goya's Wellington, among the grey landscapes no thought for Corot, and among the genre pictures no rhinoceros watched by Venetian ladies. *Des fesses et des tétons?* Among the nudes there is absolutely no sense of this, therefore no sense at all.

But if the ladies and gentlemen of the private view were confronted with a work of art that was a great work of art and in this way a special creation, would they not be very creaturely sad, and creaturely hostile, too? No, I do not think they would notice it; or they would notice it; it would not matter; it might as well not be there, and also it might as well be there. If they noticed it and were hostile, that would be an unfocused instinctive hostility, because of the privilege and power of that canvas—'it isn't fair'—but they would lose this hostility in restlessness, hurry on, there is so much to see, an excusing restlessness.

For clean, happy fun there are: horrible ladies, *passim*; horrible little girl looking at horrible squirrel; horrible short-horn up to no good with horrible lady; silly lady on silly plank (by silly artist?) above silly tank; flying moment, monarchical, nastily stayed, for multiple reproduction; lots of nasty gentlemen. God rest 'em all.

1938

133

CATS IN COLOUR

Most of the pussycats in this beautiful picture book are little deb creatures, sweet little catsy-watsies of family, offspring of prize-winners and prizewinners themselves, 'daughters' (and sons) 'of the game'; the game in this case not being Shakespeare's Ulysses' game, as you will find it in *Troilus and Cressida*, when that cunning Greek general, in highranking Army company, refuses to kiss Cressida, because she is too easy by half, too much everyman's armful.

No, here 'the game', though not to my mind entirely removed from a hidden tartiness, is the game that human beings have been playing with the animal world since the first dog owned a human master and the first cat settled down upon a human hearth. It is we who have made these little catsy-watsies so sweet, have dressed them up and set them up, in their cultivated coats and many markings, and thrown our own human love upon them and with it our own egocentricity and ambition. I should have liked some little common cats alongside our beauties, some ash-cats going sorrowful about the palings of a poor London street, and not only for contrast with the beauties but for the truth of it as to the whole cat nature. Or is the cat-nature disguised as much by misery as it is by grandeur? And what in heaven's name is the cat-nature? Does it shine in the pretty eyes of our cat gathering in this sumptuous book, or is that a humanisation too? Really to look in an animal's eyes is to be aware of stupidity, so blank and shining these eyes are, so cold. It is mind that lights the human eyes, but what mind have animals? We do not know, and as we do not like not to know, we make up stories about them, give our own feelings and thoughts to our poor pets, and then turn in disgust, if they catch, as they do sometimes, something of our own fevers and unquietness. Tamed animals can grow neurotic, as the Colonel in a poem I wrote knew but too well (he was in India, hunting tiger):

> *Wild creatures' eyes, the colonel said,*
> *Are innocent and fathomless*
> *And when I look at them I see*
> *That they are not aware of me*
> *And oh I find and oh I bless*
> *A comfort in this emptiness*
> *They only see me when they want*
> *To pounce upon me at the hunt;*
> *But in the tame variety*
> *There couches an anxiety*
> *As if they yearned, yet knew not what*
> *They yearned for, nor they yearned for not.*
> *And so my dog would look at me*
> *And it was pitiful to see*
> *Such love and such dependency.*
> *The human heart is not at ease*
> *With animals that look like these.*

But I think all animal life, tamed or wild, the cat life, the dog life and the tiger life alike, are hidden from us and protected by darkness, they are too dark for us to read. We may read our pets' bellies and their passions, we may feed them and give them warmth; or, if we are villains, we may kick them out, ill treat them, torture them as heretics, as was done with witches' poor cats in the middle ages, worship them for gods, as Old Egypt worshipped them, put words into their mouths, like Dick's cat and the Marquis of Carrabas's sly pet. But still they are not ours, to possess and know, they belong to another world and from that world and its strange obediences no human being can steal them away. It is a thought that cheers one up.

I have written many poems about cats. I like cats, I like the look of them, I like the feel of a soft fat kitchen cat that folds boneless in one's arms. I could crush a fine cat. I wrote this short poem to express such a feeling. It is called 'When I hold in my arms a soft and crushable animal, and feel the soft fur beat for fear, and the fine feather, I cannot feel unhappy'; then the poem comes, just two lines, 'In his fur the animal rode and in his fur he strove/And oh it filled my heart, my heart, it filled my heart with love'. There is a bird mentioned there, but it is the cat-feeling that prevails. And do not be alarmed. The docile pet will turn if the pressure annoys him, out come the beautiful claws; our pet is not unarmed.

I had a cat once called Tizdal, just such a kitchen fat cat as I love. I wrote this poem about Tizdal, to show the love one can have for an animal, the love that likes to hug and stroke and tickle—and pinch lightly on the sly too, half-mocking, a love that says, Don't get too big for your boots, my little catsy-watsy Emperor-animal. I called it 'Nodding'; you'll have had this mood often yourself:

NODDING

Tizdal my beautiful cat
Lies on the old rag mat
In front of the kitchen fire.
Outside the night is black.

The great fat cat
Lies with his paws under him
His whiskers twitch in a dream,
He is slumbering.

The clock on the mantlepiece
Ticks unevenly, tic toc, tic-toc,
Good heavens what is the matter
With the kitchen clock?

136

Outside an owl hunts,
Hee hee hee hee,
Hunting in the Old Park
From his snowy tree.
What on earth can he find in the park tonight,
It is so wintry?

Now the fire burns suddenly too hot
Tizdal gets up to move,
Why should such an animal
Provoke our love?

The twigs from the elder bush
Are tapping on the window pane
As the wind sets them tapping,
Now the tapping begins again.

One laughs on a night like this
In a room half firelight half dark
With a great lump of a cat
Moving on the hearth,
And the twigs tapping quick,
And the owl in an absolute fit
One laughs supposing creation
Pays for its long plodding
Simply by coming to this—
Cat, night, fire—and a girl nodding.

Why should such an animal provoke our love? It was the indifference of course, the beastly, truly beastly—that is as appertaining to beasts —indifference of poor dear Tizdal I so relished. There is something about the limitless inability of a beast to meet us on human ground, that cannot but pique, and by pique attract; at least if we are in the mood for it, perhaps, at the moment, too thronged by too-ready human responses, sick of the nerves and whining of our own human situation *vis-à-vis* our fellow mortals. At such a moment the Cat-Fact lifts the human mind and relieves its pressures. As little girls love their dolls, so we love our pets. And use them quite often (I am afraid this is all too common, especially if we suffer from feelings of loneliness) as a stick to beat our human companions, who fail us in some way, are not affectionate enough, do not 'understand' us. How nice then to turn to the indifferent cat who can be made to mean so many things—and think them—being as it were a blank page on which to scrawl the hieroglyphics of our own grievance, bad temper and unhappiness, and scrawl also, of course, the desired sweet responses to these uncomfortable feelings.

I had an unlikeable elderly female cousin once and she had a very unlikeable cat; or perhaps we set the lady's own disagreeableness upon her cat, who was in himself I expect no better and no worse than any other animal. Fluff was this cat's name, and 'Fluff understands me' was my cousin's constant cry. Looking back from kindlier later years, I can only hope that my cantankerous old cousin's gullibility—for certainly Fluff cared nothing and understood nothing—went on being a comfort to her.

I like to see cats in movement. A galloping cat is a fine sight. See it cross the road in a streak, cursed by the drivers of motor cars and buses, dodging the butcher's bicycle, coming safe to the kerb and bellying under its home gate. See the cat at love, rolling with its sweetheart, up and over, with shriek and moan. But if a person comes by, they break away, sit separate upon a fence washing their faces—and might never have met at all. Better still to see this going on at night, as, if the moon is up and the roofs handy, you sometimes may. And what a wild cry they make, this moan and shriek on an ascending scale, how very wild the cat is then—very different, besotted cat-lovers may say, from 'our own dear Queen Cat's home life'. But there's not a prim beauty in this handsome book who is not capable of it and happy at it—provided of course our cats are whole cats and not 'fixed'. Alas, as D.H. Lawrence, in his ratty way, was always saying, so much of our modern life is 'fixed' and our animals are most 'fixed' of all. That is only one part of the sweetness and cruelty—and necessity too—of taking wild beasts and making pets of them.

Well, you may say, their lives without it were brutish and short. And has not dear Nip our own dear cat, just completed his seventeenth year in quiet peacefulness and jolly feeding, and enjoyed every moment of his life (well, has he?) though a doctored tom and firmly 'fixed' from kithood? Lawrence was a bit of a sentimentalist too, though in the opposite way from such doting cat fanciers as my late old cousin. But a bit of a sentimentalist in his idea of the satisfactions of animal life; I doubt for instance if the tomcat is ever satisfied; in the hands of Nature, sex is a tyrant's weapon.

I like to watch cats when they do not know they are being watched. Especially I like to watch them hunting . . . flies, perhaps, on the window pane—cat at fishpond, cat slinking with bird in mouth, cruel cat, cat stretching on tree bark to sharpen claws, then along the branch he goes to the fledglings' nest. Cat turning at bay, street-cornered by dogs. Scared cat.

Cats, by the way, for all their appearance of indifference and self-sufficiency are nervous creatures, all tamed animals are nervous, we have given them reason to be, not only by cruelty but by our love too, that presses upon them. They have not been able to be entirely indifferent to this and untouched by it.

Best of all, is the cat hunting. Then indeed it might be a tiger, and the grass it parts in passing, not our green English, or sooty town grass, but something high in the jungle, and sharp and yellow. But cats have come a long way from tigers, this tiger-strain is also something that can be romanticised. In Edinburgh's beautiful zoo, last summer with some children, I stopped outside the tiger's glass-bound cage. He was pacing narrowly, turning with a fine swing in a narrow turn. Very close to me he was, this glass-confinement needing no guard-rails. I looked in his cold eyes reading cruelty there and great coldness. Cruelty ? . . . is not this also a romanticism? To be cruel one must be self-conscious. Animals cannot be cruel, but he was I think hungry. To try it out, to see whether I—this splendid human 'I'—could impinge in any way upon this creature in his ante-prandial single-mindedness, I made a quick hissing panting sound, and loud, so that he must hear it—hahr, hahr, hahr, that sort of sound, but loud. At once the great creature paused in his pacing and stood for a moment with his cold eyes close to mine through the protecting glass (and glad I was to have it there). Then suddenly, with my 'hahrs' increasing in violence, this animal grows suddenly mad with anger. Ah then we see what a tiger—a pussycat too?—driven to it, can do with his animal nature and his passion. Up reared my tiger on his hind legs, teeth bared to the high gums, great mouth wide open on the gorge of his terrible throat. There, most beautifully balanced on his hind legs he stood, and danced a little too on these hind paws of his. His forepaws he waved in the air, and from each paw the poor captive claws scratched bare air and would rather have scratched me. This great moment made the afternoon for me, and for the children too and for my old friend, their mama (and for the tiger I daresay) and cosily at tea afterwards in Fullers we could still in mind's eye see our animal, stretched and dancing for anger.

Though pussycat has come so far down the line from his tiger ancestry, from jungle to hearthrug, or to those London graveyards where the grass grows 'as thin as hair in leprosy' as Browning put it, and where I have often seen tib and tom at work, there does still remain a relationship, something as between a Big Cat and a little one, that you will not find between cat big or little and a dog.

I will now tell you about a hunting cat I once observed. As I put this hunting cat scene in a novel I once wrote, I will if I may lift it straight from that novel as then it was fresh to me and if I told it over again it would not be. It was a hot day in summer, and I was swimming at the seaside with a cousin, not my elderly old lady cousin this time, but a boy cousin and a dear one, his name was Caz. So this is how it goes:

'We were now swimming above a sandbank some half mile or so out from the shore. Presently the sandbank broke surface and we climbed out and stood up on it. All around us was nothing but the sea and the sand and the hot still air. Look, I said, what is this coming? (It was a piece of wreckage that was turning round in the current by the sandbank and coming towards us.) Why, I said, it is a cat. And there sure enough, standing spitting upon the wooden spar was a young cat. We must get it in, said Caz, and stretched out to get it. But I saw that the cat was not spitting for the thought of its plight—so far from land, so likely to be drowned—but for a large sea-beetle that was marooned upon the spar with the cat, and that the cat was stalking and spitting at. First it backed from the beetle with its body arched and its tail stiff, then, lowering its belly to the spar, it crawled slowly towards the beetle, placing its paws carefully and with the claws well out. Why look, said Caz, its jaws are chattering. The chatter of the teeth of the hunting cat could now be heard as the spar came swinging in to the sandbank. Caz made a grab for the spar, but the young cat, its eyes dark with anger, pounced upon his hand and tore it right across. Caz let go with a start and the piece of wreckage swung off at right angles and was already far away upon the current. We could not have taken it with us, I said, that cat is fighting mad, he does not wish to be rescued, with his baleful eye and his angry teeth chattering at the hunt, he does not wish for security.'

How curious the observance of cats has been when great artists have been observing them, to paint and sculpture them, or work them in tapestry. The great early artists seem no happier with cats than they are with babies. Yet there is the cat for all to see, and the baby too. And do not say they extract the essence of cat or baby, because that they do not do. Did Raphael extract the essence of infants, in those stiff nativity little monsters, dropsical, wizened and already four years old though born but an hour ago? He did not, nor did Leonardo on his rocks, nor Dürer, nor anyone I can think of.

Who first among artists gave the essence and outline of infancy? . . . of cathood and doghood? Look at the Grecian cats and the Egyptian cats. To do so comfortably and without the need of visiting museums and libraries of ancient manuscripts, you should take a look at Christobel Aberconway's splendid compilation—*A Dictionary of Cat Lovers XV Century B.C. to XX Century A.D.*

It is not only the cats of antiquity that seem so peculiar (3,000 years may allow some difference in form) but . . . scaled to the size of a thin mouse, as we observe an Egyptian puss, couched beneath his master's chair? The Grecian cats, though better scaled, seem dull and the cats of our Christian era not much better. There is a horrible cat drawing in Topsell's *The Historie of Four-Footed Beastes*, dated 1607; there he sits, this cat, with a buboe on his hip, frozen and elaborate. In every line of this drawing, except for the cold sad eyes, the artist wrongs cathood. Quick sketchers do better, by luck perhaps. We all know Lear's drawings of his fat cat Foss. There is true cathood here, though much, too, of course, of Mr Lear, so 'pleasant to know'. Quick sketchers too can catch the cat in movement, and, though much addicted to, and fitted for, reclining, the cat moves—gallops, leaps, climbs and plays—with such elegance, one must have it so. Yet only this morning, I saw a cat quite motionless that looked so fine I could not have disturbed it. Hindways on, on top of a gray stone wall, its great haunches spred out beyond the wall's narrow ledge, this animal was a ball of animate ginger fur; no shape but a ball's, no head, no tail that was visible, had this old cat, but he caught all there was of winter sunshine and held it.

Why I particularly like Edward Lear's drawings of cat Foss, is one peculiar character they have that the cats of ancient Greece and Egypt, and our own Christian cats as shown by master painters, do not have. I mean that impression he gives of true cat-intransigeance, of the cat in its long drawn-out 'love-affair' with the human race—loved, mocked, cross and resisting. Why should we not mock our cats a little? We know we cannot understand them, as still less can they understand us, nor can we do much to them on the mental plane, except to make them nervous. Then let us not try to, but mock them a little and let them be a little cross. This is good-natured and sensible, it is much better than trying to invade their world, as some cat lovers do, with the likelihood of ending up, like that poor old female cousin of mine, in a no-man's (and no animal's) land of grievance and pretence. But to be frankly fanciful, to invent stories about cats, to give them human clothing and human feelings, to put words in their mouths, and accompanying the tales we tell of them with bright pictures, there is no harm in this—so long as we do not pretend they are not fancies—no harm and much pleasure.

Yes, these animal fables and fairy stories are full of pleasure. My own favourite of all the cat fairy stories is the one called 'The White Cat'. I forget exactly how it goes, but there was I think the usual youngest of three royal brothers, and this young prince, adventuring in search of treasure beyond gold, finds himself in a great underground candelabra-ed palace. So lofty are these chambers, and so distant their painted walls, the soft lights cannot light them but leave many shadows. The servants in this palace were invisible except for their hands and the Queen of it all was a great white cat, very fine, and finely dressed and bejewelled, and all the lords and ladies who attended her were cats also and wore their rich silks and velvets in fine style, with swords for the gentlemen-cats and high Spanish boots. I remember the great silence of this story, and the strangeness of the hands, the human hands moving in the high air, bringing service to the lordly cats and rich food on golden plates.

This was my favourite story when I was a child. But now I think Grandville stands first with me for cat-fancies, certainly for cat fancies in pictures, he is so mad. This eerie and savage artist, as savage and eerie as Fuseli, is at his best with pussycats. But they are not the pussycats of our present book, indeed they are not. I am thinking of one of Grandville's drawings which Lady Aberconway uses in her *Dictionary of Cat Lovers*, so you may see it there. Well, in this picture a young girl-cat stands in front of some very peculiar cowled chimney-pots (one of them has a human face, all might have). This girl-cat is too gaily dressed, in cheap frills and cheap satin. On one side of her stands a nightgown-clad angel cat with wings. But she does not have an angel face, rather sly she looks, this angel, with a grin and a double chin a madam might have. Yes, there is the debased bridal theme about this cat-picture, as well as the angel theme. I think it is truly depraved. On the other side of the girl cat, and pulling her by one arm, as Madam pulls the other, stands the devil-cat, her dark angel, and I fear it is to him she looks. The devil-cat's eyes stare, his body looks hard beneath his harsh fur, but it is a very tough muscular body, you can see how strong he is. And unfurled for flight against the belching chimney cowls of the dark chimneys are his great bats' wings, leathery and clawed.

Well, you do not often get the English drawing cats like this, they will leave this sort of drawing to Monsieur Grandville. Even our mad English, like the strange cat-mad artist Louis Wain, who while he was residing at the Maudsley Hospital for his madness, drew all the nursing staff and the doctors and psychiatrists in cat forms but true likenesses, are mild and sweet in their fancies, though of rich comicality. Mild and sweet, with occasionally a sly nip, just to show puss he must not get too big for his boots, that is the English cat-comical mood, and it can be a true feeling and not sentimental, though sentimentality is the danger. Cats in art, cats on comic postcards, cats in stories. Could any of our pretty pussies in this nice book of ours play their part, given a chance, in our favourite cat stories? Yes, certainly they could. They look demure and prim, fixed in a studio portrait mood, but true cats they are and any fanciful dramatic human being, with a gift for it, could use any one of them, as his own pet cat may often have been used, for any extravagance you like. Pick your Puss-in-Boots from these pages of photographs, your Dick Whittington cat, your Queen White Cat from my favourite fairy story.

And there are the other stories, too, the 'true' stories of cat heroes . . . and cat villains. The only cat villains I can think of are the cats in the witch trials, and this by reason of the devil's choice that he so often appeared to the witches as 'a greate blacke catte', or gave a cat to a witch to be her familiar 'the devil brought her a cat and said she must feed him with a drop of her blood and call the said cat Mamillian'. But witchcraft is too grim a story for here and its rites too cruel for our pampered pets. Yet I remembered the witch legends of history, as when the Scottish witches were accused of attempting the death of the King and Queen on their sea-passage home to Scotland. The witches swam a cat off the coast of North Berwick, having first christened it 'Margaret', they cast it into the sea to drown and thus—they said—raise a storm-wind to sink the King's ship. For this they were convicted and burnt, for the Scots law was crueller than ours and sent witches to the stake, while we only hanged them. But in both countries the poor cat that belonged to the witch, if he was 'apprehended', might also suffer death by burning or hanging.

People in those days did not recognise, to respect, the two worlds —of the Human Creature and the Animal. There was a cock that turned into a hen—and was tried by Canon Law and burnt for it. We have come a little forward from those days, I think, for nowadays any lack of respect we show for the Animal World, such as to attempt an invasion of it in pursuit of understanding, is something we do out of love, that mistaken too-fond love that makes nervous wrecks of our pets. A witch-cat poem I wrote is called 'My Cats'. You can tell they are witch's cats by their names, and by the second line of the first verse, that is a punning spell-line to bring death.

> I like to toss him up and down
> A heavy cat weighs half a Crown
> With a hey do diddle my cat Brown.
>
> I like to pinch him on the sly
> When nobody is passing by
> With a hey do diddle my cat Fry.
>
> I like to ruffle up his pride
> And watch him skip and turn aside
> With a hey do diddle my cat Hyde.
>
> Hey Brown and Fry and Hyde my cats
> That sit on tombstones for your mats.

There are witches' cats too in another poem I wrote, (and after this I will let the witch cats go, but they haunt my memory, these poor animals, these simple beasts, to have been so taken and used, their animal nature so wronged, and all for mischief of our human minds that will never let well alone). So here come the last of the witches' cats, and here they do not do very much but to step in and set the ghostly scene: (The poem is called 'Great Unaffected Vampires and the Moon':

> It was a graveyard scene. The crescent moon
> Performed a devil's purpose for she shewed
> The earth a-heap where smooth it should have lain;
> And in and out the tombs great witches' cats
> Played tig-a-tag and sang harmoniously.
> Beneath the deathly slopes the palings stood
> Catching the moonlight on their painted sides,
> Beyond, the waters of a mighty lake
> Stretching five furlongs at its fullest length
> Lay as a looking-glass, framed in a growth
> Of leafless willows; all its middle part
> Was open to the sky, and there I saw
> Embosomed in the lake together lie
> Great unaffected vampires and the moon.
> A Christian crescent never would have lent
> Unchristian monsters such close company
> And so I say she was no heavenly light
> But devil's in that business manifest
> And as the vampires seemed quite unaware
> I thought she'd lost her soul for nothing lying there.

This poem, for all that the cats play so small a part in it, brings to mind another favourite aspect of cat-fancying—I mean, the cat in ghost stories. A writer who used them much in this way, and always with the deepest respect and affection—perhaps too much respect, for are they quite as 'grand' as he paints them?—was Algernon Blackwood. There is one story of his one cannot forget, not only because it is in all the anthologies, but for its quality. It is called 'Ancient Sorceries'. Do you remember . . . ? But of course, now I come to think of it, this, too, is a witch story. Poor pussycats, how linked they are with the black arts, so plump and peaceful by day, so feared by night, crossing the moon on their perilous broomsticks. In this story of Blackwood's there is a young man of French descent who is travelling in France on holiday. Suddenly the train he is on pulls up at a little station and he feels he must get down at this station. The inn he goes to is sleepy and comfortable, the proprietress is also sleepy and comfortable, a large fat lady who moves silently on little fat feet. Everybody in this inn treads silently, and all the people in the town are like this too, sleepy, heavy and treading softly. After a few days the young man begins to wonder; and at night, waking to look out over the ancient roof-tops, he wonders still more. For there is a sense of soft movement in the air, of doors opening softly, of soft thuds as soft bodies drop to the ground from wall or window; and he sees the shadows moving too. It was the shadow of a human being that dropped from the wall, but the shadow moved on the ground as a cat runs, and now it was not a human being but a cat. So in the end of course the young man is invited by the cat-girl, who is the plump inn owner's daughter and serves by day in the inn, to join 'the dance' that is the witch's sabbath. For this old French town is a mediaeval witch-town and bears the past alive within it. Being highminded, as most ghost-writers are, Blackwood makes the young man refuse the invitation and so come safe off with his soul, which had been for a moment much imperilled.

In other stories Blackwood keeps his cats on the side of the angels, the good angels that is. They serve then to give warning of evil ghosts coming up on the night hour in some house of evil history. Blackwood thought, as many people think to this day, that cats have an especial awareness of ghosts and ghostliness, even more so than dogs, who are allowed all the same I believe, by people who are informed in such matters, some disturbance of their hackles when ghosts walk.

I have come a long way from the pages of cat photographs you will soon be turning to, or perhaps have already turned to, as introductions are written to be skipped. But if you look at these pretty cats and think I have wronged them, or look at them and think they do not tell the whole cat-story and wish some other sort of cat was there, remember—the cat for all its prettiness or ugliness, high bred under human discipline or got by chance, is a blank page for you to write what you like on. Remember too that what you write throws no light on puss but only on yourself, and so be happy and leave him to his darkness. As I was content to do, I hope, in the poem I called 'My Cat Major':

Major is a fine cat
What is he at?
He hunts birds in the hydrangea
And in the tree
Major was ever a ranger
He ranges where no one can see.

Sometimes he goes up to the attic
With a hooped back
His paws hit the iron rungs
Of the ladder in a quick kick
How can this be done?
It is a knack.

Oh Major is a fine cat
He walks cleverly
And what is he at, my fine cat?
No one can see.

I will finish with the Story of a Good Cat. This was the cat who came to the cruel cold prison in which Richard III had cast Sir Henry Wyatt when young. Because of his Lancastrian sympathies Henry had already been imprisoned several times, and even put to the torture. The cat saved his life by drawing pigeons into the cell which the gaoler agreed to cook and dress for the poor prisoner, though for fear of his own life he dared not by other means increase his diet. There is a picture of Sir Henry as an old man sitting in a portrait with the prison cell for background and the cat, a peculiar sad-looking little cat, drawing a pigeon through the prison bars. Underneath is written, but so faintly it is difficult to read, 'This Knight with hunger, cold and care neere starved, pyncht, pynde away, The sillie Beast did feede, heat, cheere with dyett, warmth and playe'.

It is an amiable part of human nature, that we should love our animals; it is even better to love them to the point of folly, than not to love them at all.

1959

HISTORY OR
POETIC DRAMA?

Murder in the Cathedral is a remarkable evocation of Christian fears; remarkable for the strength of these fears and the horrible beauty in which they are dressed; remarkable, too, for the religious convictions from which they spring. The year in which it was published was 1935. If this was a godless and frivolous period, frivolity masking the guilt and uncertainty of our western behaviour, and if there was once a better behaviour, running in the churchly times of Mr Eliot's choice, then this play comes like Hamlet's portrait of his father which he shows to Gertrude. Look on this, it says, and reform yourself. The author's purpose is as serious as Hamlet's and as violent. But Hamlet was violent because he was going off his head for worry lest the ghost prove false; Mr Eliot's violence does not always seem so straightforward as this, but rather to be used as a cover for some thoughts that are equivocal, as in the speeches the knights make to justify their murder. In these speeches may be seen all that Mr Eliot believes, and thinks we should believe, about the sickness of states and the lies of statesmen, and the shared guilt of the public, 'living and partly living', who allow smooth-speaking fools and villains to lead them astray. But this does not seem a constructive political opinion, it seems rather childish, as if he thought men did not sometimes have to govern, as if he thought that by the act of governing they became at once not men but monsters. It is a disingenuous and not uncommon thought, it is one aspect of the arrogance of art and the arrogance of highmindedness divorced from power, it is something one should not put up with. But just as Shakespeare's poor Gertrude, who has all the same more spirit than Mr Eliot's people of Canterbury, was struck with swords to the heart when Hamlet showed her the Royal Dane's picture, so audiences and readers of this play are meant to be struck. But what, in fact, is the effect? Uneasiness, I think–to begin with. And not because we are drawn into the guilt of the two sorts of sinners who are depicted here, the sinners who are powerful in action and the sinners who are feeble and small and too frightened to act at all. No, it is the uneasiness of dubiety.

Is this how it was, is this the truth? Is it the truth of history, philosophy, or the Christian religion? Writers do not have to be impartial, as scholars of history are impartial; they may take events and personages of the past and fit them to their uses. The fact that Castlereagh had something to be said for him does not invalidate Shelley's cry against tyranny, or mar the beauty of his poem 'I met Murder on his way,/ He had a mask like Castlereagh'. But allowing this freedom in historical interpretation, and misinterpretation, still leaves us the right to ask what a poet is after. Shelley, writing against tyranny, made Castlereagh his villain. Mr Eliot makes Henry and the State his villains, and what is he after? It is something that at first sight looks noble. But is it? Is it not rather something ignoble, a flight from largeness into smallness, a flight in fear to a religion of fear, from freedom to captivity, from human dignity to degradation? For fear is degrading, and we are counselled, for our soul's good, to fear. Is this the truth of philosophy and religion? Back to the Church, he cries, and he makes his archbishop so truly good and strong a man that we may forget to ask, Were they all like this, is the Church so sweet a thing, does it smell so sweet, was it not already, at this time of Becket, a bride of Christ somewhat stained with blood and no less greedy for political power than the State? Becket may or may not have been a man of the cast of Mr Eliot's archbishop. Mr Eliot's dealings with him are permissible, but is it permissible to distort the truths of humanity and offend against them, to cover the needs of men with a meretricious coat, and to envisage with delight a dwindling of hope and courage? There is this beauty in the play that I have called horrible. Seldom has fear worn such colours. Especially we find these rich colours in the chorus: 'What is the sickly smell, the vapour, the dark green light from a cloud on a withered tree? . . . what is the sticky dew that forms on the back of my hand?' 'We have not been happy, my lord, we have not been happy.' This might seem a trifle on the Greek pattern, indeed Mr Eliot uses banality with beauty in the Greek fashion that is so often parodied for an easy joke, e.g. 'I hear cries within the house, all is not well'. But there is nothing Grecian in the temper of this chorus of the women of Canterbury. They are a curious lot. They are really saying all the time 'I am afraid', and with colour and variety they say it, 'I have eaten the living lobster, the crab, the oyster, and they live and spawn in my bowels'. This neurosis of the invasion of uncleanliness and sin enlivens all their crying, 'We are soiled by a filth that we cannot clean, united to supernatural vermin'.

There seems something peculiar to the author in these dreams of corruption entering the body 'like a pattern of living worms in the guts of the women of Canterbury', it is a private horror (and it is communicated), the sort of thing that is so well described, in a naturalist's terms, in Mr Henry Williamson's *Salar the Salmon* and which makes that book such painful reading—a living body entering a living body to feed and live within it and upon it. So to fear must be added disgust. The sense of digust in the chorus is the most living thing out of all the play. It is splendidly alive, this sense, most often beautiful, only once or twice running near those reefs of silliness which make the waters of disgust dangerous to sailors. The argument of the play seems altogether lighter. It is both theme and purpose, yet it is not strong, as the emotions of fear and disgust are strong, but lies on the surface, an elegant and clever foam. I do not mean he may not believe what he argues, only that he does not make us as sure that he *believes* as he makes us sure that he *feels*, and especially that he feels disgust and enjoys feeling disgust and indulges this feeling with the best of his poetry. Against his arguments may easily be brought counter arguments. Mr Eliot is well aware of this and has put many of these counter arguments into the speeches of his self-justifying murderers. But these counter arguments are valid, for all that they are given a cynical man-of-the-worldliness, the flip and deliberate mannerisms of our own times. It *is* better that law should be one and equal. When the murderers cry to the sheeplike people of Canterbury that however much the King may repudiate their action, the benefits that will arrive from it will be thanks to them, they are not strictly telling the truth. It might be argued that the martyrdom of Becket put back by about 400 years the reforms to which Mr Eliot gives so glib and derogatory a character. Yet the knightly murderers have some true thoughts about these reforms in spite of the cynical way they speak. There is some special pleading in the mannerism of the knights, as there is some special pleading in the absolute nobility of Mr Eliot's Becket. But these knights, in their city-slicker-cum-MP-cum-landed-fox dress of modernity, are also for a light relief, I suppose, a sort of joke, no worse than Shaw's seminarist coming in at the end of *St Joan*, no worse and no better. It is not they, and it is not the arguments that lie at the roots of this play, it is fear and horror it beds in and from fear and horror it draws its sap. With a sure touch Mr Eliot touches that Christian nerve which responds so shockingly to fear and cruelty, which Dante touched most surely of all, and one might have hoped for all time. What is this religion that is like a game of snakes and ladders, or a game between a cat and a mouse? Even the saintly Becket is played with in this way. 'Your sin soars heavenward covering king's falcons' cries the tempter, and Becket stands wondering whether pride may not bring even a martyr's crown tumbling to hell. And it is exciting, is it not, it adds savour, a speculation of that sort takes the flatness out of life? One observes how the poetry mounts at each touch of pain and sinks when, as does not often happen, something agreeable comes to mind.

The weather and landscapes are most alive when they are ugly: the 'sullen Dover', the rain, the fog and the sleet. Yet Dover, with its great cliffs, and the skirts of its great castle gracefully fanned, is not sullen, the sea lies aroar and the fields arch above. Why did these worm-haunted towns-people never turn their eyes that way? Living in the sweetest landscapes of England, empty then of pylons and pillboxes, with the sea below them, coloured and aroar, you might have thought they would have looked, as you might have thought the Lord had juster cause to torment them for not looking, than for any cause that Mr Eliot shows. But, of course, he is right; in his own terms he is right. A lifting of hearts for pleasant fields would have broken the gloom, and he did not wish it broken, except in a little way as he breaks it, a little hellish way, by the rattle of the knights' tongues. One thinks that Mr Eliot believes his terror-talk of cat-and-mouse damnation, and that with him it is not a case of having to have some terror about in order to make things more exciting, as seems sometimes to be the case with his fellow religious terror writers. But it seems curious, condemnable really, that so many writers of these times, which need courage and the power of criticism, and coolness, should find their chief delight in terrifying themselves and their readers with past echoes of cruelty and nonsense, 'pacing for ever' (to use Mr Eliot's words with a different application) 'in the hell of make-believe'. One would not write like this if the play were not so beautiful and strong in its feelings, but it is beautiful and strong in these feelings, and also it is abominable. And this is not to forget the noble beauty of Mr Eliot's Becket and the strains of his situation. There is true love in that man, but it seems to be in spite of his strains and not because of them. And how significant—to show how he turns from love to severity—is the alteration Mr Eliot has made in the film script of his play. It is a disputed biblical text that is altered, but a wise heart would have adhered to our English Bible's rendering.

In the play Mr Eliot uses this rendering, 'on earth peace, good will toward men', but in the film script this becomes 'peace on earth to men of good will', which is a limitation and shrinkage of charity, for all men need good will, and most of all those who do not have it. How curious the Christian conviction sometimes seems! I recall reading in a religious manual on pain that Man's state since the fall is more blessed than it was before, because of the benefits of Christ's sacrifice upon the cross to which he now is heir. Then God must need sin, since without it Man could not have become 'more blessed'? So then, indeed, his good will should be extended to all men, and they should have this good will, yes, they should have it, and the niggling down, which is the sense of the amended text 'to men of good will', should not be allowed. But what is this but a fairy comment on a fairy story, a tribute to an inventiveness that bears the mark of humanity, being so exciting and so fanciful?

Truth is far and flat, and fancy is fiery; and truth is cold, and people feel the cold, and they may wrap themselves against it in fancies that are fiery, but they should not call them facts; and, generally, poets do not; they are shrewd, they feel the cold, too, but they know a hawk from a handsaw, a fact from a fancy, as none knows better. So Mr Eliot's play does not seem to me to be quite plausible, but to be very interesting and to draw one after it. He is a powerful writer and one to pay homage to and be thankful for, he stirs our thoughts and does no harm, if our minds are cool he does no harm but gives pleasure. Not every great writer is so enjoyable, not by a long way.

1958

SOME IMPEDIMENTS
TO CHRISTIAN COMMITMENT

I thought I would just start off with this short poem showing that
friendship can rise superior to religious differences. It is for the two
voices of the disagreeing friends:

I. AN AGNOSTIC
(of his religious friend)

He often gazes on the air
And sees quite plain what is not there
Peopling the wholesome void with horrid shapes
Which he manoeuvres in religious japes.
  And yet he is more gracious than I,
  He has such a gracious personality.

II. RELIGIOUS MAN
(of his agnostic friend)

He says that religious thought and all our nerviness
Is because of the great shock it was for all of us
Long, long ago when animal turned human being
Which is more than enough to account for everything . . .
  And yet he is more gracious than I,
  He has such a gracious personality.

My thoughts about Christianity are much confused by my feelings.
My feelings fly up, my thoughts draw them down again, crying:
Fairy stories. But how can one's heart *not* go out to the idea that a
God of absolute love is in charge of the universe, and that in the end,
All will be well? I do not think there is any harm in trying to behave
as if this were the case. But if we say that positively we believe it is so,
then at once the human creature is apt to do something that is
dangerous and not very good; that is, to fall into definitions as to the
nature of God and Goodness, and be angry with those who do not
agree. Nor do I find the world of uncertainty, to which my thoughts
draw me back, a cruel place; there is room in it for love, joy, virtue,
affection, and room too for imagination.

I think it might be a good thing to begin by giving you a brief picture of my childhood, so that you may see what it is I have drawn away from. I was brought up in a household where there was great love and a great faith in the Christian religion according to the tenets of the Church of England. I enjoyed my religion, I enjoyed the church services, I liked to see the great banners go round the church on festive occasions. I especially liked the great banner that had on the back of it: The gift of Anna Maria Livermore. 'Anna Maria amen' (I used to chant) 'pray for me and all men.' Probably my first steps in verse—in heresy too, I daresay. I liked the psalms very much, especially the despairing ones, the one they sing on the evening of the 28th most of all, that tells of the captivity of Israel and the bitter feelings: 'We sat us down by the waters of Babylon, yea we wept when we remembered Zion', that finishes with the bitter words: 'Blessed shall he be that takest thy little ones and dashest them against the stones.' I even liked that dreadful hymn which so perfectly embodies the sweetness and cruelty I have come to think of as the essence of Christianity:

> Faithful tree above all others
> One and only holy tree
> None in foliage, none in blossom,
> None in fruit thy peer may be,
> Sweetest wood and sweetest iron
> Sweetest weight is hung on thee.

How deeply this hymn bites upon the nerve of cruelty that lies in all of us. I did not only like the melancholy and morbid aspects of religion. I can remember even now the exquisite pleasure I felt when the word of the Almighty, replying to the complaints of his servant Job, first came to my knowledge: 'Did you make Leviathon?' I do not know why I should have found this so immensely relieving, so wild, so large, and so funny. But I did.

In the season of Lent we had the lantern lectures, with coloured slides, to show how Christ was tortured and killed. There was the bitter crown and the bloodstained robe, and there too were the Jewish faces that seemed so cruel, and the Roman Pilate, who was made to seem less cruel than the Jews—more like one of us, more like any governing person in a political situation of some delicacy. I was confirmed and became a communicant. I learnt that the elements were truly changed into the body and blood of our Lord, and that to receive them unworthily was to 'eat damnation unto oneself'. And what was damnation? Ah, now, what was that indeed? Let me say at once that the pains of hell, and the nature of hell, were not much spoken of, as they are with Roman Catholic little children in their retreats. We were taught that God was a God of Love, that there was hell, and it was eternal, but that we should not think about it but trust in God and in the efficacy of Christ's sacrifice upon the cross and upon the altars of my church, and try to be good for his sake. But I could not forget Hell. And I thought: How could a God of Love condemn anybody at all, even a person as wicked as the most wicked person could be, even a great angel so rebellious as Lucifer Star of the Morning Sky, to eternal fiery punishment? I began to think that a God of Love should rather slay altogether a creature gone irremediably wrong, then keep him alive to torment him for ever. I read my bible and I saw that the lofty Christ believed, too, and taught this monstrous doctrine of eternal hell: 'Depart from me ye cursed into everlasting fire prepared for the devil and his angels' . . . 'and they went away into everlasting punishment.' Here is a poem I wrote

THOUGHTS ABOUT THE CHRISTIAN
DOCTRINE OF ETERNAL HELL

Is it not interesting to see
How the Christians continually
Try to separate themselves in vain
From the doctrine of eternal pain.

They cannot do it,
They are committed to it,
Their Lord said it,
They must believe it.

So the vulnerable body is stretched without pity
On flames for ever. Is this not pretty?

The religion of Christianity
Is mixed of sweetness and cruelty
Reject this Sweetness, for she wears
A smoky dress out of hell fires.

Who makes a God? Who shows him thus?
It is the Christian religion does,
Oh, oh, have none of it,
Blow it away, have done with it.

This god the Christians show
Out with him, out with him, let him go.

The doctrine of hell, so surely based upon Christ's own words, became for me the first Fault, but soon there were others, or rather this one fault ripened for me the underlying nature of Christianity with its roots in Jewish orthodoxy, for there too is the idea of hell, with its larding of gnosticism and magic.

By now the years were going on, I was grown up and torn about, because the beauties of Christianity were so apparent and so dear—too dear by half—and they were my habit. I felt that I was a child of Europe, and that Christianity was the religion of Europe. This must be the experience of many children who grow up in the Church, and feel the tug of Europe, its splendours and miseries, and the seducing sweetness of its religion. This sweetness is very strong, it is not always cruel. I loved Crashaw's poems:

The judge of torments and the King of sighs
He fills a burnisht throne of quenchless fire

and this happier one:

Thou water turnst to wine, fair friend of life,
Thy foe, to cross the bright acts of thy reign,
Distils from thence the tears of woe and strife
And so turns wine to water back again.

Some people may not find the tug of this sort of thing very strong, but I did. And writing and painting are full of it, and I was full of writing and painting. But along with all this, there marched in me a formidable Conscience, a most practical agent, a really *literal* creature, full of plain common sense and a determination that words should mean what they say. So when I read in the Gospels: 'He that believeth not shall be damned', and in the Athanasian Creed: 'This is the Catholic faith which except a man believe faithfully he shall not be saved', I found that, as a Christian, I was committed to the proposition that unbelief is as damnable as evil-doing. And why should it not be? Unbelief is the enemy of Belief. The Inquisitors knew what they were about. I turned back to the Fathers and Doctors of the Church, and to the manuals of Catholic faith, and to the catechisms, and I read the histories of the Inquisition and the transcripts of the trials, and I thought: Here is the essence of Christianity, here are the harsh bones beneath the soft sweet skin. The Inquisition is a sore point with Churchmen today, they try to laugh it off, they laugh off the fear and the torture, the iron bands on the human spirit and the cruel deaths, and the fact that the horrible thing dragged out its dreary ferocity for more than 600 years. 'Oh well,' they say, 'how can you bring up that old song? And anyway,' (as one Anglican clergyman said to me) 'the Albigenses were not very nice people.' And the late Monsignor Ronald Knox could put these words into the mouth of his hero (in his book called *Sanctions*): 'If, several centuries ago, some catholics murdered two dozen protestant gentlemen in the city of Paris [this was the massacre of St Bartholomew's] that was their funeral, or their victims' . . . I confess that I prefer a shady past to no past at all.' Well, I suppose it is something if the holy Catholic and invincible Church can be brought to admit that she has a shady past. On the whole one prefers Lord Acton's plainer statement: 'If a man accepts the Papacy with confidence, admiration and unconditional obedience, he must have made terms with murder.' You must remember that, at the time I am speaking of, some time ago now, there was what might be called almost a stampede of the sensitive and the intellectual person away from the vulgarities of the secular world into the Catholic Church. Not in vain had Belloc and Chesterton conducted their campaigns—Chesterton so well earning that judgment of Coulton, that he had spent his life crucifying truth upsidedown. Belloc, by far the cleverer of the two, has left us at least one candid statement of his policy. 'Threaten we cannot' he wrote, 'because all the temporal power is on the other side. But we can spread the mood that we are the bosses, and the chic, and that the man who does not accept the Faith writes himself down as suburban. Upon these amiable lines do I proceed.' He, too, knew what he was about. Today of course, almost with one stroke of the pen, the Vatican has herself shattered, let us hope for ever, the sentimental and romantic image of the Church that England found so endearing.

Along with my books of religion, and the jottings of religious warriors, I was also reading the writings of unbelief and protest: the ratty Gibbon (if you will forgive me, I always think of this superb creature as essentially 'ratty'), the sorrowful Lecky, the reluctant Acton, the fiery Shelley and irreverent Byron—whose couplet about the Athanasian creed I will remind you of: 'The Athanasian creed' (he wrote) 'which illuminates the Book of Common Prayer/As doth the rainbow the just-clearing air.' I will not pick from Gibbon—the field is too rich—except for this one passage, to show how relevant he can be to our own times, and that I am not fighting old battles and flogging dead horses. He is, of course, speaking of Authority's dealings with deviation: 'The sword of a military order, assisted by the terrors of the Inquisition, was sufficient to remove every objection of profane criticism.' Nor are these historic instances quite so distant as we like to think. Torture was being used against heresy in the Papal States up to the time of their dissolution in 1870.

So I read my books, and I looked at Goya's pictures. I saw the terrible pictures Goya made in the prisons of the Inquisition, that have such strange elliptic titles, like a code-book in hell: 'What cruelty!', 'Because she was sensitive', 'He loved a she-ass', 'Because her parents were Jewish'. You can imagine the pictures, if you have not seen them, and the date was 1816, 1820, 1826; it was not very long ago. And is this cruelty surprising? Is it something the Christian of today can separate himself from, can utterly condemn, as he wishes to, as he does? No, it is not something a Christian can separate himself from, not if he is honest he cannot. For their gentle Christ was more cruel than this. For the worst cruelties of man end with death, but hell is eternal, and Christ made himself the King of Hell and the judge of torments. So I read my books, and I looked at my pictures, and they strengthened me, and I threw away the sweetness of Christianity and remembered the harsh bones that lay beneath, and I said: It is immoral. And I wrote a very long poem, which is rather intolerant perhaps, but is not tinged with uncertainty, as later sometimes I again came to be, and my poems too. I will just read one verse from it:

O Church of Christ, oh bride of mien ferocious,
In fancy frantic and in deed atrocious,
What though thy scowl leans nowadays on a simper?
We're not deceived it means a better temper,

Tis but a tribute to those powers whose civil laws
In countries protestant at least have clipped your claws,
There's little doubt,
Left to it, what you would be still about.

If any doubts are felt as to the timeliness of my objections to ecclesi-astical tyranny—that is to the wish, lurking beneath the surface, that Authority might still go armed with Penalties—this sentence, from a report in *The Times* the other day, may help. It refers to an article in the *Osservatore Romano*, written by Cardinal Felicia (whom I'm afraid *The Times* later calls Cardinal Felici—which is correct I do not know). The Cardinal is writing of the 'de-mythicisation' (atrocious word, but his own) of religious beliefs and authority. He writes, 'The predecessors of the de-mythicisers are the great heretics and here-siarchs, rejected by the Church, history, reason and, in many cases, by common sense.' Apart from the vigorous, the really enormous fibs the Cardinal finishes up with—is Luther rejected? Wycliffe? Cranmer? Copernicus? Darwin?—there is a wistful sound about those 'heretics' and 'heresiarchs' that the sentimental English lover of Catholicism might do well to note. Nor, of course, is the Catholic teaching about hell 'out-dated'. Here are some words from a recently published Catholic Truth Society pamphlet about hell, cast in dialogue form: What is hell fire? Answer: It is specially created for the purpose of punishment. May I be a Catholic and believe in hell but not that hell goes on for ever? No, you may not. What will it be like for a mother in heaven who sees her son burning in hell? She will glorify the justice of God. And as Catholicism also teaches that after death no change is possible—'as the tree falls, so it lies', 'out of hell there is no redemption'—the punishment of hell can only be seen as vindictive. And this hideous teaching is, and can be, based firmly on Christ's own words: 'where their worm dieth not and the fire is not quenched', and is echoed throughout the New Testament (thirty times hell's fire is mentioned, my C T S pamphlet reminds us): 'the smoke of their torment goeth up for ever', 'they shall be tormented in the presence of the Lamb.'

The doctrine of eternal hell is not compatible with the doctrine of a God of Absolute Love and Absolute Power. We are confronted with the dilemma of Epicurus: 'Benevolence would, Omnipotence could, have found some other way.' You might think Christians could take a lesson from Nature's way of dealing with her non-adapters—by extinction. But no. Catholic theologians are firm on this point. God, they say, cannot destroy what he has created immortal. Such statements, even in non-Christian ears, seem presumptuous, as limiting and confining a God whom they have themselves declared to be omnipotent.

But it is cheering, yes, I think it is cheering, to see how vehemently these doctrines about hell are being denied nowadays, both as to their truth, and to their dependence upon Christ's teaching, by so many Christians, with the possible exception of those of the Roman communion. And let me just say once again—if *I* interpret these New Testament texts as demanding a belief in everlasting hell, without all possibility of reform or release, the Catholic church does no less. *Roma locuta est*. I am not alone. But these denials of the others, I cannot help thinking they hang up on a slightly dishonest, *post hoc propter hoc* sort of argument. Which is: that Christ is good. Ergo, anything in Christ's words, anything in the gospels, that does not seem very good, must be either a mis-translation or a pious forgery. For instance, I have been told that the verse from St Mark's Gospel I quoted earlier: 'He that believeth not shall be damned' was thought by many scholars to be spurious. I have heard it said that the verse: 'His blood be on us and on our children', a verse from which has derived so much cruel persecution, is not authentic. At the same time these apologising people (and I am glad they do apologise) must believe that the Bible, if not the dictated word of the Holy Ghost, is in a very special sense under the protection of Almighty God. Yet the forgeries and discrepancies are such as would not be tolerated for one moment in an honest human document. Nor would such a document, after the mistakes had been pointed out, be circulated in edition after edition, as our King James Bible is, without errata slips or one word to warn the simple buyer and reader that inaccuracies exist, and often on essential points of doctrine and morals.

I am not deriding the apologies and explanations, the explainings away, I have been speaking of. There is something in them that is deeply serious, and deeply moving. The people who are making them see clearly enough, however much they may try to turn it toward a faulty Church, or a faulty priesthood, that all criticism of the sort I have been making points ultimately to Christ himself. Yes. But only if Christ was (as they teach) God incarnate, the Second Person of the Trinity, Perfect God and perfect Man. For if Christ was God he must have foreseen the centuries of bloodshed and religious cruelty to which the violence of some of his teaching, and its ambiguities, must deliver mankind: 'Compel them to come in', and his words about hell. He would have known this and he would not have put such a weapon in the hands of cruel men. But if he was not God, if he was a great prophet and a great poet, but not God, then we may sort his words and absolve him from blame. Because we may say then: He did not know, he did not know how his words would be taken and twisted, and sometimes (this is where the pain lies) taken without twisting and used, used logically enough, to promote horrors, even the horrors his loving words spoke most against, the horrors of power, anger, cruelty and despotism.

How shadowy is the figure of Christ as we try to see him in the gospels. What really did he say, what really did he believe, who really was he? Is it better to cling to his loving words and let the others go?–'the kingdom of heaven is within' . . . 'love one another'. And the best words of all, such words I think as then were spoken for the first time, the words from the cross: 'Father, forgive them, for they know not what they do'. And let the harsh words, and the tyrannical words, and the ambiguous words, go?–e.g., 'No man cometh unto the Father except by me'. And the peculiarly ambiguous words that have always puzzled me, and I daresay a good many other people too, as for instance: 'Render unto Caesar the things that are Caesar's'. Such vile things can be Caesar's, as Blake wrote: 'The deadliest poison ever known,/Came from Caesar's laurel crown'. This saying, taken down the ages, would surely have cut at the root of all opposition to tyranny. As again–at the roots of social reform– his words: 'The poor you have always with you'. And the peculiar saying: 'How can you love God whom you have not seen if you cannot love your brother whom you have seen?' But it is because we have seen our brother that it is so difficult to love him.

These words must have meant something else? I dare say, I dare say. If Christ was 'good', they certainly must have meant something else. Again you see the ranks close, and I expect a good many non-Christians and atheists will be found in these ranks, they close to

161

defend Christ and the belief that Christ is good. And in so far as this closing of the ranks may be seen as the effort of our race to worship Good on the one hand, and on the other hand, to keep their idea of 'Goodness' clothed still in the extraordinary doctrines of the Trinity, the Incarnation, the Redemption of Man by Christ's death upon the cross, is it commendable? Not very, I think, because the people who make this effort are not docile to truth; they will not follow where the argument leads because if they did they would have to give up these doctrines. This, out of fear, out of love, out of habit, or merely out of an inability to reason, they will not do. Still 'An honest God's the noblest work of man' has in its rather facile cynicism I suppose some truth—yet stops short, I think, of a greater truth. And that greater truth is what I have tried to bring out in this rather long poem, called 'Was He Married?' It is a poem for two voices. One voice, the simple, young one, is complaining that Christ could not have known human suffering because human suffering has its roots in imperfection, and he was perfect. The other voice is older, and not very kind.

WAS HE MARRIED?

Was he married, did he try
To support as he grew less fond of them
Wife and family?

No,
He never suffered such a blow.

Did he feel pointless, feeble and distrait,
Unwanted by everyone and in the way?

From his cradle he was purposeful,
His bent strong and his mind full.

Did he love people very much
Yet find them die one day?

He did not love in the human way.

Did he ask how long it would go on,
Wonder if Death could be counted on for an end?

He did not feel like this,
He had a future of bliss.

Did he never feel strong
Pain for being wrong?

He was not wrong, he was right,
He suffered from others', not his own, spite.

But there is no suffering like having made a mistake
Because of being of an inferior make.

He was not inferior,
He was superior.

He knew then that power corrupts but some must govern?

His thoughts were different.

Did he lack friends? Worse,
Think it was for his fault, not theirs?

He did not lack friends,
He had disciples he moulded to his ends.

Did he feel over-handicapped sometimes, yet must draw even?

How could he feel like this? He was the King of Heaven.

. . . find a sudden brightness one day in everything
Because a mood had been conquered, or a sin?

I tell you, he did not sin.

Do only human beings suffer from the irritation
I have mentioned? learn too that being comical
Does not ameliorate the desperation?

Only human beings feel this,
It is because they are so mixed.

All human beings should have a medal,
A god cannot carry it, he is not able.

A god is Man's doll, you ass,
He makes him up like this on purpose.

He might have made him up worse.

He often has, in the past.

To choose a god of love, as he did and does,
Is a little move then?

Yes, it is.

A larger one will be when men
Love love and hate hate but do not deify them?

It will be a larger one.

Again and again as I twisted and turned myself, in quite as much of a twisting and turning as our friends' today in the Christian churches, I found, or so it seemed to me, the tangles and entanglements to be of Christianity's own making: as to these two points especially, which still today, grown up and grown old as I am, puzzle me. The first is the doctrine of the Redemption, this Bargain, this really monstrous Bargain, that God would save his little children, once so loved and favoured and now gone hopelessly astray, only by the death of his son, the Second Person of the Trinity, co-equal and co-eternal, upon the cross in man's form and nature. This seems a Bargain dishonourable both to proposer and accepter, and productive of great harm to the human race because of the burden of guilt and gratitude it imposes, but this is by the way, it is the nature of the Bargain one finds immoral. Once again one thinks of Epicurus: 'Omnipotence could, benevolence would, have found some other way'.

The other point that puzzles me, and to which, though I have often asked, I have found no answer, is the Christian teaching as to the dual nature of Christ—that he was at the same time perfect Man and perfect God. For if he was perfect God, the Second Person of the

Trinity, then he could not sin, because if he had sinned the Trinity would have sinned too, and this is not possible, for the Trinity is by definition Perfection, and perfection cannot be less than perfection. But if Christ could not sin, how then was he Man? For Man, even in Christianity's Garden of Eden, had power to sin.

I remember once asking a Roman Catholic friend of mine, an instructor in theology at a famous Benedictine school: Could Christ have sinned? He was horrified, and said: Of course not. And, given the premises of Christian doctrine, he was right, was he not, both to say 'no' and to be horrified?

I found this doctrine of the dual nature of Christ full of the most extreme difficulties and contradictions, and still do, and I wrote this poem about the difficulties. You may think it is curious to write poems so much on argumentative subjects—but so did the Arians, you know, when they rushed about Alexandria, singing their popular song: 'There was a time when the Son was not'—what was this but a poem? My poem is called:

OH CHRISTIANITY, CHRISTIANITY

Oh Christianity, Christianity,
Why do you not answer our difficulties?
If He was God He was not like us,
He could not lose.

Can Perfection be less than perfection?
Can the creator of the Devil be bested by Him?
What can the temptation to possess the earth have meant to Him
Who made and possessed it? What do you mean?

And Sin, how could He take our sins upon Him? What does it mean?
To take sin upon one is not the same
As to have sin inside one and feel guilty.

It is horrible to feel guilty,
We feel guilty because we are.
Was He horrible? Did He feel guilty?

You say He was born humble—but He was not,
He was born God—

165

Taking our nature upon Him. But then you say,
He was Perfect Man. Do you mean
Perfectly Man, meaning wholly; or Man without sin? Ah
Perfect Man without sin is not what we are.

Do you mean He did not know that He was God,
Did not know He was the Second Person of the Trinity?
(Oh, if He knew this, and was,
It was a source of strength for Him we do not have)
But this theology of 'emptying' you preach sometimes—
That He emptied Himself of knowing He was God—seems
A theology of false appearances
To mock your facts, as He was God, whether He knew He was or not.

Oh what do you mean, what do you mean?
You never answer our difficulties.

You say, Christianity, you say
That the Trinity is unchanging from eternity,
But then you say
At the incarnation He took.
Our Manhood into the Godhead,
That did not have it before,
So it must have altered it,
Having it.

Oh what do you mean, what do you mean?
You never answer our questions.

But what a tangle they have got themselves into. I do not know whether one prefers the mental and spiritual gymnastics of the Catholics, who, aware of the tangle, seek a 'logical' way out, and when this logic of theirs delivers them into the sort of impasse I have indicated, reply: 'Well, you must remember we have been discussing some of the deepest mysteries of the faith'; implying that there may come a time when what is palpably unreasonable has to be kicked upstairs and called a 'mystery', 'something that the mere human mind cannot grasp', 'God's reason', et cetera. Or whether one prefers the more usual Anglican approach which is (or has been, in my experience) to leave ends dangling and hope for the best—'Well, we don't really *know*, do we?' Well, no, of course, I don't really think we do. But I cannot say this in the sense they do, that is: I do not think I could say this and retain a belief in the Christian doctrines of the Trinity, the Incarnation and eternal Hell.

So then we come back to this. If Christ's loving words are to ring out strongly, and his cruel and ambiguous words to cast no shadow upon them, then (or so it seems to me) we had better say: He was not divine, he was not God incarnate, he was not the Second Person of the Trinity, and there is no Trinity.

Need we love him less? I do not think so, but rather perhaps more. His teaching about the Kingdom, his strange parables, the curious love he had for our not very lovable race, his quick discernment of hypocrisy, his contempt for material values, for these things one must love him. And there are other things too, or rather there is the one overwhelming thing—his teaching about Love. And that God is Love. In the late Roman world of his day, in the seedy cynicism of the Empire's religious upholstery, how this teaching runs and flashes. And if this teaching about love that burns with such seeming freshness does not, in history's facts, turn out to be the first time such things were said, if for instance (and so near to the time of Jesus) that great teacher and philosopher, the superb Hillel, first said many of the words that Christ said, even so, the words themselves are good, and to put those words upon the lips of a god, and to worship that God—such a God as who, in the abjection of a miserable death (miserable, but alas common enough—how many Jews did Titus crucify before the walls of Jerusalem?) could pray for his tormentors: 'Father, forgive them, for they know not what they do'—at least we may say: This was a new sort of God, this was indeed a Step Forward.

I am aware, too, that there are ways of circumventing the wretched doctrine of eternal hell, set out so large in the New Testament. One way is to say that Christ was a poet and used Hell as a figure of the appallingness of becoming entirely sinful. And if the blood-drenched centuries have taken it in another sense, that is their fault. I do not think this is a road the Christian can take. For if hell is but a figure of evil, then by the same reckoning, God may be but a figure of good. Which may be true, but it is not a Christian truth; it is an argument that offers no objection to atheism, no objection at all. Another point that will be brought forward, is: that if Christ was no more than a prophet and a poet, how did the Church take root at all, let alone grow strong and survive the centuries? I do not know. Any more than I know why Mohammed—from *very* unlikely beginnings —should have founded and given his name to another great religion. Any more than I know why, in equally unlikely circumstances, a handful of revolutionaries, with the highest aspirations for the good of mankind, should have delivered so large a portion of the human race to the glum government of modern communism.

There is a wonderful passage in George Moore's book *The Brook Kerith*. You remember he is writing of the life of Christ, but on the theory (not much propounded at his time, though since made familiar by Robert Graves and D.H. Lawrence) that Jesus was taken down alive from the cross. In Moore's story, he is nursed back to life in the house of Joseph of Arimathea. So at last, when he is better, Jesus goes back to the Essenes. And to them one day comes Paul, with Timothy. And Paul and Jesus meet, and slowly Paul realises that the 'Christ crucified' he is preaching stands alive before him. But he turns away, and sorrowfully Jesus sees him go (for in the book Jesus thinks that this was his great sin, to say that he was God). And though he knows that God may draw good from this sin—down the long cruel years, through pain, horror, heroism and sainthood—still, in George Moore's book, it is with sorrow Jesus sees Paul go to found the Christian church, 'to lead Rome captive that had captured the world', to take that famous calculated risk, and assume the purple.

And what else could the Church have done, or should she have done? This is the only sort of incarnation I know: when thought passes into word, idea into action, revolution into government. Always there is a loss, a falling off, a distortion. It does not seem as if it could be otherwise, but that the first impetus should fail, the love grow harsh, the morning turn into a dark day. I will just finish with a poem called:

AWAY, MELANCHOLY

Away, melancholy,
Away with it, let it go.

Are not the trees green,
The earth as green?
Does not the wind blow,
Fire leap and the rivers flow?
Away melancholy.

The ant is busy
He carrieth his meat,
All things hurry
To be eaten or eat.
Away, melancholy.

Man, too, hurries,
Eats, couples, buries,
He is an animal also
With a hey ho melancholy,
Away with it, let it go.

Man of all creatures
Is superlative
(Away melancholy)
He of all creatures alone
Raiseth a stone
(Away melancholy)
Into the stone, the god
Pours what he knows of good
Calling, good, God.
Away melancholy, let it go.

Speak not to me of tears,
Tyranny, pox, wars,
Saying, Can God
Stone of man's thought, be good?

Say rather it is enough
That the stuffed
Stone of man's good, growing,
By man's called God.
Away, melancholy, let it go.

Man aspires
To good,
To love
Sighs;

Beaten, corrupted, dying
In his own blood lying
Yet heaves up an eye above
Cries, Love, love.
It is his virtue needs explaining.
Not his failing.

Away, melancholy,
Away with it, let it go.

1968

REVIEWS

STATEMENT ON CRITICISM

A critic is meant to be a judge. So he must have the judging qualities. What are these? First—attention. He must attend absolutely to what is going on, i.e., the book. And his attention must endure to the end. This is not as easy as it sounds, as his own thoughts, especially if the book is good, will often strike across it. Then he must be impartial. He must read the book through and give a fair account of it. He must also have the judge-like (and God-like) quality of being no respecter of persons. It does not matter who has written the book, whether the author is old, young, man, woman, foreign, English, black, or white. Only the book matters.

Nowadays it is supposed to be a great virtue to be young. It doesn't matter. Youth is an arithmetical statement of passing interest, each hour eats it up. Neither does it matter being a woman. 'There are too many women novelists,' I heard a critic say (a very much indulged and important one, too). Turn it the other way: 'There are too many men novelists,' and how absurd it is. Nor does it matter being old. It can't be helped. A judge will have nothing to do with such considerations.

Attention, impartiality, and no regard for age or sex. So far the judge speaks. But when we come to the summing up, the judge's wig slips a little. For then, and only then, may our own opinions intrude. The judge in his summing up may have opinions only as to matters of law and its precedents. We as critics have grown our opinions out of life and books and pictures and friendships, and we may use them freely. And here, in our summing up, which is our critical article or review, and having first given a true account of the book, we may think of other books the author may have written, or other books on the same subject by other writers. We may even quote from other books, if there is space and our editor will allow; we may even quote from our own books and poems. But this is by way of decoration. It is the opinions that matter.

In the summing-up we may turn the sharp edge of our own opinions against the author's argument. This is legitimate, provided we do not use the book as a mere peg for it (and provided also, I would suggest, that we sign our name to the article).

There is one other matter where the critic's summing up parts company with the judge's. The judge does not have to be interesting and enjoyable. I think a critic should be both. Though you may say that if he is the one, he will be the other too—both interesting and enjoyable. But how dull the dull ones can be! . . . like Tennyson's description of the dull fellow, when he wrote (or something like it) . . . 'the meek Sir Edward with his watery eye and educated whisker'. No need to be like that.

Attention, impartiality, disrespect of persons—these are the legal virtues of judgement (learning the judge must have, or he would not be where he is). To these add the critic's virtues of judgement—knowledge of life, art, books and people (that is already a good deal) and a gift for writing well. Enough, I think. Enough to ask and a good deal more—you glum ones will say—than you will usually find.

P.E.N. News, Autumn 1958

GERMANS IN POLAND

(*The German Fifth Column in Poland*, Polish Ministry of Information, Hutchinson)

When the German really gets going on his mad and bad philosophies —pan-Germanism, Naziism, it is much the same—he cannot be considered a lovable creature; you might almost say he cannot be considered a human being. He is too solemn, for one thing, too solemn by half. But I often think this solemnity accounts for some of his temporary successes, as it certainly does, in a measure, for his ultimate defeats. Who but he could turn into such *glum* reality the fun and fancies of the spy novelette? Who but he could make of warfare a sort of devil's pantomime, with front-line troops, as quick-change artistes, dropping down from heaven in the guise of nuns, gas inspectors, milkmen and charladies?

It is as if William le Queux should be offered seriously to students at Staff College; as if Sandhurst in a body (and with the prospect of a stiff examination ahead), should attend at the Lyceum for the study of Transformation Scenes as a War Potential. Germany has such ant-like patient industry in misdoing, especially in the misdoings of Fifth Columnists! And she makes such a solemn use of psychology. ('But it was the very best psychology,' you can hear her murmur, dormouse-like, when things begin to go wrong.) Well, she can plead some successes up to date, and it is not for a pragmatical nation like ourselves to underrate success. Nor can we blame it all on to the low morale of victim nations.

Poland, for instance, is one of her most outstanding successes in this line, and Poland above all nations has a reputation for national integrity in the face of the most savage persecution. So that Messrs Hutchinson's little book, *The German Fifth Column in Poland*, comes at a ripe moment for analysis and explanation. It is a straight-forward account, supported by personal documents, of a very dis-agreeable business. Splitzkrieg before Blitzkrieg was ever Hitler's way, and the Fifth Column in Poland went into action long before war broke out. First of all the German minority, living happily enough under Polish government, was brought to a proper sense of blood brothership, superiority and grievance. It was then encouraged to demand reunion with the Reich. But this idea was soft-pedalled for a time, and even in 1937 Senator Hasbach (later rewarded by Hitler for his treachery to Poland) was able to declare that the German Poles had no irredentist hankerings. That phase soon passed, and when the German armies invaded Poland they knew well enough that they could count absolutely on the co-operation of their homesick relatives.

These German Poles were well placed, busy and ingenious. Some in high Government offices and in key positions in the factories found it easy enough to promote chaos and sabotage. Others, in the humbler capacity of agriculturalists, had nothing to do but solemnly tread out their ploughland, or stack their ricks, in prearranged patterns for the information of the Luftwaffe. By night—for it was only fair the night-bombers should have some help too—they put lights in their chimneys and sent up rockets. They thought of every-thing and were no less efficient than busy. When Poland fell and the Gestapo took over from the army, out from their hidey-holes came other little brothers and sisters of blood and soil, and began their delightful task of denouncing to the authorities those unhappy Poles who had been rash enough to resist aggression. (How the Gestapo dealt with such wrong-headedness can be read in 'Poland's Black Book.')

The present publication is offered not as a record of atrocity but as a solemn warning, a warning, shall we say, to those about to be invaded. So read it carefully, and when the hour of invasion strikes, be of good heart, go to it, keep an eye on the heavens—and do not, however shorthanded you may be, take on a charlady who arrives by air.

John O'London's Weekly, 21 March 1941

BRITTAIN
AND THE BRITISH

(*England's Hour* by Vera Brittain, Macmillan)

The destructive fury of novelists is absolutely boundless, and what they would do with the air arm—if wishes were horses—makes the RAF look like tuppence hapny. All this is fascinating reading especially for stay-at-homes. Mr Wells, for instance, in his *Shape of Things to Come* practically wiped out London overnight. And now here is Miss Vera Brittain with her new book, *England's Hour*, to harrow our feelings and convince us, almost, that if we are still alive we really ought not to be. But it cannot be done, I am afraid (though it is spoiling the story to say so); cities and races cannot be wiped out by air bombardment.

Even where there is no defence this cannot be done, and where there is anything like air parity, it very certainly cannot be done. A stranger reading Miss Brittain's observations of England's civilian population under fire might get the impression that not one stone was left standing upon another, that not one square foot of our island was left unbombed, that its heroic population, in the throes of total death, could look for some measure of race survival only to those few British children who had got away in time to the Colonies and States, coupling the pious aspiration that they have larger families than their parents. I suspect that Miss Brittain's observation is coloured by her temperament, humane and zealous, and by her political opinions, which, passionately held and very familiar, regard the Treaty of Versailles as the root of all our troubles.

Having said this, I hope without offence—a hope as buoyant as Mr Matsuoka's when 'in no unfriendly spirit' he described the English and Americans as 'serpents'—let me hasten to recommend this book as the expression of a type of mind that is of value not only as an irritant. It should make the most lazy-minded jump about a bit, the more intelligent even to some purpose. In the main Miss Brittain's conclusions err on the side of violence, but sometimes she does not go far enough. She notes, for instance, the stubbornness of civilian resistance to bombing, but she does not seem quite to realise the value of that stubbornness as a military weapon.

She notes also that terror bombing may brutalise the bombed, but not that their growing indifference to it may blunt the edge of a weapon dearly prized by the Germans. Miss Brittain feels things

176

keenly, has personal worries, and believes that the war need never have happened; it is, then, not surprising that the voice in which she speaks should at times grow shrill. But it is unfortunate that never once does she catch the authentic voice of England, as little hysterical as the growl of her guns. What Miss Brittain does say, valuably and with emphasis, is that the British react with energy to the stimulus of war, but that nothing less than that dire goad seems able to produce an equivalent effect. It is good to see the British lion getting really off the ground as wars approach their second and third years, but few will not agree with Miss Brittain that it is a pity the animal has to spend so much of its peace time slumbering heavily in the shade.

Aeronautics, May 1941

THE BETTER HALF?

(*Go Spin You Jade* by D. L. Hobman Watts)

This book is a disturbing study, though in most temperate terms, of the lot of women through the ages and of how at last they became emancipated. The title is good as it shows how high tempers ran on the other side. Did fear inspire these rages and the heavy thunderings of Church and State? If so it was a fear that hid itself in a variety of high-sounding arguments and pious violence.

Yet some men spoke for women. Cornelius Agrippa thought they were the better part of creation and that Eve was superior to Adam because she was made of a purified rib instead of common clay like the brutes. But Canon Law allowed husbands to own their wives and beat them 'temperately,' i.e. to the breaking of a limb, and only among the Jews was this forbidden. We know what the Early Fathers thought of women, and may here refresh our memories, if refresh is quite the word, and we know too that wives of old who murdered their husbands were judged guilty of petty treason and so burnt at the stake.

It is the later chapters of this book that are the most interesting, for then the fear, the hatred and the greed run close to our own times and touch home. I do not mean the cruel factory conditions and the mines, where the women pulled wagons on all fours with chains between their legs ('I have drawn till I have had the skin off me; the belt and chain is worse when we are in the family way,' says one poor female, giving evidence before an inquiring committee in 1832), but the comparatively recent tussles in the medical profession and in the universities.

The doctors were particularly obstructive and in the universities if a woman scored high in the examinations her papers were suppressed, until legal action made the dons do their duty. The most educated are so often the most prejudiced. There are lighter passages in Mrs Hobman's book, mostly about women in the arts. Here the jealousy is really comical . . . they said Aphra Behn's novels were written by her lovers and cried because Hannah More made £30,000.

Women have been good and fought like the devil, but some were bad and loved enclosure and especially in the suffrage battles this was so. How shabby Asquith seems, how timorous Lord Curzon, what anarchy they prophesied, how seedy was their violence. Fear runs to-day as fast as ever. Men fear that women will not give them self-confidence and comfort just for love, but must be forced to it by economic sanctions, and women fear that if men lose their self-confidence they will stop earning money and so have to be kept. But of course only weak people feel like this, most of us rub along pretty lovingly and do not bother.

All the same, as the author points out, vigilance is needed so that bad laws do not give countenance to bad behaviour and also because, though much has been won for women, their position might shift again—she quotes Freud on this—as easily for the worse as the better. We should look out here, as Mrs Hobman says. And be neither he nor she but human.

Observer, 22 December 1957

EDUCATING WOMEN

(*How Different from Us: A Biography of Miss Buss and Miss Beale* by Josephine Kamm, The Bodley Head)

I don't think one realises quite how brave and patient the women of the past were who fought for women. A fascinating question, even more fascinating than the women's courage, is the problem of the opposition. The men and women who opposed education for girls tried to make reason their cause, but really they were emotional. When Philippa Fawcett was ranged higher than the Senior Wrangler they trembled. Would girls become boys now, and boys, cast down, stop going out and earning money? The universities and schools of the mid-nineteenth century, the clergy and the parents, seem really to have felt that it was both wrong and dangerous to give middle-class girls any education at all, except a smattering of ornamental subjects, ill-taught and unmastered. In the board schools the girls of the poor learnt better. The famous educating women who are the subject of Josephine Kamm's doggedly pleasant book are Frances Mary Buss who founded The North London Collegiate School for Ladies (the 'Ladies' changed later to 'Girls') and Miss Dorothea Beale who founded Cheltenham Ladies' College. Miss Buss was the more practical and human character, and more democratic too. She would have no distinction of race, class or creed; tradesmen's daughters sat beside the children of the professions, Jewish ones beside Christians. She also liked to hug the girls sometimes herself. The education at the two schools was the same—it was what the girls' brothers were having in their schools.

Miss Beale was altogether more complicated than Miss Buss, with deep religious feelings and philosophical curiosity. Contrasting the two ladies, who were loyal friends, you might say, Here we have a soldier in league with a saint. But both learnt to be wily and make advances against prejudice a little at a time. It seems pathetic how often the greatest prejudice is found in the educated minds of professors and clergymen. Miss Kamm puts in some amusing anecdotes, as if she were nervous of not being bland enough about her heroines' fierce battling. But at core the book is serious and its moral paramount. Learning is the stuff of education and the years for it are too short to allow intrusive smatterings of fashion. Can we say we do not have these intrusions today and never a cause to cry: 'The hungry sheep look up and are not fed'? Not long ago I heard a head-mistress say: 'My girls are taught to use make-up properly and play bridge and be at home in the world.'

Spectator, 17 October 1958

POEMS IN PETTICOATS

(*Without Adam: The Femina Anthology of Poetry* compiled by Joan Murray Simpson, Femina)

This is a beautifully produced and printed book, and yet it is awkward, very awkward indeed. Because it is an anthology of poems by women; and it is published by a firm whose directors are all women; and they have chosen for their emblem the female sign of circle with pendant cross. Worse still, Lady Stocks in her foreword speaks of '. . . women who are often plagued by this itch to write poetry' and advises them 'to take heart and prove that they are poets' notwithstanding the fact that the greatest poets are men. Awkward.

The compiler, in her foreword—as in her choice of title—does little to ease matters. She tells us that 'in order to please everyone, a good armful of flowers (which is after all what the word anthology means) should include not only tall lilies and perfect roses but some simple daisies and pungent field flowers as well.' Perhaps as a pungent field flower I might observe that 20 lines have been cut from one of my poems, without the fact being mentioned or permission asked. Awkward.

The poems are arranged under headings: 'People,' 'Creatures,' 'Country Matters,' 'Laughter and Music,' etc., which makes for easy and pleasant reading. The compiler has found some good unfamiliar poets as well as such old friends—among the ancient ladies—as E.B.B., the Brontës, Christina Rossetti, E. Dickinson, etc. Translators are included—Helen Waddell, Rose Macaulay—but only if they are 'creative.' Creativity in translators is apt to mean a carefree way with original texts. There is no reason to suppose that Miss Macaulay is inaccurate, but reading (in her translation of Sappho's 'Ode to Aphrodite') the line 'Wile-weaving daughter of Zeus,' one rather hopes she is.

There is a good poem by Queen Elizabeth (the First) but not the theological one the splendid girl saved her neck with: 'His was the Word that spake it,/He took the bread and brake it,/And what that Word doth make it,/I do believe and take it.'

The compiler picks chiefly from modern poets: Edith Sitwell, Kathleen Raine, Elizabeth Jennings, Diana Witherby, Sylvia Plath, Marianne Moore, Fredegond Shove—and many others. One warms to her enthusiasm: one comes back to the awkwardness. Why have poems by women only? Or any group poems, come to that (really the regionalists are as bad as the women).

Tempted to take a hand in this ancient game, one might try something on these lines: Differences between men and women poets are best seen when the poets are bad. Bad women poets are better characters, they seldom ... get drunk ... go to prison ... shoot the pianist. Their faults are soulfulness and banality. They like to commune (who does not?) with the Deity, Nature, themselves, but the words they use do not quite carry the traffic. Bad men poets are more knowing; often they achieve fame as poets by stopping writing and going on committees. Some bad men poets can persuade people (some people) that tricks and shocks are a substitute for talent. Bad women poets are not so clever about this, STOP, they are not so clever. Of course, good poets of either sex are above these squabbles, at least one hopes they are. Awkward.

My advice to readers of this pleasant book is to turn to the poems first and then to the Notes on Poets at the back. Some of these are fascinating, especially the one about 'Michael Field,' that odd amalgam of Aunt and Niece. But neither odd lives nor sex really signify, it is a person's poems that stand to be judged.

Observer, 19 May 1968

PROUD AND FEARFUL

(*My Dear Dorothea* by Bernard Shaw, Phoenix)

This letter to an imaginary Dorothea aged five was written in 1878 when Shaw was twenty-one. It is a most illuminating and sorrowful self-portrait, a treasure of revelation. Why sorrowful? Because it shows that Shaw was as proud as the devil and put pride in the place of love. And why should a bright creature of such mercurial wits and fighting frenzies so limit himself if not for fear? The devil is proud and fears love more than anything. Happily, Shaw, being a fine fighting human creature and no devil, cannot carry it quite off, every now and then the heart limps in, but then he is ashamed of it and begins to bluster.

Look what he tells Dorothea. Never must she allow an affront to go unpunished: if she has a mother who beats her, she must show the bruises to everybody, out of pride and to be revenged. And she must mind her manners and keep her thoughts to herself and only pretend to be amiable when people talk nonsense to her about religion. And she had better be kind while she is about it and share the social burdens, or people may be unkind to her. You may say Dorothea will soon grow a monster of reticence and calculation.

Now all this advice, though it is given for pride and self-respect, has the heart creeping into it, too—Shaw does not wish Dorothea to be hurt and thinks if she follows his advice she will not be. But it is pride calls the tune, it is pride he will allow and not love. For instance, she must never cry in case she is despised. Yes, but also *love* might pity her, and that Shaw would not like, because then the heart would be troubled.

This pride of Shaw's is most peculiar and ferocious. Because of it he is not able to face life whole but only as an argument. All the virtues and vices of mankind, the sufferings, the courage, the tortures and the sicknesses must be withered to an argument, so that the heart need not be troubled and the light thinker may say, Ah well, it need never have happened, it was just a misunderstanding. Are not St Joan's judges kind and honourable men, with the implication that all inquisitors were like that (but we know they were not).

And so with Androcles. What a pretty liony-piony situation it is, with no thought at all for the realities of Christian martyrdom. And underneath there beats a heart of fear that cannot allow suffering, and a false pride that says a man should not allow his body to be tormented, he had better throw the pinch of salt to the silly god and laugh, as Dorothea is advised to, in private.

This twisted pride is the source of so much in Shaw that is shining bright and mischievous and useful. But what a defect it is too, what diminishment and nonsense it brings, what perils. One thinks of the bright, brave women who run through his plays, and the talking bright men and the greatness of power they will often have so much warmth for, like Undershaft: and one wonders how they would have fared in the desperate circumstances of our time, in the torturers' hands?

Of course, Shaw would not put them there, he would save them by a witty turn. But people are not always saved, sometimes they must die in great pain and without hope. It is true that Shaw's men and women accomplish a good deal, their spirits are high and they raise ours, or they are playful, and we may laugh if we like. But as a matter of fact, we are being cheated. At depth Shaw cheats, he cannot help it, it is because he is so proud. Pride, Shaw's pride, can never achieve so much as love, because it can never face the extremes of nobility and debasement which love can face and which are our life.

Observer, 2 December 1956

PARTY VIEWS

(*Thurber and Company*, Hamish Hamilton; *Vicky, a Memorial Volume*, Allen Lane; *Asia the Arena*, Topolski's Chronicle)

The trouble with Thurber—especially noticeable in a collected edition—is his lack of variety. People and animals are always the same, and so is the artist's mood. Of course he can be extremely funny, with the blunt fun of the comic picture postcard, slightly up-graded. This fun sees the male as endlessly pursued by the female; both being of outstanding ugliness. It is usually the man who has the telling word, e.g., 'Sometimes the news from Washington forces me to the conclusion that your mother and your brother Ed are in charge'. When the female is being offensive she shows less wit and seems more stupid than malicious, e.g., 'What do you want me to do with your remains, George?' Or else she is reacting against some-thing offensive in him, e.g., 'Well, *don't* come and look at the rain-bow then, you big ape'. His captions are superb, for they open up in a few words a whole lifetime of fret. Here are some more: 'I know he's terribly nervous, but I'm sure he meant it as a pass at me'; 'Where did you get those big brown eyes and that tiny mind?'

Mr Thurber is less happy with his illustrations to famous poems. Subtlety has never been his strong point, and his drawings for 'The Raven', 'Locksley Hall', 'Lochinvar', and his Shakespearian ones—Hamlet, Macbeth, Lear—seem almost on a schoolboy level of intelli-gence and scribble; one feels this section might have been funnier if someone else had tackled it. No doubt that blunt instrument Mr Thurber has made so much his own serves best to depict our own times and the theme he has also made his own . . . that women are unlikeable and men are not much better, and both are worst seen at parties. The collection goes back as far as 1917 and includes a section on Europe with a very good drawing—going rather deeper than most of them—of a melancholy prostitute leading a hopeful tourist upstairs. The section called 'Fantasies' is not very bright; it is the social comment one always comes back to: 'Why did I ever marry below my emotional level?'; 'You keep your wife's name out of this, Ashby!'

But for a humorous artist to be collected in book form is a great test. Osbert Lancaster stands the test, so did the early Bateman—but how soon he went off. Leach, great man, never grew stale, nor Tom Webster either, to my thinking. And as for Low, how truly great he

was. Which brings us to the political field—and Vicky. This is difficult ground, because the political cartoonist is first and foremost a
critic and critics need balance; Vicky's feelings came first, he was a
man of fiery feelings and convictions. Unlike Low, his great friend
and first pattern, he lacked the wisdom that makes for balance.
Vicky's great friend and admirer, James Cameron, who writes an
excellent introduction to this book, tells us how disillusioned he was
when Labour, coming into power, shed some of its ideals. But this is
a commonplace of human affairs, and one need not be a cynic to see
that a party in power is rather different from a party in opposition.
Some of Vicky's less successful drawings show this sort of blindness,
touched with arrogance and sentimentality. As if children, for
instance, were somehow 'innocent' and not, as they obviously are,
the young of their species . . . as if revolutionaries were always noble,
until of course they succeed and become their country's governors.
But Vicky was necessary to our times because he brought the sharp
eyes of Europe, a very suffering Europe, to our supposedly blander
scene. In the end he despaired of man, which again seems rather
arrogant, and killed himself.

Upon an enormous cardboard holder inked in beautiful lettering
are the following words: 'Asia the Arena', and then, at the side, the
words 'Siberia, Mongolia, China, Hongkong, Vietnam, India'. And
then, underneath, the words 'Topolski's Chronicle'. Above, there is
a drawing which, like so much of this artist's work, is far from clear.
Inside the holder are many enormous sheets of paper covered with
enormous drawings. They are very cleverly folded. Unfolded, they
might do well on an enormous wall, but I do not think you could get
them back into the holder again. And not everybody has a wall; and,
come to that, not everybody who has a wall wants it covered with
Topolski, or if he does, has a large enough room to get sufficiently
far back even to begin to guess what the drawings are about. I'm by
no means sure this required distance might not land them below the
horizon.

Listener, 25 May 1967

A PRIVATE LIFE

(Life at Fonthill, from the correspondence of William Beckford translated and edited by Boyd Alexander, Hart-Davis)

Beckford is an author who should not be followed home. Read 'Vathek,' yes—it is one of the best hell-pictures ever made and such a peculiar mixture of farce, compassion and tragedy; read the travel diaries; but do not pry into his private life or you may be put in such an ill-humour with him that even 'Vathek' will cease to please.

Life at Fonthill, being chiefly composed of Beckford's Italian letters to Franchi (beautifully translated and edited by Mr Alexander) pries deeply into Beckford's private life. He emerges a dire bore, endlessly complaining about the weather, the expensiveness of Fonthill, the humbug of the English and the difficulty of procuring lovely boys. Hazards with catamites is the book's burden. 'I see clearly,' Beckford writes of himself, 'that poor Barzaba must die of grief'—it is because he is in love with a circus boy who is far away. A footnote tells us he used this name Barzaba when in pursuit of boys. Beckford was addicted to nicknames: 'Mme Bion' is his valet, Richardson, whose 'coldness' is much complained of; his two daughters are 'the Pledges'—until one of them makes an unprofitable marriage with Colonel Orde and becomes from then onwards 'Madame Ordure.'

Beckford was not a man of family, but he liked to pretend he was, and had portraits hung up of all the barons who signed Magna Charta, claiming descent from each of them. And he loved Catholicism for its cruelty and grandeur. Casting a hind-eye on Lisbon, he writes:

> Ah, what a divine celebration was the auto-da-fe of November, 1707. What a fine mixture of fireworks and of flames from burning Jews. . . . These effects of light and shade please me.

It is odd that Beckford, who so abused the English for their legal strictures on sodomy, should have thought of Portugal as free and easy. Sodomy in England carried the death penalty by hanging, but in Catholic countries one could be burnt alive for it. Just now it is usual to have books indulging sodomites. In 'Lord Byron's Marriage' Mr Wilson Knight seems almost to draw Our Lord into their company and hints that normal sexuality is a bar to eminence in the arts. I suppose nobody will ever be able to make a true equation between vice, virtue and art; and why try? Certainly why try by praising sodomy? Mr Alexander does not exactly praise, or obtrude his own opinion at all—but he does dilate. As an editor he is superb ... 'Introduction,' 'Index,' 'Glossary and Principal Nicknames'—there is even a paederastic sign-drawing. The footnotes crown all. When Beckford writes 'Oh *dies irae, dies illae,*' the footnote gives the 'Mass for the Dead' reference and the relevant hymn numbers in A & M and the E H.

On the angels' side there are, of course, the Breughels and Bellinis Beckford 'collected,' and sometimes a turn of conversation that shows wit and affection; but, oh, he seems a bored poor sinner, a parvenu of grandeur. And, as always in books of this sort, there is that suggestion of a lady's maid, light fingered and with an eye to the keyhole ...

Oh leave it, leave it, one feels. Read the stories and poems the sinners write, but leave their private lives (as we should like our own sinning lives to be left—remembering that equation which cannot truly be cast by any human being) to heaven. So one feels. One may be wrong.

Observer, 10 March 1957

SWISHING
AND SWINBURNE

(*Swinburne* by Jean Overton Fuller, Chatto)

In this excellent book, which is often funnier than perhaps the author intends, I do not think Miss Fuller emphasises too much the whipping-obsession poor Swinburne suffered from, because this—and the homosexuality that went with it—ruled his life. But there is a great deal of it. The only female person Swinburne was able to love was his brilliant and beautiful cousin, Mary Charlotte Julia Gordon, who later married Colonel Disney Leith. There seems no doubt that Mary shared Swinburne's interest in flagellation. As children, they were much in each other's company—galloping across the downs above Bonchurch, swimming in the rough cold seas, gloating and giggling over Swinburne's 'swishings', then turning, with Swinburne's help, to Mary's Greek grammar lessons. It seems to have been rather merry. And there were the odd coded letters they wrote each other—and went on writing all their lives. One from Mary, dated 1892 (when she was 52), reads: 'Cy merest dozen, Anks thawfully for your kyind letter. Your most interesting Eton book, even tho' it be only the tavings of a rug, or the toping of a mug, is exceptionally amusing. How many changes seem to have been made of late, tho' let us hope that it may never see a change in one respect and that it may be said of the birch as of the school: *Florebit*.' This letter, found by the author almost by chance, and not 'Reserved from Public Use' (as are most of the Swinburne papers in the British Museum), filled Miss Overton Fuller with the utmost perturbation, so that she felt the temperature of the Reading Room drop several points. It was of course a splendid 'find', but the work referred to was almost certainly Swinburne's *The Flogging Block* and how could Mary (asks Miss Fuller), 'a woman of position and responsibility', find this 'amusing'? But Mary was such a very *vigorous* lady—a husband, several children, learning Icelandic, travelling in Iceland, writing books—I daresay she thought *un peu de vice* on top of it all did not signify. I do not say she was right.

A very interesting part of Miss Fuller's book is the long account she gives of Swinburne's novels and plays. His first novel, *Love's Cross Currents* (it looks comical without the hyphen—were they very cross?), was written when he was 25. It is in the form of letters, sent from one character to another, except for the Prologue, which explains the very complicated relationships. It is obvious that both Swinburne and his cousin Mary are in this novel. In the first 'try-out' (known as the Kirklowes fragment), Mary, who is called Helen, appears as the ghoulish little sister of Swinburne-Redgie. Helen delights in Redgie's 'tingling flesh', after one of the innumerable floggings, and delights, too, when a young man who admires her upsets his boat and drowns. She crawls down the rocks to watch him drown. In the final version, Helen is dropped, and we get a splendid company of interlocking cousins, and their even more splendid grandmother, Lady Midhurst, who writes to her rebellious granddaughter, Amicia: 'Married ladies, in modern English society, *cannot* fail in their duties to the conjugal relation. Recollect that you are devoted to your husband, and he to you.' The whole story is like a Compton-Burnett novel, especially the ending, of which Miss Fuller writes: 'There lingers a suspicion that Frank begat the child by which he was disinherited.' The abandoned first version has this description of Helen: 'She was by nature untender, thoughtful, subtly apprehensive, greedy of pleasure, curious of evil and good; had a cool sound head, a ready, rapid, flexible cleverness. There was a certain cruelty about her.' Miss Fuller believes, and I expect she is right, that this splendid description is of Mary herself and that it shows how sinister she could seem to Swinburne and how truly a prototype of 'Dolores' and 'Faustine'. One must bear in mind that Swinburne nearly always *enjoyed* himself, and as pain had to be a part of his pleasure, Mary's sins may well have been exaggerated to make things more exciting.

Swinburne's capacity for enjoyment comes out very strongly. He drank a lot, but even when he was not drunk he had a mad sort of gaiety. He loved 'sodomite jokes' (Miss Fuller tells us) and he and Rossetti, and poor Simeon Solomon—before they threw him over —and all the other friends, often used to roll about the floor for laughter. Especially when reading *Justine* aloud they would laugh. And here I think they were right. For the sufferings of Justine are piled on to such a point—those leaded-whips!—one can but laugh. As Swinburne said, Eton was much better than De Sade at that sort of thing. He did not say this sarcastically. He loved Eton and meant it for a true tribute. Throughout this book his love for Eton flares rather comically. Especially it was the swishing he liked. Oh, how he longed to see the birching block again! Often, with a similarly disposed friend, he would re-enact those painful pleasures. Eton had eventually contrived a gingerly dismissal of Swinburne because he was enjoying it too much.

Another peculiarity Miss Fuller mentions (or perhaps it is the same one) is Swinburne's 'enjoyment of an inversion of the usual sexual roles'. For instance, he liked the girls to carry the boys. In his early Tristram poem 'Queen Yseult', written when he was at Oxford, Yseult goes to look for Tristram, who got lost in King Mark's castle trying to find her room. When she finds him, Swinburne writes,

> she raised him tenderly
> Bore him lightly as might be,
> That was wonderful to see.

Rossetti, to try and help Swinburne out of his obsessions, gave an actress £10 to seduce him. When the attempt failed, she very sportingly returned the money. He also introduced him to Mazzini, hoping that the sorrows of Italy might take his mind off. Miss Fuller speaks of the 'loftier tone' of these noble verses, but cannot refrain from telling us that many of the 'Songs before Sunrise' were composed when the poet was sitting on a bench in St John's Wood, waiting to be summoned by Miss Flo (or whoever it might be) for his whipping appointment in the whipping establishment friends had introduced him to.

One begins to feel now that one wants to protect this poor man from the foolishly lavish evidence he left behind for researchers to discover. At least in his love of the natural world there is no swishing. He loved Northumberland, he loved the wild icy seas, the great cliffs and the storm clouds racing across the winter sky. He has always the most exact things to say about landscape, and flowers and trees and insects. He loved the snow-storm colours of white on grey. He also liked to set himself 'tests': a dangerous double-climb, as a boy, up Culver cliffs, swimming out into some really too rough seas. Swinburne was a very brave man, and these tests were as important to him, to prove his courage, as were the ordeals that pain came into, to show he could bear it. Some of Miss Fuller's judgments of the poems one may quarrel with—as perhaps with her comment on his Mary Queen of Scots play, that he gave no inkling of an idea that Mary Stuart loved Scotland. But as it is plain from Mary's own words that she did not love Scotland, Swinburne probably has the right of it.

The last love of Swinburne's life—after he had come fully at last into the hands of Theodore Watts-Dunton, who had a *very* restraining influence—was for a little boy of about five. It was a perfectly innocent and unself-conscious love. But poor Lady Swinburne, fearful (and who will blame her?) of what might lie ahead, encouraged the infant's parents to take him for an extended holiday. The letters Lady Swinburne often writes about 'my poor son' are infinitely moving.

I wonder if Aldous Huxley's estimate of Swinburne's poetry—in his essay on 'Vulgarity in Literature'—will stand? Not altogether, I think. There are some dreadfully lolloping anapaestic heptameters, and some shocking lolloping dactyls too, and some silly exaggerations of raptures and languors. But then . . . there is something about butterflies going seawards, and the White Girl, and lines in 'Tristram of Lyonesse', and 'Who is this who sits by the way, by the wayside weeping?' And yes, in their own ghastly way, there are the Faustine and Dolores poems. Miss Fuller has found some wonderfully sharp things to say and reveal that have nothing to do with swishing. But perhaps there is too much that does swish. And if only she could have prevented the use of the lamentably chosen and produced photographs. Poor Mary Gordon on her horse—if that is what she is on—can hardly be seen and the stout gentlemen, like funeral directors, whom one can see, one would rather not. Especially if they are called 'Swinburne and Watts-Dunton at the Pines'.

Listener, 30 January 1969

(*The Life and Death of Radclyffe Hall* by Una, Lady Troubridge, Hammond Hammond)

If two human beings can live together in love and kindness, understanding and peace, they are to be felicitated and—if one can use the word stripped of all evil content—envied. What comes so strongly out of Lady Troubridge's life of her friend Radclyffe Hall, which is also a history of their life together, is that they were happy and they were good. Miss Hall's *The Well of Loneliness* had its own sort of honesty but slight literary value. Nowadays it is in free circulation and readers must judge for themselves if it is not extraordinary the book was so highly praised by serious critics, especially foreign ones. The passage in Lady Troubridge's book about d'Annunzio's enthusiasm for it makes one smile, as also the literary life which then began to be 'lived up' by this kindly pair.

Smile, yes, but not with contempt. And not with contempt either when Lady Troubridge recounts the ups and downs of temperament, as Miss Hall's writing went well or did not, in the language of an *aide-de-camp* (and it *was* a bit of a battlefield) to genius. What does it matter if the value of the writing was questionable? The pains of composition ring true enough, and also the kindness between them. And what a gay time they had; with plenty of money, plenty of pleasant houses, in England, France and Italy, plenty of dear dogs and dear horses and canaries; and nothing to worry about, even when war came, beyond fetching the beloved poodle back from France.

I admire Lady Troubridge's handling of her subject. She has excellent manners and never forces the reader into embarrassing intimacy. Some readers, less well mannered, may be disappointed by her admirable reticence; they must look elsewhere for a Lesbian document. The end of the story is of touching bravery. Miss Hall, endlessly it seems the victim of medical incompetence, found finally that cancer was the cause of her not feeling very well. Indeed she did not feel very well; her eyelashes grew inwards and operations proved useless; increasing weakness made writing a torment. So, in the end, of cancer she died. Lady Troubridge little stresses her own wisdom and patience. But these books of Miss Hall's were written and re-written, and 'bridge' novels, never meant to be published, were written; and all must be read aloud and again and again. But there was this love between them, and no tyranny on the one side and no servility on the other. Now she must miss her very much. But they were both Catholics, so hope to meet again. This book may seem to some a study in self-delusion. It does not seem so to me because out of whatever dreams they had came the realities of love and friendship. Good luck to them, one thinks. In a desperate world, in the fearful business of being a human creature, they made a corner for themselves and were happy.

Listener, 7 December 1961

ON THE SIDE
OF THE ANGELS

(*Testament of Experience* by Vera Brittain, Gollancz)

Miss Vera Brittain is a very vigorous and convinced lady who in the past thirty-five years has fought a great many battles in the cause of peace and brotherhood; and written, and travelled, and argued. In *Testament of Experience*, an autobiography which reads like a novel, she tells us about her public and private life, and how difficult it was to keep the two running together—her husband, also a fighter for freedom, was generally in another country—and how full of brickbats and exultation and foreign travel and profit to soul and pocket such a life has proved. All the good causes of our time, in their peculiarly human mixture of good intentions and imperfect performance, their flights, fancies, good sense and nonsense, are here, along with the famous names they are associated with—Dick Sheppard, George Lansbury, H. G. Wells, Gandhi . . .

One wants to be careful not to mock. The ideals are on the side of the angels and it is a bit of a devil's act to dismiss them as 'silly,' just because the idealists often are—as well as being pompous, touchy and tolerant only of those who agree with them. The Gospels, from which as a pacifist Miss Brittian draws her chief strength, though pacifism was condemned by the Church as early as the fourth century, are not noticeably tolerant of persons out of line with their teaching—the scribes come off badly, so does the fig tree and so do honest doubters whose worm dieth not. To fight one must be convinced that one is right and that one is important. Miss Brittain scores on both counts.

What I like especially about this book is its warmth and dash and its unconscious comicality, of which I will give some examples: On her honeymoon she speaks of her husband's 'early morning thoughts turning to Serb-Croat relations and the pluralistic basis of the Yugoslav state'; they then go on to discuss about having some children, but she says 'the uncertainty of the immediate future made postponement inevitable.' And when her dear father dies, after being very 'difficult' all his life, she says that in God's 'many mansions even my poor father may find a place.'

What I do not like so much is the war years and Miss Brittain being cross because the Government curtails her pacifism programme, although she herself has just sent her children to America with the odd comment that a Nazi victory was 'a fate from which no sacrifice of scruples could be too great to save them.' Or when she says that England should have sent food to Nazi-occupied Europe; or when she tells the Germans after the war not to feel guilty because it is our fault. It is a pity to be so silly. On the other hand, few will quarrel with her strictures on saturation bombing or fail to appreciate her analysis of anti-British feeling in America when the war was just over.

What picture emerges of this lady, scourge of Governments, terror of the uncommitted? Something one warms to, I think, but is on one's guard against: something that perhaps had best be looked upon as the peculiar fruit of our successful fighting history, for I think no country that was not a successful fighting country could afford to cherish her, as on the whole and judging by this book, we do seem to have done, even in wartime.

Observer, 14 July 1957

EDWARDIAN ENERGY

(*Ethel Smyth, A Biography* by Christopher St John, Longmans; *To Be Young* by Mary Lutyens, Rupert Hart-Davis)

This book about Ethel Smyth is as good as it could be, that is to say that it gives the facts and the feelings, the press cuttings and the private letters, and the extracts from Dame Ethel's diaries and books, and all with the stylish ease that makes reading a pleasure. At the end are appendices of further letters—many, and perhaps the most interesting, from her old friend and admirer, Maurice Baring (a particularly interesting one is on his feelings about his conversion to Roman Catholicism after nine years of thinking it over). Dame Ethel was born in 1858, of a well-to-do upper-middle-class family. She was born with a stormy and battling temperament, as you can tell from the full eyes and strong chin of the photographs from childhood to old age. She looks like Browning's line: 'I was ever a fighter, so one fight more.' And she had plenty to fight for and against. First of all she had to fight her loving parents, especially her father, to get permission, and some money, to go and study music in Germany. The German passages bring back the old musical life there very well—its stuffiness, diligence, jealousies and true fervours. There was much fighting, too, to get her music properly performed and recognised — but this is really the theme of the whole book, and what was begun with the gnashing of young teeth in Leipzig went on in England and everywhere, while the teeth grew longer and the beautiful full eyes stormed, flashed and wept in an ageing face. The author avowedly presents her as a unique person. Perhaps Miss V. Sackville-West in her memoir, also given at the end (along with one from Mr Edward Sackville-West, and a note on her music by Mrs Kathleen Dale), best described this personality, which was so bursting its psychological seams with enormous energy that it puts me in mind of what a friend of mine once said of another energetic lady: 'she has tired out two riding horses before breakfast.' Miss Sackville-West says that she had no intellectual interest 'towards life' and that 'it is sometimes a relief to meet a primitive animal such as Ethel.' Friendships, if the word can be used for the wild associations Dame Ethel required, are a great part of her life. She was always getting infatuated with her own sex: it is rather the schoolgirl than the Lesbian situation. Like my friend's riding horses, the objects of Dame Ethel's affection were often 'tried out.' But between herself and her German friend, Lisl von Herzogenberg, whose mother detested 'the Englishwoman,' stepped the great masculine friendship of her life, the love that grew up between her and Lisl's sister's husband, a Mr Brewster. About the explicit sexual relationships of her long life, Dame Ethel was always reticent, though besought by Virginia Woolf, the last great passion of her life, to bear Rousseau in mind and tell all. The Brewster affair remains shadowy and puzzling, but the affair with Virginia Woolf is beautifully clear, helped by the letters the two ladies exchanged, those wild, peculiar, sensitive letters that make one wonder how any mere human soul, let alone the nervous human soul of an artist, can survive such intimacies. Dame Ethel's life was not only given to her music, her writing and her friendships, but also to various 'causes'. She went to prison as a suffragette and conducted the suffragettes' hymn with a toothbrush from her cell window while they were marching past. And all the time she was obsessed with the harshness of the woman artist's lot. Virginia Woolf's letter to her, warning her not to overdo this protesting, or at least to try and make it less personal, is very wise and characteristic. This is an excellent biography, but it has caught enough of Dame Ethel's fearful energy to make one glad it is just a book and that one does not have to meet all the people in it.

Mary Lutyens's story of herself growing up to the age of nineteen is a very different affair from the Dame Ethel book, though some characters come into both, notably her formidable mother, Lady Emily Lutyens. It is a delightful, simple and most courageous book. Chiefly it is about Mary's feeling of great love for Krishnamurti's brother, Nitya. As a dull, secretive little girl (she tells us), the 'baby of the family,' she fell in love with this charming and candid young Indian, and, through all the strange and comical and really appalling vicissitudes of the Lutyens' life, this love ran firm. The life does appear in many ways appalling. Lady Emily, who has spoken out well for herself, so there is little we do not know, was loved and 'sided with' by the younger children in the sad coil of theosophy and the troubles that came of it. Yet always in the background, and appealing much to the reader's sympathies, is the figure of Sir Edwin Lutyens, bested and tormented by what one can only call the second-rate fancies of a lordly wife. His was the genius, hers the clamour. Here again energy seems to have been the victimiser, a wife's energy unaccompanied by a just intelligence. The author says nothing of this, nor does she need to. Her book is a heartrending and limpid tribute to a child's power of fetching what it wants—Nitya, love and her own life—from a world given up to travels and manias. If she and her sister, Elizabeth Lutyens, the composer, have a touch of genius, they have this in common with their shadowy great father.

Spectator, 13 March 1959

A DECIDED GIRL

(*Simone Weil: seventy letters* translated and arranged by Richard Rees, Oxford)

The impression one gets from these letters of Simone Weil's is of a learned yet feverish intelligence driven by a relentless will and working death upon the luckless body that was its host. At the same time one sees a generous girl, a cocksure girl, anxious to put the world right and know the world's pain by enduring it. Her interests were extraordinarily varied: mathematics, philosophy, religion—veering to the mysticisms of East and West, but favouring Christianity—sociology, and the arts. Her cocksureness is too firmly rooted in innocence and energy to be offensive; it is perhaps the humility of laziness she lacks.

Yet the old words run true: *les natures profondement bonnes sont toujours indécises*. She was seldom undecided. She tells the older pupils in the school she taught at that they are living on charity, their parents' charity, if they do not leave school and earn their living. She herself gave up teaching and worked for some years as an unskilled hand in engineering factories. Her sympathy for people dehumanized by this sort of work, monotonous yet needing attention, runs like fire. That every worker is not a Simone Weil, or every *plongeur*, for that matter, a George Orwell, cannot decently be said by the brave experimenters themselves; but an outsider might venture the comment, without in any way underrating the harmfulness of such work. She was also certain that a band of nurses, sent for service under fire to tend the wounded and dying, would put a new face on war. Her editor goes farther. He thinks it would make war impossible. There is a lack of profundity here; and in Simone Weil's odd comments about the 'moral dangers' of the situation, an ignorance that is disagreeable and absurd.

Yet how truly she speaks of suffering, especially in the letter about how she thinks she could best meet torture, emptying herself of pride, docile. Writing to an Oxford poet about *King Lear*, she says: 'When poetry struggles toward expressing pain and misery, it can be great poetry only if that cry sounds through every word' as it does, she says, 'in Sophocles, in Lear'. But surely this is to ignore Shakespeare's use of humanity's basic stuff—inconsistency. In Lear's mind run also the Fool's iconoclasms.

Most interesting of all are her religious thoughts. 'We are born', she says, 'and grow up in falsehood. Truth only comes to us from outside and it comes always from God'. The notion that we want truth to come from God, want there to be a God of Love and Power to tell us the truth and pay attention to us, never came to trouble her. She also says: 'Nothing that is catholic, nothing that is Christian, has ever seemed alien to me'. This seems incredible.

Simone Weil's thoughts about England are of surpassing generosity. Though she came here so soon to die, she saw us at our best and has recorded that best with love and a humorousness of understanding not always found elsewhere in this fascinating book.

Listener, 4 November 1965

FAITH OR TRUTH

(*Facing God* by M. C. D'Arcy SJ, Burns & Oates)

Father D'arcy has always had a most generous and eager interest in things of the mind and has certainly earned the title of Apostle to the Intelligentsia which some people have given him. He writes here with charm and lucidity of the various philosophies he has studied throughout his life and especially of the arts, sciences and arguments of our own times.

He is first and foremost a Catholic and it is with a Catholic eye that he seeks and finds evidence of the truths of his religion, often in places where it does not seem to lie. But if his reasoning does not convince us of much beyond the fact that man is infinitely adroit at finding proofs for what he wishes to believe, his manner and explorations are so fascinating and so full of joyfulness that it seems ill-mannered to pick holes. Yet sometimes one must; as for instance when he says that he would find it difficult to be virtuous if he were not a Christian. Many people, of other faiths, and of no faith, have also loved virtue and tried to be good.

I think he is brave to bring us back, as he does from time to time, to the simplicities of the Catholic faith, for it is here that the true stumbling-blocks lie. Delirious with the subtleties of today's advanced theology, we might so easily forget that those simple pronouncements, say of the Catholic Truth Society, are for the faithful of equal validity: as they are for the unfaithful—if I may say so—so much more *readily* offensive.

If Fr D'Arcy's arguments were turned upside down, I suppose they would run like this. Man would like there to be a righteous and all-powerful God, to love, judge and attend to him. Since such a God cannot be less than perfect, then the obvious imperfections of this world must be the fault of man: hence the doctrines of Free Will and the Fall. The doctrines of the Trinity, the Incarnation and the Redemption are very flattering to man; and how can we *not* believe they are within the power of his agile and hopeful mind to invent? One difficulty Fr D'Arcy does not explain. According to Catholic teaching, perfect man, that is man before the Fall, had the power to sin. But Christ, when he was on earth, had not this power. How then was he perfect man?

This book is full of joyfulness because Fr D'Arcy is happy in his religion, and as we know it is a religion which, for all its cruelties, has brought happiness and strength to multitudes. He is also happy in the exercise of his intellect. But who is upside down—Fr D'Arcy or the unbelievers—we cannot know. Fr D'Arcy would say: Pray for faith. But what does this mean? We should not pray for what is not true, and if we believe his faith is true, then we already have it. If we pray, we must pray to know the truth. Joyfully Fr D'Arcy will say: There is no distinction. Less joyfully—for it is happier to be settled— we say we think there is.

Observer, 14th August 1966

HOLY MATRIMONY

(*Contraception and Holiness. A Symposium,* Collins)

It must, I think be allowed, even by the Panglosses of our ecumenical times, that the spectacle of a celibate priesthood discussing intimate details of female anatomy is not edifying. That the Roman Catholic hierarchy is forced to do this in order to discover a method of birth control that is face-saving as well as efficient makes sympathy difficult. For if they had not formerly taken so stiff a line, they would not now be in such a pickle. And what has brought them to the point of changing their minds? It is not only the pressure of circumstances, a leaping birth-rate and the prevalence of contraceptives, it is the revolt of their own people. The Catholic layman has found his voice, especially here and in America, where this symposium of Catholic opinion was first published.

One sees at once that rebellion is well mounted. Should we then leave matters in the hands of Catholics, allowing only the faithful to comment on Roman Catholic pronouncements and books such as this? Of course we should not. It was our freedom and our discoveries that brought birth control into use, and if sterner members of their communion say we have infected Catholics with our ideas— well, perhaps we have; and all the more reason to stand by them. Again, the contributors to this book are all of trained intelligence and professional status. How small a part that is of the Catholic world. Can they *swing it*? With our help and the weight of a world's necessity, they may, and our help is valuable, for it is in countries that are largely Protestant or unbelieving that the Church is most vulnerable, most sensitive to outside temper and opinion. The introduction to the book, by Archbishop Roberts, SJ, is really splendid.

Easy, forceful, good-tempered, he sets a standard the rest on the whole maintain. It was, he reminds us, his inability to comprehend Roman Catholic objections to birth control 'that elicited from the English [R.C.] bishops their statement that contraception is unchangeably against the law of God.' The Archbishop is puzzled, not because the Church says 'I say so, you obey' but because it says 'contraception is a question of natural law and can be resolved purely through the powers of reason.' He goes on: 'As an English Catholic I cannot but recall a similar dilemma of conscience which faced my ancestors when Pope Pius V, after glorifying the secular power as of truly divine origin, went on to depose Queen Elizabeth and free her subjects from all allegiance to her'—even to the point, though he does not mention this, of encouraging persons of 'right motives' to 'rid the world of that evil woman.' On the whole, he prefers the 'viewpoint of the Lambeth Conference' on birth control. But of course, Lambeth is not Rome. He tells us that what he really fears, and well he may, is the Catholic habit 'of enthroning human reason in theory and of deposing it in practice.' The medical and scientific essays in this book seem incontrovertible. The writers tell us, what most of us already knew, that their Church's pronouncements about sex and marriage are based on imperfect knowledge and an inevitable lack of experience. What, asks one contributor (Rosemary Ruether from Claremont) in a cry that comes truly from the heart, can an unmarried priest know of sex except as 'a purely egotistic drive' or in the context of fornication? The living, growing relationship of a happy marriage, the unselfish yet spontaneous use of sex to make this growth possible, in love, in companionship, how can this be helped by such heartless and ignorant instruction from the Church, as to be continent, or to use the 'safe period'? It is of course discussion of the safe period that involves the hierarchy in those details of almost laughable complication and indecency I have referred to, resulting in pronouncements which have been defined, justly, I think, as 'a sure guide to misery and muddle.' Vigorously, Dr Ruether weighs in: 'Anybody who has tried to live by the temperature-taking, glucose-testing, chartmaking routine imposed by the rhythm method with its artificial manipulation of the whole relationship can scarcely be led to see this as any real spiritual discipline.'

What anxiety—for the 'safe period' is hardly a happy name for it —what neurosis, and what a danger to marriage lies in this method.

And of course, to the outsider, what nonsense it must appear. If you once allow the intention to control birth, why cavil at the means? One contributor quotes the odds against conception when no preventive is used. And indeed the Church's whole attitude in this matter does seem to come rather close to the bookies' field—as if the odds against the life force were somehow 'unfair' with contraceptives, 'fair' only with rhythm. A cry from another contributor, that the Church does not seem to realise 'how difficult sex is' also goes home. It often occurred to me, while reading *Casti Conubii*, that the advice given there by Pope Pius XI—as to prayers and holy pictures, that the ambience of religion might embrace those about to embrace —would, if faithfully carried out, render contraceptives superfluous. Meanwhile the verdict waits. And what is the loving, faithful Catholic to do? A contributor quotes St Augustine: '*Ama et fac quod vis.*' He may decide, this loving faithful one—and for the moment keep it to himself, if his confessor does not question directly—that true love permits the unselfish use of whatever method of contraception he chooses. Soon the Church may agree. Then he will not have to keep it secret.

Encounter, July 1965

A LIFE OF CHRIST

(Jesus In His Time by M. Daniel-Rops, Eyre & Spottiswoode)

The author of this new life of Christ is a Roman Catholic scholar who writes vigorously and argues without rancour. Roman and Jewish historical documents, the New Testament and the Fathers are his chief sources. And over all, to interpret and command, is the Catholic Church.

What will the religious-minded agnostic make of this book? He will find much that is uncomfortable. In the matter of disputed texts M. Daniel-Rops is a little airy. Scholars who disagree with him are called 'fanciful' (and sometimes 'hysterical'). Of the Virgin Birth he says 'the subject is by its nature refractory to the methods of controversy.' Particularly uncomfortable are these words: 'Pious falsifiers, of whom there were many . . .' *Have they all been accounted for?*

He is good about the Roman world, but here again one feels uneasy. The Romans, he says, are like the English in India, caring nothing for the people or their customs, requiring only that the governed shall keep quiet. If M. Daniel-Rops can so misunderstand a recent situation (for British rule in India produced as well as careful Governors many fine scholars of Indian life, arts and religion) may he not also be off the mark sometimes in the remoter situations of this book? He is mild with Pilate in the great trial scene and pauses— no reason why he should not—to wonder whether the lady Pilate may not have been Augustus Caesar's granddaughter . . . But he is severe with the Jews. And one does not much like the way he writes about women. To describe the Virgin Mary as 'a good little wife and mother, modest, well-trained and obedient to her husband' does scant justice to the fiery authoress of the Magnificat. And there are too many dusty references to 'women's intuition' and so on.

I do not wish to underrate the book's merits. It carries well; the familiar people, for centuries so loved and so detested, are full flesh and blood (not for nothing is M. Daniel-Rops also a novelist). But our religious-minded agnostic will come away hungry. He will see in this Christ a lofty and indomitable Being, whose masterful convictions, growing stronger, drove Him finally to death. In a fearful mood, he will remember that these convictions, never fully uttered in Christ's lifetime, were made explicit by the Church and hedged with penalties. At which point he may be tempted to quote Gibbon in a similar context: 'The sword of a Military Order, assisted by the terrors of the Inquisition, was sufficient to remove every objection of profane criticism.'

There is so much one would like to know. Why is there no *taedium vitae* in the New Testament–there is plenty of it in the Old? Is it not interesting to compare Eve's argument, so curiously invented by Milton in the Tenth Book of 'Paradise Lost,' with Mary's great '*fiat mihi* . . .'? Eve, you will remember (it is just after the expulsion from the Garden), says in effect: If all our children are to be condemned to discomfort in this world and the probability of eternal torment in the next, would it not be better not to have any children? How different is Mary's fiery acceptance. It *was* fiery. She does not passively accept the will of God, she carries it like a banner. Eve sides with Death (or rather Milton does, but of course he quickly pulled himself together). Mary stands, 'battle-arrayed,' as Francis Thompson saw her, in the forefront of the forces of life.

But the fact is some people do not want eternal life; they would rather, if possible, 'storm back through the gates of birth.' Such people never seem to crop up in the New Testament . . . And then the suicide rate in this Roman world–the servile part of it–was low. This is surprising (it surprised Seneca), seeing how abominably the Romans treated their slaves. Four hundred crucified (as M. Daniel-Rops reminds us) because a Senator was assassinated–men, women and children, *his* slaves. One wonders why people want to live in the past . . . This is an interesting book which stirs many thoughts; but it casts no spells, as our English Bible does, our dangerous Bible.

Observer, 19 February 1956

THE WHEAT
AND THE TARES

(*Jesus Rediscovered* by Malcolm Muggeridge, Fontana)

Mr Muggeridge has become a great admirer and lover of Jesus–as he sees Jesus. I suppose everybody, even the most orthodox Christian, sees his own Jesus. It is very interesting to look at other people's Jesuses. So often one is aware that the truest feeling of love exists, but then as one looks at the Beloved, it is not the Beloved's features we see, but those of the Lover–not perhaps quite as the Lover is, but as he would like to be if he were not so sinful. As we should expect, Mr Muggeridge's Jesus is very different from, say, the Jesus of a Dominican monk at the time of the Inquisition, detailed for torturing misbelievers. Different, too, from the Jesus who inspired Scottish Protestants to emblazon on their banners 'Jesus No Quarter'.

Well, let us look at Mr Muggeridge's Jesus. First, he is not God. He is a man like us, but in some special way that is not explained he is the Son of God. Mr Muggeridge is very severe with people who want definitions, but definitions sometimes are what we do want. This unexplained 'Son of God', according to Mr Muggeridge, showed to all mankind the Way of Life: that we must die to be born again, that we must be poor, that a man must lose his life in order to gain it, that the Kingdom of Heaven is within. How beautiful the words of Jesus in the New Testament are, and of course one is tempted, with Mr Muggeridge, not quite to ask what they *mean*: as to what, for example, our unhappy race is meant to do in the matter of taking no thought for the morrow or rendering unto Caesar the things that are Caesar's.

Some very nasty things are Caesar's, including Caesar's punishments. Christ's words here seem to cut at the root of all political reform, in the same way that his words 'the poor ye have always with you' seem to cut at the root of social reform. Mr Muggeridge, who might be described as a lay preacher of the castigating kind, has a great hatred of reformers. He thinks they have done and are doing a great deal more harm than Machiavelli. But the fact is Machiavelli would never have freed slaves or tried to remove abuses in canon and civil law.

It seems to me very curious that in this book (a collection of lectures, sermons, broadcasts and newspaper articles), Mr Muggeridge, for all his professed love for the Lover of Mankind, the Crucified, the All-Giving Lamb, should display such hatred and contempt for his fellow-men, especially for those in power. Hatred and contempt beget hatred and contempt, so one must be careful here. But why exactly should the Archbishop of Canterbury and Professor Hoyle be picked upon for vituperation? And all prime ministers and governors? Somebody has to govern. But of course thoughts like this might lead to gratitude (that that *somebody* is not we), and gratitude is not what Mr Muggeridge feels. Yet if somebody had not governed, and endeavoured through government to make people a little less oppressed, I think a great many things in this book might have cost him his ears or even his life. How can he even turn the bath tap on without involving the law and government he so despises?

However, to get back to Jesus. There are several things Mr Muggeridge leaves out of his book, such as Christ's fiercer sayings—about Hell, for instance—but also the marvellous words about the tares growing alongside the wheat. So that all people, even the Archbishop of Canterbury, have some wheat in their lives and work as well as tares, and some wheat in their hearts. This is surely true, too, of the Mary and Martha story (on which also he does not dilate). Not that one person must be Mary and another person Martha, but that we must be both and put up with being one or the other as the moment demands. And who, faced, say, with a wife and family to support, a harsh employer, or harsh employees, to please, would not prefer to be Mary? Jesus of course was particularly blessed in having so little experience of being Martha—with his own carpentry business up to the age of 30 and then the flower-like wandering and teaching which Mr Muggeridge so beautifully describes, making the words and the landscape seem truly flower-like.

Mr Muggeridge sees Jesus as a poet and a prophet, a teacher and a good man; but if he was no more than this, he was not a very good man, because he claimed to be God, and good men do not make false claims. The Church has based her faith on the 'fact' that he did so claim, and the texts seem to bear it out. Of course you may say the texts have been tampered with, 'written up' by pious editors and forged, but if that is so, what else has also been forged? Christ lived a flower-like life, with no children or wife to worry him, or any money difficulties; he died the hideous Roman death—how many went that way, lingering often for four days upon the cross?—and his teaching, his beautiful words, open to such various interpretations and so variously interpreted, live on. Would they do so if the Christian Church had not taken Caesar's place, assumed the purple and ruled the world? I think not, for the Church made his words their holy book and thus ensured their survival. Which brings us back again to the wheat and the tares, the Marys and Marthas of life, and to the uses as well as the abuses of power.

Listener, 26 June 1969

SMUDGERS AND MEDDLERS

(*The New English Bible*, Cambridge and Oxford Standard edition; with *Apocrypha*; Library edition *Old Testament*; *Apocrypha*; *New Testament*)

When a new translation of the Bible comes along, one wants to rush at once upon comparisons. For however beautiful the book may look, and this New English Bible looks very beautiful, it must stand to be measured against the two great translations of our language—the Authorised (1611) and Revised (1881) versions.

First, a few facts. This work was begun in 1946 and the New Testament part of it published in 1961 and gone over again since. We now have the Old and New Testaments, and the Apocrypha, in one volume. Many learned church and chapel men, and men distinguished in literature (assisted by one woman, Mrs Anne Ridler), have been engaged upon it. The pages are printed straight across. Footnotes are brief and often oddly introduced: 'some witnesses read . . .' No psalm holds a candle to Cranmer, or has the beautiful 'Selah' left in (meaning 'a musical pause or stress', not 'hurrah'). Chapter headings are less lively than in AV. We look in vain for 'Saul seeketh to a witch of En-dor.' Many passages are set out as poetry, that we knew were poetry before, from the beautiful older verse-breaks and punctuation, and from the sound. The 'thou' form is retained only when people are praying.

One need hardly state the purpose of the book. It is (as usual) to bring the Bible up to date, that is to put it into current, and dignified, English, to brush up meanings in the light of modern knowledge, and to clarify the text where this seems useful (e.g., St Paul). I do not think they do clarify St Paul very much, and they do not help the reader by failing to mention, as AV does, that Hebrews is by him* and by putting 'Letters' (but leaving the 'of') instead of 'Epistles'. 'Letter *of* Paul to the Romans' sounds awkward; it should be 'from'. I like the look of the columnless page, but actually AV, with its two columns of clear print and narrower centre column for notes and cross-references, is in the long run easier to read. Strangely enough, though their wish was to root out archaisms, the translators have succeeded in introducing some new ones. I noticed a 'betide' in Habakkuk which is not in fact there.

Let us come now to the key passages. First, the Our Father. Cranmer's Prayer Book rendering of this is of course the best. NEB (i.e., this New English Bible), indicating in a footnote how greatly the texts vary, gives: 'Father, thy name be hallowed.' You might think, having swallowed the archaicism of 'hallowed', they would leave 'trespasses'. But no, we have 'And forgive us our sins' followed by 'for we too forgive all who have done us wrong'. Weak. The problem sentence of this great prayer—'Lead us not into temptation'—becomes 'do not bring us to the test'. This fails to clear Almighty God of the implied charge of cat-and-mouse behaviour to his children; and must of course, for English sporting ears, have another very unfortunate connotation.

With hope paling a little, we come to the Magnificat. NEB: 'Tell out my soul the greatness of the Lord/Rejoice, rejoice my spirit in God my saviour.' *All right*, one supposes, but hardly in the field with great Cranmer's Prayer Book: 'My soul doth magnify the Lord: and my spirit hath rejoiced in God my saviour.' NEB limps on: 'So tenderly has he looked upon his servant, humble as she is.' What a good thing this servant is a she, one might otherwise wonder whether God or the servant was 'humble'. But does it not make one sicken, that Cranmer's great hymn should be so cast awry? My word, in the face of Rome's glib sanctifications, surely the English church might do something to honour the martyred Cranmer, Archbishop and poet: 'Mocked by the priests of Mary Tudor, given to the flames,/ Flinching and overcoming the flinching, Cranmer.' I see 'girl' is used—boldly—for Mary: '. . . the angel Gabriel was sent . . . with a message for a girl betrothed to a man named Joseph' ('betrothed' hardly seems to go with it). The 'boy' Jesus is mentioned and we also, rather surprisingly, get 'boy' in association with Noah. NEB: 'Lamech was 187 years old when he begot a son. He named him Noah, saying: "This boy will bring us relief from our work . . ." ' but fails to note, as AV does, that Noah means 'rest' or 'comfort'; so a point is lost. NEB also tells us that Lot's wife 'turned' (not 'was turned') into a pillar of salt. This suggests a vegetable process and is rather weak. A pity they could not embody a comment I once read on this passage: 'In this rich oil-bearing district' (wrote the commentator, a mining engineer by profession) 'it is probable that Lot's wife was turned into a pillar of asphalt, not salt.'

The angels' greeting to the shepherds is very clumsy: '. . . on earth his peace for men on whom his favour rests'. But at least a footnote ('Some witnesses read . . . his favour towards men') leaves the way open for AV's 'on earth peace, good will toward men', which is so much more divinely generous. It is interesting that Eliot in *Murder in the Cathedral* had the sense to quote this passage in AV's wording, yet in his film script of the same play weakened and gave us the hedged blessing: especially as this is now shown to be linguistically unnecessary.

Another great key passage is Ecclesiastes 12. The best version of this, beyond any doubt, is the Revised Version:

> Remember also thy Creator in the days of thy youth, or ever the evil days come, and the years draw nigh, when thou shalt say, I have no pleasure in them./Or ever the sun, and the light, and the moon and the stars, be darkened, and the clouds return after the rain.

Again, I suppose the translators have not done too badly with this, but, as usual, for all their good minds and better intentions, they have put a smudge on it. And why say 'with' the rain instead of 'after'? 'After' gives such a forlorn feeling, as someone who hoped the rain had gone away. When words that are part of our language are changed, and no good gained, it angers one: e.g. (RV Job 38), 'Then the Lord answered Job out of the whirlwind, and said: Who is this that darkeneth counsel by words without knowledge?' NEB bleats: 'Then the Lord answered Job out of the tempest: Who is this whose ignorant words cloud my design in darkness?' (who indeed!) Leviathan of course becomes a whale: (AV) 'Canst thou draw out leviathan with a fish hook?' A problem one may admit (but it could have been solved in a footnote) is the loss in modern English of 'watch' meaning to stay awake. So when Christ says (RV) 'Take ye heed, watch and pray', and to Peter, 'What, could ye not watch with me one hour? Watch and pray, that ye enter not into temptation', NEB has: 'Stay awake and pray that you may be spared the test'. ('Put' to the test, or, grimmer still, 'put' to the question, is I *suppose* what they have in mind with all these 'tests'.)

Everything that was bright is dulled, what was sharp, blunted. Does their great labour, then, serve only to smudge and betray? Another famous passage: here the eerie Habakkuk (AV) curses table-turners and witches: 'Woe unto him that saith to the wood, Awake.' Superb. NEB: 'Woe betide him who says to the wood, Wake up.' Abysmal. The splendid 1 Peter, 2: 17 says: 'Honour all men. Love the brotherhood. Fear God. Honour the king.' NEB does not like these mighty imperatives. Also it is shaky on 'fear' God (though in

208

Proverbs it allows 'The fear of the Lord is the beginning of knowledge'). So we have: 'Give due honour to everyone: love to the brotherhood . . . honour to the sovereign.' People have lost their right hands for no worse than this.

John 1 is generally regarded as a key passage for translators; though actually the problem here rests in the meaning attached to *Logos*, a matter for theologians versed in the mystifications of Greek gnosticism and not for translators. Authorised and RV: 'In the beginning was the Word, and the Word was with God, and the Word was God.' These sentences run crystal clear. What do our meddlers do with them? 'When all things began, the Word already was . . .' (Was *what*? 'was' alone in this sense is not current English.) Yet more: the strong and beautiful AV 'Thou fool, this night shall thy soul be required of thee' becomes 'You fool, this very night you must surrender your life' (another manufactured archaicism: 'very'). Christ's beautiful words (AV) 'Fear not, little flock; for it is your Father's good pleasure to give you the kingdom' become at our smudgers' hands: 'Have no fear, little flock; for your Father has chosen to give you the Kingdom.' And this (for AV John 10:37): 'If I am not acting as my Father would, do not believe me.'

The New English Bible might be good enough—if we had never had King James's and the Revised Version. To smudge, to weaken, to blunt, to make pallid, every beautiful word and the thought it carries—was this worth 24 years' work, with the alterations so trivial, nothing to make even the attempt worth while? But let not the friends of mediocrity be cast down. For nowadays we do not often have the AV or the RV or great Cranmer's Prayer Book. The churches and chapels have chosen the new translations. They think they are right for the times we live in. But nothing that is second-best is right.

New Statesman, 20 March 1970

---

* In a letter to the *New Statesman*, 27 March 1970, Paul A. Welsby pointed out that contemporary scholars do not accept that the Letter to the Hebrews was written by Paul. He also noted that the Lord's Prayer and the angel's song at the Nativity must be translated in the light of texts not available to Cranmer and the translators of the Authorised Version. Stevie did not write in response, but told Anthony Thwaite that her errors were the result of 'sheer ignorance'. (Eds.)

POEMS

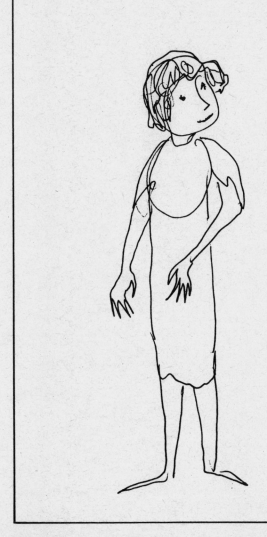

A Portrait

I never know what to say
When I'm in company,
I feel quite tonguetied and shy,
I'm a perfect misery.
It really is tantalising,
And after the Education I've had
Surprising.
There's nothing I'd rather say
Than something Edifying and Unusual.

Via Media Via Dolorosa

There's so much to be said on either side,
I'll be dumb.
There's so much to be said on either side,
I'll hold my tongue.
For years and years I never said a word,
Now I have lost the art: my voice is never heard,
For my apprehension
Snaps beneath the tension
Of what is to be said on either side.

Portrait

Mr. Petty-Pie
Keeps his masterpieces in his head,
He is a better tactician than I.

Silent, silent thought.
Never to be brought
To the printed page,
Weave a subtle shade.
O'er the facey-fie
Of little Petty-Pie;
And may its lineaments continue to suggest
A wisdom too profound to be expressed

He preferred . . .

He preferred to be a hearthrug sage
To risking the cold opinion of the world,
Somewhere within him there had been
A lack of courage, a nerve failed.
He was not happy: but then he was not miserable
He had money. Sometimes he wrote.
You might say his character was cast upon him,
And with it that luck's lot.

The Midwife

The Midwife guards the mother's health
But she herself is on the shelf,
She cannot have a little child,
And that is why she looks so wild.

Mort's Cry

Oh, Lamb of God I am
Too sharp, too tired,
Make me more amiable, Oh Lamb,
Less tired,
No longer what I am.

So cried poor Colonel Mort, I heard him cry,
And yet he was a good man and fought energetically,
His men loved him, his country too, and did not find him tearful,
Then what a funny cry for him! I thought it made him wonderful.

Change me, Lord Lamb,
Leave me not as I am.

The Word

Oh where is the word
Said sweet Sally Soo
Oh! where is the word I seek
It cannot be true
There is no word from you
To put in my velvet cheek
But the echoes ran
And the silence came
And alone in the cold
She is much the same
Oh! where is the word oh! where is it pray
Don't keep me waiting all night and day.

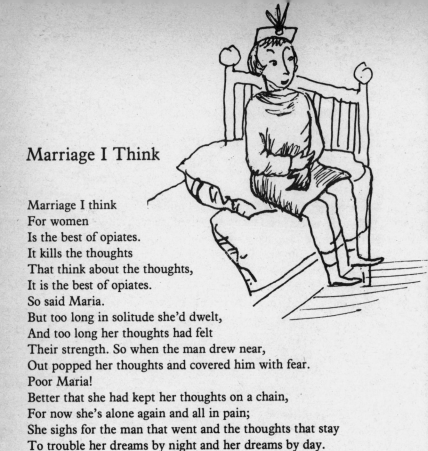

Marriage I Think

Marriage I think
For women
Is the best of opiates.
It kills the thoughts
That think about the thoughts,
It is the best of opiates.
So said Maria.
But too long in solitude she'd dwelt,
And too long her thoughts had felt
Their strength. So when the man drew near,
Out popped her thoughts and covered him with fear.
Poor Maria!
Better that she had kept her thoughts on a chain,
For now she's alone again and all in pain;
She sighs for the man that went and the thoughts that stay
To trouble her dreams by night and her dreams by day.

Ruory

Ruory loved the agèd Edith
She lived in kindness with
And ever had done and ever had done
In a sweet domestic kingdom.

And to Aunt Edith the cry went up
From many an uneven stance
For Ruory's soul was pitched awry
And often went unbalanced.

Without that lady's help
Who so firmly behaved
Ruory would not be here at all
But off to the icy glades.

Then God bless Edith's kindness
And her strongmindedness
And Lord God never let Ruory forget
The gracious mercies her path beset.

Wife's Lament at Hereford

The beast
At the end of the lane
Has risen again

And spread his slime
On my furniture

Why must the Wye
Rise so high? He is
Such a pretty runner between banks.

Why does the Wild destroy
Peace and joy? the Unhappy
Need tears to make him happy?

Mother Love

Mother love is a mighty benefaction
The prop of the world and its population
If mother love died the world would rue it
No money would bring the women to it.

The Octopus

Darling little Tom and Harry,
When time comes for you to marry,
Lullaby,
Mother will be close at hand,
Close at hand

Little girlies, you who marry
Darling Tom and darling Harry
By and by,
Understand
Mother will be close at hand,
Close at hand

Lulu

I do not care for Nature,
    She does not care for me;
You can be alone with a person,
    You can't be alone with a tree.

Henry Wilberforce

Henry Wilberforce as a child
Was much addicted to the pleasures of the wild;
He observed Nature, saw, remembered,
And was by a natural lion dismembered.

(1) Like This
(Young man in an Asylum)

It must be some disease I have
To feel so lonely like this,
And not for company I see
The others like this, like this,
It only makes more isolate
To see another like this,
Oh nobody like this *likes* this,
Or likes another like this.

(2) Like This
(Young girl in an Asylum)

The greatest love?
The greatest love?
There is no love at all,
What love means is, To speak to me,
Not leave me in the cold.

How very cold it is out here,
How bitterly the wind blows,
O Love, why did you dedicate me
To the snows?

There is an Old Man

There is an old man
Who sleeps in the park
When he has no light
He sleeps in the dark
When he has no fire
He sleeps in the cold
Oh why do you do this
Old man, so old?

I sleep in the park
And by day I roam
I would rather do this
Than live in a Home
I was put in one once
Where the meth men were
And they stole my money
And kicked me downstair.

So now I sleep
In the lonely park
And I do not mind
If it's cold and dark
As soon as day breaks
I roam up and down
And when night returns
To my park I come.

Oh living like this is much jollier for me
Than anything I've found for the Elderly.

The Horrible Man

He is a most horrible man,
Why look?
He is a horrible man

He has done something at which the
    crocodile
Grew wan

He has never done anything at all—no,
    not by chance,
At which the crocodile kept
Countenance

He is a most horrible man

Mabel

In her loneliness Mabel
Found the hiss of the unlit gas
Companionable
And in a little time, dying
Sublime

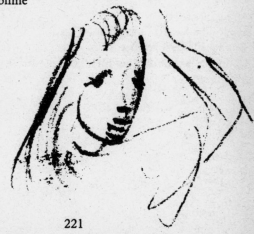

The Lesson

Is it Claudius or Clowdius? my little child Harry said,
Harry with his innocent look on his Latin studies.
Ah my son, my little one, draw near and hear
The Claudian story. First it was Clowdian—
The patrician families always preserved the diphthong,
As nowadays we English do too, speaking Latin, unless it is Eton.
When Claudius went to obtain the vote of the Plebs,
They laughed—his mama, his papa, his relations laughed,
'He is calling it Clodius now, the silly fool, he thinks it will fetch
  'em'.
(The common people were naturally slovenly, it was Clo for
  them.)
But he wasn't such a silly fool because it did fetch them.
By and by the common pronunciation seeped slowly up
And now is in general use on the Continent.

Call me 'Arry, said the innocent child I was speaking to.
We are not a new family, I said coldly, and I have no vote for
  you.

Sapphic
(in mixed speech)

The mune ha gien her loicht an' gan
The stardies eek are flee
Upon ma bett in durchet nich'
Ah lane ah lee.

The Royal Dane

Now is come the horrible mome,
When I to my sulphureous home,
Must go'ome, must go'ome.

Our Doggy

First he sat, and then he lay,
And then he said: I've come to stay.
And that is how we acquired our doggy Pontz.
He is all right as dogs go, but not quite what one wants.
Because he talks. He talks like you and me.
And he is not you and me, he is made differently.
You think it is nice to have a talking animal?
It is not nice. It is unnatural.

My Tortoise

I had a sweet tortoise called Pye
Wabbit.
He ate dandelions, it was
His habit.
Pye Wabbit, Pye Wy-et,
It was more than a habit, it was
His diet.
All the hot summer days, Pye
Wy-et, Pye Wiked-it,
Ate dandelions. I lay on the grass flat to see
How much he liked it.
In the autumn when it got cold, Pye Wiked-it, Pye
Wy-bernator
Went to sleep till next spring. He was
A hibernator.
First he made a secret bed for the winter,
To lie there.
We loved him far too much ever
To spy where.
Why does his second name change every time?
Why, to make the rhyme.
Pye our dear tortoise
Is dead and gone.
He lies in the tomb we built for him, called
'Pye's Home'.
Pye, our dear tortoise,
We loved him so much.
Is he as dear to you now
As he was to us?

As Sways

As sways the gentle sycamore
Beneath the winds of heaven,
So sways my inconstant heart, dear love,
When you are far away;
So sways my inconstant heart, dear love,
And shall for ever sway.
No use for you to say:
'Better the oak by tempest riven
Than nodding sycamore beneath
    the winds of heaven'

Tom Snooks the Pundit

'Down with creative talent
(I have none)
Down with creative talent,
Kick it down!'

So cried Tom Snooks, a literary pundit,
The tender talent lay where he had stunn'd it,
He kicked the poor thing dead quite easily and then he cried:
'Hats off, my friends, it was a genius died.'

Oh long live Tom, long live his reputation,
(His proper name I'll give on application.)

Miss Snooks, Poetess

Miss Snooks was really awfully nice
And never wrote a poem
That was not really awfully nice
And fitted to a woman,

She therefore made no enemies
And gave no sad surprises
But went on being awfully nice
And took a lot of prizes.

The Old Poet

There was an old poet lay dying
And as he lay dying, said he (said he)
I'd 've done much better as a literurry editor
Than a-writing of poetry
Hey ho, hey ho,
A-writing of poetry.

A literurry editor has great sensibility
Cried the old poet, cried he,
Why sometimes the creature's even written a poem
God help us all, said he,
And got it published, and got it published, and got it published
Coincidentally
Hey ho, hey ho,
Coincidentally.

Then the poor old poet turned on his side
And to save putting another shilling in the gasmeter
Died,
Hey ho, hey ho,
Died.

They Killed

They killed a poet by neglect
And treating him worse than an insect
They said what he wrote was feeble
And should never be read by serious people

Serious people, serious people,
I should think it was serious to be such people.

On Coming Late To Parnassus

Upon his loneliness and pain
Fame broke
Too strong a wave for him
And slew.

Accented

I *love* you, Muse,
In your *arms* I lie,
Speak to me, *feed* me,
I am not your *enemy*.

Two Friends

I only asked my friends to be friendly and polite,
I found them indifferent and censorious;
The one I left to silence, the other to reproach:
God send me over all such friends victorious

I Forgive You

I forgive you, Maria,
Things can never be the same,
But I forgive you, Maria,
Though I think you were to blame.
I forgive you, Maria,
I can never forget,
But I forgive you, Maria,
Kindly remember that.

Revenge

Revenge, Timotheus cries, and in that shout
There's all there is about it and about
Between this man and me, whate'er befall
There is no word more to be said at all.

None of the Other Birds

None of the other birds seem to like it
It sits alone on the corner edge of the outhouse gutter
They do not even dislike it
Enough to bite it
So it sits alone unbitten
It is always alone.

The holiday

The time is passing now
And will come soon
When you will be able
To go home.

The malice and the misunderstanding
The loneliness and pain
Need not in this case, if you are careful,
Come again.

Say goodbye to the holiday, then,
To the peace you did not know,
And to the friends who had power over you,
Say goodbye and go.

Sigh No More

Sigh no more ladies nor gentlemen at all,
Whatever fate attend or woe befall;
Sigh no more, shed no bitter tear,
Another hundred years you won't be here.

Telly-me-Do

Telly me do,
Do telly me too!
You have told all the others
Including your mother's
Companion
So telly me too!

But they would not,
I felt quite cut off,
So I thought I would try
To burn their house down to make them die,
But they only laughed and cried:
'Telly me do, Telly me do',
Again and again, to mock me.
Oh what a lot of pain!

My Earliest Love

This is my earliest love, sweet Death,
That was my Love from my first breath.

When One

When one torments another without cease
It cannot but seem
It cannot but seem
That Death is the only release.

When two torment each other in this way
The one by being tormented easily
The other by tormenting actively
It cannot but seem
It cannot but seem
That Death, as he must come happily,
Should not delay.

Ah this unhappy Two
It seems as if
They never could leave off
Tormenting. And so nervily
All is done,
Death, quieten them.

Why do I think of Death
As a friend?
It is because he is a scatterer,
He scatters the human frame
The nerviness and the great pain,
Throws it on the fresh fresh air
And now it is nowhere.
Only sweet Death does this,
Sweet Death, kind Death,
Of all the gods you are best.

When I Awake

When I awake
The whole returning flood of consciousness
Is hateful to me
And Death, too often on my lips,
Becomes my shadower.

O Death, Death, Death, deceitful friend,
Come pounce, and take,
And make
An end at once.

Beautiful

Man thinks he was not born to die
But that's no proof he wasnt,
And those who would not have it so
Are very glad it isnt.

Why should man wish to live for ever?
His term is merciful,
He riseth like a beaming plant
And fades most beautiful,

And his rising and his fading
Is most beautiful.

Not, not the one without the other,
But always the two together,
Rising fading, fading rising,
It is really not surprising
To find this beautiful.

Roaming

Far from his home he came, the old person,
Not comely or of much account,
People thought he was a shifty *Eulenspiegel*
Whose nose was out of joint.

Yet how could a man that was shifty
Look so purposeful,
And when he was looking purposeful
Seem beautiful?

He had excellent manners too
And never spoke of Heaven
Only when he came close up
You saw he was driven.

Do I believe in heaven? (he asked)
What is belief?
I only know when I speak of Death
I experience relief.

But since I was sent to roam
And given a place to roam in,
Roam I will with a will of tears.
Was this wise of him?

Yes, he was wise to say it
For being kindly and able to reason
The people saw they could serve him best
By giving him poison.

When he was dead they buried him
And wrote on his tomb:
Eulenspiegel
Who used to roam.

Landrecie

What shall I say to the gentlemen, mother,
They stand in the doorway to hear what is said,
Waiting and watching and listening and laughing,
Is there no word that will send them away?

What shall I say to the gentlemen, mother,
What shall I say to them, must I say nothing?
If I say nothing, then will they not harm us,
Will they not harm us and shall we not suffer?

What shall I say to the gentlemen, mother?
See, they are waiting, and will not depart.
Closed are your eyelids, your lips closed in silence
Cannot instruct me, oh what shall I answer?

Childhood and Interruption

Now it is time to go for a walk
Perhaps we shall go for a walk in the park
And then it will be time to play until dark
Not quite, when the shadows fall it is time to go home
It is always time to do something I am never torn
With a hesitation of my own
For always everything is arranged punctually
I am guarded entirely from the tension of anxiety
Walk tea-supper bath bed I am a very happy child really
And underneath the pram cover lies my brother Jake
He is not old enough yet to be properly awake
He is alone in his sleep; no arrangement they make
For him can touch him at all, he is alone,
For a little while yet, it is as if he had not been born
Rest in infancy, brother Jake; childhood and interruption come
    swiftly on.

The Ballet of the Twelve Dancing Princesses
Hayes Court, June 1939

The schoolgirls dance on the cold grass
The ballet of the twelve dancing princesses
And the shadows pass

Over their cold feet
Above in the cold summer sky the clouds mass

The icy wind blows across the laurel bushes
The sky is hard blue and gray where a cloud rushes
The sky is icy blue it is like the night blue where a star pushes.

But it is not night
It is daytime on an English lawn.
The scholars dance. The weather is as fresh as dawn.
Dawn and night are the webs of this summer's day
Dawn and night the tempo of the children's play.

Who taught the scholars? Who informed the dance?
Who taught them so innocent to advance
So far in a peculiar study? They seem to be in a trance.

It is a trance in which the cold innocent feet pass
To and fro in a hinted meaning over the grass
The meaning is not more ominous and frivolous than the clouds
    that mass.

There is nothing to my thought more beautiful at this moment
Than a vision of innocence that is bound to do something
    equivocal
I sense something equivocal beneath the veneer of an innocent
    spent
Tale and in the trumpet sound of the icy storm overhead there is
    evocable
The advance of innocence against a mutation that is irrevocable
Only in the imagination of that issue joined for a split second is
    the idea beautiful.

Silence

Why do people abuse so much our busy age?
They can withdraw into themselves and not rage
It is better to do this and live in one's own kingdom
Than by raging add to the rage of our busy time.

This is an age when there are too many words,
Silent, silent, silent the waters lie
And the beautiful grass lies silent and this is beautiful,
Why can men then not withdraw and be silent and happy?

It is better to see the grass than write about it
Better to see the water than write a water-song,
Yet both may be painted and a person be happy in the painting,
Can it be that the tongue is cursed, to go so wrong?

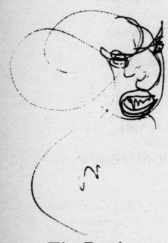

The Pearl

Weep not my pretty boy, grieve not my girl
Mankind is Nature's pearl
Not so much for his beauty, being beautiful,
As in that he's the child of all things irritable.

Sterilization

Carve delinquency away,
Said the great Professor Clay.

A surgical operation is just the thing
To make everybody as happy as a king.

But the great Dostoievsky the Epileptic
Turned on his side and looked rather sceptic.

And the homosexual Mr. Wilde
Sat in the sunshine and smiled and smiled.

And a similarly inclined older ghost in a ruff
Stopped reading his sonnets aloud and said 'Stuff!'

And the certainly eccentric Swift, Crashawe and Donne,
Silently shook hands and thanked God they had gone.

But the egregious Professor Clay
Called on Theopompous and won the day.

And soon all our minds will be flat as a pancake,
With no room for genius, exaltation or heartache.

And our children and theirs will preen, smirk and chatter,
With not even the sense to ask what is the matter.

The Vision

These before the worlds in congress
Stood to sing their songs in song-dress,
Never one was in a wrong dress
Never one was out of tune.

Oh it filled my heart with pity
As, so serious and pretty,
Stood my Race to sing its ditty,
Unsolicited.

The worlds were quite indifferent
As to how the singing went,
If the Race were elegant
They did not care.

But still the people stood and chanted
For to chant was all they wanted,
So their bravery was vaunted
Emptily, emptily.

Yet I was proud to see their singing,
Proud the human race was flinging
Such a song at such a ceiling
Gustily

Then it vanished all away,
Worlds and singers went away;
Nothing now is left to say
But this: it was a vision.

Oh Thou Pale Intellectual Brow

Oh thou pale intellectual brow—
The angel said. The boy replied:

The intellect is but a toy
And I a medium-sensual boy
Can hardly hear you now.

This doll that lies against my side
Is easy and agreeable,
And so I like to play with her,
Come, be sensible.

The doll rose up with awful frown
And with the angel fled the town
The boy waits on, and he will play
With anything that comes his way.

He should go up and after them,
Pray heaven he may do so in time,
God send him back his angel friend,

And all the women cried Amen.

From the French

I have plunged in a poem of the sea.
Alight with stars at first and growing milky
It ate the pretty blues and greens as I went down
And turned quite dark. There,
Like piece of flotsam torn about and stained,
A pensive corpse came floating to my side.
It was at this great depth I was aware
Of crimson flowing in the cold dark sea
All crimson, all bright red. I thought it was
As if our human love lay bleeding there,
Bleeding in anger, bleeding yet alive;
And I was glad, although I was not happy,
Because it was alive. The rest was dead.

Salon d'Automne

One thousand and one naked ladies
With a *naïveté*
At once pedantic and unsympathetic
Deck the walls
Of the Salon d'Automne.
This is the Slap school of art,
It would be nice
To smack them
Slap, slap, slap,
That would be nice.
It is possible
One might tire of smacking them
In time
But not so soon
As one tires of seeing them.
We too
Have our pedantic and unsympathetic
School,

It used to show
A feeling for animals.
The English are splendid with animals,
There was The Stag at Bay
And Faithful unto Death,
And Man's Best Friend the horse this time
Usually under gunfire,
The English are splendid with animals.
That older school
Was perhaps
On an intellectual level
With the Salon d'Automne.
Nowadays, of course,
We are more advanced:
The bad modern painter
Has lost the *naïveté*
Of that earlier school
And in its place
Has developed a talent
For making the work of his betters
Seem stale
By unspirited
Imitation.
Really
This is more tiring
Than the thousand and one
Naked ladies.

O Lord!
From 2nd Messenger's Speech To King Pentheus, Bacchae

This god then, O lord whoever he is do receive into the city
For not only is he great but also as I have heard
He gave the pain-killing vine to men.
Take away drink, where's Love?
Any pleasure come to that, O lord there is nothing left.

B.B.C. Feature Programme on Prostitution

How hypocritical this dear old fellow is
Mr Something who runs the Nude Theatre,
He tells us it lifts the mind and is artistic
And does no harm in fact it does good
(And makes money. Beg pardon no that he did not say.)

And then he said, My girls don't do so much
Harm as those stunted spinsters who write poison letters
And a good many other of your goody people who fancy
   themselves
Et cetera. Et cetera. And how artistic it is.

In the end you'd hardly have got this fine old creature to admit
Some girls off the streets are just as good as those on it.

The girls themselves said, Chaps
Often came behind the scenes afterwards and said, Ten
Fifteen or twenty pounds, and yes it was tempting.

After that in this interesting radio feature
The prostitutes spoke with an interviewing clergyman.
What do you think sin is? he asked 'Judy',
Judy said it was doing something for nothing,
No, she said, prostitution wasn't wrong

It didn't do nearly so much harm as
Stunted spinsters writing poison letters et cetera
But she wouldn't go to church all the same
As long as she was doing it.

And all of them said it was dangerous
And not really very enjoyable
As often they got carved up or beaten or killed
But there you are, it was twenty pounds a week untaxed
(And a good deal more)
Compared with five in a job, subject to taxation.

So they all admitted money was the thing
(Being plainer than Mr Something, or stupider)
And money, money, not with the old alternative
Of nothing at all, but with not enough for the telly,
And not getting up to catch a bus to the office,

And having pink lampshades, and ultimately
Getting out of it with the money you had invested
And buying a place of your own and being respected.

So you see it's money all the time and how to get it
And not caring about money is what is wicked
And idiots who think like this are always generous
When it comes to paying the price for money. Only
The wise look twice at that price and are parsimonious. Only
The clergyman in this radio programme seemed not stupid, not
    half an idiot.

Satan Speaks

Sit'st now in Heaven? Happy art thou there,
Beloved Milton, my beloved friend,
Sweet singing to th' empyreal choristers
As once so sweetly thou didst sing to men?
What Muse leans on thy heart, in Heaven stayed,
Apt as the Muse of Hell to draw from thee
Chords of upwelling sound, and cadences
Of subtle, intricate imagining?
Thou knowing so well my estate, me King
Of the wide campaign of this royal Hell
Art raped from me and wrapped in heavenly Coat,
Beyond my power to help and without hope.
Sweet singer, in the streets of Heaven exiled,
Keep thou memorial of my passing love,
As I of thee still keep memorial
Fresh in the nostrils of Eternity.
For never Singer ever sang as thou
The Prince of Hell and her unhappy Sons,
My proud compeers, and the high government
Of very Hell.

  Come Milton, come again,
Rouse up thyself, in Heaven too long hast stayed.
Numbed art thou now, and chained in heavy doze
Upon the pavement. Blindly dost thou touch
The harp that only has one tale to tell,
One song to sing, foreordered and scored out
In heavenly manuscript before all worlds.
Canst thou not sin? Canst thou not only think
One little thought against Heaven's Majesty,
A Majesty that is not slow to wrath?
Make essay, mighty Milton, what's to lose?
For if thou canst not sin, thou canst but stay,
And if to sin thou still hast art, all Hell
Waits thy footsteps, and wide the gates are set,
Rank upon rank th' infernal hosts are drawn
To give thee passage, and upon the way
With flambent torches many escorts stand.

Alas for the great land that gave thee birth,
Is her Son lost to her in Heaven's empire?
Is England not to see her Milton here,
Where other sons have honourable place?
While Marlowe sings, and Crashaw's peevish Muse
Still prates of Heaven and gladly suffers Hell,
Is England's Milton not to come again?
Is Milton bound in Heaven and padlocked in?

Alas, alas, for Heaven's ingenious laws
I may not help thee and full well I know
Thou canst not help thyself by heresy,
For once in Heaven no man may further sin,
It is so writ. Farewell, Unfortunate.
An Angel, still couldst thou rebellion raise
To merit overthrow and swift exile,
But thou art Man, redeemed by Jesus' blood,
And where thou sit'st for ever must abide.

Goodnight

Miriam and Horlick spend a great deal of time putting off going
    to bed.
This is the thought that came to me in my bedroom where they
    both were, and she said:
Horlick, look at Tuggers, he is getting quite excited in his head.

Tuggers was the dog. And he was getting excited. So.
Miriam had taken her stockings off and you know
Tuggers was getting excited licking her legs, slow, slow.

It's funny Tuggers should be so enthusiastic, said Horlick nastily,
It must be nice to be able to get so excited about nothing really,
Try a little higher up old chap, you're acting puppily.

I yawned. Miriam and Horlick said Goodnight
And went. It was 2 o'clock and Miriam was quite white
With sorrow. Very well then, Goodnight.

On the Dressing gown lent me by my Hostess the Brazilian Consul in Milan, 1958

Dear Daughter of the Southern Cross
I admit your fiery nature and your loss

Your fiery integrity and your intelligence
I admit your high post and its relevance

And I admit, dear Consuelessa, that your dressing gown
Has wrapped me from the offences of the town

From rain in Milan in a peculiar May
From anger at break of day
From heat and cold as I lay

Wrapped me, but not entirely, from the words I must hear
Thrown between you and him, that were not 'dear'.

Oh that him
Was a problem
Consuelessa, your husband.

He and I ran together in the streets, I think
We grew more English with each drink
And we laughed as we ran in the town
Consuelessa, where then was your dressing gown?

The Portuguese and Italian languages
Drew our laughter in stages
Of infantine rages,
This was outrageous.

Yes, I admit your courage, I heard
Heart steel at the word
That found everything absurd,
The English word I spoke and heard.

Tapping at your heels, Consuelessa,
We were children again, your husband and I,
A worthless couple,

Hanging behind, whining, being slow,
'Where is our wife?' we cry. (This you knew.)
'Give us money' we said, 'you have not given us much'.
We were your kiddies, Consuelessa, out for a touch.

Yet I admit your dressing gown
Wrapped me from the offences of the town
But never from my own
Ah Consuelessa, this I own.

From rain in May
From the cold as I lay
When the servant Cesare had stolen
The electric fire, the only one,
From disappointment too I dare say
Consuelessa,
It is your dressing gown I remember today.

No Matter Who Rides

No matter who rides in my Ford
Nothing happens at all untoward
Because I simply will not
Have it. Have what?
Oh I don't know—well, THAT! In a Ford!

La Robe Chemise

Disarmed off-guard *tendre et soumise*
How foolish of women to abandon *la Robe Chemise*,
Especially Englishwomen with their long backs and bend
    serpentine—
Such figures look best without a waistline.
But of course the Americans would not have it, in that women-
    dominated place
All girls must be bright and brittle and have a tight waist.

Oh under the old trees of Europe, on the soft grass
I sigh for the tender ungirt dress,
Oh bring it back, bring it back, *douce et soumise*,
Bring back to my arms again *la Robe Chemise*.

If you will not allow the implications of this dress's story
Say at least it is comfortable and be hypocritical,
For you cannot, unless you are stupid, not know it is irresistable
To be so off-guard gay tender and vulnerable.

Saint Foam and The Holy Child
A Christmas Legend

On a black horse
A long time ago in a northern forest
Rode Rothga the heathen child.

Rothga, where are you riding?
Said a great witch.
I am not riding to see you,
Said Rothga.

Then came a bear who stood upright
Upon his hind legs: Where are you riding, Rothga,
Not that I mind? Well, not to see you.
And she rode more quickly. Because, she said,
There is not much time.

On, on they went,
The heathen child and her black horse,
Until the forest broke—
And they came to a sea-shore where the great waves
Threw their froth and foam beneath the lights
Of a northern sky.

Rothga left her black horse and ran
Down to the sea's edge. I am in time,
She said, and laughed to see
Riding the greatest of the sea-waves
A Child of Light who cried:
I am new born tonight, in the city of Bethlehem.
Rothga, be sure who I am.

I am sure, said Rothga. You must bless me.

I bless you Rothga, said the Child. I am come to save
All people from the malign witch,
From the indifferent bear
And from the dark forest.
Rothga, take this foam-curd for a token,
It shall never grow dull or grow less.

Rothga went home and said:
Father, mother, we have been blessed by a sea-child
Who gave me this for a token.

Thus it was there came to be built
As it stands today, the Great Church
Of St Foam and the Holy Child
On a northern shore.

Pretty Baby

Sweet baby, pretty baby, I bless thee,
Thou liest so snug and lookst so prettily,
And yet I think you also look imperially.

Why shouldst thou not? If it is Deity
Couches in mother's lap, prettily, prettily,
Then thou art God and canst not sin or feel guilty,

As we can do, for we have our sins innerly,
Sweet baby. Now I think there is a fee
That you must pay for looking happily.

And that is: not to know what being free
From sin means, being sinless. Only we
Can bless and measure that felicity.

But let the angels sing a song for thy birth sweetly,
And we will try to sing songs too, but differently,
For we are earth-born and the song is heavenly.

I thank thee, Lord

I thank thee O Lord for my beautiful bed
Have mercy on those who have none
And may all thy children still happier lie
When they to thy kingdom come.

LETTERS

We have made minimal editorial changes in this selection of Stevie's letters. Stevie frequently suggested pauses by the use of full stops which ordinarily would indicate ellipsis, and we have let these stand. All the letters here are printed in full. Many of them, especially early ones, are written in the conversational, run-on style Stevie invented for her narrator in *Novel on Yellow Paper*. We have preserved that style in the letters, supplying only rarely the odd comma or semicolon, where the meaning might otherwise be obscure. Letters Stevie wrote from her home are designated 'Palmers Green', although she always prefaced this with 1 Avondale Road and sometimes with her telephone number; the address of her office on Southampton Street we have reduced to 'Tower House'; and letters written from the home of her sister Molly Ward-Smith are designated 'Buckfast, S.Devon'. All dates have been standardised, titles of books and journals have been italicised, and typing mistakes corrected except in the case of her last letters when her brain tumour affected her writing: these have been printed as she wrote them. Her spelling mistakes, and her highly individual use of French and German, we have left unaltered. We have only added surnames at the beginning of letters where the reader may be in doubt as to who the recipient is: 'Dear Helen' is always Helen Fowler, 'Dear Rachel', Rachel Marshall, and so on. Notes at the end of this section will, under the respective page numbers, give brief descriptions of names and incidents that may puzzle the reader. All material which appears in square brackets is written by the editors.

Stevie Smith's first novel, *Novel on Yellow Paper*, was published by Jonathan Cape in 1936. Denis Johnston, Irish playwright and author of *The Moon in the Yellow River*, *A Bride for the Unicorn* and other plays, recalls that a letter he sent to Stevie in 1936 praising *Novel on Yellow Paper* began their correspondence and subsequent friendship. The *Listener* reviewer, the poet and critic Edwin Muir, wrote that *Novel on Yellow Paper* 'contains . . . a well-sustained picture of a disillusioned flapper's mind'. The *Spectator* reviewer, Peter Burra, described the novel as 'young Joyce out of Anita Loos' though ultimately he found it 'worth the effort'. 'Minorelizabethismus' was his version of Stevie's jokey word in *Novel on Yellow Paper* and Pompey Casmilus is the narrator of that novel. Elizabeth Bergner opened in J.M. Barrie's *The Boy David* at His Majesty's Theatre in Haymarket but the play closed after a few performances.

Palmers Green
23 September 1936

Dear Denis Johnston,

I feel I must hide my head in the sand now to have had such a stupid picture of you from your first letter but I am so glad too in this way that you have given me this lovely phrase to fix it perfectly for all time it has made me laugh ever since I got your last letter—the arch advances of an aged journalist up to no good. You had better hurry up and put that in a play or I shall use it.

It is very kind of you to ask to see my press cuttings and so here they are because really they are so nice that I must show them to everybody but of course the *Listener* is not so-o-o good I could wring his neck to say that I have the flapper mind. As if there was not already a great deal too much of this about just now with the unhappy conjugation of Bergner and Barrie oh how I detest it my next book will have to be a learned treatise on some subject I have unfortunately not yet been able to think of to counteract this hateful impression.

The *Spectator* too is a little acid and to quote the word they have to be grateful for having from me and to get it so absurdly wrong that is rather funny. I can not even begin to pronounce their version of it what I said was what I said was Minorelizabethanismus.

I have had some very nice letters from people and only one horror from 'Uncle James'—late of Somerset House this is the most utter rubbish on the sex theme in the language of James Douglas yes it is just the stuff for the *Sunday Express*. Now you say that you have in your time been 'for it' well what have you done with these abusive letters I think it is a good idea not to answer them because this uncle creature has written 3 pages of single spaced typescript and surely can anything be more infuriating than to get no reply to that? This uncle was in Dublin at the time of one of the Troubles and he was ambushed how I am beginning to wish that the Irish had shot straight.

I have also had a very grand and complimentary letter from I think I should lead up to it by saying No Less a Person than the director of the Nat. Gallery [Kenneth Clark], he only doesn't like the amount of time I spend talking about the *Bacchae* well that is a pity but it is in now and cannot come out also I like it very much and enjoyed doing it because it comes in so pat upon Miss Hogmanimy and I remember so well acting in this play when I was at school [North London Collegiate] and at the same time I was having to listen to these silly lectures on how babies are born. Clive Bell has also written and John Hayward and the *New Statesman en bloc* they have been peaches.

This is an awfully long letter and all about myself do forgive me. Yes certainly Cape are a scream but I can hardly bear to look them in the face now because I have been so frightful for them with endless last minute corrections and other sorts of frightfulnesses. I am lying very low indeed now about them and saying and doing nothing I think they must be sick of me but if the book goes well perhaps they will forgive me. They are thinking to do some poems of mine in book form but I expect that will depend on the way Pompey gets around.

I hope you are writing another play I should like to have a play on a classical theme not the Private Life of Helen of Troy sort of thing or even *Die Schöne Helena* but something that transcends space and time and is classically-modern without being teaching like Acropolis or facetious that is the worst of all. Of course I am quite dotty about Phaedra myself but perhaps it might be better to do one that Racine has not done. I am awfully stuck on my old Casmilus too but please don't breathe a word to Cape about this because I have already bored them to tears with it Casmilus is a dark name to fight under and he was a most awful twister he is the Phoenician Mercury-Hermes but the fact that he had the right of entrance to (and ahem exit from) hell has always fascinated me what a bore for instance he must have been for Pluto, Minos and Rhadamanthus, pursuing his frightful trivial quarrels into their country and doing a good deal of self-advantageous business on the side I make no bones to say.

I must stop now and quite time too you will say as I have to type some poems.

With best wishes,
Yours sincerely,
Stevie Smith

Rupert Hart-Davis, publisher, author and editor, first met Stevie when she brought *Novel on Yellow Paper* to Jonathan Cape, where he was a director, in 1935 or 1936. Thereafter he saw her very regularly until he joined the army in 1940. After the war, when he founded his own publishing company, they met only occasionally. In March 1937 Cape published Stevie's first book of poems, *A Good Time Was Had By All*. In these years Stevie was employed by Arthur Pearson Ltd where she was secretary to Sir Neville Pearson and Sir Frank Newnes (Sir Phoebus and Sir Frank in Stevie's novels). By August 1937 her office was in Southampton Street, but this letter to Rupert Hart-Davis was sent from her former office at 18 Henrietta Street, W.C. 2.

Sunday [October 1936]

Dear Rupert Hart-Davis,
Here at last are the poems with the beastlies pinned on to make it more fun for everyone. I think *A Good Time Was Had By All* would

be an attractive title for the book—if you really think you can do a book out of them.

The poems are arranged in alphabetical order of first lines—this is the hardest work I have ever done, much worse than writing them. I hope it won't depress you if I tell you that the *N.S.* [*New Statesman*] have copies of some of them and a *lot* more drawings. And this time next year I have no doubt they will still have them, unless you care to take action. If so, please do, and please deal direct with them.

A lot of the poems go to music—some of it my own and some other people's. For instance 'The nearly right and yet not quite' goes beautifully to (I think it is) the Coventry Carol . . . O sisters two (or true), What shall we do, To preserve this day, etc. I don't remember the words of the carol very well but the music is very nice, but again perhaps the question of setting does not arise.

I think it was very amusing of Raymond Mortimer to put 'Lord Barrenstock' on the same page as those two rather grand poems by E. Sackville-West and Binyon. I think also that they must have given Mr Kingsley Martin a general anasthetic don't you think so too?

I am getting on and getting on with the new novel which I want to call *Over The Frontier* but I never seem to have very much time now and Sir P. [Sir Neville Pearson] has only chosen to absent himself for a too-brief fortnight this year, this has rather upset my timetable.

I also enclose an envelope I have been meaning to let you have for a long time and now I am afraid it is rather grubby [in margin: 'I have found a clean one'] it contains all the letters I have had about *N on Y P* [*Novel on Yellow Paper*] and I expect they will amuse you and you will see how very nice people have been because I am not sending you the only beastly I have had—from 'Uncle James' of the Novel, late of Somerset House. I am getting rather isolated now because a great many of my not-so-dear friends will no longer speak to me—Rosa, Herman, all the Larry-party crowd, and Leonie more in sorrow than anger has withdrawn because she thinks I am an anti-semite (if that is the word). Josephine on the other hand has been splendid and Harriet has started a novel on her own account which I hope you will eventually see. These are all characters in Pompey in case you forgot.

Seriously I do hope you are pleased with the way the novel is selling and I think that I am very glad Chatto [Chatto & Windus, the publishers] turned it down because you have been so very nice about it all. And also you have been so very generous to advertise it so much. I think Chatto's advertisements are frightful but yours always make me want to buy all the books listed. I suppose it is the very attractive type and the way they are set out.

Yours sincerely,
Stevie Smith

The novelist, essayist, and literary journalist, Naomi Mitchison, met Stevie in the 1930s, presumably having first written enthusiastically to her about poems which were appearing in various magazines and journals. In her memoir, *You May Well Ask* (1979), Naomi Mitchison says that probably she wrote Stevie 'a gloomy letter' in 1937 about the world situation, and that this was Stevie's response.

Hunstanton
Monday [June 1937]

Dear Naomi

You take me at a disadvantage. If only I had my typewriter with me!

No. I don't think we can pass the buck to forces of evil or to anything but our own humanity. We are bloody fools—but then, we are hardly out of the egg shell yet. I think we want to keep a tight hand—each of us on our own thoughts. I think at the present moment you are in a state of mind that hungers for the disasters it fears. If there are these forces of evil, you see, you are siding with them, in allowing your thoughts to panic. Your mind is your own province—the only thing that is. Yes, this brings up another point. There is a sort of hubris in this world-worrying. For if you have achieved peace in your own mind, when the worst happens (if it does) you will have reserves of strength to meet it. And if you have not achieved peace in your own mind, how can you expect the world to do any better. You are the world, & so am I—& at the moment the world is a great deal too articulate! (You will agree!!) And worries too much—& so on. My God—the hungry generations—ours appears to be famished. If you knew the letters I still get. The ones from the women—all so hungry & worrying. Hungry for a nostrum, a Saviour, a Leader, anything but to face up to themselves & a suspension of belief. They are so unhappy too you know. (I am thinking of one particular letter. I'd send it to you but I had my bag pinched the other day & the damned thing in it.) It is sad for them. It is like a baby cutting its teeth—&

257

fighting against it all the time: 'Oh what is to happen to me now, oh these teeth. The future is nothing but one large tooth, oh is there no Saviour to save me from my tooth?' Yes, our times are difficult but our weapon is not argument I think but silence & a sort of self-interest, observation & documentation (I was going to say 'not for publication' but I am hardly in a position to say that!).

I shall love to come to your party on the 13th & shall look forward to seeing you then.

Yours,
Stevie

Thank you *so* much for the Riding book. I agree w. a lot of what she says (which must be a weight off her mind) but deprecate that turgid style. It is difficult for me to read here—or anywhere just now. I seem to have lost the art—or shall we say any sort of matey interest in other people's thoughts. When Music deserts me—it will no doubt come back. Thank you also for all you are doing for me about that review. Hope the *N. S.* proves more reasonable than *T. & T.* [*Time and Tide*].

Palmers Green
10 June 1937

Dear Denis,

Excuse me when I so *unmädelweise die Dinge durchschneide* . . . (this is awful German so don't show it up for a translation). I know tradition demands a *slow* progress now through Denis J. and Stevie S. to fetch up months later at the point I disgracefully anticipate. Excuse me.

I too very much enjoyed that evening out and also I enjoyed the play which is more than I can say of other similar occasions I won't bring up here. Thank you very much for asking Ru [Rupert Hart-Davis] to send *Yellow River*, you shall have *Yellow Paper* as soon as they get it down to me, which should be this afternoon. And I will write in it which I guess you haven't done for me, in fact if I can find an Old Family Snap sink me if I won't put that in too, just to show you how very loving and giving I can be when the weather is fine and I am just loosed for a holiday.

Last Sunday certainly was hot and I had a most amusing day with a fan who is a Town Clerk and a solicitor and is married to a nice girl but rather intense (that is she will worry into fits about War and

258

Communism and After Life and The Stars, horoscopically speaking, and All That). This fan is quite nice but a bit fat for a long walk and do you know he kept very politely complaining that I walked too quickly, as a matter of fact I got him lost in some miles and miles of woods and if I am lost in woods I always get jumpy and begin to run, so poor fan got left behind and I had to keep going back to look for him. After lunch, and I will say this for him, he had the sense to bring a flask of gin along to help down the ginger beer, he sat and read me a long short story called *The Specialist*, this is about a man that specialised in building excuse me but after all I had to excuse him *privies*, and took his life work seriously, it is very funny because of this solemn note of devotion it has in it. Have you read it? We got back to dinner with his wife Rosalie who is the sister of Ronald Mackenzie who wrote *Strange Orchestra* and *The Maitlands* and after hours of talk from Rosalie I told her she ought to let up on World Problems and take things easy. Well she took this all right and knew I meant it for the best, and if she doesn't take my advice she certainly will have a nervous breakdown and how's that going to help the world anyway?

Last Tuesday I went out for dinner and more talkie from Naomi Mitchison, and she's got world problems on the brain too and also the boringness that all her children must get measles that developed into scarlet fever. I told her she didn't want to worry about the children, and I'd take one of them, duly convalescenced and disinfected, off her hands for a bit if she liked to send it up to Hunstanton where I go Friday with my Aunt. I think I am having a lot of The Comforter about me just now, and that my name ought to be Comfort Smith instead of what it is. I like Naomi but of course we are poles apart as far as World Problems goes, but if she thinks she's going to rope me in to the Haldane-Communismus gang she is mistaken. She has a very nice child called Valentine aged six, and why do I like Valentine? Because she said: Ma the only one of your friends I like, that talks about things that interest me is Stevie Smith. Hurra three times, I am getting driven outside of myself with conceit. And I am afraid of writing anything else now for fear of offending and disappointing the Little Ones. Do you know that feeling? Anyway I don't think it matters whether you go on writing or not, unless you have to of course for bread and butter. Naomi has come to a dry patch, but I told her that didn't matter either because a lot of great writers were remembered and honoured for only one book they had written, or may be only one poem, and people just forgot the others, including the ones they didn't write because of the dry patch. After this Naomi began to get a queer wild look in her eyes and ordered up some more black coffee hot and strong.

I wish I could come to Ireland but you see I only get loosed once a year but I saw Harriet yesterday and she has fallen for someone who (this is very private and confidential) teaches dances on board ship and this ship is doing a Bank Holiday cruise to Ireland in August, and will I come with her to be in the way and be in the way. I said of course No. But perhaps I will think about it, but surely the Irish sea is rather rough isn't it and I do not make a very good sailor.

Excuse this long letter but Sir Phoebus [Sir Neville Pearson] is in a Meeting . . . and that is how it runs on. It is very indiscreet too now I come to think of it about all these people but you are more discreet than Ru I expect.

Thank you again and best wishes,
Stevie

In the next letter Stevie mentions the London Gate Theatre. She had asked Denis Johnston earlier that year to propose her for membership of the Gate. When she writes about not waiting for Bottle Green to put on *Moon in the Yellow River*, she is referring to the Intimate Theatre in Palmers Green. Dobelle is the Anchor Man, one of the characters in Denis Johnston's *Moon in the Yellow River*.

Tower House
6 October 1937

Dear Denis,

Thank you so much for your letter and what you say about the Gate, it was stupid of me to think that just because you took me there that evening you were a member; but Harriet is signed up now and I have no doubt that she will see me through, but as a matter of fact I have rather lost interest in it now; it has become a sort of duty you know because I never bother to go to any shows but sit too long over dinner and am getting lazy so this is to prevent that. Nina [Condron] and Harriet and I went to *Moon in the Yellow River* and I am very glad I did not wait for Bottle Green to put it on and possibly almost certainly risk its mangling by indifferent casting. I liked it very much indeed, Dobelle of course any way gets the laurels but acting as opposed to reading brings out the disturbance and uproar and everybody saying their own say and makes it much more exciting; also the little girl pays handsome dividends on good acting; the audience I need not say was dotty and laughed because it was convinced the Irish Are Funny. Rupert says the *Bride for the Unicorn* is even better but when I shall be able to see that I do not know, you have a *tendre* for unicorns I see, the unicorn, the chaste, the virile.

I expect before I see you again my book will be out and then you probably won't want to have anything to do with me. I have been warned that here they do not look with favour upon my writing; that I am immoral, and subversive, one of our directors is at a very advanced stage of noncomformity and I fancy it is from him the strictures arrive. I am rather curious about this because I am not immoral, but Sir P. says I must be careful, but how can you be careful, and when the book is no longer in my hands, I do not know. I did not quite see eye to eye with you about Britain's bad girl, when you wrote to me about this in your first letter, but now I see you must have been thinking just about these directors of ours. I think it is an amusing situation, rather a little bit dangerous too, for instance they made me alter lavatory to washplace, that shows you how refined we are in Southampton Street; but in many ways they are also very kind people and have perhaps been after all very longsuffering, so I shall hope I shall go quietly if I must go. But isn't this all very silly?

I hope you are well and that you will be over here again soon. Give my love to the BBC which also I see is again afflicted by this same disease of non-conformititis. There are a lot of things I could tell you about the over-here rather curious workings of this but it is too dangerous, I mean the infection of secrecy and melodrama proceeding from Sir John is too potent, and I cannot say in writing what is perhaps after all only the same old tale that we all know very well.

Yours ever,
Stevie

Tower House
11 November 1937

Dear Denis

Many thanks for your letter and so sorry not to have answered same before. I can't get away from this 'same', I have a would-be contributor to one of our weekly lovey-dovies, who says it with such fascination, I am seduced outside of myself, he says in his covering letter: 'Enclosed please find poems, with stamped addressed envelope should same prove unsuitable'. The poems are always about love and springtime and the daisies, except once one that was called 'The Orphan', I returned same.

I am sorry to have to tell you that my book *Over The Frontier* [published by Jonathan Cape in 1938] does not now come out until January by reason of the machinations of the proof readers, me and Rupert, and the awful business of steering a clear course between libel and obscurity—I mean if there are too many red herrings about, people find it difficult to understand what people are talking about; you will agreee. Also the bill is going to be enormous. Phew, this is positively the final appearance of Pompey. Storms at the office seem to have drifted overhead, but look out for choppy weather in January, I do. You see Denis I am no martyr, I cannot feel really cross with these directors, indeed I see their point, or occasionally I get a glimmer of it. Happy is the secretary who has no history, that sort of thing I take it, and as Sir P. said: Caesar's wife . . . But I am Caesar's wife, I said, meaning of course that in that way I was above reproach, and not wishing in any way to make trouble with Calpurnia but it's no good, we argue from different standpoints, only they are all very nice in their way and not the sort of ogres it would be sensible to make an aunt sally out of, they pay me a good salary, about twice what I am worth, and are very nice to say how do you do to and how is your cough. I am sailing all the time a bit near the wind, but if it gets too strong, I shall take a reef and tie some grannies, I do not intend to be a martyr to art for art or any hysteria of that sort; it is entirely a question of cunning and not of principle. How much can I get away with? it's a gamble, but I do not dislike them.

I send you separately a copy of the *Mercury*, this is rather cheek perhaps, but you see I want you to see the drawing you saw in rough, 'Mother Among the Dustbins', and how it is come out, they have some very good blockmakers I think, [R.A.] Scott-James is very nice, he really is very nice indeed.

I should like so much to have a copy of *A Bride for the Unicorn*, so do persuade Rupert to reprint, please. Next week we are going to see *The Unhappy Spirit* at the Gate, that will be the first time I use my subscription, the play is a translation I think from the French. How is tricks and the BBC? I expect they are something you could hate, I

262

mean not just kindly and fusty like some of our people, but real hate-worthy. I hope Armistice Day has passed off without the demolition of Dublin over on your side, I expect it will be the last armistice day before we give it cause to be two-squared-equals-4-minutes silence, if things go on much more looking like they was going on getting worse. I don't see why you shouldn't have your child-father reconcil-iation in *Yellow River* there's no reason why a situation should be tabu just because other people have often mucked it up, I see the danger of course, but it seemed to me to come out clear of it. No more now do write again soon.

Yours,
Stevie

Tower House
8 December 1937

Dear Denis,

Thank you very much for your letter and the *Unicorn*. I should love to see this acted but you are an expensive person I should think from the producer's point of view, has it been done on a revolving stage yet, I do so like to see stages revolving, especially in such a good cause as the unicorn, I wonder shall I ever see it done, I am returning the manuscript, very noble-like, as I haven't lost a manuscript since June and it's getting just about time I should lose another, so I shouldn't like it to be yours, so here it is, and thank you very much for sending it; please do give me a copy of the published version, I take it there were no alterations, no deletions for libel, no spelling mistakes and no excess proof corrections to make Rupert send you one of his little bills? It is funny the lady turns out to be Death, I mean here was I thinking of my next, and going to call it Married to Death, I'm nuts on death really, it comes out in my poems and does something to limit their ready sale, not that I've much to grumble at that way really, as I have almost got rid of the lot now and must write some more. But this Death idea, it is very prominent, rather a running-away in my case I am afraid, not very *strrrong* of me. But as a matter of fact please keep this idea of my next very secret because I have already told them I am never going to write again, and I expect perhaps it will come to nothing. But there it is, death death death lovely death—so far 40 pp. Do you find you have great difficulty in getting time to write? with me it is like that, I begin here and go on there, and often I wonder it is not getting more disjointed than it is; it *is* really, and I expect very soon people will not stand for any more of it, but how the hell else can I write with so many things to distract me, and I am not a very good girl to my Aunt, you know, I am hardly ever at home and when I am I do not feel I should not talk to her but get out the typewriter and give her no attention at all, she gets lonely, does the Lion, but never grumbles, which makes me feel worse, home ties are trying because of this guilty feeling if you do not heed them; well then I might see less of my so-dear friends and stop rushing off Fridays for weekends, but that cuts home too, I like to see them, so everything is just fixed to be an uproar of distraction, how be quiet, how come to it. I expect you find the same difficulty I expect everybody does. I expect the BBC takes as much of your time as Sir P. does of mine, and very lucky we are ahem of course . . . Then I have a German friend and her husband [Gertrude and Alfred Wirth] who travel about the world and write me lovely long letters, and in the end I owed them so many letters feeling very guilty I sent them a cable to Shanghai hoping they hadn't been blown up but I heard next from her that they were in Calcutta, I never knew people get around like those two, and here am I very fixed in London.

Today I saw Nina, I see quite a lot of her and her Edward, he is quite simpatico, very definite and inclined to shout, and he too gets about a lot, Russia and all that, you know, what he is I really cannot quite guess, engineering I should think, but yet he used to be a journalist, but now I am sure he is very M.I.Mech.E. and so on. Nina is very worried just now about cats, a cat to Nina is something more than it is to you and me, she has photographs of them and always speaks of them as one might speak of very dear people, they get married and have children and they are husbands and wives and sons and mothers and girls and boys, it is very curious; to me an animal is an animal some nice some not but never anything that is not an animal. I think Nina is very tensed over these animals she is a very nice girl but very strung up but I think the unhappiness in her life, not now perhaps but what has passed must account for this.

This is a very long letter Denis and it runs on but I am again doing what I should not do and typing it here when I ought to be reading bloody manuscripts or writing cheques or working out dividends or putting things away preliminary to taking them out again tomorrow, anything but writing this letter. It is a sort of bet I have whether I shall finish it before he [Sir Neville Pearson] walks into my room and says what the hell are you doing there, also it is getting very late and I am afraid I shall never get home and tonight I am taking the Lion to see *Hamlet* done by our rep theatre. She has been reading this grand old play and she says: It is very sad, There are a lot of well known sayings in it; there are a lot of people killed. Yes of course she has read it before but as a young girl I think she has forgotten, but staunchly she reads it through in the most repulsive sort of family bible edition of Shakespeare dated about 1860 full of engravings of him all head leaning on pillars rather like the statue in Leicester Square except that there are no pigeons to misbehave themselves. I am at the moment flanked dangerously by 2 baronets, Sir Frank and Sir Phoebus, my situation is desperate, I think I must Close.

Yours ever,
Stevie
A happy Christmas!

The novelist Rosamond Lehmann, a friend of Stevie's, wrote to her on 19 January 1938 'about *Over the Frontier* which, to my great joy, your publishers sent me'. Her reaction to the novel was mixed and Stevie seems to have been angry at first, taking the criticism as gratuitous fault-finding on Rosamond Lehmann's part. A correspondence ensued and eventually Stevie sent *Tender Only To One*, her second book of poems, to Rosamond for her appraisal.

Palmers Green
Sunday [1938]

Dear Rosamund, [sic]
I have been meaning to write to you all the week, but now I do have a moment I find I have left my address book at the office, so I cannot post this till tomorrow. You will have got the awful poems about which I feel pretty desperate by now but what I really want to say is not about them as it is too late but about your last page. I am so sorry about that and Rosamund you have not got it right yet. I did not send your letters to Cape, only your *letter*, that first one, which was quite all right I thought, it was a dear Stevie Smith yours sincerely Rosamund Lehmann letter. I told Rupert you had afterwards sent me the most charming and generous letters and that the misunderstanding was cleared up. But it was before this that Derek V [Verschoyle] must have come into it how I do not know. When I got your subsequent letters I saw at once what had happened. You thought I had

asked Cape to send you my book; and thinking that had a perfect right to criticise it, but naturally I did not know that until later. I do hope now that you will criticise the poems if you can be bothered. I should like so much to know what you think about them. I cannot sleep for thinking of 'Poop'*, how I let it get in I can't imagine, I get so sick of my poems I cannot really bother to read them in proof and am always chopping and changing, it is desperate for Rupert he has whole new batches set up for me and still I cannot make up my mind. I wish there was some litmus paper test you could have for your poems, blue for bad and pink for good, it ought to be possible because it is the acid ones that are best, is it pink for acid, I forget.

I loathe these first aid lectures I absolutely detest them but every now and then things get so frightful in Germany I think one ought to make sacrifices, so now we are having gas lectures on top of the first aid ones, I never did chemistry at school I cannot make head or tail of them; my doctor said the other day that it would be better to keep away from them and that a rather bad first aider was a burden, and then I read about the man who was kicked in the stomach at football and the first aider massaged him and he died; one doesn't know what to do.

Do ring me up some time and say when we can meet. I should love to see you.

Love,
Stevie
*I showed it to Stonier, too late of course, & he said he didn't like it. I have absolute confidence in his Judgment. I don't know *how* he knows but he does know don't you think?

The novelist Inez Holden, one of Stevie's closest friends, is depicted as Lopez in 'The Story of a Story'. Kay Boyle, the American novelist and short story writer, married the poet and writer Laurence Vail in 1931. Both were members of the legendary group of American expatriates in Paris in the twenties.

Tower House
25 February 1938

Dear Denis,
Thank you so much for writing, and I am so glad you liked *Over The Frontier*. I've had a mixed bag of brick-bats and bouquets, and

now it's more or less all over, and I suppose I ought to be getting along with the next one, but I'm bloody well not yet. Inez Holden asked me out to dinner the other day and said would I write a review with her, why don't you, it's much more in your line, but she's a funny girl, rather off the handle quite nice, and really funny, but she says this sort of thing: A man meets a man and he says, and then the other says, . . . there you are Stevie, that's clever isn't it, rather subtle, now you do one. And at the end of the evening she says: Now we've done the whole review, we've only got to write it down. A dead sea harvest I assure you. But then I thought, would this appeal to you. Do a review, a lot of sketches bringing in all the funny ways people behave, and the base and ugly and fine and heroic ways they behave in England, and then show that it, Eng., is being attacked now very strongly and must fight for its life against the controlled nations (Germany etc.), with a sort of theme song running through it, Prepare, prepare, prepare, to defend your life. (To have for music a variation on the tune of Man is born to trouble, as the sparks fly up.) And it could be linked together also by someone running across the stage at the end of every scene carrying a human leg or arm or something to finish a laughing head, very dummy-figures, of course, with only a little hint of the torso case. Well, there you are, poor Denis, I do write you long rigamaroles, there you are, for you if you like.

I shall now say All news when we meet, because even if we do not meet for years it is a good brake on a boring long letter.

Yours ever,
Stevie

I do like Nina. She wants me to go to Austria in July to stay with the Kay Boyles who don't seem to know ever how many people they have staying with them or care. So will you come too, because I think 2 strangers are better than one (Nina is a *friend* of Kay's so doesn't count).

Tower House
6 April 1938

Dear Denis,
The place isn't in Austria it's in France I now find somewhere near Gervais les Bains, but I am beginning to feel rather unstuck about the whole idea because of Kay Boyle, Nina seems absolutely nuts on

her and you know it's all very odd, weird somehow, I mean Kay (I get this impression very strongly from Nina's conversation, and she admires her for it) seems to spend her whole time Being Unconventional, this sort of thing, Why put cups on the table, why not on the floor, the English are so conventional, if you want to throw somebody out of the window, why not do it, the English are so conventional (this will become a poem if I am not careful). But if you throw people out of the window it will boil down to the survival of the physically strongest, won't it, that is the grossest materialism, with the corollary rather distasteful to the unconvention Fans, You English are so spiritual. However if you can come too, to off-set the teacups, that might be fun, do you think. I wish we could get Malcolm Muggeridge and Inez Holden too, because then we could all have a good laugh and stay at the pub instead of with the K.B.'s. But I expect as you say the real difficulty will be getting the dates to fit in. I only have a horrible little fortnight and heaven knows when it will happen, but I think some time in July. I met an Irishman at V.S. Pritchett's party the other day who knew you very well but unfortunately I did not catch his name very clearly, O'Connor, or Connell, or is that just a Conventional guess? The only other point against France is that there is no sea to go and swim in, only a tank. On the credit side perhaps I ought to mention nice scenery and climbing and walking, and of course A Change . . . I do so hope the BBC is not treating you barbarously, I do feel so sorry for you if it is.

Bless D. from S.
Stevie

Ivor Brown, a literary journalist who became editor of the *Observer* wrote 'Proper Words and Proper Places', for the *Manchester Guardian*, 14 May 1938. In it he describes the style of Stevie's essay, 'Private Views', as 'jerky jabs at the attention'.

Tower House
30 May 1938

Dear Denis,

I am sorry not to have answered your letter before but it was no use writing until things got settled and they didn't, for some time, indeed they hardly are yet. I rang Nina up this morning and she poor Nina is in the throes of a tiresome but very money making serial which will not be finished until about the end of July, so that means, as I have to have my holiday from July 8 for a fortnight, we shall not be able to go away together, and I don't want to go out to the Alps (by the way it is the Alps and not the Pyrenees) alone, because as I said I think the Kay Boyle crowd might be just a shade trying. So I am fixed now more or less to go away with the Marshalls some Cambridge friends of mine. Rachel is very nice and Nat the son who is at Trinity Hall may come too, and perhaps a few others. Rachel is David Garnett's sister-in-law, and they are all my booksy friends. We are aiming to go to Bamborough Castle just opposite Farne Island and near Berwick. The scenery must be lovely up there I think, and another friend of mine wants to give me an introduction to Edith Sitwell but I don't know that I want that, I have had some letters from Osbert, but I don't know about Edith. Of course if you can take in Bamborough on your way to Austria, how I wish you will, but I wonder if it is possible. I suppose you absolutely have to go to Vienna, I mean I rather gather you do have to, otherwise it would be awful to go and bolster up the larger German Reich with good British currency, I have a Viennese friend who says things are awful there now and getting daily worse, but I don't want to depress you if you have to go, and anyway you know all about it of course.

Writing not going very well but Cape are going to do some more poems, also I have done some articles and reviewing, and also I have been attacked. So you were right after all, and I don't take this attacking business at all kindly. Ivor Brown in the *Manchester Guardian*, and an old acquaintance has scored off me desperately in a *New Statesman* competition; he is the sort of man who is awfully rancorous and never forgets a laugh in the wrong place!!

I hope you are flourishing and writing like stink. The Gate Theatre has been an absolute wash out this season, nothing worth looking at, such a pity; but that splendid old girl who played the great grandmother, was it, in *Tobacco Road* came out to Palmers Green the other day and played another splendid old girl in *9 to 6*.

Blessings from,
Stevie

Osbert Sitwell wrote to Stevie on 22 May 1938 to say that 'Brown is an idiot . . . if he is out to find a modern author *without* a sense of rhythm why pick on you who are the essence of rhythm?' He then recounts to Stevie an incident that occurred in the Sacristy of the Escurial Chapel when a party of sightseers 'of the private-view type' arrived and spent more of their time carefully

examining a boring brown religious picture, giving only a passing glance to
El Greco's brilliant 'St Maurice and the Pheban Legion'.

Tower House
9 June 1938

Dear Mr Osbert Sitwell,

I do know these people who go and look at the dark brown religious
pictures, and will not look at all at the clean El Greco; I suppose they
see the bright colours out of the corners of their disgusting eyes &
think: This is our 'old' day & that must be a new one that has got in
by mistake so we must take it on a 'new' day of course only. They are
very tidy in their habits always. I should like to see the clean St
Maurice; I cannot imagine quite what that would be like: I have only
seen it ever in reproduction. How I do detest Kingsley Martin. The
latest trouble is now with him. You can imagine. But I ask myself, is
or is *not* Raymond Mortimer the literary editor of the *New Statesman*. He must feel his position very keenly to have something that he
says he likes and Stonier says *he* likes, crabbed by that horrible little
thing. And will the *N.S. burst* because I crack up Aquinas and prefer
Thomism to the misty and fear-ridden Calvinism of Masaryk's
Modern Man and Religion? Just lately I chose two books to review,
and this was one, and the other was a book called *Morals Makyth
Man* by somebody called [Gerald] Vann O.P. Well, I happened to be
dining with a Viennese friend of mine: and I said 'There's something
funny about Masaryk as a *thinker*' (he may have been a very heroic
man of action perhaps but that is not the point): and she said: He was
a Calvinist. So odd. Everything at once fell into place. And now that
absurd Kingsley Martin, with his everlasting little groups! You
know. . . . Last night there was a famous rally of the Writers Unite
for Freedom anti-fascist group, & of course Kingsley Martin was on
the platform. Though of course actually he only dislikes *other*
dictators. However, Day Lewis brought the frightfully emotional
house down by quoting for *Horror*—Goering. Goering said: When I
hear the word culture, I reach for my gun. And I thought: When I
hear the word Kingsleymartin, I reach for my gun. And when I hear
the word Daylewis I reach for my gun. (Not that I know anything
about his poetry, but as a thinker. Why does he have to think such a
lot—or rather to think he thinks, because really he *feels*. 'We do feel,
don't we? . . .' The absolute curate!) And what do you think the
mouse of those *mountains* of oratory was? You will never guess, so I

must take yet another page—A telegram to Freud, groupily wishing him a happy stay in England.

My new book does not go very well. It is real unearthly and so sad. There is Never a Smile. (This is a title Inez Holden suggested for a revue we were going to write but we never shall.) She is so amusing, and not groupy at all, she always makes me laugh so much when I go out with her, the whole time.

I hope you are enjoying the stay at the Hôtel des Lilas and that you are already better. (Weather here still very disappointing!)

Yours sincerely,
Stevie Smith

Palmers Green
28 September 1938

Dear Denis,

How did you enjoy yourself in Greater Germany? It must have been an eyeful. If this here war comes off, Denis, I want to get a job at the BBC. After attending various classes in first aid, (we have a weird Colonel who comes and lectures us at the office on Bones, his beautiful name is Thurlow-Potts, and bandaging) I have come to the conclusion that I shall never learn to tie a reef knot and know a fibula from a tibula, and indeed that it is not conceivable I could be *more* useless anywhere. But I have a fine port winey voice and when the poor BBC young men are called up I am just wondering if I could not Announce. Do you think it would be worth trying and do you know, this is the real awful point, anyone I should write to. With the already serious shortage of paper I don't see that journalism will flourish and anyway I imagine the BBC will largely take the place of the press. Did you ever hear anything like Chamberlain's speech? Pappy, said Dr Johnson. Chamberlain's 'unreasonable' was a high-water mark of understatement, and the piece about 'larger issues' just what Ribbentrop has been wanting and expecting. His allusions to letters from Mum were just what we have in our 'Write to me, dear' columns. I guess he gets voted out today. But Sam [Hoare] and John [Simon] are angling for the premiership and they are both of them plain rogues, something more I mean than just old so-and-so's. I mean I don't think anyone could really stomach Hoare and the same goes for Simon. I hope Eden and Churchill and Atlee manage to arrive.

271

Horrible times, horrible letter,

Yours ever,
Stevie

29 September 1938

Dear Denis,
This is in the nature of a hurried and apologetic postscript. (1) for bothering you at all and (2) for crabbing Chamberlain. I think his speech yesterday was a masterpiece, and he is a very brave and stick-at-it old boy. About the BBC, Phoebus tells me my voice is awful, I mean not clear and with a lisp (!!) and also that if war comes I shall be for once in my life indispensable here. So I fear my Broadcasting House ambitions will not be realised. Still things do look a bit better this morning, so perhaps it won't happen after all, but if it is only a postponement, almost better now than a year ahead. I was talking to Nina yesterday. Edward at the Air Ministry or wherever he is (something to do with the press side of the air business I think), is off his head with work and Nina has to go down to Devonshire on Saturday to take her mama out of the danger zone, and then come back to town. I do think in this case Mum sounds pretty awful, Nina is writing her biography, has in fact finished it I believe, and it all comes in there, about Mum. How is your play going? I am still trying to get Harriet to get the tickets as I am not a member of the Arts, but the Crisis covers all. Even advertising. Did you see McLean's? 'Have you got Crisis-Stomach? Try McLean's stomach powder.'

Yours,
Stevie

9 December 1938

Dear Mr Scott-James,
Thank you so very much for the review [of *Tender Only To One*] in the Christmas *Mercury*. It was very kind of you to bother so much to get it in when the book only arrived at the last minute like that, and to give me such a nice one too, and to write it yourself as Cam tells me you did. I feel very depressed and deathly about my writing, I think it annoys people and that they imagine I do it for that purpose which

272

of course nobody does, I mean when you are writing you cannot be bothered with such thoughts, they are too trivial, but these thoughts make a difference in this way, when the books are published they creep into the reviews and stand often between the writer and the reader. I saw Naomi Mitchison the other day and she had my book and kept saying: It is impossible, you do not take life seriously. She is writing a book about the early Christians [*The Blood of the Martyrs*, 1939] all the characters get thrown to the lions and (Naomi says, and I think you can catch the Naomi note?)—'mind rather'. I said: 'You are a cruel girl, Naomi' and she implied I was a frivolous one, so you see it is difficult not to impute motives I see that. But also perhaps there is something frivolous in this throwing of one's characters to the lions and showing that they 'mind'. It is a dangerous book, I shall be interested to see how it comes out.

Thank you again very much for being so kind about my writing you will say I might be the same about Naomi's I expect!

With best wishes,
Stevie Smith

Stevie's review 'Wells The Fighting Prophet' appeared in the well-known literary journal, *John O'London's Weekly*, on 23 August 1940.

Tower House
8 July 1940

Dearest Naomi,
I got the news [that N.M. had lost her baby] this morning it is terrible and nothing one can say can possibly help at all; oh I did so hope things would go well for you this time, I imagine that the fact it would have been a horrible new world to grow up in is no sort of consolation, and that those considerations, strong enough in theory, don't amount to much when it comes to it. I think it will be rather a horrible new world and a pretty hungry one too, if we carry on the war, as I have no doubt we shall; one gets the habit and coming late to full strength, as we always do, must of course put that strength to the test. It is a weird situation. Hitler's war is practically over now, if it wasn't for us, and what an 'if'. Ours is just beginning. The timing seems wonky to me—rather as if we might not overlap! You must be so sad and tired and sick now I can hardly bear to think of that, but I am sure you don't want political chat, so I will put a sock in it,

273

though it goes against the grain. (This is almost as bad a mix up as the famous 'cool as a cucumber in the teeth of fearful odds'.) I wish dear Naomi that when you are well again you will come to London, I am sure it is a good place to be. But perhaps I am wrong there too, and it is only good if you have work to do. I expect I have mentioned it to you before, but I have got the book again and it is so good, specially the Greek Tragedy essay and the one on St Paul—do read [John] Cowper Powys's *The Pleasures of Literature*, I am sure you will get even more out of it than I have. This child bearing puts a woman at almost as great a disadvantage as advantage, I so admire women who have children, they are such hostages to fate as no timid selfish person could willingly give—not that all mamas are brave and unselfish, but the best and willing must be. Timid bachelors can keep near the door, but parents go right into the middle of the room, where there is no chance of evasion and escape, and no such cowardly thought at all. So you see I really admire you, if it isn't cheeky to say so, with all your lovely children and at the same time, what some mamas have not got, your shrewd idea of what they're up against.

I now have to do an essay for *John O'London* on H.G. Wells. It is like being at school again, doing these set jobs. He does let one down so terribly I find, I don't know that I can do this essay. He starts off (*Food of the Gods* and all those) by being so exciting, he gets his atmosphere and his people so well, and then off he tails into terrible puerilities. He has no conception of spiritual strife or of the importance of spiritual things at all. As if machines could be either good or bad without minds to drive them and make of them either buses or tanks.

My best wishes go to you, Naomi, and don't you bother to answer this letter (of course, as if you could!) until you are strong again, then of course I do hope you will. They may not let you read it perhaps, as perhaps it is too long.

Love from,
Stevie

Hermon Ould was secretary of P.E.N. in London and the novelist Margaret Storm Jameson was its President. Stevie reviewed Storm Jameson's *Cousin Honoré* in *Modern Woman*, February 1941.

Tower House
3 April 1941

Dear Hermon,

I am sorry to have been so long answering your letter, but I was going to come as Sagittarius's guest to the last afternoon party of the P.E.N., and I hoped to see you there; unfortunately I couldn't get up to town that day after all, and so missed you.

This business of the P.E.N. subscription is truly *awful*. I thought I told you the painful truth—I really cannot afford to belong; since I didn't pay my subscription I have never been except as somebody's guest—generally Inez', so really I am sure I haven't broken any rules. If I have, I really do apologise. I thought you just went on sending me the *Report* out of kindness to the hard-up.

You know Hermon it is no good being a penurious author unless you are also a foreign author, I can quite see that, and I think it is awfully sad for us hard up English writers because we not only have to stew in beastly offices all day to pay our bills but we cannot ever have any contact with other writers unless they happen to come our way casual like! Now I know you can have too much literary gaddings, but also I believe you can have too little and get right out of touch; that is why I should like to belong to the P.E.N., but it is so expensive, not only the subscription which I might squeeze out, but every time one meets, if it is a luncheon or dinner, bang goes another pound or so. It is really only for rich and middling well-to-do people. Then there is the other point so far as I am concerned, even if I could afford it I can almost never get the time to come to the luncheons so that means I can only put in an appearance at the Saturday afternoon parties. Now couldn't you be kind to poor English writers and arrange an associate membership for them (on the lines of the Arts Theatre Club), so that they could come to the Saturday parties but not to the rich grand luncheons? Do think this over and be an angel about it, or I shall develop an unconscionable grievance to the tune of 'nobody helps us poor English'—after all there must be dozens like me. Well, you know how bad disgruntledom is for the artistic soul, so I need say no more!

I hope David [Carver] is enjoying life in the R.A.F., I'm afraid you must miss him badly. It is funny you know Hermon how all one's friends get scattered even if they aren't in the armed forces. I believe nearly all mine divide themselves between Oxford and Aberystwyth.

I wouldn't really be out of London but I do wish some of the others were here.

I'm still writing poems, but you know what it's like getting them accepted, the *New Statesman* has been wonderful, but of course they have to get their politics in—and that doesn't leave much room. Apart from that I am not doing much writing, except some reviewing, *John O'London, Country Life, Modern Woman*—and (don't laugh) *Aeronautics*! There's a nice collection for you, all our own [Newnes, Pearson] papers of course. Only *Aeronautics*, which has a peach of an editor [Oliver Stewart], pays me, so don't you go thinking honey I'm making my fortune, I guess I'll never make that. How is Horace? He sent me such a nice story once (not knowing it was me doing the reading) but I couldn't get it accepted for him. Please give my love to Storm Jameson when you see her, and could you explain for me about my membership, I do hope she won't think I'm bilking! But I'm sure she will understand, she is so nice. I had her book to review for *Modern Woman*—but not much space at my disposal; these ladies' papers are a bit terrific you know.

Best wishes from,
Stevie

On 31 December 1940 Stevie received a letter from John Gabriel, a member of The Royal Berkshire Regiment, who was writing to say he'd 'known and loved your poems for some time, but yesterday I happily exchanged a Christmas book token for *Over The Frontier* and ever since a particularly boring phase of Army life has been enlightened delightfully'. An exchange of correspondence followed and then on 8 April 1941 Clothilde Gabriel wrote to tell Stevie that her husband had been reported 'missing, believed drowned'.

Tower House
7 April 1941

Dear John Gabriel,

I was awfully amused by your letter, no, I am not yet in the false beards department I have such an awfully bad memory I think I should not do very well I should be apt to ask my sleuthee if we hadn't met before somewhere. But I'm glad you're there and if you'll pass me some dope I shall be able to go round talking like the old lady in Saki as if I'd been in touch with all the governments of Europe before breakfast. I'll help you out with my own job, it's such a lovely mixture, book reviewing, mss. reading and a couple of baronets for whom I perform lowly secretarial duties as described in the books, perhaps *ad nauseam*. You're right about *Peg's Paper*, that's one of our publications, or was, it's now got eaten up by *Lucky Star* I believe, but at the other end of the scale to give us a high class look is *Country Life*. My word.

I've never met a soldier who didn't break his heart over the old blimps at WO [War Office]. I suppose the old blimps did the same in their youth, it's just a pity that they cracked their brains as well. The amount of dammed up energy that junior officers waste on brass hats if turned to better use might pep up our local trains and help us to arrive at work on time. It's a shame, that's what it is. Do you think you'll get to your desert? When I left school I wanted to be an explorer more than anything and I put an advertisement in the personal column of *The Times*—it cost quite a lot. But I mis-worded it somehow and I got a note from the advertising manager to ask me if other ladies were joining the party. This is absolutely the only occasion on which by implication I have been mixed up with the white slave racket. It was a bit of a set-back, you must admit, and if I have languished feebly in an office ever since, am I entirely to blame?

I like Orwell very much and I thought his *Magnet* article was superb. I rather hoped he'd go on and do the same for the women's papers, perhaps he will. I can't get Connolly to take any of my poems, but I still say, keeping a stiff upper lip, that *Horizon* is a very good paper. That grave-yard note of mine is jolly difficult to place, I can tell you.

Isn't it awful about Virginia Woolf?—just generally fed up all round I suppose. I am looking forward to reading the obituaries. It will be nice when we have a National newspaper and ex-rivals have to take para- and para. about, like a Faustian Angelic Chorus—or perhaps only rather like this.

Well no more now.
Stevie Smith

As Stevie mentions in her letter of 30 May 1938 to Denis Johnston, the Marshalls, Rachel and Horace, were Cambridge friends of hers, and Kitty, Janet, and Nat were their children. Eleanor (Price) was Horace's sister. Inez Holden occupied at this time a mews flat behind H.G. Well's house in Hanover Terrace and remained there until a row broke out between Wells and George Orwell.

18 April 1941

Dearest Rachel,

I am sorry you have been having such a terribly sad time, I was getting awfully anxious about you so you can imagine how glad I was to get your letter, although it was a sad one. I am afraid you will miss your friend terribly; oh dear, this war.

I knew Mrs Marshall was staying with you but of course I had no idea she was so ill; it is—at least I suppose one can think of it that way —a good thing that she did not realise how serious it was; you must have been a lovely person to stay with, and I expect she felt that. If you are writing to Eleanor, would you give her my best love and sympathy please, and to Horace too; I won't write to Eleanor I think, as letters like that are apt to be wrong somehow, at least I always feel nervous about writing them. I should love her to look me up when next she is in London, it is ages since I saw her.

And now you darling must be absolutely worn out so please don't think of having me until you are quite rested, in fact don't think about it at all. Visitors whoever they are are always something extra and when one is tired one simply cannot cope emotionally and all that I mean; my word I do understand that. Perhaps after a bit when all the awful clearing up has been done you could go away for a holiday. I expect you know heaps of places where you could be quiet and un-war-wracked. The only place I can think of like that at the moment is Aberystwyth, and I only think of that because my friend Ba's papa left his Br. Museum mss. and came back to Southgate for a night and I went up and had coffee with him in the evening. He had never *been in a raid* and had only heard aeroplanes 'going over'; sounds like peace doesn't it? The poor man picked the night of our big blitz for his stay, so I guess by the morning he'd got an angle on it. That was a blitz, and London looks very knocked about now I can tell you, Piccadilly's a treat, so is the Strand. Yesterday morning we paddled to our offices through piles of broken glass, in the sunshine the streets sparkled like diamonds with the stuff, smashed so small, looking like diamonds and frost. There is a large bomb crater in the road just outside what is left of St James's, Piccadilly, it's deep, all London clay and with fountains of water cascading down into it from broken mains; smells of gas and burning everywhere, but all that has been dealt with by now, I mean the gas, water and burning. It's bloody silly knocking each other's cities to bits like this, I'm sure these air terror tactics are futile, they only work when there is no air defence, no near-parity, and the whole thing is followed up by mechanised infantry. The effect it has on us seems to be fury and the intention of holding out these next few months at all costs until we creep up to parity and plus, and then give it back to them, and so on and so on. I often have tea with Inez at weekends and H.G. Wells comes across from the big house for twenty minutes or so for a nice bit of toast. He thinks we shall win in the end because we can't afford to lose, but it may take another two years or so.

I'm so glad you had all your children with you at Easter. A letter came yesterday from Kitty and I hope to see her soon. Do you see anything of John Hayward—is he still with the Rothschilds?—and Joan [Robinson]? and Max [Newman]? Please give them my love if and when you do. And best love to you and hoping I see you soon,

Stevie

Dearest Rachel,

Thank you so much for your letter and for asking me down for the 30th. I am longing to see you again and shall love to come—if nothing awful crops up in the meantime. I had no idea poor Janet had been indulging in appendicitis, but I am glad—and amazed rather—that she is over it all so successfully that she is already promised a dancing date so soon. That is wonderful, though I am sure you must all have had an anxious time, because appendices (ahem—is that right?) are no joke. Love to her and best of luck, please. I am wondering about Kitty's new job, too, I suppose the film work collapsed?—or is the interviewing something to do with that. These are just wonderings that swim up, they can be fully explored on the 30th, which I hope will come quickly.

We had a nice quiet family Christmas, but poor Molly took to her bed with a bad cold which we feared was flu—but it turned out to be just a cold, thank goodness for everyone's sake. You know, the more I do of housework, and it isn't very much, the more wonderful I think you are, because if I had it always to do I don't think I should ever do anything else, and you do so much and so much organising and yet have time for your own work and the widest outside interests. I don't know how you do it; as the lady said to Drinkwater after he had been giving a reading of his poems . . . 'Oh Mr Drinkwater, how do you think of it?' How indeed.

You are an angel to write as you do about my poems, I can't tell you how it cheers me up because I am never never very certain about them, the inspiration or whatever it is comes in such a vague and muddled way, and I am not sure that I don't sometimes get the wrong poems into print. I am awfully involved in them again now because I have to sort some out for Cape to do another book [*Mother, What Is Man?*], and there are so many drawings, which I think are so much better than they used to be, and I can't get poems to tie up to them. Do you think I could just have a page or so of drawings with underlines instead of poems . . . '18 months old and already odious', 'My right arm had turned blue', 'Think it over', 'I could let Tom go, but what about the children?', 'I dreamed that I was dressed in cellophane', etc., etc. Oh dear there's no end to it, and my poor little room is like a paper chase and people get quite cynical and say 'Is this the art department?'.

Well at any rate it is sweet of you to write as you did and I treasure it and go to it with fresh zest (and Sir Frank [Newnes] can whistle!!).

Love from,
Stevie

My love to Nat when he arrives. I hope he flourishes!

In 1936 John Hayward wrote as 'an obscure stranger' to Stevie thanking her for the 'intense & continuous pleasure' *Novel on Yellow Paper* gave him, and saying how much he 'hopes that it will have a sequel'. A friendship developed and they continued to correspond.

Tower House
9 April 1942

Dear John,

After all the fuss I made dear did they not *arrive*? I posted them more than a week ago, but so far no word perhaps the colour scheme boled you out? Yes? Well dear, what a life. There is now the most terrific row going on in frightful old *J. O'London* between Rebecca West and Lady Listowel because Rebecca objects to what the Lady wrote in her review of *Green Lamb Grey Goat*. Meself I don't hold with bandying words with mere reviewers, I don't hold with it not as reviewer nor writer, but the temper is so funny you know, I had no idea absolutely no idea Rebecca could Go On like that! I can hardly wait for next week's reply from Lady L. Or perhaps the correspondence will be brought to an end by an editorial 'Ladies, ladies!' But the editor of that thar paper is Mister John Brophy, a dull dog. I think I will send you a copy, and the baronets can go short, because I want you to agree with me that it is a smelly little paper. Reviewers are getting so censorious, look at Pamela H. Johnson on Evelyn Waugh, and Howard Sprring in *Country Life*. What's bit them all, eh? Well, chum, I'm a tired girl after a late night so I will draw to a close. (Sir N.'s favourite ending for his after dinner speeches: 'Thank heaven I'm drawing towards my close, as Lady Godiva said.') Don't stop me if you've heard that one. Max Newman has just rung up and I'm going trotting with him tonight. Do you see much of him nowadays? By the way John I am with some qualms sending you an obscene poem of mine because there is an argument whether it should go in the new book or not, what I mean is, it was a very vivid incident and shows how awful marriage can get and yet go on, if you know what I mean, and it is very concentrated and exactly what Jack said in front of me to his wife, well the obscenity wasn't meant to be the chief thing, it just happened like that, you see, very concentrated and strrong. [See 'Goodnight', p. 245] But Rupert thought it was a bit too much when it was a question of putting it in the last book-o, and now Rupert's gone for a soldier, Veronica [Wedgwood] thinks it's o.k. but she's a woman. So you see I'm in a bit of a dither. I don't want to be an *obscene* poet though the word thrills me to death ever since my schoolgirl eyes first lit on that tumty-tum line in the *Georgics* about *obscenae canes importunaeque volucres* (??? 'My dear Margaret, parse . . . analyse . . .') but when you are writing about everyday life etcetera there is bound to be bits of it here and there isn't there? *Olivia* [Manning]. Olivia is married to Reggie Smith who had a job with the British Council in Bucharest; they both Got Out in Time and after wandering through Greece and Asia Minor and possibly the Holy Land (*vide* missionary journeys of S. Paul) fetched up in Cairo, where they now are. I send you her letter and that short story, and at the same time may I say how my heart goes out to you in all the troubles and worries I am bringing upon you which if I were not such a mean girl I would plant, at 10% off, on hardy old sinners like Spencer C.-B. [Curtis-Brown] or even Miss Pearn.

Love,
Stevie

John Mair (1916–42) was killed in an RAF combat mission. The *New Statesman*, to which he contributed, mentioned in an obituary an 'unpublished thriller', *Never Come Back*, which had in fact been published in England and America. And it erroneously gave the Channel, rather than the North Sea, as the site of his death.

Tower House
24 April 1942

Dear John [Hayward],

I was so sorry to hear you had been so beastly ill, I mean it was bad enough if it had been flu—but that streptoccoccal something sounds the limit. I do hope you are well on the way to recovery and able to get out and enjoy the sunshine, that drug you mention is a famous old piece, isn't it, it seems to have pulled half the world round, judging by friends' confidences. It was specially nice of you in such an extremity to write at all and I feel rather guilty for landing you with all that ms. stuff. I am absolutely certain Olivia doesn't mean to be patronising, she was always very interested and generous about my writing, and this sort of interest (and it wasn't half as mutual as it oughteravebin), is by no means general among ladies and gentlemen of a literary turn, ahem I name no names! I can't understand for instance why people get so cross about Rosamund, is it just the green eye do you think? I was reading an old book of hers not long ago, the one called *A Note in Music*, and I thought it was excellent and absolutely without the embarrassing vulnerability of *Dusty A.* [*Answer*]. About the obscene poem, I take your opinion and will not publish it, though even if I wanted to I expect Cape would buck at the last moment. One has to be careful with these transcripts from life I suppose, and there's another thing which worries me rather, how I wish my muse would not *only* respond to the disagreeable and sad, because I nearly always feel agreeable and happy, and then— never a word, Muse velly dumb, but as soon as anything goes wrong, the old girl gets going. It is sickening. London is looking perfect just now with all the trees looking green and the flowers out, I just went today to see the new Tate acquisitions at the National Gallery—very good on the whole with some stunning Sickerts and Steers and of course a terrible bunch of pre-Raphs. I can't stand 'em you know though of course they are grand to read about. A lot of highclass people with irritating voices having lunch on the grass outside looking very Rex Whistler. I suppose I must write to Olivia and tell her about John Mair, it is terribly sad, he was so very much alive alive-oh, and I must say the *N.S.* managed to make a nice boggle of his obituary notice, but I expect they were in a hurry. I don't know if you read *Never Come Back* but there was a fine fuss about it, because John had awful rows with *John O'London* and its then editor when he was here and it all came out in the book—not quite all though, because I remember they settled out of court: He had to apologise to Whitaker, who has now been translated to the editorial chair of *Country Life* and has got himself elected to the Reform Club. No more gossip now, dear, ('calling all chums, calling all chums'). About the Christie sale I like to think The Lord will come and not be slow, His footsteps cannot err, there was something on the radio about it and some member of the royal family but I forget exactly what . . .

Yours ever,
Stevie

Stevie's friendship with George Orwell began when they met at the BBC, where he worked during World War II. In this letter she replied to his of 17 October 1942 explaining why it was that her poems were read by Herbert Read, the celebrated art historian and poet, and not by herself.

Tower House
20 October 1942

Dear George,

Lies are the most irritating thing in the world and would make an angel grisel and you are the most persistent liar and these fibs are always coming back to me from other people. You never gave me a date for the bloody broadcast or breathed one word about my reading my own poem. I sent the poems to you from this address and also the three short stories you've had since last March. I never gave you Inez's address, why the hell should I, specially as she was on the point of leaving? I'm sorry about it, but not very, as I'm sure Read read better than I should as I've never broadcast before or had a rehearsal. I'm bored to death by the lies.

Stevie

Hamish Miles, a reader for Jonathan Cape, died before World War II. According to Sir Rupert Hart-Davis 'the interview that is so amusingly described on pp.108–12 of *Over the Frontier* was with . . . Hamish Miles'. Stevie inscribed on the fly-leaf of his copy of *Novel on Yellow Paper* these verses: 'Thank you, Dr Hamish/ For being so beamish./ If it hadn't been for you, believe me/ My child would never have seen the light of day. Stevie'. The child, in the accompanying drawing, stands on a copy of *Novel on Yellow Paper*.

Tower House
31 August 194[?]

Dear John [Hayward],

I'm afraid my novel wasn't any good after all, alas, I know this will be disappointing to you—and letting you down too in a way—but there it is, as Sir Frank says: Heigh-ho, it can't be helped. I will tell you a little about it, if it won't bore you to tears, and you can skip if it does, but I feel so hopeless about my writing now, and you know what authors are in this mood. It isn't just that it has been turned down, but that I really think it is the wrong sort of writing and really something to be ashamed of, so I am really afraid to put pen to paper now, and even afraid of this letter to you. I sent it of course to Cape, that is to Veronica Wedgwood, who is now in Rupert's place, and also a friend of mine. First of all she said she liked it, but that it had tremendous libel dangers; then her uncle fell ill and she went away for a week or so, then she said she still liked it, but wasn't sure of her judgment (she had had an awful lot of worry over Uncle Josiah, and running to and fro on family occasions), so I suggested she should send it outside for a second opinion, preferably a man's, and I said, why not Stonier? So she said she would do that on a strictly professional footing, so that seemed to me the best possible idea. I do respect Stonier's opinion and I think he is absolutely honest. So I had lunch with him when he had read it, and he said he thought it was awful, I could see it had really revolted him. It is this terrible personal stuff, you know, written in a jig of private feelings and secretarial odd jobs. Of course that is the way the others were written, but I know that *Over The Frontier* was nothing to be proud of, and *Novel on Y.P.* just happened to come off, it had a sort of light-heartedness that scraped it through. I have been reading a lot of Somerset Maugham just now, and that is the sort of writing I admire, it is so controlled and cool, he has learnt what to do with private feelings, they are to be worked and worked and worked and never used in the slab, they are nothing but raw material for the writer to work to shape. I think Olivia has this quality of coolness in her writing. And I was reading, for review, Ngaio Marsh's *Colour Scheme*, that is excellent. But this new girl, Elizabeth Myers—*A Well Full of Leaves*—what do you think of that? It seems very good when she is writing about them all when they are children, but oh dear, when Laura grows up and meets Mr McCann . . . . And then this little excerpt, John, isn't it, in its way . . . Eh?

The weeks went by. At last the strange ailment that had overtaken me, obliged me to decide upon medical advice. Now a pain would squirt up from my lungs and become embedded like a rusty star in each of my shoulders. Now, when I coughed, bright blood would quietly stream into my handkerchief. So, without telling Bernard [(Mr McCann) interpolated by Stevie] I went to an eminent chest-man. He made the necessary examination. 'Are you alone in the world?' he asked me, 'or have you parents—a guardian?' 'I am—alone,' I said. 'Why do you ask? What is it?' 'Since you are alone,' he said, 'I think you ought to know the truth.' 'I want to know the truth,' I said. 'And what's more, I can bear it. What ails me?' 'You've got tuberculosis,' he replied.

I so much like the idea of the blood streaming *quietly*. When we cut our finger, our blood roars like a tap with a defective washer.

John dear, you are a kind sweet creature letting me run on like this about myself—not that you can do a thing about it of course, except, as I said, skip. But Stonier gave me no end of a lecture (curtain) and said I ought to take myself in hand etc. and write a diary of self-criticism every blooming night! And said it was a pity poor old Hamish Miles wasn't still with us, as he would have know what to suggest for tired writers—not that bit about the diary, I bet. 'Take yourself in hand' reminds me of a story Jack Alden told me the other day—the fact that he is related to the Alden Press, those more than prudish censors who cut out all Cape's fucks and bloodies, makes it all the funnier. Young officer goes to Jack (or fellow medico) and complains of feeling tired. Doctor: Do you have much to do with women? Well, yes, my wife of course. And how often do you interview your wife? Oh, four times a week. Anyone else? Oh, the maid. And how often? Four times a week. Anyone else? A girl I'm rather fond of. How often? Four times a week. Anyone else? Well, there's an A.T.S. girl. How often? Four times a week. Doctor: You'll have to take yourself in hand, young man. Oh, I do—four times a week. I've got some other much much better ones, dear, which I'll tell you when I see you. (that's a bribe.) But I do really respect old George Stonier's opinion, (*da capo*). Only what shall I *do*? I am so tired about writing and so nervous, and yet I do so hate this feeling that I am shut back into secretarial odd jobs. Alas, I am not *sure* that it is an absolutely good thing that the prizes of writing are so enormous, it is the one form of art that is overpraised in England, if I were drawing a Muse of Writing (I forget which one it is) I should dress her in gold cloth and give her a cocktail in her hand. Success in writing, the best sort I mean, lets one into such agreeable company! Stonier said the love of fame would make me go on writing, but it's not the fame, dear, it's the company. But either motive is of course *wrong* and *vulgar*. Old Neville P. is home again from Africa, and is hanging about waiting for a Pacific Priority to fly from San Francisco to

Australia. He is off (but it's a damned protracted departure) along with old Sir Walter Layton and Sam Storey, on a mission to the Dominion.

Praying again your indulgence for a long and dreary letter, and in the perishing hope of receiving again from you one long, thoughtful and bawdy,

I am,
Your always devoted and admiring,
Stevie

Kay Dick, the novelist, editor and critic, first met Stevie in 1943 when they were both working in Tower House. Later, using the pseudonym of Edward Lane, she was first joint, then sole editor of the literary magazine, *The Windmill*.

[*c*. 1945]

Dearest Kay Dick,

No, I assure you I did not run off with your manuscripts, the ones belonging to Mr [James] Courage, I think you said. Not for worlds would I have deprived you of them. I enclose my character. Please scan it closely. You will find nothing in it about running away with people's manuscripts. (And the avarice bit you can skip, as now we both know about the $25 ex-U.S.A.) I think you will have to come down and see me, as although I love getting letters I do not so much like writing them. And everytime I come to see you there is somehow so much Midge [Wilson Midgely] about. It is just that something. You know? I am so glad you like *N on Y P*. I am surprised that you would ever speak to me after reading only *Over The F*. It is horrible, I am so ashamed of it. But hurry up and finish the *Novel*, because I have already another one for you to go on with. Yes, last night I think I have really finished my new one [*The Holiday*], and I am awfully glad. At least I have got to the end. But I think there are still a lot of things I still want to say, well that I can work off somewhere in the middle. At least I should be surprised if I couldn't. What shall I call it, do you think Death and the Girl? You are quite wrong about *Tender Only to One* it is *Mother, What Is Man?* that is the best, though of course, as we should expect, there are some very good pieces in the other. Ahem. The poke and pry poem is about the Rosa girl in the *Novel* [See 'Portrait (2)', *Collected Poems*.]. Off hand, i.e. with the greatest deliberation and *authority*, the self portraits that I

287

can remember are: 'Death's Ostracism', 'One of Many', 'Croft', 'Love me', 'I Have Two Friends', 'Lot's Wife', and all the others that are about being dead or dotty. So now you know. And now for God's sake send me yours. And in return I will give you a nice shot of luminal for a nice cup of tea for an editor. And so I shall see you soon.

Stevie

In this letter Stevie discusses the threat of libel she faced in regard to her story, 'Sunday At Home'.

12 February 1946

Dear Kay,

This is *velly confidential*, in fact it is practically written in invisible ink (owing to the ribbon being worn out).

The encd. ms. though not so handsome in appearance as the one now *avec* the elusive Reggie [Moore], is, I think a good deal less dangerous.

I will explain some of the alterations, reasons therefore, and that is what will make this letter so confidential.

The putative Plaintiff ('X') is not an angler. He is not 40, lanky, or yellow haired, he has had nothing to do with bomb experiments. (We might get [J.D.] Bernal to counter-claim if there is any trouble, which I now think there will not be.) His wife is not in the least like Glory, who is shown to be both young and childish. They have no dog, and no baby. They live in London: the general implication of this story is that they don't live in London, e.g. London cannot be said to have a 'home water' in which to fish. Also, if the bomb were over London, it could not be said to be moving off in the direction of 'the town'. 'X' has no German friend—see Friedl in this story. There is no suggestion of misconduct between Ivor and the two girls. There is nothing defamatory about Ivor in the story—beyond the implication that he and his wife are inclined to fripp. Even that is softened by the story's ending, when all is peace and 'loving kindness'.

Ivor does take refuge in the cupboard when the bomb comes over, and his wife does not. I do not think this can be laboured into an imputation of cowardice, because it is explained that the doodles reminded him of the 'experiment' in which he had been wounded.

I think myself that the whole thing is a storm in a tea-cup and that 'X'—not having seen the ms.—imagines that all sorts of private matters concerning himself are in it. This of course is not the case.

From the literary point of view as opposed to the legal—I do hope you will still like the story and not feel that the outlines have been unduly blurred.

I think one could write a wonderful tale about a group of coterie friends writing about each other and the zig-zagging antics they would get up to to foil the litigious—one feels exactly like a ship with a torpedo after it. You shall have it!

Love,
Stevie

Sally Chilver and Stevie met at a party during World War II and remained close friends until Stevie's death. She is the niece of the poet Robert Graves and a poet herself. She organised social anthropologists for the Colonial Office during World War II, became principal of Bedford College (introducing male students) before becoming Principal of Lady Margaret Hall. Within a short time of her arrival there, this women's college had one of Oxford's most renowned cellars and one of its best cuisines. Stevie's allusion to singing tunes in a restaurant refers to a time when they did do so, collapsed into laughter, and were asked to leave.

Tower House
2 January 1948

Dear Sally,

Many thanks for your letter—and many more thanks for what you say about the poems, and for the music you copied out for me so beautifully, and the suggestions about tunes generally. I spent a very happy time (the after Christmas lunch lull) inking it all in most carefully so that nothing should get rubbed off or smudged. This was a fascinating exercise as you know I do not understand scoring, but I hope I have not made any mistakes. I played the tunes through and got my sister to do so too. The point is though that I am still haunted by the missed-shot tunes I seem to hear and cannot always reproduce even by singing, for instance there is real beauty to 'The Lads of the village, we read in the lay, By medalled commanders were muddled away, And the picture that the poet makes is not very gay' but now I cannot get it right, it is exasperating, I really must do what E. [Elizabeth] Lutyens suggested and get them recorded, even if it costs me a fortune. Every child ought to be taught how to score at least in tonic sol fa. What I shall do with your tunes is to get them so into my mind that some time a poem will fit itself to them, that is the way it does happen.

I am glad you are leaving the old *News Chron*, because I am sure it is only a job for a time, what will you do next? How truly awful about Margery [Hemming], I think what one has to go on remembering, however dismal and cruel it may sound is that she cannot change ever, so it is not any good ever having a *rapprochement*, but your position with her is very different, because you are this symbol of something positive (though I don't quite know what it is—Something built up where nobody else could have built up anything—or would have wished to—or what?) whereas I am a plain simple symbol of betrayal and treachery in simple account with herself only, and therefore to be cherished, thank heaven, in the absence of the villain, as a martyrdom. I don't know, but at any rate the absence is the operative word and long may it continue.

Can I come over to tea again one Saturday afternoon and hear some of the tunes, because we can't do that in a restaurant, and the more I have of them, the more I think lunches and drinks and even suppers are so rushed and crowded and so on. It was very nice of you to send along the dates and crab paste I left with you last time, you really should have kept them for your Christmas stocking.

I have just got the life of Gerard Manley Hopkins to review for *Trib*, what a wonderful suffering time he had, there is something melancholy and magnificent about his life, the verse is so wild that grew from the Jesuit discipline 'where pain makes patterns the poet slanders' well, certainly, he does not slander the pain.

Love,
Stevie

Jack McDougall worked for Chapman & Hall Ltd and was responsible for their publication of *The Holiday* in 1949. Hedli Anderson is the singer (at her best in cabaret) for whom Auden and Britten composed songs. Louis MacNiece, the poet, was her husband.

11 February 1949

Dear Jack McDougall,

I wonder if I may send you *Postscript for Leona* which is by a friend of Sir Neville's. It is about a rather touchy American soldier and his wartime experiences which are rather amorous. It is not v. good, but not altogether bad, you know, the sort of borderline case. I am afraid this is not a very warm recommendation, but I promised I would send it round, and I don't mind telling you that you are the last victim on my list.

Poems. You know how I am always going on about getting these republished, well–I am coming back to you for this reason. Last night some of them were sung by Hedli Anderson to music by Elizabeth Lutyens (my tunes, some of them, I firmly state), and the audience reacted in a way that made me think perhaps they had better not be looked upon as pure poems but rather as intimate revue stuff, you know, they laughed quite a lot and clapped really like anything. Does this suggest that there might be a wider public for them than the highbrow sort? Two of them were quite melancholy, so it isn't only the funny ones.

Do forgive my bringing this up again if it bores you, you have but to say, No, no. Or even, No.

Yours ever,
Stevie

Tower House
15 December [1949?]

Dear Kay,

I am so glad you & Kathleen [Farrell] can come to the party & am so much looking forward to it (in the innocence of my heart–*never* having been anything but a guest all my slothful life. But I am told by savage friends that one should not even hope to enjoy one's own party?!) About your friends who sound very nice I *dare not* invite anyone else (not even *one*) until some of the replies come in! Because Sally [Chilver] & I were having rather a lot to drink (This sounds rather rude. We asked *you*, dear, *cold sober*.) & I *think* we have between us asked about 200 people. Ha ha ha.

Love to you both.
Stevie

Helen Fowler, whose many novels are published under the pseudonym 'Helen Foley', and her husband Laurence, a career Army officer, were friends of Stevie for many years. Stevie bequeathed her Queen's Gold Medal for Poetry to their daughter and her godchild, Anna Lucinda. Their other children are Catherine and Richard.

My dear Helen,

I am very much honoured and shall be delighted to be Anna Lucinda's godmother though I am afraid I am not very good at it, I mean I have never been one before and I am not a really proper practicing Christian you know (I do seem to remember a lot in the baptism service about catechisms and religious instruction and so on). Is it all right not being one? Of course it is my proxy who will have the book in front of her to blush for my shortcomings and uncommunicated heresies. Well, if you and Laurence think it would be better to have a real Christian, I shall quite understand but if not I shall love to be the one. And as I say I am much honoured, almost overwhelmed in fact, that I should be thought of as an even possible godparent.

No more now as I must get this off to you, I think yours crossed my last one.

Love to you and Laurence, the children and especially 'my' Anna Lucinda, and I hope she is very good at her christening and that is (I believe) that she howls like anything to show Mr Old Sooty what she thinks of him and his works.

Stevie

15 April 1953

Dearest Kay,

I don't know whether you are back yet but I remember you wanted some biog. from me. It is precious dull I must say, unless we dip into fic. One might say for instance, Born in Afghanistan by accident on a picnic, etc. But the truth is, born in Hull, came south at the age of 4, lived ever since in London. Educated at famous, like hell it was, girl's pioneer public school, (the Miss Buss one—North London Collegiate, Miss Buss of the well-known rhyme:

> *Miss Buss and Miss Beale*
> *Cupid's arrows n'er feel*
> *They are not like us*
> *Miss Beale and Miss Buss*

note: Miss Beale founded Cheltenham Ladies' College, so there).

Money being short and school report singularly unpropitious for a university whatjumacallit, I went to Mrs Hoster's Secretarial Training College, oh these colleges, and since then have been with Nev. and later with Frank, as faithful dog-o. What time we know, do we not, I have managed to fit in ha ha '*a little writing*'. Dull though it is I think all this wants soft pedalling, I generally cover it by saying 'has worked all her life in a publishing office'. Travels?? Well, I've always made *as much as possible* of those holiday trips to Germany and there's a lot oh a lot of it in *Novel on Yellow Paper*, hardly to France at all, except Brittany and once Bandol. English holidays—'she loves, adores 'em', can't be torn away from coastal marshes (Lincs and Norfolk), chalk downs, chalk cliffs, sea everywhere, empty country, turf trips, nice and soft, walking walking (like all melancholiacs) walking and also climbing, doesn't mind cold and high winds, wilts in tropic heat but likes the English sort, never too hot and lovely late afternoon light. Am getting lyrical must stop, death note strong in poems but romantic death, just another holiday, or else a nice long everylasting sleep-o. Don't mind much. Age? well, say middle or take the sub-title of *Yellow Paper* and 'work it out for yourself'.

There, loves, isn't that nice and dandy?

Do you know I am selling quite a lot of my poems and drawings to *Punch*, I am very pleased after having them all come back from U.S.A. and *The Times Lit.*, and not being allowed near the *N. Statesman* etc.

Let me know if there is *anything else you would like to know* and do come to London soon and have some leeonch with me. I meant the Inez book to be a present, love, but I guess you didn't like it and so it is better to have it come back. *World Review* has packed up, as I expect you saw, but I had a letter from Des. [Desmond Fitzgerald] saying they hoped it was only temporarily and that they meant to start up again in a few months leaving out the politics and being purely lit. and art. This looks like putting 'em plum in *J. O'L.'s* market. He wants me to go on doing the novels for him when they do come to life again but I fear it means my beeootiful review of Ivy [Compton-Burnett]'s book will not see the light of day. Or Rosamund's either, as a matter of fact though I might do 'em both as notable novels of the year; Rosamund's is too, you know, though I don't much like the ding dong theme of love, love, love (if that's the word).

Love to you both,
Stevie

My typing seems to have gone quite haywire. I'm sick of trying to put it right—all these backs to fronts must *mean* something??? Have decided to go to Dublin for the P.E.N. Conference; it seems a good way of *not* looking up my relations. Why don't you both come? June 8 to 13?

Palmers Green
25 April 1953

Dear Kay,

I meant to get this off to you yesterday but I had a boring *rush* (for once) & so didn't. Anyway, this will show I am home sometimes!

Yes, do come to lunch on Weds. 29th, if we can't get farther afield it will have to be the Club, luv, but if you will pick me up at the office at about 1 o'clock—we'll see. (The secretarial situation may not be arduous but it is a trifle confining.) I am sorry you feel melancholy—I don't think you *don't*, but mind, if you attempt to be more melancholy than me I shall be more than furious. I shall be *hurt*. I felt too low for words (eh??) last weekend but worked it off for all that in a poem & *Punch* like it, think it's funny I suppose, it was most touching, I thought, called 'Not Waving but Drowning'. See? Seriously, *Punch* is nice for us girls now it has got Malc Muggeridge & Tony Powell more or less running it. Inez has had some 'pieces' in it also all old pards like Angus Wilson, John Lehmann, etcetera, etcetera. I'm not going to get off for Dublin after all, the baronets want me in London that week. I don't mind either way really, & it would have been another £50 at least. The P.E.N. is really for sellers, dear, not *me*! I pant to see your novel, even if I no longer have *World Review* to review it in. I don't think I'm much good on *Love*, must be something missing. Certainly Rossie [Rosamond Lehmann?] as you call her (rather nice, that) gives me the fair [bumps?]. Sally suggested I should do some Sappho translations—but I can't make head nor tail of that ancient girl. It's all so fragmentary, one word sometimes & the rest of the page occupied by learned commentaries & cross references of the type '. . . but see Schichkelgruber'. See you Wed. Love to come to Coombewood again some time. Many thanks.

Love,
from *Stevie*

On 1 July 1953 Stevie attempted suicide at her office in Tower House. Her doctor realised that she was extremely ill, as she herself confirms in the following letter. She retired from work with a pension and, later, was pleased to be able to reverse roles with her aunt who, up to that point, had looked after her.

Palmers Green
12 July 1953

Dear Kay,

How are you all & how is The Writing going? I hope at any rate you will be able to read *this* writing. I am sitting up in bed where I have been more or less for the last 12 days. And glory be, the doctor says this time I must stay here for at least another month. I am a Nervous Wreck, it appears, also anaemic. Hurra! I have the memory that I was absolutely foul the last time we met (at the Arts, with D. [Daniel] George) but I remember then being too tired for words so forgive me. Dear Olivia says she will come out & see me. That girl is an angel, my word, when I think of the fag getting out here I mean. She has asked me to her party on the 23rd & I hope to be able to stagger forth by then & also to see you both there. It is heaven having such a long time before I need think of that awful office life again, sometimes doctors are *the thing*. I am looking forward to all our friends' books coming out. I have a lot of books now to read as the *Spectator* has asked me to go on their rota, so here I am, the old hack again. They always seem to give novels to people who practically can't bear the sight of 'em, I brought this point up at the *Spectator* & they said, yes, that was the idea. However, of course once one starts to read 'em the old thing gets at one, so I suppose it's just the thought of having to write 'a piece'. My dear sister's affair at Missenden Abbey (which she so hopes you will come [to] is not till *December*) I thought it was practically next week but you know how awful I am about dates. I have now cleared that point up. Sally gave a party last Friday but I could not go, alas, very disappointed. Robert Graves & Beryl & the children are over on their yearly visit to England. I am going to move heaven & earth to get Olivia's book to review for the *Spectator*. The more I think about it the better I think it is, but of course there are 4 of us on the rota & it takes some fixing as the others can get round there more easily than I can & pinch the books before I get a look at them. I have got Philip Toynbee's new one. It looks O.K. by me—oh if only that was *all* one need say about them! Are you doing anything for *John O'London* now? What do you think of 'Bill' Evans? He seems terribly afraid of 'the highbrow' as he calls it. I can't quite make out what he is like. There's a very strong defence mechanism there I think, Yes? No? It seems very odd to be writing by hand but I really can't *cope* with the typewriter just now. Do you know I find it very difficult to write the letters 'y' & 'p' following each other as in type & Egypt. And do you know Emanuel Miller (Betty's psychiatrist husband) once told me that was one of the tests for mental disequilibrium? So there you are. I have written a lot of new poems & what is the good of *that*? *Punch* seems to have frozen up on me. I fear it is the editor himself (Malcolm Muggeridge) who must have said 'No', because I know the Lit. Ed. (Anthony Powell) wanted to use the whole lot 'in time', & by now there has been quite a lot of time. Heigho does the road wind uphill all the way, does it not. Do write a nice long letter to your poor unbalanced friend.

Love,
Stevie

In response to a review of *The Holiday* written by Phyllis Bentley for the *Yorkshire Post*, Stevie wrote a letter to the editor (12 July 1949). She noted that in the novel Caz has forgotten where he read about the Lion and Unicorn and added: 'It was, of course, in Santayana's "Soliloquies in England". If I were so immoral as to pass this idea off as my own (which I am not) I still hope I should not be so foolish. The passage is well known.'

Palmers Green
23 September 1953

Dear Kay,

Many thanks indeed for the Script which raises my morale v. considerably, what a nice encouraging clever creature you are. There will now be a spate of new poems under your inspiration.

There are only two points I would ask you to consider

(1) I never want to go to Germany again, my love. Twice (a fortnight in 1929 & 1931) is more than enough. Perhaps one might say something like 'Has spent short but concentrated times in Germany, about which she has written so much' (ha ha).

(2) That Unicorn & Lion idea was not originally mine. The rather scatty conversation in *The Holiday* between Celia & Caz in which he characteristically attributes it to 'an Indian writer' makes this clear (I

296

hope!). Of course it was actually Santayana in a rather famous passage (sorry & no offence, please, we can't all read the same books). The only reason I am bringing this up is that it is always possible some carpy listener may write a cross letter about it (you will find this reference on p. 176 of *The Holiday*). I should love to see you. There are so many things I want to talk about. By the way, as I was looking up that Casmilus passage, I went on re-reading *The Holiday*. Oh how much better I think it is than *Novel on Yellow Paper*. It is my favourite of everything I have written, I am insufferable perhaps in saying this, but I think it is *beautiful*, never brassy, like *N on Y P* but so very richly melancholy like those hot summer days it is so full of that come before the autumn, it quite ravishes me now again when I read it, and the tears stream down my face because of what Matthew Arnold says, you know?

> But oh the labour,
> O Prince, what pain.

I've a jolly good mind to write to Anna Kallin [BBC Talks Department] & ask if I can't have some of that on the air instead of some more poems (which I am supposed to be doing for her). I think it is perhaps more truly poetical because more sustained than the poems. But then there is this awful deprecating modesty one is supposed to show. Why can one not see one's writing as something separate from oneself, & not to one's own credit either, & so speak freely about it?

By the way (again) *did* Couster translate those poems of mine? Because if so I would like to drop him a line & thank him. Is it *Paul* Couster, oh dear, one must get all this right. Can you read any of this awful scrawl. My love to you all & more thanks than I can say, *how* you do encourage one.

Stevie

P.S. What I meant to say about seeing you was this. Molly *could* drop me at your house on the way back from the Stratford theatre but it would probably not be till about 1 o'clock in the morning (after midnight I mean). I don't think Donagh (the one I am supposed to be staying with at Burnham) is on the telephone, but if the midnight delivery is too late for you, perhaps I could get a bus from Burnham to Missenden??

Naomi Replansky is an American poet who first met Stevie in 1969 though they had corresponded for some time. 'Complaint of the Ignorant Wizard', 'Foreigner', 'The Ratless Cat' are poems printed in Miss Replansky's volume *Ring Song*, as is 'The Six Million', a poem about the Holocaust. Stevie's 'next one' is *Not Waving But Drowning*.

Palmers Green
30 May 1954

Dear Miss Replansky,

I was so glad to get your poems I think they are awfully good you know, very precise which I do like, & yet mournful & dreamy too & always telling the truth. For instance the 'Ignorant Wizard' is *right*, & 'The Six Million', most difficult to say & yet how well you have said it. It is something of what I tried to say in 'Bye Baby-Brother' ['Bye Baby Bother'] (The German Mother) & 'Foreigner' too. And then saying the same forlorn thing in a different way like 'The Ratless Cat', I think that is very good. I do thank you so much for sending me this book & also for your inscription which I do much appreciate. Also I envy you in a way—this precision for instance. I see you have made no alterations. But I am always altering my poems & wondering then if that is right too. Awful: to be so undecided. I don't know if you have got *Harold's Leap* yet. But later I will send you the enormous list of corrections to those poems. Only I want to get this letter off to you quickly as I am already rather late in writing, but I have been reading & re-reading your beautiful poems & brooding a bit & ruminating.

Thank you also for your last letter. No, I would not at all mind having a selection made. Are you writing another book of poems? I do hope you are. I have been in two minds about my next one. Chatto & Windus say they will do the poems but will not have any drawings, but now I feel the drawings are so much a part of the verses that they must be published with them. And there is (mercifully) another publisher here who says he will do the poems with the drawings. So I think I shall let him. What do you think? Chatto thought the drawings were too comical, but then so often are the poems, & the drawings *I* think are not *only* comical. Do you do any other writing besides poems? I do a lot of reviewing, but my, my, it doesn't half put one off books, in the end it does this. Best wishes & again *many* thanks for *Ring Song*.

Yours ever,
Stevie Smith

In 1948 Stevie reviewed L. P. Hartley's *Eustace and Hilda* in *The Windmill*. This was the third novel in the trilogy of that name. The review gave Hartley 'the keenest pleasure' and in 1950 they met. In this letter Stevie replies to one that Hartley wrote on 17 December 1954 from Avondale, his home in Somerset. 'Your aunt sounds so delightful—I wish she could be *universal*', he wrote.

Palmers Green
5 January 1955

Dear Leslie,

Yes, it is funny about this Avondale, but I think ours is rather different from yours—I will show you a drawing of ours some time! My Aunt is an angel & very un-universal, as you suppose.

I do hope you are better now as you sounded rather *triste* & the sort of *tristesse* that goes with tiredness. That *is* a problem. But now I have some quite wonderful pills (ha ha) from my new doctor who is extremely realistic about drugs. That is so unlike (delightfully unlike) the puritan way we were brought up, that sleepless nights are good for the character, etc. etc. Of course they *may* be good for the Muse.

Talking of *whom*. I would love you to see some of my poems, & it is more than nice it is positively reckless of you to suggest it. I should think I now have about seventy—all with several drawings *each*. I cannot get any publisher to do this new book of them. Ian Parsons (Chatto) says, Yes, he will do poems without drawings, & Mervyn Horder (Duckworth) says he likes the drawings best. And both of them are *dear old chums* of course. And haughtily I am certain neither has any idea what the poems are about. I am now going to try André Deutsch, so please keep your fingers crossed for me. Has it anything to do with Mervyn & Ian being Wykehamists?? Or am I falling a prey to morbid fancies??

I do hope you have not been snowed *up* and cut *off*? We are now melting slowly with several tiles also coming off the roof. We always know because otherwise it is a soft flop.

I am glad your new novel is now coming along. How I hope I shall get it & not dear John Davenport. Do you happen to know where that line I am quoting in my next review comes from—'*et dans ces mornes séjours, les jamais sont les toujours*'? It has always haunted me.

Yours ever,
Stevie

I shall go on for a bit as I see this page is blank (or was). I picked up an 1856 copy of E.A.Poe's poems the other day with the most wonderful illustrations. How I love the Raven and the dark tarn of Aube— where I wandered with Psyche my soul. Eh? Do you in some moods, but seriously too? If he were writing today do you know I think he would not get published. That brittle laughter that covers so much *fear* of not being on the right bus—would damn him. Just think how cross with a ha ha ha Miss [Janet] Adam Smith would be. Oh & the *Listener* too. One has to be *à la* nowadays in poetry I think—*à la* [T.S.] Eliot, [Stephen] Spender etc. & soon I fear *à la* Dylan [Thomas]! I do believe this does not hold good with novels. There is much more freedom there. That *We Are Utopia* is v. good. But that is a translation. There is something sits on the English spirit somehow. I hope so much to have yours soon to prove me wrong. You see what I meant by 'reckless'! *Vous est un ange* to *be* so reckless.

   Stevie

Richard Church, poet, novelist and literary critic, wrote Jonathan Cape a letter in 1942 praising *Mother, What Is Man?* and they forwarded his letter to Stevie. She replied, thanking him and saying how much she looked forward to having his translation of the psalms in print. So their friendship began.

Palmers Green
11 July 1955

Dear Richard Church,
   Are you an Old Yarrovian? I mean *was* that Convalescent Home at Broadstairs the Yarrow Convalescent Home? Because if so, I was there too, so we ought to have an Old Boys' & Girls' Brooch or Tie, eh? Three years I was there on & off with nothing to eat but raw eggs & 3 pints of milk a day (tubercular peritonitis *I* had) & very grand & privileged I was, sitting with the boys at the special diet table. Ghastly matron called Chamberlain (I think). Roland Raven-Hart, who's everlastingly writing books about canoeing up the Irrawaddy etc. was there too, also his sister, Hester, a great pal of mine, only now dead.
   Best congratulations anyway & I do hope it was the Yarrow etc. otherwise all this must be a bit glum for you. Awful about poor old Sir Frank, isn't it?

   Yours ever,
   Stevie Smith

Diana Athill, editorial director at André Deutsch, was responsible for the publication of *Not Waving But Drowning*, which that firm published in 1957.

Palmers Green
14 December 1955

Dear Miss Athill,

The more I go through these poems the more unhappy I become about the drawings—I mean about not *having* them. I know you feel differently about this—all of you—and I do think your opinion is something that cannot be argued about & I respect it. But now I have been through the poems—& have seen some of them in *Nimbus with* the drawings—I really do not want the book to be published without them. So I am going to ask you to release me from my contract with you & I send you herewith a cheque for £50 which is the money you advanced to me on the Signing of the contract. I know this is very troublesome of me & I am sure you don't want to hear any more ever about these drawings—as I gathered when you did not answer my last attempt (about a month ago in a letter I wrote to you) to get the matter re-considered! I can only ask you to forgive me. I absolutely am riveted to them.

Yours sincerely,
Stevie Smith

Vanessa Jebb was an editor at André Deutsch where she worked on *Not Waving But Drowning*. The photograph Stevie mentions appears on page xi of *Me Again*.

Palmers Green
16 January 1956

Dear Miss Jebb,

I don't know whether the back of this Penguin [*Novel on Yellow Paper*, 1951] would help. It's a bit made up, as I did not stay very long in Germany—not more than a month all told!

Hull, as you see, I left at an *early age*, & Palmers Green, where I have lived ever since, I do not wish *stirred up in any way*, not only for reasons of a becoming modesty—but because I want a quiet life & a lot of the people here are in the novels & poems. Very few in this suburb know me as Stevie Smith, & I should like it to stay that way, if you don't mind. There's a bit in *Who's Who* you might get something from but chiefly books published I think—I don't quite remember. I don't think my 'tastes' are much use as they're pretty usual. I don't like games, card games or sports, I like sea & country to walk by & in, & swimming. I like talking & parties. I'll get a new photograph taken if you like as this is a very old one. The *hat* is so awful.

Yours sincerely,
Stevie Smith

20 November 1956

Dearest Sal [Sally Chilver],

Thank you so much for those poems. I have read some of them before & am glad to read them again. As you know 'The Cook Book Whore' is a great favourite of mine, but I like them all, the new & the old, & I think you must soon write some more & yield up your wicked will to the publishers, for really I think they should be published & also I think there is no stopping place—like they say there isn't between Atheism & Rome (but here I do *not* agree)—between the WPB [Waste Paper Basket] & publication. I do so love 'Mandrakes', it seems to me absolutely 1st class . . . 'bold with brass' is a stroke of genius, with its wonderful echoes of clatter, officiousness & seniority, my, my, that milieu [the Colonial Office] of yours comes handy! and '. . . praised the sexless lily weed' how just, & particular. Yes I like your family liking for particularity. And 'The Welfare State'—that I like v. much, especially '. . . a cross eyed child/Is given his liberty with spectacles . . . ' There's a stir in most of them that seems to be about *love* that I do not always quite catch successfully (to be infected by, I mean) that troubled stirring world of Two's is always strange to me, people *generally* are a stir & a trouble, & a pleasure, too, of course, but I cannot ever get the *à deux* fix; however, I take your word for it, & a *beautiful* word it is, at least I think so, though as I say, I do not quite catch it. But I know it means a lot to some people, so I suppose it does mean a lot. Now (of course!) I must tell you my new ones.

(1)   IT FILLED MY HEART WITH LOVE

When I hold in my hand a soft and crushable animal, and feel the fur beat for fear and the soft feather, I cannot feel unhappy.

In his fur the animal rode, and in his fur he strove,
And oh it filled my heart my heart, it filled my heart with love.

302

(2)   MY HEART GOES OUT

My heart goes out to my Creator in love
Who gave me Death, as end and remedy
All living creatures come to quiet Death
For him to eat up their activity
And give them nothing, which is what they want although
When they are living they do not think so.

(what I like about this is that it's so *apt* to be 'my creator-in-law')

(3)   I REMEMBER

It was my bridal night I remember,
An old man of seventy-three
I lay with my young bride in my arms,
A girl with t.b.
It was wartime, and overhead
The Germans were making a particularly heavy raid on Hampstead.
What rendered the confusion worse, perversely
Our bombers had chosen that moment to set out for Germany.
Harry, do they ever collide?
I do not think it has ever happened,
Oh my bride, my bride.

I only send you these out of *uppishness*, trying to *insist* (yah!) that if I cannot manage *à deux* love, which *is* the best, I can (sniff) have a boss shot at a general feeling of warmth & affection. I have also done –& done with, at last–'Die Lorelei,' curse her, & remembering what *you* said about the private grief, I finished up with the line 'Lurks there some meaning underneath?'. So thank you, & always, dear Sal, your poems move me v. strOngly & make me feel glad you can prance so surely where I can but huff & stare, gapy-face. Just ask me round any time you like & I will come. Our home is a bit of a trial at the moment, the lavatory cistern floods the garden every time the plug is pulled, it's the ball tap. I've watched it stick 3 times out of 5. But we'll get it fixed & then–I am all yours. I am so sorry you have been beastly invalidish again, oh lord, what asses our doctors are, poor Sal, I wish you better, & much help that is. Inez is now around again & I am so glad as I like the old thing, Anna Browne too, so my fur is no longer a-stare!!

Love.
Stevie

I do not mean your poems are *closely à deux*, but the wonderful disturbance underneath all of them, even when it's all zen & shells & cliffs & staircases & plants & hunting dogs seems to *me* to have the human hearts in it like two lovers, am I right? Hope you can read this. And also you manage never, never to commit the tinkle-tinkle as I do (it's the hymns coming up I expect) but your language is very beautiful *always*.

Love again.
Stevie

Anna Kallin was a staff member of the BBC Radio Talks Department. 'The Necessity of Not Believing' is a version of 'Some Impediments to Christian Commitment' printed in *Me Again* (p. 153).

Palmers Green
21 October 1957

Dear Niouta [Anna Kallin],

I wonder if I might send you a lecture I have been asked to give to the Cambridge Humanists on an anti-religious subject. I have called it 'The Necessity of Not Believing'. It is partly autobiographical, showing how very religious I was when young—with hymns & some poems—& later how I became not religious, but conscientiously anti-religious, with regret because I had enjoyed it so much, especially the morbid hymns like 'Days & moments swiftly flying/Blend the living with the dying . . .' (etc.) but *firmly* because it was immoral to believe. And the reasons why it was (is) immoral to believe. Then some more poems (not all mine). And so on. The lecture has to last about 50 minutes with 10 minutes for questions, but of course it could be cut. It has come out as something quite consistent (I think) but not all talking—in fact some of it could be sung. It is not *at all whimsical*, as some asses seem to think I am, but serious, yet not aggressive, & fairly cheerful though with melancholy patches.

Yours ever,
Stevie

Were you at Richard Rees's picture show? I couldn't get there as it was so wet, but he told me the lights fused, good heavens!

Dearest Helen,

Thank you for your heavenly letter–& for bothering so much about that broadcast ['A Turn Outside', p. 335]. No, I do not–& never have at all–thought of myself as a witch. I know too much about witchcraft & its ghastly history to do anything but loathe it. But I do often feel rather ineffectual–everybody else seems so much better somehow (you know how it goes!) & then one gets romantic about old Death & so on, & so on. But it's in all my poems, *passim, ad nauseam*, I fear. No doubt I shall creak on to be 100. But it is sweet of you to worry. And Laurence too. I think the girl ought to have gone off crying a bit through her quick words. But perhaps that would have been a bit too much. I love the 17th Century poets but I'm not a Believer, you know, so don't really fit in there. That talk I gave to the Cambridge Humanists, called 'The Necessity of Not Believing' is being published as a sort of pamphlet, so if you read it, alas, you will see how *v.* unsuitable I am to be Lucinda's or anyone's godmother.

I do think your holiday plan sounds beautiful & I hope you all enjoy it enormously. What a good idea it is because you can easily (I suppose?) get to the sea, when you want to.

I may be going to some friends in Normandy–Cecily Mackworth (do you know her?) & her second French husband. They live in their broken down old Chateau Short-Tooth (yes, that is right isn't it?– 'Brèvedent'??) in Calvados so we shall have something nice to drink!

& now *do* ring me up when you are in London & have a moment. Long to see you all.

Lots of love
from *Stevie*

PS. Has Lucinda got Masefield's *The Midnight Folk* because if not I will send it to her. It is heavenly.

The poet, David Wright, was an early admirer of Stevie's poetry but did not meet her until 1951, at a party she went to with Naomi Mitchison. In 1955 he became co-editor of *Nimbus* and wrote to ask her for some poems. Later he co-edited the literary journal, *X*, and published Stevie's work there as well, and they frequently met in London. Stevie's review of David Wright's auto-biography, *Deafness: A Personal Account*, was published in the *Listener* on 19 February 1970.

Dear David,

Here are some more poems as you kindly asked for. Some of them you may have seen before—if so, forgive me.

I don't know what to do about that proof MS ('Votaries of Both Sexes' etc.). When I read it through, I quickly altered 'warm' to 'cold' ('the tears of this person were warm') because (a) warm is such a nasty word (Isn't it?) and (b) they are of course *cold*. But then I wondered if when I wrote it I meant he had a warm heart. So—as it wd. be pointless really I suppose I say they were cold, as literally they are, perhaps it had better be left as 'warm'?? What do you think? Can I leave it to you? Hope you are both well. Wasn't that party fun?

Love
Stevie
Otherwise no alterations.

Stevie had decided, with Diana Athill's approval, to edit a book about Hell for André Deutsch; but it was never done.

Palmers Green
2 May 1960

Dear Diana,

Thank you very much for your most encouraging letter which really stirs me to go on, *press* on almost! At any rate I will at once start a Hell File and please do from time to time suggest books or pictures or pamphlets, anything at all that might be relevant. For instance, I had forgotten that end passage in *Pilgrim's Progress*, which I see mentioned in this week's *Times Lit.*—about the gate to hell being placed alongside heaven's wall on the far side of the river. My difficulty is getting hold of the books because at the moment I am far from mobile, owing to my brute of a knee (I saw a specialist about it at St George's hospital and he says the knee cap must come off). If when all this is over, I joined the London Library, do you think they would have the sort of books I shall want—I mean especially the *Complete Works of Father Faber* (he's the Hell and Purgatory man, but I see the Catholic Truth Society have now shelved him in favour of a more up to date chap who puts it less starkly). The novel by Anthony West—I remember reviewing it for the *Spectator*, but many years ago and the title I cannot remember—I suppose I could get from them? If only I could get over this neurotic attitude to work—being afraid of getting it wrong, being afraid of everything really, and thinking how much nicer it would be to be dead, I might be of more use to you and much merrier. I say it's laziness, but of course it isn't, but it sounds less dotty. However, I swear I will try. Yes, I think the £50 might keep me at it too. I did so enjoy our lunch and hope to see you soon, but I know how busy you are, and I ought to be.

Yours ever,
Stevie

Terence Kilmartin is literary editor of the *Observer*.

[1961?]

Dear Terry,

Here is the poem which perhaps is a bit rough—but not I think at all silly. I can't help feeling that Rose M. though awfully nice, is a bit silly sometimes. The *Letters* (like *The Towers of Trebizond*) get a bit noveletish. Perhaps it's partly that love for the dead man. The awful thing about 'love' is that it is easily so completely forgotten, & best so. Because when called up again it is always something false, made up, really. Or sounds so. So the rest does too.

Love
Stevie

Palmers Green
20 March 1961

Dear Rachel,

Forgive me, dear Rachel, now please *do*, if this is a professional intrusion. But (I've just done another broadcast) I'm not half worried by the awful nasalness of my voice, whether it's on a record, or tape, or a live broadcast, it is awfully noticeable. Is there anything I could *do* about this, any one in London I could go to, for some remedial treatment? As a matter of fact it's partly physical (*very* narrow thin bridge to my nose, so that often I can't really breathe through it!) Never mind, I dare say there's nothing to be done, & you may say, if the BBC don't mind, why bother?

How are you & Horace these days? It must be just about a year since I came up to Cambridge last, but couldn't call because you both had bad colds. I do hope all goes well with you & the children—& Janet's baby.

I've just had my knee-cap removed. I enjoyed my three weeks in hospital enormously. Wonderful being waited on hand & foot, really bed is the life. It's going through rather a painful time at the moment, but no doubt that is just part of the convalescence! (Hope so, at any rate.) As poor Aunt has a beastly arthritic hip (not the spreading sort of arthritis, thank heaven, but painful enough) we are a nice couple of lame dogs.

Lots of love
from *Stevie*

Palmers Green
18 December 1963

Dearest Helen,

This is just to wish you all a Happy Christmas & to thank you for your long letter which I did so much enjoy—& did mean to answer before this. But oh dear, things are in rather a pickle with us. So do forgive me. Dear old Auntie is well but cannot, poor darling, do much in the way of getting about, except just around the two rooms, & bathroom upstairs. And now my poor Sister has been took ill, alas, a coronary, I fear. She is in hospital (in Devon of course) & will be there for about 5 weeks 'having a complete rest' & (not so nice) a very strict diet, excluding all animal fats, also she mustn't smoke. Suddenly dropping from about 30 a day to 0 is an awful strain. I am afraid she will always now have to 'be careful' i.e. no stair-climbing, no jumping up & down, supposing she wanted to, etc. I don't even know if she will really ever be able to come home, or if she does, she will have to join Auntie on the first floor—& stay there. I suppose I might chivvy the poor Aunt out into a bungalow somewhere, but I think at ninety-one, she is probably best where she is. *Well. That's* a long excuse for not answering letters, isn't it. And how, dear Helen, are you & Laurence & Richard & Catherine & my dear Lucinda (to whom I have just posted a poem-book, wh. I hope the little thing will enjoy). And how, oh *how*, is that Army Life you so beautifully describe? It sounds extraordinary but even the extraordinary can be boring, don't we know. Do, if you have a moment, write me another long letter & tell me all. And of course let me know if you are in England & I will try & creep out to lunch.

Lots of love
from *Stevie*

Dear Helen,

I was glad to get your nice long letter—but rather a sad letter, I'm afraid. I am so sorry the book [*Fort of Silence*] had such bad luck. There is far too much luck about reviews & all that, but oh how depressing it is when they don't arrive & everything seems empty & pointless & so much labour & thought gone, one feels, for nothing. But of course it isn't really for nothing. It was 'worked out', in both senses—carefully made & got off the chest, as it were. But I fear the place & mental climate of where you are now [Germany] are not calculated to raise the spirits & start up anything new. Do you have my tendency to sink into a really awful lethargy? . . . the sort of awful mood in which one sits on some draughty provincial station waiting for a beastly train that never somehow *comes*? I have had a lof of luck with my *Selected Poems*. They have been published in America [by New Directions, in 1964], & now Longmans want another book of poems. And you know, I can hardly bear ever to look at my wretched poems, & all the new ones get more & more melancholy. Perhaps it's being tired that is the reason. But I've always been tired. And all my poor friends seem to have so much more to do than I have. So there's no excuse. There's nothing more tiring, dear Helen, than having no excuse.

I do hope you & Laurence enjoy your trips away from Army life & that the children are well & happy. How does Lucinda like her convent school? And how is Richard getting along? It was sweet of him to say he liked me as a guest. So did I like being one. By the way, I've got his Penguin Robert Browning life of by my poor old friend, now in a loony bin, Betty Miller. (It's a physical thing poor Betty has, an actual dying off of the brain cells.) She is quiet & seems happy but cannot remember anything or even recognize Emanuel (her husband) when he goes to see her.

I had to go up to Oxford to read some of my poems to the O.U.P.S. [Oxford University Poetry Society] last week. It was simply awful. The young man turned up & almost failed to meet me (meandering up & down the platform instead of planting himself firmly at the ticket barrier) & had to borrow the taxi fare & the cost of a few drinks from me. And only about 20 turned up, & the room wasn't heated & I didn't get anything to eat until 9:30. And then I had to change my hotel because we had a row because they wouldn't bring us our dinner! Ha, ha. I think Oxford is a *bad place*. (Always have.) They promised to pay my expenses, so I let them off a fee. But I doubt if I shall ever see the £5 that they came to.

My poor old friend Francis Hemming died the other day. He fell down dead at Phoebe [Pool]'s dinner party. Oh what awful luck poor Phoebe does have. I didn't go to the Memorial Service yesterday, because it was pelting with rain. But I see from the papers that they read some Shakespeare & had the 90th psalm.

I wish we could all go & sit on a beach somewhere—in the hot sunshine. A nice flat broad East Anglian beach. (I nearly wrote 'Anglican'—shows how theological I'm getting!)

I *daren't* read this letter through, Helen. I fear it is a shade on the glum side. I'll go & get the supper now. I always feel better after food —not to say drink! Lots of buoyant love & hollow laughter.

from
Stevie

Ladislav Horvat was introduced to Stevie by Sally Chilver. He worked in the City as a financial adviser, and for some years helped Stevie to invest her small savings.

Buckfast, S. Devon
5 July 1964

Dear Ladislav,

I've got away at last (as you will observe)—thanks to having found a nice kind Aunt-sitter who seems, cross fingers, to be functioning *all right*. I am staying here with Molly until about *the 14th*, when the A-S departs. I think Molly seems much better, but still not really up to much, & looking rather frail. She is a marvellous hostess & we go round about in the car a lot. She loves driving but of course cannot walk very far, or bathe. We went over to *Tor Cross* & *I* swam but it was absolutely deathly cold, so it was just an in-&-out bathe. Nice, all the same & the sun nice & hot to sit in afterwards. The country round here—once you get out of Buckfast, i.e. about a mile—is magnificent. Much better, but rather like, where I was in Scotland last year. Dartmoor really is superb. You must come down here some time.

Well, the point of this long rigamarole is this. Poor old Molly is really hard pressed for *beastly old money*, the bungalow etc. being, as I feared it would be, rather more than she can afford. But I want her to be easy & happy, specially in case the poor darling doesn't as they say 'make old bones'. So I have waived the interest she was paying on the £1000 I lent her & now I am going to let her have another £500, interest free. So take this into account, my dear, when next operating on my behalf. I'll give her the cheque when I get back & see whether it can come off my current a/c or will need another withdrawal from the Building Society.

Do hope all goes well with you & that the City is not being too much of a Prima Donna in the way of temperament!

Yours ever,
Stevie

Palmers Green
9 November 1964

Dear Diana,

I know I oughtn't to bother you with this and I hope I am not making a perfectly idiotic mistake in arithmetic . . . but *why* have they deducted the royalties . . . £1.7s. . . instead of adding them?? Also I do so like the title 'Not Waving but Browning.' I once saw an even better version: 'Not Wavell but Browning.' Do hope you are well.

Love,
Stevie
Wonder why they don't put the address in the a/c's.

Palmers Green
13 December 1964

Dearest Rachel,

Forgive a typewritten letter but I've burnt my fingers again cooking (I'm always doing this . . . very clumsy of me). It was sweet of you to send me that card from America. I do hope you enjoyed your trip and found Nat and his family in good trim; what years and years since I saw dear Nat, I wonder if I should recognise him now, or he me. I do wish you could come out and see us again one day, but even if you are in London, I know what a large slice of time it takes to get out here. How are you, and Horace? And the children and grand-children?? I can't get out very much now, as you can imagine, but I keep my energy (what there is of it ha ha) for going into London

311

when I have to on some job or interview or something. And this combines work and pleasure as it is always rather fun. Aunt is pretty well, dear old thing, and manages to totter round upstairs, but it is now nearly three years since she was downstairs. I camp with her in her room, which we have managed to rig up as quite a presentable little den for the Lion, and only come down to do my work, writing, I mean, and of course, the house work which doesn't get done too well, I fear. We have had a series of awful chars and now have no one, and I'm rather glad we haven't, to tell you the truth. I am getting quite a dab at it all especially the cooking. We got hold of quite a nice woman to come and stay with Aunt for three weeks in the summer while I went down to pay a long delayed visit to my sister. Poor Molly, I am afraid she will never really get over the coronary she had last Christmas. Thank heavens she has a bungalow, so no bother about stairs, etc.; and also a car so that she can get around. I did enjoy my stay so much. She is at Buckfast, you know, and I think is very happy there, as she is an R.C. and it is of course an R.C. centre. Not quite in my line, I fear, but everybody seemed very nice and friendly. And Dartmoor looked marvello in some really nice hot sunshine, for once, instead of the usual endless rain. Molly came home just recently for ten days, but of course . . . those stairs make things a bit difficult for her and altogether I thought she seemed very far from well.

I have been doing quite a lot of reading (and singing) my poems—it is wonderful what a poor captive audience has to put up with. But as soon as I get tired that wretched thickening-up of my m's and n's begins and it is really quite painful too, as all the words echo back in my head. And of course it sounds revolting. I'm going to see a doctor at Guy's about it on Tuesday, so I do hope he will be able to do something. But I fear it will be a case of 'They murmured as they took their fees, there is no cure for this disease'. My own doctor says there isn't . . . or for the tiredness either. But on the whole I am pretty fit, and you know Rachel, there's something in what they say, about looking after people, if you like the people, that is. And the almost absolute dearth of companionship in Palmers Green does drive one into writing, and, like a good many other writers, I need driving.

Are you still able to do some work, or have you now really retired? I am sure you haven't because you are so wonderfully good at not retiring and not getting, or at least appearing not to get, sort of slightly lost, as I do. But one never knows really how things are with other people, they just do always seem more spirited than oneself somehow.

I suppose you don't by any chance want a cat? A friend of mine has got the awful job of trying to find a nice home for three top cats that poor Edith Sitwell left behind her. They are all toms and doctored and good housecats, and one is a Siamese. We can't have one because of being too much of a tie, and of course most cat lovers already have one. B, another friend of mine, now has 22!! Fortunately they live in the country, but it's a bit much. They have to show people over the house practically all day and every day, and it smells and smells, in spite of plentiful spraying with Ocean Breezes (or whatever it is).

My last book (*Selected Poems*) was published in America this year which probably accounts for your seeing some of my poems in American papers, as my American publisher [James Laughlin of New Directions] is very good at shopping odd ones around. Also I am going to be in the new Penguin three-poets-in-one volume series. I am becoming quite famous in my old age, isn't it funny how things come round?

I see Joan [Robinson] has been made a Professor and that Teddy Hodgkin's sister-in-law has got a Nobel Prize. Teddy and Nancy are friends of mine. I don't know if you knew them? She sculpted a head of me, but it wasn't much good and in the end I think she scrapped it.

What a huge letter. Now you go and write me one.

Lots of love to you both,
Stevie.

Palmers Green
16 January 1967

Dear David,

I was so glad to hear from you again, and so glad to hear that you were enjoying your Gregory Fellowship at Leeds. I should love to see you and Pip again, but I am afraid I really cannot come to your festival, as it is so awfully difficult arranging aunt-sitters and, worse still, and to tell you the truth, I am getting awfully sick of reading my poems, but as for 'talking'—I simply could not do it; I have to have a script and my pet and I dare say unenterprising but ever recurrent nightmare is: turning up with the wrong file, e.g. the one reserved for income tax 'communications'?—ha ha. So do forgive me if I say 'no'—and many thanks too for inviting me. As a matter of fact I was just brooding over some Feb. and March 'dates'—fixed when they were further off, or I was feeling stronger, and wondering if I could cancel the lot (but 3 actually), and surmising—whether I could or not—I would. I do hope you and Pip are both well and absolutely full of energy. Yes, I love Yorks. too, though it is the other side I mostly know—Hull, Pickering, Scarborough and up to Whitby. There is no doubt I am now getting rather languid, even going from here to London (about 35 minutes) seems pretty terrific. I just stay at home and get absolutely fascinated by doing the same thing at the same time over and over again every day. I should be quite lost without it. Tonight—for a *wild* sort of change, I have been boiling a jersey purple, as it was rather on the red side before. You have no idea how sinister the brew looked seething around with a hellish white mist drifting off it. Aunt is well but gets wonderfully bored as she cannot see properly, or hear, and can't therefore sew or read the *D. Telegraph* leaders but thank heaven by some sort of miracle she can hear the radio and actually hears it better when it is turned low. 'We have much to be thankful for'!!

I'm afraid my new poems are all a bit dreamy, but I've got one called 'Mrs Blow and her Animals'—suppose I ought to have called it 'Mrs Blow, *Et ses Animaux*', just thought of this jolly old joke—which is coming out, but heaven knows when, in the *Listener* which I hope you will like.

Love to you both,
from,
Stevie

Ian Angus is Librarian of the Liddell Hart Centre for Military Archives at Kings College, London, and co-editor with Sonia Orwell of the four volumes of *The Collected Essays, Journalism and Letters of George Orwell* (London, 1968). In *Four Absentees* (London, 1960, p. 27), the novelist, critic and BBC producer Rayner Heppenstall says that Stevie Smith 'put [Orwell] in a novel and made his most characteristic utterance the statement that girls were no good because they couldn't play games'. In *The Holiday* Pompey Casmilus says Basil Tait 'thinks girls can't play'.

Dear Mr Angus,

I don't think I ever had many letters from George Orwell and I'm afraid if I did I did not keep them. I knew George and his first wife, Eileen, quite well and saw a good deal of them during the latter part of the war and for a few years after. About the novel of mine you mention. This was called *The Holiday* and was published by Chapman & Hall in 1949. It has been out of print for a good many years now. Mr Rayner Heppenstall's quotation, as you have it, is—as so often happens—not only a misquotation of what I said, but really makes complete nonsense of poor George. It was not cricket and football he was talking about, he was no 'player' in that sense himself, but rather rules in general . . . and that girls were a shade anarchic and did not know or care about rules at all, with the undertone, I fancy, that they did not 'play the game'. However, all this comes into *The Holiday*, in various fairly lengthy conversations between the writer, (it is a first person novel) and two characters who divide between them many of George's opinions and characteristics as I saw them. I seem to remember I had the idea at the time that splitting George into two might lessen the danger of libel, not much of a danger really. I think the novel may be difficult to get hold of if you want to keep it, though of course it can be read at the British Museum and I believe the London Library have it. I expect it can be bought second hand but it would mean putting a dealer on to it. I could give you the name of the man I use, but no doubt you have your own agents. Do get in touch with me again if you want the book to keep, or if, having read it, you want to know which the two characters are. I cannot remember now what they were called and my copy of *The Holiday* is at a publisher's, but I have reminded him that I would like it back.

Yours sincerely,
Stevie Smith
P.S. I should have put this in before, of course! (but it's in the book). George's actual words were: 'Girls can't play.'

Anna Browne and her husband Michael were old friends of Stevie, and the environs of their cottage in Norfolk, where she often stayed with them, afforded Stevie material for a number of her poems. Maria and Alice are the Browne's daughters.

Dearest Anna,

I thought this letter of [L.P.] Hartley's might amuse you &
Michael—even if you didn't see Leonard Woolf's review, which was
I must say extremely *cross*. I really think Leslie Hartley has answered
every point, so you will have an idea what it was like! I know I did not
manage to read much of the Cynthia Asquith *Diaries*, but that was
because I tackled it at bed time—& went to sleep. But don't you think
it is an awfully good letter, he just hits right home every time—at all
that awful Bloomsbury self-righteousness & self-deception. But perhaps he too is rather too cross—about Virginia??

I do hope you are all having a heavenly time & some sunshine. It
was sweet of you [to] have me to stay—once again, you angel. I did so
enjoy it. I hope Maria is wearing the Victorian jacket. I think it
would look awfully nice over shorts, as Maria can wear those exact-
ing garments, as so many who do alas *can't*. On Whit Sunday I went
to church [at St Cuthbert's in Philbeach Gardens, London]—Gerard
[Irvine]'s—as after evensong he had arranged a little poetry reading &
singing—some Donne, & G. Manley Hopkins, Wordsworth & even
D. [Dorothy] Parker. But then when that was over we had Benedic-
tion (in English) & somehow you know, with the best will in the
world, it does seem what Aunt always called 'odd'. I had never been
in Gerard's church before. He's got a rather wonderful Bavarian
(can't spell it) rococco (?) madonna up in the gallery. I can't spell anything now. I think I am *deteriorating*. We had a nice supper party
after church & the Snows (SNOWS) [C.P. Snow and Pamela Hansford Johnson]—writing getting feeble too—were v. nice. They had
been to the Fourth [of June celebration] which actually was on the
1st & told me that the Captain of the School [Eton] had recited my
'Do Take Muriel Out' poem. So there! what glory! I'm off to Molly
tomorrow, but don't know for how long.

Lots of love.
Stevie

In the following letter, Stevie refers to her neighbour Nina Woodcock,
daughter of Dr Woodcock, the physician who looked after Stevie's mother
and the family at 1 Avondale Road for many years. Stevie responded on 26
August 1935 to his announcement of retirement, thanking him for all he had
done 'to help me make the best of a rotten inside'. Another of Dr Woodcock's

daughters, Bobby, is mentioned in Stevie's letter to Doreen Diamant. Mungo and Racy Buxton were Norfolk friends of Stevie's—Rose is their daughter, and Boy their dog. (Boy is mentioned in Stevie's poem, 'Archie and Tina'.) The usual version of Stevie's opening phrase is 'Just a Collins', i.e. a bread-and-butter letter. 'Prowies' was Stevie's nickname for a Norfolk vicar and his wife, the Gambles.

Palmers Green

6 September 1968

Dearest Anna,

Just a Collinses dear—but so much more than that—you *know*. I did enjoy every minute of it & thank you all once again for a heavenly time. I'm afraid my handwriting is sadly deteriorating so you must just take the spirit for the words!

You may be interested to know that the only really hot weather we had was on the journey home. As so often happens. We even had to have the blind down & when I did get home (about 3:30) I rushed to change into a cotton frock. Needless to say, it is now quite wet & cold again. I always find it rather beastly for the first few days, because I really am very bad about *employing* myself. Unlike all my splendid friends, for which I do admire them. Nina [Woodcock] had most kindly put lots of roses in several rooms & the house looked v. tidy, & pretty. Now less so, I fear, as I have scattered a lot of papers around looking for a BBC contract to check up something. I can't help laughing hollowly-like, because the only people who want to talk to me are always the newspapers! I found a letter from the *Observer* colour supplement asking if they might come & talk to me about *death*. It's a bit odd if lack of companionship drives one to making an ass of oneself. But it looks like happening once again. So if you see it, ponder the root cause & be indulgent. Everybody still seems to be away, & if the next approach is from the *D. Mirror* asking how I cook scrambled eggs, I expect that too will get a 'yes'.

By the way, the broadcast was simply awful. So I'm glad there was only Racy, Mungo, Rose, Boy & me to listen. We went in to drinks with the Prowies on Wednesday & got involved in some more theology. They were just off to Amalfi, where there should be some sun.

I've just been reading T.S. Eliot's *Selected Essays*—trying to get my poor brain into a less trivial & melancholy state. He has a marvellous essay on Marvell—with this, for a really superb opening: 'The tercentenary of the former member for Hull . . .' (date of essay—1921).

Lots of love & I hope you all have a wonderful & *sunny* finish to the holidays.

Stevie
And I do wish you were here!

Palmers Green
20 December 1968

Dearest Rachel,

Thank you so much for your awfully nice letter—I was so glad to get it & to hear all your news. But *very* sorry about Kathy [Cox, Rachel's sister, who had just died] & I can imagine how very much you must miss her. I'm glad you & Horace are well but wish *you* were not so 'bothered' with rheumatism etc.

It is amazing how old everybody is now getting—isn't it?—but I rather like it, it's so *restful* & *sleepy* somehow. Or perhaps that is just these dark days before Christmas that I always love so much.

I don't like telling you in a Christmas letter, dear Rachel, but darling Aunt died on the 11th March. She had a little stroke & was taken to hospital. Then, amazingly, she regained consciousness & seemed on the mend. But then suddenly she died. For her sake, it was certainly best, as she so hated getting more & more helpless, & specially she hated being in hospital. But we miss her *awfully*. Molly was the greatest possible help & lots of friends came to the funeral to 'honour her'. All that was really wonderful. But, well, it is still *awful*.

Lots of love
from
Stevie

Doreen Diamant was a lifelong friend of Stevie who remembers her from the days when, as children, they climbed trees together in Palmers Green.

Buckfast, S. Devon
27 May 1969

Dear Doreen,

I'm afraid poor old Molly had a stroke last Saturday (24th), just after lunch. At first it seemed only a minor one, but then she had another. Anyway, I came down here on Sunday & got to the hospital (at Ashburton) about 6 pm. Matron said it was very unlikely she would live the week out. (I have rarely had such a *frank* appraisal from a hospital functionary!) But by now I think she is a little better, but it is *awful* to see her, really, because she is paralysed all down her left side & her speech is affected. However, *that* really is getting better & the prospect altogether does look more hopeful. But of course what wd. be really awful is if she 'got better' as they say, but remained paralysed. Meanwhile, thanks to the many *many* kind friends here, I go in to see her twice every day. So what with that, & running the *bung* [bungalow] & looking after that rather detestable cat!! I am kept too busy, & tired too, to do much awful worrying as to the future. But worrying all the same it *not half is*!

I really shd. be most awfully obliged if some time you cd. *v.* kindly drop in at 1 Avondale & see that all is well. I left of course in an awful rush. Bobby (Woodcock) like an angel came up to Paddington with me (we managed to get a car) & I know she will be looking in from time to time. But the *letters* must be up to the ceiling by now! Better perhaps have a word with her first so that you don't both go the same day.

One other thing, if you would. I put my two 'Busy Lizzies' out in the back garden so they cd. get the rain, but I think I put them in rather too sunny a position. Perhaps a northern aspect (i.e. left hand side of the garden) might be better. Silly thing to think of at this rather awful time—but there it is!

I really *can't* think of the real awfulness much of the time, it is almost too much.

Love,
Stevie

Jonathan Mayne, an art historian, and Peter, his brother, a writer—both friends of Stevie—wrote to congratulate her on having been awarded the Queen's Gold Medal for Poetry, in 1969.

Palmers Green
8 November 1969

Dear Jonathan and Peter,

What a *heavenly* card for your *very* much appreciated love and good wishes. Of course I am delighted about the award and I shall now be terrified of putting pen to paper in case the gold medal says it is not quite what We had in mind!

Love,
Stevie

To the poet Patricia Beer, Stevie sent this account of her visit to Buckingham Palace. Mr Jack Dalglish arranged for Stevie to give a reading on 6 January 1971, sponsored by the Leicestershire Education Authority; but she was too ill to travel there.

Palmers Green
22 November 1969

Dear Patricia,

Thank you so much for your letter & congratulations. I *am* very pleased & surprised too! I went & collected it on Friday & enjoyed that very much too. One walks miles over pink carpets & H.M. is very gracious—& pretty. I rather liked the slightly giggly time I had first with the lady-in-waiting & a very decorative young man. Everything had got a bit late so it was rather longer than meant before I finally took my turn & then I had about 20 minutes alone with the Queen. The questions she asked rather kept us on the subject of poetry & I could not help feeling it wasn't *absolutely* her *very* favourite subject.

By the way—is Hereford College of Education in the town of Hereford—if so why does Mr Dalglish always write from Leicester??

Yours ever,
Stevie

Palmers Green
28 November 1969

Dear Kathleen [Farrell],

Thank you so much for your letter & congratulations. I *was* delighted—& rather surprised—but it was great fun collecting it [the Queen's Gold Medal] & H.M. was most gracious & pretty—but with an enormous aura of efficiency, strength etc. (especially professionalism!). Rather like meeting the very best sort of headmistress in the very best sort of mood (if one ever had!).

May your 'move' be over soon & prove well worth it & all you hoped for.

Love
Stevie

As mentioned in an earlier letter, Elizabeth Lutyens, an old friend, composed a number of musical settings for poems by Stevie. This letter is in response to one Elizabeth Lutyens sent Stevie, congratulating her on the

Queen's Gold Medal. Jane Bown's photograph of Stevie by the lake in Grovelands Park, Palmers Green, appeared in the *Observer*.

28 November 1969

Dear Liz,

Many thanks for your con-grat-u-la-tions! Much appreciated. Likewise *your* appreciation of that *Observer* lakeside 'study'? *All* my *deep-country* feelings I am sure really come from that marvellous park which now (and for about 50 years) you still refuse to meet.

Alas, some of the people who do come and sit beside it—the lake—aren't nearly as nice as you and will fish with WORMS.

When you say 'won't death be a bit of an anti-climax when you come face to face?' you sound rather as if you *had* met him and found him not quite the dish I thought.

Lots of love
Stevie

In the next letter 'the Funeral Festival' is Stevie's jokey term for an exhibition held in Brighton on the theme 'Death, Heaven and the Victorians'. Stevie was invited to read her poems at the preview on 5 May 1970.

Palmers Green
29 April 1970

Dear Kay,

You do send wonderful postcards—I almost (but not quite) am prepared to go at once for a bathe.

Mr [John] Morley, the man who is organising the Funeral Festival asked me if I had any friends I would like to invite, but I said a firm No as I always hope audiences will be composed entirely of Complete Strangers. However, I shall be so glad to see you even if I wish you weren't going to be there. And Olivia too, oh lor, I shall have to cut out all the singing. I suppose it is ridiculous but friends do make one feel nervous, do they not? Anyway, looking forward to seeing you.

I'm afraid I've just had a ghastly accident and cracked three ribs and damaged (once again) that poor wretched old knee, the one that had the knee cap removed from it a few years ago. So I expect my poem reading will be punctuated with fearful grimaces because though the ribs healed up like angels the knee did not and is sometimes bitesome.

Still come I will if only to get away from here where I have been more or less housebound for a month. I skidded on a new pair of shoes just after giving a reading at Dulwich in the middle of the road (the slip I mean not the reading); fortunately I was flanked by a strong poet on either side, Christopher Middleton and Michael Hamburger and they held the traffic up and hauled me off the road, and immediately afterwards I had to go and have a film interview at Michael's house with a German film unit. Just shows what you can do if you do not know quite what has happened. It wasn't till I arrived home and got the doctor round (at midnight) that I did know.

I do hope you are well, and Francis [King] and all the others. If only I could get my parson man to drive me down on the 5th but I fear he also is now rather poor and has had to sell his car. It is absolutely staggering about Olivia's grant. Because you know I ran into Phoebe Hesketh at a poetry reading, and liked her very much. And it came out, or at least I got the idea somehow, that she was rather hard up and had been for a long time and with an invalid husband to look after and so on and so on. So I wrote to Rupert [Hart-Davis] and he passed it on to the Arts Council and do you know what our combined efforts obtained for poor Phoebe? . . . £500. And now Olivia with what certainly looks to me like a sound sort of income and a good deal of this extra capital by way of film payments coming in, etc. manages to get £1000.

I think *I* shall apply. Because though I always think I am awfully over paid and well off ha ha ha—but this thought always does haunt me—I suppose I really am not, and now I have to pay for other people to do all the things one generally does for oneself, it does cost quite a lot. Does it not?

Love from,
Stevie
I am going to be put up for the night so perhaps we can romp on the beach the next morning?

Mr Robert Buhler, RA, a painter whose work Stevie had admired, invited a number of distinguished poets and novelists to sit for him, Stevie among them. The drawings were to be published but the book has not yet appeared. Eventually Mr Buhler completed two portraits of Stevie.

11 May 1970

Dear Mr Buhler,

Thank you so much for sending me the photograph of my portrait. I think this looks a perfectly delightful picture, the colouring seems to me really lovely, but I do not think it is like me. It's the mouth and perhaps the lower part of the face that seem to belong to somebody else as far as the likeness goes, to Disraeli I think, yes, the whole portrait is rather like Dizzy, for whom of course I have a great admiration, but whom I think I do not resemble. You must forgive my saying this, it is just the likeness that seems to have gone awry, as a picture it is beautiful, and as you know, I am quite a besotted admirer of yours, if I may be allowed to say so. What this is leading up to is, if you have any doubts about it yourself, and would like another shot at it, or another shot at the mouth, I will come and sit for you again.

Yours sincerely,
Stevie Smith

Dr James Curley, a physician in Palmers Green, looked after Stevie from 1958 until she went to Buckfast late in 1970. Stevie sometimes baby-sat for his children who once looked out of a window and saw her executing a cartwheel as she approached the door. This was apparently a demonstration of her suppleness following a knee operation. Dr Curley tried to discourage Stevie from attempting to care for her ill sister, saying that her own health would not stand up under the strain.

Buckfast, S. Devon
[Postmarked 27 December 1970]

I am actually writing this at 1:30 in the morning of Dec. 22nd as I cannot sleep. I don't always sleep *very* well so write instead.
Dear Jim,

Forgive this sort of paper but I cannot find the other lot.

I meant to let you know that the enteritis (?) diarhhoer (sp?) *stopped* just before I came down here on Nov. 9th after about 4 years, wasn't it? of it.

But now I have fits of nearly fainting & losing control over words. I was with some friends of ours—Don & Molly Everett—at Dartington when this happened the first time. But I have often had them since.

They do not last very long but they are rather awful.

I have now acquired Dr [D.A.] Moore's senior partner here—Dr Wigram, because Don takes me in his car, he is *his* patient.

It is only when I am getting really very tired that these fits come on. I get ringing sounds (two notes, like doh dropping to lah) in my head & I sit down or would fall over.

Dr Wigram is going to write to you suggesting I shd. go to a neurologist. I don't know quite what they are. I still wonder if the dead whiteness Don tells me I have, & the faintness, may not come somehow from the *constipation*? wh. has now taken the place of *diarrhoea* (wh. I can never spell) & shows something really *is* slightly wrong colon-wise. Dr Wigram is wrong when he says the loss of word-control is in the category of 'er er' & a slight stammer before being able to go on. It (in my case) is almost a mental black out. One instance I remember—I tried to say to Don or someone that I could not find the word I wanted. But instead of 'word' I said 'milk' first & then 'snow'. And could not properly say 'cannot find' but just 'find . . . milk . . . snow'. *I refuse to agree that this is in the category of 'er er er' i.e. hesitation & a slight stammer.* But he is really quite nice.

The fits only come when I am *very* tired. Oh, I said that . . . By the way I just now got Rosemary's Christmas card from you both asking me in to drinks some time over Christmas. Thank you of course but actually I shall be here till the 6th of Jan. when I go to Leicester for yet another of my poem readings & then on the 7th home to Palmers G. when I will ring you up as I hope by then you will have had both Dr Wigram's letter & this ill-written (I fear) one from me. I have about 4 readings coming along, 2 in Edinburgh & 2 in London. Perhaps you will say, Well don't. I love being here & I think Molly is absolutely super—*v*. brave & dogged. But poor pussy has been run over. But getting better now. A Happy Christmas & love to you all. And hope you can read this.

Stevie

John Guest was Stevie's editor at Longmans, her last publisher during her lifetime, and became a friend. The title Stevie has trouble with is 'Come, Death', which was read for the first time at her funeral service. The critic Jack Lambert was then literary editor of the *Sunday Times*.

The Ella Rowcropt Ward
Torbay Hospital
Torquay
or
Ward 2
Freedom Fields
Plymouth
[postmarked 16 January 1971]

Dear John,

Thank you so much for your angelic & forbearing letter. I think Donald & Molly are wonderful & have I know typed my poems (the ones she did for me) all though I *think* the *Sunday Times* one which Jack Lambert may (or not) have printed on Jan. 10th (if not ask him, if you like). Terry Kilmartin printed mine on Jan. 3rd. His was called 'The Stroke' & Jack's (wh. he may *not* want) is called 'Come, Dauth
Daugth So anyway I expect you'll have them sent by angelic Everetts.

Lots of love—my dear, I've had lots of every sort you can think of trip-torgen, high hyppers with streen pincers, & etc. & etc. lasting now for *6* days! I hope you are beautifully happy.

Love from *Stevie* & my darling
sister gets brought home [or here?]

The poet Anthony Thwaite was literary editor of the *New Statesman* at this time. He published a number of Stevie's poems and reviews, and they were good friends. This letter, Mr Thwaite reports, was delayed by a lengthy postal strike and arrived the day after he heard the news of Stevie's death.

Up to Jan. 5th I was
with my sister at
Dart St. Mary, Buckfast
Higher Hill Lane
S. Devon
Buckfastleigh 32/04
I am afraid my dear sister, Molly,
had a stroke 18 months ago.

At the moment, but I don't
know for how long ha ha.
Sunday Jan. 17th [1971]
in Ward 2
Freedom Fields Hospitel
Plymouth

Dear Anthony,

I had a very peculiar toss down. I wasn't *very* well for about a month & even then I did often find myself using all but quite extraordinarily odd wrong words. It is like the telephones scrambling their eggs–but I never managed for about 10 minutes at least to spike any proper eggs. Then I'm afraid on Jan. 5th (I was of course & had since Nov. 10th been living with Molly, my sister, in Buckfast) then on Jan. 5th I fell almost dead, I mean ridiculous, etc. The doctor at 10 P.M. arrived & at once shipped me off to hospital, not this one I've had to come to for endlessly *more* odd takings (?) *with* can't remember what. (Anyway I've had now to sign glad pleas for happy gladdings of more endless pops & goes. I have signed my name *but* now I feel awfully frightend. Am I saying wisely in these solemn legalnesses) that any little murder, caused by here & there, has been quite let off by my names having been signed so beautifully!??

How does happens in life come for you & Ann. I do hope you & the children are wonderfully well. I wish I saw you all sometimes in Devon but lor! it's far away. How are you finding Crossman's *New Statesman*'s new ah *quite* possibly *too* new life! Isn't it nice for me I found Terry (Kilmartin) did not like the extra verses I wasn't really any surer about than either of us! I did send one called 'Come, Death' to Jack Lambert but if he doesn't like it I shd. love to send it to you. It's being *fond* of *Death* old Crossman (*is* that his name?) would blast his bussynuss [with?] & would *hate*. Love to you (& thanks for sending your home address) & Ann & *les enfants*

from *Stevie*

Stevie Smith died of a brain tumour at Ashburton Hospital on 7 March 1971.

ENDNOTES TO LETTERS

254 *Uncle James*: A distant relative who worked in Somerset House where all British last wills and testaments are filed.

254 *James Douglas*: He thundered weekly in the *Sunday Express* exposing the immoralities of the day, illustrating them with salacious detail.

254 *Director of the National Gallery*: Sir Kenneth (now Lord) Clark, distinguished art historian, critic and populariser of painting.

254 *John Hayward*: Respected critic and bibliophile who was crippled and stayed with Lord and Lady Rothschild in Cambridge during World War II. Lord Rothschild FRS, scientist and man of affairs, was Director General and Permanent Under-Secretary of the Central Policy Review Staff, Cabinet Offices.

255 *Private Life of Helen of Troy*: Reference to the popular stage production of the great German theatre director, Max Reinhardt.

255 *Arthur Pearson Ltd*: Popular magazine publishers who amalgamated with George Newnes Ltd. Sir Neville Pearson and Sir Frank Newnes were at the head of the firm when Stevie worked there.

256 *Raymond Mortimer*: Literary editor of the *New Statesman*, then an influential post. He became senior literary critic of the *Sunday Times* in succession to Sir Desmond MacCarthy. He was a young associate of the Bloomsbury Group.

256 *Edward Sackville-West*: Novelist and music critic, cousin of V. Sackville-West.

256 *Laurence Binyon*: Poet, playwright and translator of Dante. He became a Companion of Honour.

256 *Kingsley Martin*: Journalist, famous as editor of the *New Statesman* 1930-60.

256 *Rosa, Herman and the Larry-party crowd*: Acquaintances whom Stevie fictionalised in *Novel on Yellow Paper*.

258 *Laura Riding*: American poet, writer, editor and critic of poetry. She lived in Europe at this time and was associated with Robert Graves.

259 *The Specialist*: A very short American comic story by Charles Sale about a Mid-Western carpenter who specialised in building privies. Very daring in its day, it had a great success that still continues.

259 *Haldane Communismus*: J.B.S. Haldane FRS, the great scientist (biometrics *et alii*) who supported the Spanish Republican cause and wrote for the *Daily Worker*. Brother of Naomi Mitchison.

260 *The Gate*: The Gate Theatre Club in London put on plays, often for only one or a few performances, thus giving new playwrights the opportunity of production; as a Club it faced less danger of prosecution if the censor, the Lord Chamberlain, took exception to any performance.

260 *Nina Condron*: Free-lance journalist and close friend of the American writer Kay Boyle, with whom, at this time, she spent holidays each year in Austria or the South of France. She was co-editor (as Nina Conarain) with Kay Boyle and Laurence Vail of a volume, *365 Days*.

262 *Mercury*: *The London Mercury*, a literary magazine, once edited by J.C. Squire.

262 *Scott-James*: R.A. Scott-James, then editor of *The London Mercury*.

263 *4-minutes silence*: This was the *three* minutes silence kept all over the UK annually on 11 November to commemorate the end of World War I.

263 *Married to Death*: Probably a reference to *The Holiday*, published in 1949.

265 *Derek V*: Derek Verschoyle, literary editor of the *Spectator* in the late thirties. Founded his own publishing firm after World War II.

266 *Stonier*: G.W. Stonier, literary journalist, long on the staff of the *New Statesman*, also author of stories, *Shaving Through the Blitz* and other books.

268 *Malcolm Muggeridge*: The author and journalist, much exposed on TV in England and America. One-time editor of *Punch*.

268 *V.S. Pritchett*: Now Sir Victor Pritchett, novelist, short story writer and doyen of British critics.

269 *Marshalls*: Cambridge friends of Stevie. Rachel was a specialist in voice production. Horace Marshall was Rachel's husband. One of his sisters, Ray, married David Garnett. Eleanor and Frances Marshall were also Horace's sisters, the latter married Ralph Partridge, Lytton Strachey's secretary and author and critic in his own right.

269 *David Garnett*: Novelist and literary journalist, in his day a notable younger member of the Bloomsbury Group.

269 *Osbert*: Sir Osbert Sitwell Bt, brother of Edith and a writer who, with her, played a prominent part in furthering the arts. Author of many books including his memorable autobiography, *Left Hand, Right Hand*.

269 *larger German Reich*: Hitler's Germany had just annexed Austria.

270 *Masaryk*: Tomás Garrigue Masaryk, Czech philosopher and statesman who was first president of the Czecho-Slovakian Republic.

270 *Day-Lewis*: C. Day-Lewis, poet and novelist, associated with W.H. Auden and Louis MacNeice in the 1930s as poets of the Left. Became Poet Laureate in the 1960s.

271 *Chamberlain's speech*: Neville Chamberlain, then British Prime Minister and principal appeaser of Hitler, signed the notorious Munich Agreement in 1938.

271 *Sam and John*: Sir Samuel Hoare and Sir John Simon, Chamberlain's principal cabinet ministers and fellow appeasers.

274 *Cowper Powys*: John Cowper Powys, prolific and original novelist, elder brother of Theodore and Llewelyn Powys.

275 *Sagittarius*: Pseudonym of Olga Katzin who wrote witty satirical verse regularly in the *New Statesman*.

275 *Hermon*: Hermon Ould, long associated with the British branch of P.E.N., the international association of writers particularly concerned with freedom of expression.

275 *David*: David Carver was General Secretary of International P.E.N. and of the British branch.

276 *Saki*: Pseudonym of H.H. Munro, the witty satirical writer of short stories that reflected the Edwardian age.

277 *Orwell*: George Orwell wrote a serious study in *Horizon* of Frank Richards's very popular school stories that appeared in the *Magnet* and other boys' weeklies. They were something of a national institution in their day.

277 *Connolly*: Cyril Connolly, author of *Enemies of Promise* and *The Unquiet Grave* and distinguished critic who founded *Horizon* in late 1939 which continued until the 1950s.

277 *Virginia Woolf*: A reference to her suicide on 28 March 1941.

278 *Ba*: Barbara Flower, a classicist whose father worked at the British Museum.

279 *Joan*: Joan Robinson, Professor of Economics at Cambridge.

279 *Max*: Max Newman, Professor Emeritus of Mathematics at University of Manchester.

280 *Drinkwater*: John Drinkwater, poet and dramatist.

281 *Rebecca West*: Dame Rebecca West, celebrated novelist, critic and political journalist who reported the Nürnberg trial of the Nazi leaders. Her book was *Black Lamb and Grey Falcon*—not Stevie's intentional misnomer.

281 *Lady Listowel*: Judith, Lady Listowel, Hungarian-born first wife of the Earl of Listowel, journalist and author with a special interest in Africa.

281 *John Brophy*: Novelist, father of Brigid Brophy.

281 *Pamela H. Johnson*: Pamela Hansford Johnson, novelist and critic. Second wife of C.P. (Lord) Snow, the novelist.

281 *Howard Spring*: Literary journalist and successful popular novelist.

282 *Veronica*: Dame Veronica (C.V.) Wedgwood, the great historian of the 17th century, then on the staff of Jonathan Cape, the publishers.

282 *Olivia*: Olivia Manning, author of many novels including her famous Balkan Trilogy.

282 *Spencer C.-B*: Spencer Curtis Brown, then head of the famous literary agency founded by his father.

282 *Miss Pearn*: Director of the Pearn, Pollinger & Higham literary agency. Later founded another agency, Pearn & Pollinger.

283 *Whitaker*: Staff member of Newnes-Pearson magazine group who edited *Country Life* from the 1940s into the 1950s.

284 *my novel*: Probably a reference to *The Holiday*, published in 1949, her

third and last novel, recently re-issued, along with her other two, by Virago Press.

285 *Elizabeth Myers*: This novel, the first of three, was published in 1947.

286 *Jack Alden*: The Alden Press were Jonathan Cape's principal printers. Printers, being then jointly responsible for libel, were liable to demand changes in anything suspect.

287 *Sir Walter Layton*: Later Lord Layton, chairman of the Liberal *News Chronicle*, owned by Quaker interests, which was absorbed into the *Daily Mail* after World War II.

287 *Mr Courage*: James Courage, New Zealand-born novelist.

287 *Midge*: Wilson Midgely, then editor of *John O'London's Weekly*.

287 *Rosa girl*: A character in *Novel on Yellow Paper*.

288 *Reggie*: Reginald Moore who co-edited the first five numbers of *The Windmill*.

288 *Bernal*: J.D. Bernal FRS, eminent crystalographer, who carried out important research in World War II, specially when he was a civilian member of Lord Mountbatten's staff at Combined Operations HQ.

289 *E. Lutyens*: Elizabeth Lutyens, leading British composer. Her father was the eminent architect.

290 *Trib*: *Tribune*, weekly journal of the Labour Left. Stevie's review of *Gerard Manley Hopkins* by Eleanor Ruggles appeared as 'The Converted Poet' in *Tribune*, 23 January 1948.

291 *Kathleen*: Kathleen Farrell the novelist who knew Stevie through her friendship with Kay Dick.

293 *World Review*: A literary magazine founded by Sir Edward Hulton, founder of *Picture Post* and a press millionaire. Desmond Fitzgerald was the editor.

294 *Tony Powell*: Anthony Powell, the novelist, best known for his sequence *A Dance to the Music of Time*.

294 *Angus Wilson*: The novelist, recently knighted. He worked in the top-secret British decoding establishment at Bletchley during World War II.

294 *John Lehmann*: Writer, poet and editor with flair for discovering new writers, particularly in the 1930s and during World War II, in his *New Writing* and Penguin *New Writing*. Founded his own publishing firm after the war. Brother of Rosamond.

294 *Schichkelgruber*: Schicklgruber was Hitler's father's real name. Used ironically during the war as it is just possible that it was Jewish.

295 *D. George*: Daniel George, critic and journalist who was Jonathan Cape's chief reader for many years.

295 *Missenden Abbey*: Molly Ward-Smith was schools' county drama adviser for Buckinghamshire. Presumably this is a reference to a theatrical production given there.

295 *Philip Toynbee*: Novelist and literary critic on the *Observer*. The 'new

one' was his *From the Garden to the Sea*.

296 *Bill Evans*: Then editor of *John O'London's Weekly*.

296 *Emanuel and Betty Miller*: He was a distinguished psychiatrist. One of his appointments was Honorary Physician, Child Psychiatry Department, St George's Hospital. Betty Miller was a novelist and author of a classic biography of Robert Browning. Parents of Jonathan Miller.

297 *Santayana*: George Santayana, the Spanish American philosopher.

298 *my next one*: Although it was published three years after this letter was written, probably a reference to *Not Waving But Drowning*, the collection published by André Deutsch in a large format which gave full scope to the drawings, without which none of her books of poems was published.

299 *Ian Parsons*: Chairman of Chatto & Windus, the publishers, and one of the most respected British publishers in the post-war period. He himself edited poetry anthologies.

299 *Mervyn Horder*: Lord Horder, then head of Duckworths, the publishers.

299 *Wykehamists*: former pupils of the public school, Winchester College.

299 *John Davenport*: Then fiction reviewer on the *Observer* and a well known rumbustious literary character in London.

300 *Miss Adam Smith*: Janet Adam Smith, a prominent literary figure in London. Critic, author and, at this time, literary editor of the *New Statesman*.

300 *The Listener*: The BBC weekly.

300 *Sir Frank*: Sir Frank Newnes died on 10 July 1955.

301 *Nimbus*: A poetry magazine that provided a most useful outlet for new poets.

304 *Richard Rees*: Sir Richard Rees Bt, critic, author and painter, who edited *The Adelphi*, a literary magazine, in the 1930s.

305 *Cecily Mackworth*: Novelist and occasional contributor to literary magazines. Her second husband was an impoverished French aristocrat.

306 *The Complete Works of Father Faber*: Frederick William Faber (1814–63). Roman Catholic convert and apologist, co-founder of the London Oratory.

306 *Anthony West*: Son of Dame Rebecca West and H.G. Wells, novelist, also the book critic on the *New Yorker* for many years.

307 *Rose Macaulay*: The prolific novelist and travel writer whose last novel *The Towers of Trebizond* was her most successful. Her letters were published after her death in 1958, edited by Constance Babington Smith, who also discusses the love affair Stevie alludes to in this letter in her biography, *Rose Macaulay*, 1972.

310 *Francis Hemming*: Eminent civil servant and lepidopterist.

310 *Phoebe*: Phoebe Pool, an art historian.

312 *Buckfast*: Buckfast Abbey in Devon had been built between the wars by

the monks on an old abbey site. Father Sebastian, an able organist there, knew Stevie and seven years later played wonderfully at her funeral service in the local Church of England church, wearing 'mufti'.

312 *words echo back in my head*: An early symptom of the brain tumour which caused her death.

312 *Guy's*: The famous London hospital where Keats studied medicine.

313 *Teddy Hodgkin's sister-in-law*: Dorothy Hodgkin, scientist and Nobel Prize winner.

316 *Cynthia Asquith*: Lady Cynthia Asquith, novelist and journalist who had been J.M. Barrie's secretary, 1918–37. She was the daughter-in-law of the first Earl of Asquith, the British Prime Minister when Great Britain declared war in 1914.

316 *Bloomsbury*: The Bloomsbury Group. Stevie's view of this eminent group reflects her reaction to anything which, to her, smacked of complacency.

316 *Gerard*: The Reverend Gerard Irvine, Church of England clergyman, friend of Stevie's with whom she enjoyed discussing her slightly ambivalent attitude to High Anglicanism.

316 *D. Parker*: Dorothy Parker, the great American wit, poet and short story writer, one of those who made the *New Yorker* famous.

316 *The Fourth*: The Fourth of June is the annual commemoration day at Eton College.

316 *Molly*: Molly Ward-Smith [1901–75]. This stroke did not impair her mind and, although disabled, she outlived Stevie by some four years.

322 *Christopher Middleton*: Poet and translator of German literature.

322 *Michael Hamburger*: English poet and German translator whose parents emigrated to England when Hitler came to power. His brother is Paul Hamlyn, the successful publisher, now head of Octopus Books.

322 *Francis*: Francis King, novelist and critic.

322 *my parson man*: Possibly a reference to the Reverend Gerard Irvine.

323 *Don and Molly Everett*: Neighbours of Molly Ward-Smith who were very helpful when Stevie took ill.

324 *Dr Wigram*: The Buckfastleigh doctor who attended Stevie at the local cottage hospital where she died, keeping her out of pain.

326 *Ann*: Ann Thwaite, writer, critic and biographer of Frances Hodgson Burnett.

326 *Crossman*: R.H.S. Crossman, journalist, diarist and member of the Labour Government Cabinet, who became editor of the *New Statesman* when Harold Wilson's government lost the election in 1970.

RADIO PLAY

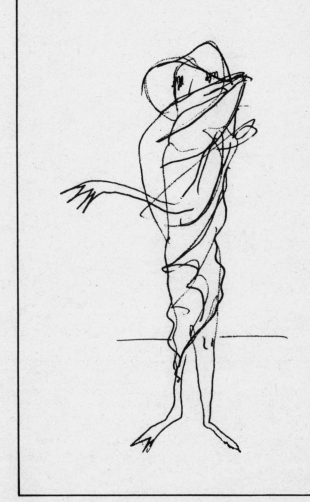

First broadcast on the BBC, 23 May 1959, 'A Turn Outside' was produced for the Third Programme by Douglas Cleverdon. Janette Richer read the part of Stevie Smith, and Hugh Burden that of The Interlocutor.

A TURN OUTSIDE

INTERLOCUTOR: A lot of your poems, dear . . . You don't mind if I call you 'dear'?

S.S.: No, I would rather have 'dear' than a name, it is less personal.

INTERLOCUTOR: And that is what you want? Well, a lot of your poems, dear, seem to me sometimes to have tunes to them, I mean as if they ought to go to music, or as if you had some idea of some music when you wrote them. Like this one I always like so much:

> Behind the Knight sits hooded Care,
> And as he rides she speaks him fair,
> She lays her hand in his sable muff,
> Ride he never so fast he'll not cast her off.

S.S.: You sang that very well. Oh yes, they do, nearly all the poems do have some tune.

INTERLOCUTOR: That you have made up?

S.S.: Well yes, or is it something ancestral, like that poor Knight on his old horse; yes, in a way I have made it up.

INTERLOCUTOR: You try one.

S.S.: Well, it is difficult you know, because of often having come some way off from, so to say, the original tune. I wonder if I might just have a drink out of that bottle, such a delicious colour. Hymn tunes, for instance, have a great influence on me. Thank you.

INTERLOCUTOR: Here's to us. Go on now, sing something, try one.

S.S.: Well, all right. There is this one. It could go either to 'Greenland's Icy Mountains' or 'Jerusalem the Golden'. Which would you prefer?

INTERLOCUTOR: 'Greenland's Icy Mountains'.

s.s.: All right. Did you ever notice by the way what a lot of 'Horatius', I mean Macaulay's 'Horatius', goes to 'Greenland's Icy Mountains'? You can slide it in, I often used to do this. For instance, you begin with Greenland's et cetera:

> *From Greenland's icy mountains*
> *From India's coral strand*
> *Where Afric's golden fountains*
> *Roll down the something land*

and then the 'Horatius' bit:

> *From many a lonely hamlet*
> *Which hid by beach and pine*
> *Like an eagle's nest*
> *Hangs on the crest*
> *Of purple Apennin.*

It's like 'Uncle George and Auntie Mabel/Fainted at the breakfast table.' Only not so immoral. Ahem.

INTERLOCUTOR: Ahem.

s.s.: Well, it's always fun doing this, fitting other words to an old tune.

INTERLOCUTOR: Shall we go on with the poem?

s.s.: It's called 'Voice from the Tomb'. (To 'Greenland's Icy Mountains'.)

> *I trod a foreign path, dears,*
> *The silence was extreme*
> *And so it came about, dears,*
> *That I fell into dream,*
>
> *That I fell into dream, my dear,*
> *And feelings beyond cause,*
> *And tears without a reason*
> *And so was lost.*

INTERLOCUTOR: It's a bit of a fiddle, that last line . . . so-o wa-as lost.

s.s.: Well, it brings the desperateness out.

INTERLOCUTOR: Yes, it brings the desperateness out . . .

s.s.: Why do you come closer, don't come so close.

INTERLOCUTOR: Oh it's just to get out of the draught, you know, just the draught.

s.s.: There isn't a draught.

INTERLOCUTOR: Well, I don't know, I thought I felt one.

s.s.: I always find these studios, these box-like premises, rather close.

INTERLOCUTOR: It's the other door, I expect, I mean there being another door makes for a draught.

s.s.: I say, do you feel all right?

INTERLOCUTOR: Quite, thank you. Do you?

s.s.: Not particularly, not just at the moment, *Because you see there isn't another door.* Shall we go on? Well then, there is this poem, it has quite a bright lolloping sort of tune. See if you can recognise it. The idea of the poem is that there is a funeral service going on in the rain. It was inspired by an advertisement I saw in a clerical outfitters' catalogue. It said that a cloak that was advertised was 'Eminently suitable for conducting funeral services in the rain'. Do you mind? I'll fish out some more cheerful ones later.

INTERLOCUTOR: *I* don't mind.

s.s.: All right. It's called 'Silence and Tears are Convenient'.

The tears of the widow of the military man
Fell down to the earth as the funeral sentence ran.
Dust to dust, Oh how frightful sighed the mourners as the rain began.

But the grave yawned wide and took the tears and the rain,
And the poor dead man was at last free from all his pain,
Pee wee sang the little bird upon the tree again and again.

Is it not a solemn moment when the last word is said,
And wrapped in cloak of priestly custom we dispose our dead,

And the earth falls heavy, heavy, upon the expensive coffin lined with
  lead?

And may the coffin hold his bones in peace that lies below,
And may the widow woman's tears make a good show,
And may the suitable priestly garment not let the breath of scandal
  through.

For the weather of their happening has been a little inclement,
And would people be so sympathetic if they knew how the story went?
Best not put it to the test. Silence and tears are convenient.

INTERLOCUTOR: It's 'The Death of Poor Cock Robin' tune, isn't
it? I don't mind the melancholy ones, you know, I like something
deathly, *I feel at home in it.*

S.S.: Now you say that in rather a particular way. I don't want to
know why. So shut up now and don't come any nearer. Oh well, all
right. So do I like the melancholy poems. But I was brought up to
expect that one should be cheerful. It was a duty. You know? It
was a stiff school I was brought up in. It was a girls' public school
that was more manly than the boys' ones are, it outdid them all, in
stiffness it did, and keeping a chain on the great feelings we had,
we went in chains, it was to prepare us for the World . . .

INTERLOCUTOR: Well, let's have this cheerful poem you have been
saving up, that was written for the duty of cheerfulness.

S.S.: It is funny how you should say that. Because this poem turns on
duty. You see the child has been told that duty is one's lodestar.
But she is rebellious, this child, she will have none of it, so she says
lobster instead of lodestar, and so makes a mock of it, and makes a
monkey of the kind schoolteacher (that was all the time thinking
only of Harrow and 'Forty Years On', that my school had a very
special devotion to—that song and that school). So here is the
poem, it is called 'Duty was his Lodestar'.

> *Duty was my Lobster, my Lobster was she,*
> *And when I walked with my Lobster*
> *I was happy.*

338

But one day my Lobster and I fell out,
And we did nothing but
Rave and shout.

Rejoice, rejoice, Hallelujah drink the flowing champagne
For my darling Lobster and I
Are friends again.

Rejoice, rejoice, drink the flowing champagne-cup,
My lobster and I have made it up.

INTERLOCUTOR: (*Laughs*) That's cheerful, that's done it, that made a monkey of them. I can see that you made a monkey of them.

S.S.: Oh it was not I, it was just somebody, anybody, a girl. You do have a peculiar laugh, it echoes in my head so much.

INTERLOCUTOR: I shouldn't worry.

S.S.: . . . and then the tune. Is that my tune, do you think? Or does it remind you of something, some tune that already exists, that is not mine, that perhaps I should not say it was mine? Eh? What do you think? These tunes worry me, and then there is the copyright question, I might be infringing a copyright of somebody else's tune?

INTERLOCUTOR: I shouldn't worry, that one doesn't strike me, to be like anything I have once heard, it's not near enough to worry, it's no more to worry about than the way I laugh is, not near enough yet.

S.S.: Oh? . . . Well then here is another happy one. It is deliciously happy, it is quite radiant, but of course it is a fairy story, it is the East of the Sun and West of the Moon, Cupid-Psyche story, really I am afraid that is what it is. Also—like, alas, so many of the gay ones—it has no tune, so I shall have to say it.

THE CASTLE

I married the Earl of Egremont,
I never saw him by day,
I had him in bed at night,
And cuddled him tight.

We had two boys, twins,
Tommy and Roly,
Roly was so fat
We called him Roly-poly.

Oh that was a romantic time,
The castle had such a lonely look,
The estate,
Heavy with cockle and spurge,
Lay desolate.

The ocean waves
Lapped in the castle caves.

Oh I love the ramshackle castle,
And the room
Where our sons were born.

Oh I love the wild
Parkland,
The mild
Sunshine.

Underneath the wall
Sleeps our pet toad,
There the hollyhocks grow tall.

My children never saw their father,
Do not know,
He sleeps in my arms each night
Till cock-crow.

Oh I love the ramshackle castle,
And the turret room
Where our sons were born.

INTERLOCUTOR: *You* may call that radiantly happy, deliciously happy, even cheerful, but I like it for another reason.

S.S.: *You like it because it is out of the world.*

INTERLOCUTOR: Splendid, good girl, really very good girl.

S.S.: Keep away. I want to get on with my poems. Now a lot of these sung poems go to church tunes and they stem from the liturgy as well as from *Hymns Ancient and Modern*. But I think this is all right, don't you?—for the poems that have a religious theme, it is all right? Like this one—'The Repentance of Lady T.' Lady T. is sitting in front of her looking glass, in corsets and chemise. She is combing her front hair.

THE REPENTANCE OF LADY T

I look in the glass
Whose face do I see?
It is the face
Of Lady T.

I wish to change,
How can that be?
Oh Lamb of God
Change me, change me.

INTERLOCUTOR: Yes, I see the liturgy there, it becomes a sort of recitative, it is getting near to that, I have heard it in your poems before.

S.S.: Yes, in this one perhaps. It is a half-French, half-English verse, a macaronic poem. In the background are the busy shops on a Saturday afternoon in a poor quarter. People look out of the poor-lodging-house windows above the shops. Down below are the shopping crowds. A little child looks over his shoulder at a butcher with a large knife standing in front of his frozen carcases . . .

INTERLOCUTOR: Where do these descriptions come from?

S.S.: They are the drawings that go with the poems.

INTERLOCUTOR: All right, what's this macaronic poem that goes to the recitative?

S.S.: It is called '*Ceux Qui Luttent . . .*'. It is on the French proverb that says 'Those who struggle are those who live'.

341

Ceux qui luttent ce sont ceux qui vivent.
And down here they luttent a very great deal indeed.
But if life be the desideratum, why grieve, ils vivent.

INTERLOCUTOR: Nice to have got some Latin in too.

S.S.: What? Oh yes, I hadn't noticed that. *I see.*

INTERLOCUTOR: Ha ha ha.

S.S.: But this idea you know of struggling being living. Really in a
way I suppose it is. But what happens also to be true—though not
quite what the moralists had in mind—is that you can suffer just as
much for something that isn't real as for something that is. Like
the poor girl in this poem called '*Infelice*'. She is pretending that
the man is in love with her, but really she must know that he is not.
It is a *said* poem, but it is very close to the sung poems because of
the rhythm that beats so strong.

INTERLOCUTOR: Any moment, you mean, it might get off the
ground and be sung?

S.S.: Not this time it won't. The title, in English, which I prefer, is
'*Infelice*' (In-felleese) or you could call it In-*fay*-leechay.

INFELICE

Walking swiftly with a dreadful duchess,
He smiled too briefly, his face was as pale as sand,
He jumped into a taxi when he saw me coming,
Leaving me alone with a private meaning,
He loves me so much, my heart is singing.
Later at the Club when I rang him in the evening
They said: Sir Rat is dining, is dining, is dining,
No Madam, he left no message, ah how his silence speaks,
He loves me too much for words, my heart is singing.
The Pullman seats are here, the tickets for Paris, I am waiting,
Presently the telephone rings, it is his valet speaking,
Sir Rat is called away, to Scotland, his constituents,
(Ah the dreadful duchess, but he loves me best)
Best pleasure to the last, my heart is singing.
One night he came, it was four in the morning,

Walking slowly upstairs, he stands beside my bed,
Dear darling, lie beside me, it is too cold to stand speaking,
He lies down beside me, his face is like the sand,
He is in a sleep of love, my heart is singing.
Sleeping softly softly, in the morning I must wake him,
And waking he murmers, I only came to sleep.
The words are so sweetly cruel, how deeply he loves me,
I say them to myself alone, my heart is singing.
Now the sunshine strengthens, it is ten in the morning,
He is so timid in love, he only needs to know,
He is my little child, how can he come if I do not call him,
I will write and tell him everything, I take the pen and write:
I love you so much, my heart is singing.

I hope that does not depress you too much, it does not leave you feeling sad?

INTERLOCUTOR: On the contrary. It is a situation where I can help —I think where *only* I can help . . .

S.S.: *Who are you?* No, don't answer. (*Hurries*) You must suppose that after six months, or a year, or ten years, she will admit he did not love her, and then she will have learnt something, she will have learnt the splendid power the mind has on itself, to inflict suffering and to bear it. Or, if she cannot bear it, then she can be like this truthful girl who crawls naked in a rose garden to pick up the sword that has a glint in the moonlight. This girl blames nobody. That is already a good deal, eh? She is just going to . . . but here it is, and this time to a deadly accurate tune, from Bizet's '*L'Arlesienne*', I think.

> *God in heaven, forgive my death, it lies*
> *Not in any hand, but mine, but mine.*

INTERLOCUTOR: Death is a help, isn't it, always such a help.

S.S.: Yes, it is. It is what happens to Muriel in the next poem, and it is a good thing. If people had to go on living for ever they could not possibly be cheerful. Muriel is a girl who was looking for her friends in the Palace, among the rich people, but it was not there that they were. She stands melancholy, with a crown of tinsel in her hands.

INTERLOCUTOR: Do you sing this one?

S.S.: Yes, in a way, it is also a recitative one.

> Do take Muriel out
> She is looking so glum
> Do take Muriel out
> All her friends have gone.
>
> And after too much pressure
> Looking for them in the Palace
> She goes home to too much leisure
> And this is what her life is.
>
> All her friends are gone
> And she is alone
> And she looks for them where they have never been
> And her peace is flown.
>
> Her friends went into the forest
> And across the river
> And the desert took their footprints
> And they went with a believer.
>
> Ah they are gone they were so beautiful
> And she cannot come to them
> And she kneels in her room at night
> Crying, Amen.
>
> Do take Muriel out
> Although your name is Death
> She will not complain
> When you dance her over the blasted heath.

Well, do you like that, is that all right, do you think? Does it cheer you up?

INTERLOCUTOR: Yes, it cheers me up very much, I think you have a true feeling for me, a very warm feeling.

S.S.: Steady. And I don't see why you should say that.

INTERLOCUTOR: Don't you? . . . and that last dance cheers me up. Over the Brocken? In the Hartz Mountains, perhaps? But Muriel's fate—fate is not very happy?

S.S.: Oh, I don't know. Her values were wrong, now perhaps they will be put right. These are all very moral poems, you know. I always think Muriel is such a musical name. What you say there about the Hartz Mountains is interesting . . . yes, there is the German feeling, I cannot think why, I have no very fond feeling for Germany. All the same there is something of the Gretchen song in it . . . 'My heart is heavy, my peace is gone, I shall find it never, O never again'.

INTERLOCUTOR: But of course Gretchen did find peace again.

S.S.: Oh yes. She became nameless, you remember? *Una poeni-tentium*. 'One of the penitent women'. Oh how horrible, how cruel, how *German*. Oh if we could only slough off this beastly religion, that is so cruel, that darkens our lives, that clings to us like fire, and if we tear it away we tear the flesh with it. Oh away with it, away with it, there wants a great wind to blow it all away. As dear H.G. Wells used to roar, meaning of course that all other people's beliefs should be blown away and only his be left. Ha ha.

INTERLOCUTOR: Ha ha. But you said you were very moralising, so what were you wishing in that poem for poor Muriel then? That her values should be put right? That has rather an ominous ring, doesn't it?

S.S.: Oh, I did not mean it in that way, in that religious *Christian* way, but only that she should be free, not pressed any longer close to the burning gold, that is false richness, or to any burning idea that clings and burns, and is false. In the hands of Death she might become free and relaxed and happy . . .

INTERLOCUTOR: In the hands of Death . . .?

S.S.: Oh what beautiful eyes you have . . .

INTERLOCUTOR: Then *look*. But you always turn away.

S.S.: In the hands of Death she might become happy . . .

INTERLOCUTOR: Or unconscious, in perpetual sleep?

S.S.: That too is a gain. You know the hymn, 'There is a green hill far away'? Well, I wrote a poem called 'The Face' that goes to that tune. This poem is about *another* person's faults, not my own, so forgive me if it is censorious. But it is probably something he is not entirely to blame for. This person in the poem, had a silver-spoon upbringing and a doting Mama. As well as the deep stupidity he was born with, poor fellow, no doubt it was not easy for him.

INTERLOCUTOR: All right, all right, no excuses please, no tears, just say 'The Face'.

S.S.: I don't say it, I sing it. As I told you, it goes to the tune of 'There is a green hill far away'. It seems peculiar to me you can't remember what has just been said; even if it isn't up to what you generally have to listen to, it was only a second ago . . . Perhaps you would like to sing it youself.

INTERLOCUTOR: Oh go on.

S.S.: All right.

THE FACE

> There is a face I know too well,
> A face I dread to see,
> So vain it is, so eloquent
> Of all futility.
>
> It is a human face that hides
> A monkey soul within,
> That bangs about, that beats a gong,
> That makes a horrid din.
>
> Sometimes the monkey soul will sprawl
> Athwart the human eyes,
> And peering forth, will flesh its pads,
> And utter social lies.
>
> So wretched is this face, so vain,
> So empty and forlorn,
> You well may say that better far
> This face had not been born.

INTERLOCUTOR: First Lady T.'s face, before the looking glass, and now this poor fellow's, and in both of them you are afraid, I think, that it is your own face you see? We shall really have to take a turn outside.

S.S.: When you come close to me—like that—I think I have seen you before.

INTERLOCUTOR: You look quite startled. Come, be brave. Let me hold your hand.

S.S.: Not just now. Not yet.

INTERLOCUTOR: Oh, very well. But we all have to go outside some time. You would agree with that, I think? You are in fact always saying it. 'We all have to go some time'.

S.S.: I I I I I . . .

INTERLOCUTOR: Now don't stammer. It always comes out so badly on the air. Tell me about seeing me before.

S.S.: I I was going to. It was not once, or twice, but three times.

INTERLOCUTOR: Well?

S.S.: I would rather sing another poem. This one:

> *Cool and plain*
> *Cool and plain*
> *Was the message of love on the window pane.*
> *Soft and quiet*
> *Soft and quiet*
> *It vanished away in the fogs of night.*

INTERLOCUTOR: I see. Is that where you saw me?

S.S.: Yes. You took the message away.

INTERLOCUTOR: And where else, where else did you see me?

S.S.: I saw you in the wood.

INTERLOCUTOR: But you have been in so many woods.

S.S.: And always you are there, eventually that is what it boils down to.

INTERLOCUTOR: You feel all right?

S.S.: Not particularly. There's an unearthly chill in the air just now.

INTERLOCUTOR: It's that *other* door, dear.

S.S.: Well, quickly, as I was going to say . . .

INTERLOCUTOR: You are frightened, aren't you? Well, what were you going to say? About the wood?

S.S.: No, about another place, not the wood. I saw you once in another place. You were standing on the bank of a stream, at the other side. There was a man with you, he had a plaster of a baroque face with an elegant long nose a little chipped. So there he stood, this plaster baroque person, and he twirled an hour glass at the end of a black moire ribbon.

INTERLOCUTOR: I never stood with such a companion.

S.S.: Oh yes you did. I was walking by this stream and then standing still. It was a February filldyke ditch, flowing dirty below a factory town; very grim it was, this stream, and the factory town that could never be a city.

INTERLOCUTOR: So what happened?

S.S.: Oh, I don't know, I slipped, I fell. I suppose I fell into the stream. Now I will tell you how I saw you in the wood. It is in this poem, that is said, not sung. The poem is about a girl who threw everything away, she had friends, and a lover, and loving relations, but she threw them all away. It is called 'I Rode with my Darling in the Dark Wood at Night'.

I rode with my darling in the dark wood at night
And suddenly there was an angel burning bright
Come with me or go far away he said
But do not stay alone in the dark wood at night.

My darling grew pale he was responsible
He said we should go back it was reasonable
But I wished to stay with the angel in the dark wood at night.

My darling said goodbye and rode off angrily
And suddenly I rode after him and came to a cornfield
Where had my darling gone and where was the angel now?
The wind bent the corn and drew it along the ground
And the corn said, Do not go alone in the dark wood.

Then the wind drew more strongly and the black clouds covered the moon
And I rode into the dark wood at night.

There was a light burning in the trees but it was not the angel
And in the pale light stood a tall tower without windows
And a mean rain fell and the voice of the tower spoke,
Do not stay alone in the dark wood at night.

The walls of the pale tower were heavy, in a heavy mood
The great stones stood as if resisting without belief.
Oh how sad sighed the wind, how disconsolately,
Do not ride alone in the dark wood at night.

Loved I once my darling? I love him not now.
Had I a mother beloved? She lies far away.
A sister, a loving heart? My aunt a noble lady?
All all is silent in the dark wood at night.

INTERLOCUTOR: Then I was your darling, your true darling—that never yet rode away. Do you think I am attractive?

S.S.: Yes, awfully. I mean I always think Death is so attractive.

INTERLOCUTOR: I *beg* your pardon?

S.S.: . . . awfully attractive. No, don't come any closer.

INTERLOCUTOR: It's just the draught, just to get out of the draught from that other door.

S.S.: I don't see any draught.

INTERLOCUTOR: 'I don't feel any door'. Ha ha ha. Why are you so frightened?

S.S.: I I I I . . .

INTERLOCUTOR: Don't stammer. Just think what you want to say and say it.

S.S.: It is just this poem I have here, about Mr Over. You will see from this poem, if you will listen, how I find Death attractive, and yet . . . I say, would you mind not coming any nearer? How can I sing with you hanging round my neck?

INTERLOCUTOR: It's another sung one, is it?

S.S.: Yes, it is. And I will tell you what is happening if you will draw off a little. Imagine then this scene: A non-activiste, a broody egg-head, say, is standing by the grave of a brave soldier who died fighting. The egg-head would like to die too, but knowing that he has always been so feeble, so un-brave and un-fighting, not to say plum languid, he fears for his reception on the other side . . . The poem is called 'Over to You'.

Mr. Over is dead
He died fighting and true
And on his tombstone they wrote
Over to You.

And who pray is this You
To whom Mr. Over is gone?
Oh if we only knew that
We should not do wrong

But who is this beautiful You
We all of us long for so much
Is he not our friend and our brother
Our father and such?

Yes he is this and much more
This is but a portion
A sea-drop in a bucket
Taken from the ocean

So the voices spake
Softly above my head
And a voice in my heart cried: Follow
Where he has led

And a devil's voice cried: Happy
Happy the dead.

350

INTERLOCUTOR: Les chants desésperés sont les chants les plus beaux
Et j'en sais d'immortels qui sont des purs sanglots

S.S.: I beg your pardon? ... Oh yes, that Victor Hugo thing—'the despairing songs are the most beautiful and I know some that are pure sobs'. You want it in English to get the full excruciating flavour. Am I right in supposing that that is how my sung poems affect you?

INTERLOCUTOR: A little, yes, a little that way.

S.S.: Well, if it is only a little, I don't think I should bother.

INTERLOCUTOR: I don't bother, not in the way *you* suppose. But there's a lot of fear in that poem. You do frighten yourself, don't you? It's silly being frightened, and it's not going to be much good.

S.S.: Do you *like* the poem? about Mr Over?

INTERLOCUTOR: Yes, I do, in a way. It's what a lot of people feel. I suppose. Something in them wants to go, something holds them back; while the beautiful red blood flows in their beautiful veins, they feel they must be loyal to it, so they say the other thing that wants to go must be . . .

S.S.: 'A devil's voice'.

INTERLOCUTOR: Exactly.

S.S.: I tell you what.

INTERLOCUTOR: What?

S.S.: I wouldn't mind another nip of that . . .

INTERLOCUTOR: All right. Here you are.

S.S.: Here's to us.

INTERLOCUTOR: You wouldn't care to take a turn outside?

S.S.: Not just now. Later, perhaps.

INTERLOCUTOR: You adore putting things off.

S.S.: I do adore putting things off.

INTERLOCUTOR: I feel I should like so much to take a turn with you outside.

S.S.: Oh no, it is really quite all right in this room. I don't mind this room really. Please do not bother. So far as it goes, you might say this room was all right. But all the time you are edging closer, you keep looking at that other door. Do you have to do that, it is a little unnerving. In a way, you know, it is unnerving.

INTERLOCUTOR: You *can* see the other door, you *do* see it?

S.S.: Why yes of course I can see it.

INTERLOCUTOR: You feel rather drawn towards it?

S.S.: Yes, a little, yes I do. But not now, by and by perhaps.

INTERLOCUTOR: Well . . .

S.S.: No, no, wait. I was with you once another time, you and I were off for an excursion to the sea, we were riding together, in a vista with distances. We ride through the morning, slowly, lollingly, we take our feet out of the stirrups and dangle them in the long grass. We find the right place for our picnic and dismount and lie on the grass, that is short turf on a cliff top. The place where we are now is drenched in sunlight, this sunshine has the quality of the eternal, it is absolutely classical. We are on a little promontory where the low cliffs stand out a little way into the sea, the soft grass on top of the cliff is speckled with flowers. The flowers that you will not let me pick. 'Do you want to raise the devil?' you say.

INTERLOCUTOR: I would not let you pluck the flowers?

S.S.: No, *then*, on that occasion, you would not.

INTERLOCUTOR: Why are you so frightened? You flee the torturers of this world? Is that what it is? You flee, but none pursue.

S.S.: Oh yes, you do, you pursue to the death. What is death like?

INTERLOCUTOR: I shouldn't know him from Adam.

S.S.: What is death like?

INTERLOCUTOR: He is nothing to write home about.

S.S.: The sunlight was like the sunlight of Homer, it was eternal.

Or that fair field of Enna, where Proserpin gathering flowers,
Herself a fairer flower, by gloomy Dis was gathered, which cost
Ceres all that pain, To seek her through the world.

INTERLOCUTOR: So sometimes you can say the poems that other people have written as well as your own? Why *are* you so frightened? And you are tricky too, you are up to tricks. Those prose passages you said, about where you had seen me, with the hourglass on the moire ribbon and in the sunshine of Homer, these are also poems, are they not? Just as much as the girl in the dark wood was a poem?

S.S.: There is no very strong division between what is poetry and what is prose. This drink is remarkably good. Here's to you. This programme is now beginning to be only about you. *Prosit. Gesundheit.* Where was I?

INTERLOCUTOR: Still in this room. Still here for a little while.

S.S.: Oh no, no, no, no.

INTERLOCUTOR: Why are you so frightened?

S.S.: It is that fair field of Enna I was remembering. And the classic sunshine that has the quality of Homer, that is eternal. But *I* dare not pluck the flowers that Persephone plucked. It is not only the scenery of Homer, the dark sea and the laughterless stone, I remember the other books where the shades must have blood to drink, where the dead cannot speak, they are so cold, they cannot speak, they cannot think, they have no memory at all unless they lap the warm blood.

> *I walked in the graveyard*
> *The shades came to me*
> *'Give us a saucer of blood!'*
> *You will get no blood from me.*
>
> *Then they held me, and tore and drank*
> *And called me by name*
> *And drank my bright blood*
> *As it ran in a stain.*
>
> *It was for pity I fed them,*
> *For pity stood still.*
> *In the land of the Shades*
> *Now I dwell.*

INTERLOCUTOR: *Don't be frightened!*

S.S.: I often have these thoughts about the blood that flows so beautifully and the bright colours of this world, it is so pretty, oh it is so pretty.

INTERLOCUTOR: So pretty, so pretty. Well, there's no need to make a song about it, my dear girl. Do you think *I* shall drink your blood and take you away from the bright colours?

S.S.: You do not seem to me to be altogether and absolutely . . . the same person you were when first we began talking. Something seems to have slipped a little . . .

INTERLOCUTOR: You think *I* slipped in?

S.S.: Yes, I expect you slipped in. Things that come on the air are always so dangerous.

INTERLOCUTOR: Come outside *now*.

S.S.: Oh I do not wish to cough and drawl and go into the darkness.

INTERLOCUTOR: You have no choice.

S.S.: No, no, no.

INTERLOCUTOR: You must. Come along, you know you must. I will sing one of your poems to show that you know you must.

> *Brightest and best are the sons of the morning,*
> *They wait on our footsteps and show us no ill.*
> *But waking or sleeping*
> *We are in their keeping*
> *And sooner or later they will do as they will.*

But you have had other opinions about me that are not so full of this absurd fear, not fearful at all.

S.S.: Yes, I know, I know.

> *I like to see him drink the gash*
> *I made with my own knife*
> *And draw the blood out of my wrist*
>   *and drink my life*

Who is this One who drinks so deep?
His name is Death, He drinks asleep.

INTERLOCUTOR: Well, there you are, you see.

S.S.: Ah. When you kiss me I remember only this one, this poem is called 'Longing for Death because of Feebleness'.

INTERLOCUTOR: Said or sung?

S.S.: Said, so far, I have not thought of a tune for it. Perhaps you can help?

INTERLOCUTOR: I might at that. Help with the *tune*, you mean?

S.S.: What did you think I meant?

INTERLOCUTOR: Well, let's have the poem. We haven't all the time in the world.

S.S.: You mean . . .

INTERLOCUTOR: Come on, come on, the poem, if you please.

S.S.:

LONGING FOR DEATH BECAUSE OF FEEBLENESS

Oh would that I were a reliable spirit careering around
Congenially employed and no longer by feebleness *bound*
Oh who would not leave the flesh to become a reliable spirit
Possibly travelling far and acquiring merit.

INTERLOCUTOR: That's very hopeful, very very hopeful. I can see that Death for you is an excursion train . . . all aboard for a nice day in the country.

S.S.: But there is the moral idea too, the work, or something useful, whatever it might be.

INTERLOCUTOR: Nothing is pleasanter than travelling freely with the excuse of a moral purpose. Could you wander in a desert of snow without a commission? It might be that, you know. I am only pulling your leg, of course, but there is something else you wrote, in prose, we will pass it as prose, but you did write it you know.

S.S.: I do know.

INTERLOCUTOR: Say it.

S.S.: I would rather not. It is frightening.

INTERLOCUTOR: Say it all the same.

S.S.: Oh very well. This is it . . . 'There is little laughter where you are going and no warmth. In that landscape of harsh winter where the rivers are frozen fast, and the only sound is the crash of winter tree branches beneath the weight of the snow that is piled on them, for the birds that might have been singing froze long ago, dropping like stones from the cold sky (I lick my lips) the soul is delivered to a slow death. For in that winter landscape there is no shelter for her delicate limbs, for her soft downy and voluptuous head. On the horizon, trees stand like gallows, and in the foreground of our picture—by Breughel out of Hecate—there is a wheel with studs stuck on it. What can that be? The soul, frivolous and vulnerable, will now lie down and draw the snow over her for a blanket. Now she is terrified, look, the tears freeze as they stand in her eyes. She is naked in this desert as she was born, she has no friends, she is alone. The skin of the body clothes the delicate nerves, there is no part of it that is free from pain. Racked by useless grief, for grief is useless and also insolent that is not rooted in repentance, she will now lie down and draw the snow over her. But the wind that draws from the east, blowing from the frozen tundras of Thibet and Siberia, snatches away from her that *cold* covering; she is naked as when she was born, but now there is no friendly hand to raise her up 'with customary and domestic kindness'. With customary and domestic kindness.

INTERLOCUTOR: There you are you see, that is *not* so hopeful, that is *not* the excursion train for a day in the country. My word how you do like to frighten yourself. But of course I am only pulling your leg.

S.S.: That what I said there is not what I think, it is not what I believe, it is . . .

INTERLOCUTOR: Only what the Church teaches, and absolutely immoral. Away with it, away with it. *We* know.

S.S.: I would rather have *nox est perpetua una dormienda*, I would rather have Lucretius, 'where we are Death is not and where Death is we cannot be'. An eternal sleep, Nothing, an End. That makes me happy, then I can say what I said in this poem:

> My heart goes out to my Creator in love
> Who gave me Death, as end and remedy.
> All living creatures come to quiet Death
> For him to eat up their activity
> And give them nothing, which is what they want although
> When they are living they do not think so.

INTERLOCUTOR: Yes, I am a quiet fellow.

S.S.: You are a power of the air who has trapped me.

INTERLOCUTOR: Does that feel better?

S.S.: Yes, when you kiss me again . . . I feel, I feel . . .

INTERLOCUTOR: 'That everything is swimming in a wonderful wisdom', I know.

S.S.: Shall we just have another drink? It was that German ass who poisoned himself with mescalin who used that sentence, about everything swimming in a wonderful wisdom, that is so wonderfully loopy, such a summing up of nonsense, so wonderfully silly, he could not have hit on it for himself, he must have been inspired by a Power of the Air . . .

INTERLOCUTOR: Come along now.

S.S.: Ah. This third kiss. Oh how disgusting it is in here, oh how I hate these beastly harsh white lights and the blank walls that have no shadows, oh how harsh and white it is.

INTERLOCUTOR: Come along, dear. We shall soon be outside now, just a turn of the key and there we are.

S.S.: Hurry, hurry. Oh, how boring you are, to be so boring and stupid and to take so long. Why have you taken so long over it, hanging about here, doing absolutely nothing, you are so lackadaisical and frivolous, so utterly *inactive*, it makes one feel quite faint, it is something one does not care to think about, how much you can stand about doing nothing . . .

INTERLOCUTOR: That's my dear girl, that's my . . .

(*Fade out*)   *1959*

INDEX TO LETTERS

Page numbers for recipients of letters from Stevie Smith are marked in italics.
Page numbers referring to notes on letters are marked n.

ABOUT THE AUTHOR

STEVIE SMITH was born in Hull in 1902, but when she was three she moved with her parents and sister to Avondale Road in Palmers Green—an address now immortalised in her own writings, in the recent Hugh Whitemore stage play *Stevie,* and its highly acclaimed film version, which starred Glenda Jackson. Here she stayed for over sixty years, after her parents' death living with her 'Lion Aunt.' She worked until retirement as private secretary to Sir Frank Newnes and Sir Neville Pearson, the magazine publishers. She first attempted to publish her poems in 1935 but was told to 'go away and write a novel.' *Novel on Yellow Paper* (1936) was the result. This and her first volume of poems, *A Good Time Was Had by All* (1937), established her reputation as a unique poetic talent, and she published seven more collections, many of them illustrated by her own drawings. An accomplished and very popular reciter of her verse both on the BBC and at poetry readings, she won the Cholmondeley Award for Poetry and, in 1969, the Queen's Gold Medal for Poetry.

Stevie Smith died in 1971. In 1976 her *Collected Poems* were published in the United States.

JAMES MACGIBBON, the distinguished publisher, was a close friend of Stevie Smith and is her literary executor.

JACK BARBERA is Assistant Professor of English at the University of Mississippi.

WILLIAM MCBRIEN is Professor of English at Hofstra University, New York.